"Cast off!" Diokles called, and the lines tying the *Aphrodite* to the pier thumped down into the akatos.

At almost the same moment, Sostratos and Menedemos saw the soldiers coming down toward the harbor.

"They aren't coming to invite us to the symposium," Menedemos said with commendable calm. "Let's get out of here."

"Back oars!" Diokles said, and set the stroke with his mallet and bronze square. "Rhyppa*pai*! Rhyppa*pai*! Come on, you lugs! Put your backs into it!"

As if sliding through glue, the *Aphrodite* began easing away from the pier.

"The soldiers are starting to run!"

"Rhyppa*pai*! Rhyppa*pai*!"

"You there!" An officer shouted. "Are you the polluted Rhodians?" More soldiers trotted down to the end of the wharf, many of them carrying bows.

"Rhodians?" Sostratos answered. "We're the *Thetis* out of Kos. Want to buy some silk?"

"Liar!" The officer turned to his men. "Shoot!"

And the deadly arrows began to fly. . . .

By H. N. Turteltaub from Tom Doherty Associates

Justinian
Over the Wine-Dark Sea
The Gryphon's Skull
The Sacred Land

THE GRYPHON'S SKULL

H. N. TURTELTAUB

TOR®
A TOM DOHERTY ASSOCIATES BOOK
NEW YORK

The Gryphon's Skull *is dedicated to Jack Horner, whose* Dinosaur Lives *gave me the idea for it. I owe him special thanks for the pleasure of his conversation, and for his patience with my questions about* Protoceratops *skulls. Any errors, of course, are purely my own.*

THE GRYPHON'S SKULL

Map by Mark Stein Studios

A Tor Book
Published by Tom Doherty Associates, LLC
175 Fifth Avenue
New York, NY 10010

www.tor.com

Tor® is a registered trademark of Tom Doherty Associates, LLC.

ISBN: 0-765-34503-X

First edition: December 2002
First mass market edition: December 2003

Printed in the United States of America

0 9 8 7 6 5 4 3 2 1

A NOTE ON WEIGHTS, MEASURES, AND MONEY

I have, as best I could, used in this novel the weights, measures, and coinages my characters would have used and encountered in their journey. Here are some approximate equivalents (precise values would have varied from city to city, further complicating things):

1 digit = $^{3}/_{4}$ inch
4 digits = 1 palm
6 palms = 1 cubit

1 cubit = $1^{1}/_{2}$ feet
1 plethron = 100 feet
1 stadion = 600 feet

12 khalkoi = 1 obolos
6 oboloi = 1 drakhma
100 drakhmai = 1 mina
(about 1 pound)
60 minai = 1 talent

As noted, these are all approximate. As a measure of how widely they could vary, the talent in Athens was about 57 pounds, while that of Aigina, less than 30 miles away, was about 83 pounds.

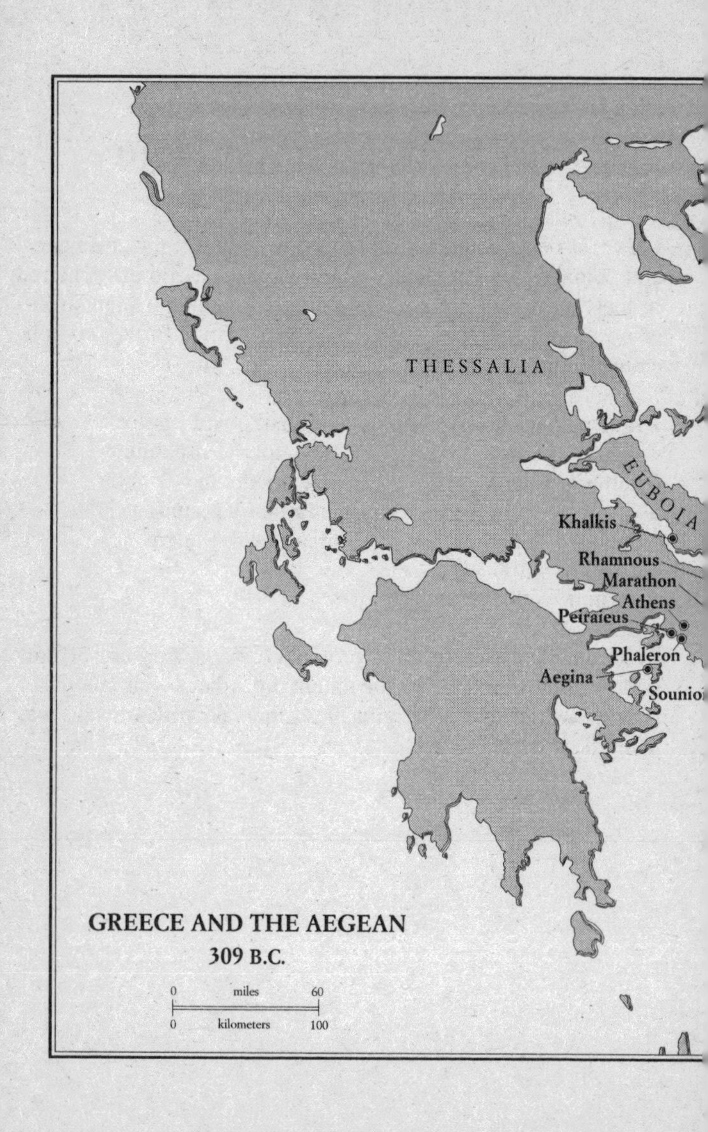
THESSALIA
EUBOIA
Khalkis
Rhamnous
Marathon
Athens
Peiraieus
Phaleron
Aegina
Sounio
GREECE AND THE AEGEAN
309 B.C.
0
miles
60
0
kilometers
100

Lesbos
Skyros
Sardis
Andros
Samos
Ephesos
Samos
Ckeos
Tenos
Ikaria
Tenos
Mykonos
Miletos
Syros
Kythnos
Delos
Naxos
Patmos
Myndos
Halikarnassos
Seriphos
Lebinthos
Paros
Kalymnos
Kos
Kos
Knidos
Rhodes
Astypalaia
Telos
Rhodes
N
Mark Stein Studios

1

SPRING. NEVER IN ALL HIS TWENTY-SIX years had Menedemos been so glad to see the sailing season come round again. Not that winter in Rhodes was harsh. Menedemos had never seen snow fall here, nor had his father. Even so . . .

His fingers caressed the steering-oar tillers of the merchant galley *Aphrodite* as they might have stroked a lover's skin. His cousin Sostratos stood on the akatos' poop deck with him. Sostratos was a few months older and most of a head taller, but Menedemos captained the ship. His cousin served as toikharkhos, keeping track of the *Aphrodite* and of what they would bring in and spend on their trading run. Sostratos had a splendid head for numbers. People, now, people gave him a good deal more trouble.

From the quay at which the *Aphrodite* was tied up, Menedemos' father called, "Be careful. By the gods, be extra careful."

"I will, Father," Menedemos said dutifully. One of the reasons he was so glad to escape Rhodes was that that meant escaping Philodemos. Living in the same house with him through the winter had been harder this year than in any other Menedemos could remember. His father had long been convinced he couldn't do anything right.

As if to prove as much, Philodemos called, "Listen to your cousin. Sostratos has the beginnings of good sense."

Menedemos dipped his head, as Hellenes did to show assent. He shot Sostratos a hooded glance. Sostratos had the decency to look embarrassed at such praise from the older generation.

Sostratos' father, Lysistratos, stood alongside Philodemos. He was a good deal more easygoing than his older brother.

But he too said, "You're going to have to watch yourselves every single place you go."

"We *will.*" Even Sostratos let a little exasperation show, and he got on with his father far better than Menedemos did with *his.*

But Lysistratos persisted: "Not just pirates these days, you know. Since Ptolemaios and Antigonos started fighting again last year, there'll be more war galleys on the sea than a dog has fleas. Some of those whoresons are just pirates in bigger, faster, stronger ships."

"Yes, Uncle Lysistratos," Menedemos said patiently. "But if we don't go out and trade, the family goes hungry."

"Well, that's true," Lysistratos admitted.

"Watch out for the silk merchants on Kos," Philodemos warned. "They'll gouge you if you give them half a chance—even a quarter of a chance. They think they've got the world by the short hairs because you can't buy silk anywhere else."

They have a point, too, Menedemos thought. Aloud, he said, "We'll do our best. We did all right with them last year, remember. And we've got crimson dye aboard. They always pay well for that."

His father gave more advice. In a low voice, Sostratos said, "If we keep listening to them, we'll never sail."

"Isn't that the truth?" Menedemos whispered back. He raised his voice to call out to the crew: "Rowers to the benches! Diokles, come up to the stern, if you please."

"Right you are, skipper," Diokles answered. The keleustes was in his early forties, his skin tanned and leathery from endless summers at sea. He mounted from the undecked waist of the akatos to the poop. His bare feet were sure and quiet as he came up the steps to the raised platform at the stern. Seamen didn't wear shoes aboard ship—and few of them bothered with shoes ashore, either.

All forty of the akatos' oars were manned fast enough to keep Menedemos from complaining. More than half of the rowers had gone west to Great Hellas and the towns of the Italian barbarians the year before. Almost all of them had pulled an oar in a Rhodian warship at one time or another. They weren't a raw crew, and wouldn't need much beating in to work well together—so Menedemos hoped, at any rate.

He glanced over to the quay to make sure no lines still secured the *Aphrodite*. Sure enough, they'd all been taken aboard. He knew that, but was glad he'd checked all the same. Trying to row away while still tied up? His father would never have let him live it down. Neither would anyone else.

Having satisfied himself, he dipped his head to Diokles.

"Good enough." As always aboard ship, the oarmaster carried a little mallet with an iron head and a bronze square dangling from a chain. He used them to beat out the stroke. All eyes went to him when he raised the bronze square. He grinned at the rowers as he cocked his right arm, then brought the mallet forward. As metal clanged on metal, he began to call the stroke, too: "Rhyppa*pai*! Rhyppa*pai*!"

The oars rose and fell, rose and fell. The *Aphrodite* glided away from the pier, slowly at first, then faster and faster. Sostratos waved back toward his father. Grudgingly, Menedemos looked back over his shoulder and lifted one hand from the steering oar to wave at Philodemos in turn. A little to his surprise, his father waved back. *But is he waving because he's sorry to see me go, or because he's glad?*

Rhodes boasted no fewer than five harbors, but only the great harbor and the naval harbor just northwest of it were warded from wind and weather with manmade moles. The great harbor's opening onto the Aegean was only a couple of plethra across—not even a bowshot. Menedemos steered toward the middle of the channel.

"Rhyppa*pai*!" Diokles called. He smote the bronze square again. "Rhyppa*pai*!" He set a stately pace. What point to wearing out the rowers at the beginning of the voyage? And what point to embarrassing them by pushing them up to a quick stroke and having them make mistakes under the critical eyes of every wharf rat in Rhodes? After all, the only reason Menedemos put a full complement on the oars was for show. Once out of the harbor, the merchant galley would either sail or amble along with eight or ten rowers on a side unless she had to flee or fight.

Menedemos tasted the motion of the sea through the soles of his feet and the palms of his hands on the steering oars.

Here in the protected harbor, the water was almost glassy smooth. Even so, no one could ever mistake it for the staid solidity of dry land. "Almost like riding a woman, isn't it?" Menedemos said to Sostratos.

His cousin plucked at his beard. They weren't fashionable for young men these days—Menedemos and most of the sailors were clean-shaven—but Sostratos had never been one to care much for fashion. "Trust you to come up with that particular comparison," he said at last.

"I haven't the faintest idea what you're talking about," Menedemos replied with a chuckle.

Sostratos snorted. "It's plain you're no Persian, at any rate."

"Persian? I should hope not," Menedemos said. "What *are* you talking about, anyhow? You pull the strangest things out from under your hat."

"Herodotos says Persians learn three things when they're growing up," Sostratos said: "to ride, to shoot, and to tell the truth."

"Oh," Menedemos said. "Well, to the crows with you, O cousin of mine." They both laughed. What Menedemos didn't tell Sostratos was that he was glad to be leaving Rhodes not because of what he had done this winter but because of what he hadn't—a sizable departure from his norm.

His cousin knew nothing of that. No one but Menedemos knew of the passion he'd conceived for his father's young second wife—unless Baukis herself had some inkling of it. But whatever he thought, whatever he felt, he hadn't done anything about it, and the strain of doing nothing had made living with his father even harder than it would have been otherwise.

He would have known blindfolded the instant when the *Aphrodite* glided out between the fortified moles that sheltered the great harbor and onto the open waters of the Aegean. The akatos' motion changed inside the space of a heartbeat. Real waves—not big ones, but waves nonetheless, driven by a brisk northerly breeze—slapped her bow and foamed over the three-finned bronze ram she carried there. She began to pitch, going up and down, up and down, under Menedemos' feet.

"Now we're really on the sea!" he said happily.

"So we are." Sostratos sounded less delighted. The merchant galley's motion remained quite mild, but Menedemos' cousin had an uncertain stomach till he got back his sea legs at the start of each new sailing season. Menedemos thanked the gods that that affliction didn't trouble him.

The chop made the *Aphrodite*'s timbers creak. Menedemos cocked his head and smiled at the familiar sound. The mortises and tenons and treenails that held plank to plank hadn't taken any strain since the akatos came back from Great Hellas the autumn before. Indeed, she'd been beached all winter, for all the world as if she were a warship, to let her dry out. She would be uncommonly fast for a while, till the pine got waterlogged again.

Fishing boats bobbed on the swells. Seeing the *Aphrodite* outbound from the harbor at Rhodes, they knew the galley was no pirate ship. A couple of fishermen even waved at her. Menedemos lifted his right hand from the steering oar to wave back. He loved eating fish—what Hellene didn't?—but nothing could have made him catch them for a living. Endless labor, poor reward . . . He tossed his head: no, anything but that.

Diokles said, "Pity the wind's straight in our face. Otherwise, we could lower the sail from the yard and give the rowers a rest."

"It usually blows out of the north at this season of the year," Menedemos answered, and the oarmaster dipped his head in agreement. Menedemos went on, "But I will take half the men off the oars now. We'll make Kaunos by sundown without hurrying."

"We'd better," Diokles said. He left off clanging his mallet on bronze and called out, "*Oöp!*" The rowers rested at their oars. The akatos eased to a halt. Diokles went on, "Starting from the bow, every other man take a rest." The rowers coming off hauled in their long, dripping oars and stowed them atop medium-sized jars of crimson dye; small, round pots of ink; and oiled-leather sacks full of papyrus from Egypt. "Rhyppa*pai*!" the keleustes sang out. "Rhyppa*pai*!" The men left on the oars went back to work. The *Aphrodite* began to move again, not with the speed she'd shown before but still well enough to suit Menedemos.

"We'll practice tactics for a sea fight a good deal on this cruise," he told the crew. "Never can tell when we'll need them. Except right around Rhodes, pirates are thick as flies round a dead goat."

No one grumbled. Anybody who went to sea knew he told the truth. Sostratos said, "If anybody besides our polis cared about keeping those vultures off the water . . ." He clicked his tongue between his teeth.

"But no one does." Menedemos called to one of the sailors who'd just stopped rowing: "Aristeidas! Go up to the foredeck and keep an eye on things. You're the best lookout we've got."

"Right, captain," the young sailor answered, and hurried forward. He'd proved on the *Aphrodite*'s last voyage how sharp his eyes were. Menedemos wanted a pair of good eyes looking out for pirates. The mountainous seaside district of Lykia lay just east of Kaunos, and, as far as he or any other Rhodian could tell, piracy was the Lykians' chief national industry. Any headland might shelter a long, lean, fifty-oared pentekonter or a hemiolia—shorter than a pentekonter because its oars were on two banks rather than one but even swifter, the pirate ship *par excellence*—lying in wait to rush out and capture a prize. Spotting a raider in good time might make the difference between staying free and going up on the auction block, naked and manacled, in some second-rate slave market.

Menedemos' eye went from the sea to the Karian coastline ahead. Mist and distance—Kaunos lay about two hundred fifty stadia north and slightly east of Rhodes—shrouded his view, but his mind's eye supplied the details he couldn't yet make out. As in Lykia, the mountains of Karia rose swiftly from the sea. The lower slopes would show the green and gold of ripening crops at this season of the year. Farther up grew cypress and juniper and even a few precious cedars. Woodcutters who went up into the mountains after the timber shipwrights had to have might face not only wolves and bears but lions as well.

When he thought of lions, he naturally thought of Homer,

too, and murmured a few lines from the eighteenth book of the *Iliad*:

" 'With them Peleus' son began endless lamentation,
Setting his murderous hands on his comrade's breast.
He groaned again and again, like a well-maned lion
From whom a man who hunts deer has taken its cubs
From the thick woods. It, coming later, is grieved.
It goes through many valleys, seeking the man by scent
If it might find him anywhere: for anger most piercing seizes it.' "

"Why are you going on about lions?" Sostratos asked. Menedemos explained. "Ah," his cousin said. "Do you have a few lines from Homer that you trot out for everything under the sun?"

"Not for everything," Menedemos admitted. "But for most things, if you know the *Iliad* and the *Odyssey*, you'll come up with some lines to help you figure out how it all goes together."

"But that's something you should do for yourself," Sostratos said. "You shouldn't need to find your answers in the words of an old blind poet."

"Hellenes have been doing it ever since he sang," Menedemos said. "Tell me any of your precious philosophers and historians will last as well." He was much more conventional—he thought of himself as much more practical—than Sostratos, and enjoyed twitting his cousin. "Why go to Athens to study, the way you did, when most of what you need is right there under your nose?"

Sostratos exhaled angrily through that nose. "For one thing, a lot of Homer's answers aren't so good as people think they are. And, for another, who says Herodotos and Platon and Thoukydides won't last? Thoukydides wrote his history to be a possession for all time, and I think he did what he set out to do."

"Did he?" Menedemos jabbed a thumb at his own chest. "*I* don't know what all he wrote, and I'm not exactly ignorant.

But you can take any Hellene from Massalia, on the coast of the Inner Sea way north and west of Great Hellas, and drop him into one of the poleis Alexander founded in India or one of those other countries out beyond Persia, and if he recites the lines I just did, somebody else will know the ones that come next. Go on—tell me I'm wrong."

He waited. Sostratos sometimes irked him, but was always painfully honest. And now, with a sigh, Menedemos' cousin said, "Well, I can't do that, and you know it perfectly well. Homer is everywhere, and everybody knows he's everywhere. When you first learn to read, if you do, what do you learn? The *Iliad*, of course. And even men who don't have their letters know the stories the poet tells."

"Thank you." Menedemos made as if to bow without letting go of the steering oar. "You've just proved my case for me."

"No, by the dog of Egypt." Sostratos tossed his head. "What people think to be true and what is true aren't always the same. If we thought this ship were sailing south, would we end up at Alexandria? Or would we still go on to Kaunos, regardless of what our opinion was?"

It was Menedemos' turn to wince. After a moment, he pointed to starboard. "There's a fisherman with a false opinion of us. We're a galley, so he thinks we're pirates, and he's sailing away as fast as he can."

Sostratos wagged a finger in his face. "Oh, no, you don't, best one. You can't slide out of the argument that way." He was, annoyingly, as tenacious as he was honest. "People may believe things because they're true; things aren't true because people believe them."

Menedemos pondered that. A dolphin leaped into the air near the *Aphrodite*, then splashed back into the sea. It was beautiful, but he couldn't point to it and talk about truth. At last, he said, "No wonder they made Sokrates drink hemlock."

That, at least, started a different argument.

WITH THE WIND dead against her, the *Aphrodite*'s crew had to row all the way to Kaunos. The akatos got into the town on the coast of Karia late in the afternoon. Sostratos spoke without thinking as they glided past the moles that closed off the harbor and neared a quay: "We won't have time to do any business today."

He was angry at himself as soon as the words passed the barrier of his teeth—*another phrase from Homer*, he thought, and wished he hadn't. He'd stayed away from Menedemos, as well as he could in the cramped confines of the merchant galley, ever since they wrangled about Sokrates. They'd had that quarrel before; Sostratos suspected—no, he was certain—his cousin had trotted it out only to inflame him. The trouble was, it had worked.

Menedemos answered as if he hadn't noticed Sostratos avoiding him: "You're right, worse luck. But I hope the proxenos will have room for us at his house tonight."

"So do I." Sostratos accepted the tacit truce.

His cousin pulled in on one steering oar and out on the other, guiding the *Aphrodite* towards a berth. Diokles' mallet and bronze square got a couple of quick strokes from the rowers. Then the keleustes called, "Back oars!" Three or four such strokes killed the ship's momentum and left her motionless beside the quay.

"Very nice, as usual," Sostratos said.

"Thank you, young sir," Diokles replied. As toikharkhos, Sostratos outranked him, and was of course the son of one of the *Aphrodite*'s owners. But Sostratos would never be a seaman to match the oarmaster, and they both knew it. Differences in status and skill made for politeness on both sides.

A couple of round ships—ordinary merchantmen—and a shark-shaped hull that looked as if it would make a hemiolia were abuilding in the dockyard not far away. One of the round ships was nearly done; carpenters were affixing stiffening ribs to the already-completed outer shell of planking. Other men drove bronze spikes through the planking from the outside to secure it to the ribs. The bang of their hammers filled the whole town.

Up on the hills above seaside Kaunos, the gray stone fortress of Imbros squatted and brooded. The soldiers in the fortress served one-eyed Antigonos, who had overrun all of Karia three years before. Kaunos still proclaimed itself to be free and autonomous. In these days of clashing marshals, though, many towns' claims to freedom and autonomy had a distinctly hollow ring.

While Sostratos eyed the dockyards and the hills and mused on world affairs, Menedemos briskly went ahead with what needed doing. Like a lot of Hellenes, he carried small change in his mouth, between his cheek and his teeth. He spat an obolos into the palm of his hand. "You know who the Rhodian proxenos is, don't you?" he asked a man standing on the pier who wasn't busy securing the *Aphrodite*.

"Certainly: Kissidas son of Alexias, the olive merchant," the Kaunian replied.

"That's right." Menedemos tossed the little silver coin to the local. He gave the fellow the name of the ship, his own name, and Sostratos'. "Ask him if he's able to put my cousin and me up for the night. I'll give you another obolos when you come back with his answer."

"You've got a bargain, pal." The man stuck the obolos into his own mouth and trotted away.

He came back a quarter of an hour later with a big-bellied bald man whose bare scalp was as shiny as if he'd rubbed it with olive oil. Menedemos gave the messenger the second obolos, which disappeared as the first one had. The bald man said, "Hail. I'm Kissidas. Which of you is which?"

"I'm Sostratos," Sostratos answered. Menedemos also named himself.

"Pleased to make your acquaintance," Kissidas said, though he didn't sound particularly pleased. That worried Sostratos: what was a proxenos for, if not to help citizens of the polis he represented in his own home town? The olive dealer went on, "You'll want lodging, you say?" No, he didn't sound pleased at all.

"If you'd be so kind," Sostratos replied, wondering if Kissidas bore a grudge against his father or Menedemos'. Neither of the younger men had set eyes on the proxenos before. *Menedemos has never tried seducing his wife*, Sostratos thought tartly.

"I suppose I can get away with it," Kissidas said. "But Hipparkhos—he's Antigonos' garrison commander—doesn't much like Rhodians. He's made it hard to keep up the proxeny, he really has."

"We're glad you have kept it up, best one." Sostratos meant every word of that. Neither a buggy, noisy, crowded inn nor sleeping on the hard planks of the poop deck much appealed to him. "And what has old One-Eye's officer got against Rhodians?"

"What would you expect?" Kissidas answered. "He thinks your polis leans toward Ptolemaios."

That held a good deal of truth. Considering how much Egyptian grain went through Rhodes for transshipment all over the Aegean, Sostratos' city had to stay friendly with Ptolemaios. Nonetheless, Sostratos spoke the technical truth when he said, "That's foolish. We're neutral. We have to stay neutral, or somebody *would* gobble us up for leaning to the other side."

"My cousin's right," Menedemos said. He and Sostratos might squabble with each other, but they presented a united front to the world. Menedemos went on, "We even built some ships for Antigonos two or three years ago. How does that make us lean toward Ptolemaios?"

"You don't need to persuade me, friends," Kissidas said, "and you won't persuade Hipparkhos, for his mind's made up."

"Will you have trouble with him because you're taking us in?" Sostratos asked.

"I hope not," the proxenos answered bleakly. "But whether I do or don't, it's my duty to help Rhodians here, the same as it's the duty of the Kaunian proxenos in Rhodes to help men from this city there. Come along with me, best ones, and use my home as your own as long as you're in Kaunos."

Before leaving the *Aphrodite*, Menedemos made sure Diokles would keep at least half a dozen sailors aboard her. "Wouldn't do to come back and find half our cargo had grown legs and walked off, now would it?" Menedemos said.

"Not hardly, skipper, especially when we haven't got any peafowl along with us this spring," Diokles said.

"We haven't got 'em, and we—or I, anyhow—don't miss 'em, either," Sostratos said. He'd had to care for the birds till they sold the last of them in Syracuse, and hadn't enjoyed the experience. *As far as raucous, stupid bipeds go, they're even worse than sailors*, he thought—a bit of fluff he wisely didn't pass on to the oarmaster.

"Come along, my friends," Kissidas repeated, more urgently than before: maybe he didn't want to be seen hanging around a Rhodian ship. Would informers denounce him to Antigonos' garrison commander? As Sostratos went up the gangplank onto the quay, he thanked Fortune and the other gods that Rhodes really was free and autonomous, and that Rhodians didn't have to worry about such nonsense.

As far as the look of both buildings and people went, Kaunos might have been a purely Hellenic city. The temples were older and plainer than those of Rhodes, but built in the same style. Houses showed the world only blank fronts, some whitewashed, and red tile roofs, as they would have back home. All the signs were in Greek. Men wore thigh-length chitons; a few wrapped himatia over the tunics. Women's chitons reached their ankles. If prosperous or prominent women came out in public, they wore hats and veils against the prying eyes of men.

"Just thinking about what might be under those wrappings builds a fire under you, doesn't it?" Menedemos murmured after one such woman walked by.

"Under you, maybe," Sostratos said. His cousin laughed at him.

As Sostratos walked along the narrow, muddy, winding streets, he realized the Karians who shared Kaunos with the Hellenes also made their presence felt. Though they were hellenized as far as dress went, more of their men wore beards than was true at Rhodes—the fad for shaving hadn't caught on among them. Some of them wore short, curved swords on their belts, too: outlandish weapons to a Hellene's eye. And, even if they didn't write their own language, they did speak it—a gurgling tongue that meant nothing to Sostratos.

"Tell me," he said to Kissidas, suddenly curious, "do men and women and even children here in Kaunos sometimes get large drinking parties together for friends of about the same age?"

The Rhodian proxenos stopped in his tracks and gave him an odd look. "Why, yes," he answered. "But how could you know that? You've never been here before, I don't believe, and that's not the custom anywhere else in Karia."

"I've heard it said, and I wondered if it was true," Sostratos answered. Explaining he'd stumbled across it in the history of Herodotos was likely to spawn as many questions as it answered, so he didn't bother.

When they got to the olive merchant's home, a slave greeted Kissidas in bad Greek before barring the door after him and his guests. Kissidas led the two Rhodians across the rather bare courtyard to the andron. The slave brought a jar of wine, another of water, a mixing bowl, and three cups to the men's room. "Supper soon," he said, mixing wine and water in the bowl and filling the cups from it.

"To what shall we drink?" Sostratos asked. "To peace among the marshals?"

"That would be wonderful. It would also be too much to hope for," Kissidas said bleakly. He lifted his own cup. "Here is a prayer the gods may hear: to staying out from underfoot when the marshals clash!" He drank. So did Menedemos. And so did Sostratos. The proxenos' toast summed up his own hope for Rhodes.

Menedemos raised his cup, too. "To making a profit while we stay out from underfoot!" They all drank again. Warmth spread outward from Sostratos' belly. He guessed the mix was one part wine to two of water, a little stronger than usual.

Kissidas said, "I can have couches brought if you like, gentlemen, but I usually dine sitting unless I'm giving a real symposion."

"Don't trouble yourself, best one," Sostratos said at once. "You're doing us the kindness of putting us up. We don't want to disrupt your household any more than we must."

"Good of you. Kind of you." The wine seemed to hit Kissidas even harder than it hit Sostratos. "My dear fellow, some people imagine that staying at a proxenos' house means they own the place." He rolled his eyes. "The stories I could tell you . . ." After another cup of wine, he started telling those stories. Sostratos heard a good one about a long-winded Rhodian of his father's generation whom he already disliked, a pleasure sweeter than most.

At Kissidas' wave, his house slave set a three-legged round table in front of each chair. The sitos—the main part of the meal—the slave fetched in was wheat bread, still warm from the oven. The opson—the relish that accompanied it—consisted of plates of small squids fried in olive oil till they were golden brown.

Like any mannerly person, Sostratos ate sitos with his left hand, opson with his right, and was careful to eat more bread than squid. As Menedemos popped a squid into his mouth with the thumb and first two fingers of his right hand, he inclined his head to Kissidas and said, "You'll make an opsophagos out of me with a supper like this."

Not wanting to be taken for someone who ate opson at the expense of sitos helped keep Sostratos mannerly. He dipped his head to show his host he agreed with Menedemos' comment. Actually, he thought his cousin was exaggerating for politeness' sake. The squids were good—like most Hellenes, Sostratos was very fond of seafood—but nothing exceptional.

"You're too kind," Kissidas said. "I forgot to ask before: what have you got aboard? With an akatos, I wouldn't expect you to be carrying grain or timber or cheap wine or oil."

"No, the *Aphrodite*'s not a bulk hauler, though she's carried grain before," Menedemos said. "We've got perfume from Rhodian roses, and some of the finest crimson dye to come out of Phoenicia since Alexander sacked Tyre twenty years ago."

"And papyrus out of Egypt, and pots of first-quality ink from Rhodes," Sostratos added.

"A few other odds and ends, too: things for men who aren't satisfied with the everyday," Menedemos said.

"The luxury trade, sure enough—I knew it as soon as I saw your ship," Kissidas said. "And what do you hope to get here? This isn't a town with a lot of luxuries to sell; we make our living from our crops, and from the timber and mines in the mountains."

Sostratos and Menedemos shrugged in such perfect unison, they might have been actors on the comic stage. "We'll go into the agora tomorrow and see what your traders have," Sostratos said. "And we'll gladly sell for silver, too. Plenty of that in these parts, if we can pry it out of people."

"I wish you the best of luck," Kissidas said. "But Antigonos squeezes us pretty hard. He—" He broke off as the house slave came in to light lamps and torches, and didn't resume till the man had left the andron. Even afterwards, he kept the conversation innocuous for a while. He had to be worrying about informers.

Menedemos, if Sostratos knew his cousin, had to be thinking about taking one of Kissidas' slave girls to bed. But no women showed themselves, and the fellow who took Sostratos and Menedemos out of the andron led them to a pair of beds in one crowded room. The lamp flickering on the table between the two didn't throw much light, but did shed enough to show Menedemos' expression. It was so eloquent, Sostratos snickered.

"Oh, shut up," Menedemos told him. "You're not a pretty girl."

"I'm not even an ugly girl," Sostratos agreed, "though I suppose I would be, were I a girl."

"That old-fashioned beard you wear certainly wouldn't help," Menedemos said.

Sostratos snorted. "Things could be worse. We could be lying there on the planks of the poop deck." He pulled his chiton off over his head, wrapped himself in his himation, and lay down. Menedemos did the same. Both bed frames creaked as the leather lashings supporting the wool-stuffed mattresses sagged under the men's weight. Menedemos blew out the lamp. The room plunged into blackness. Sostratos fell asleep almost at once.

WHEN MENEDEMOS WOKE up in the Rhodian proxenos' guest bedchamber, he needed a moment to remember where he was. His cousin's snores from the other bed soon gave him a hint. Gray morning twilight was leaking through the wooden shutters over the window. Outside, not very far away, a jackdaw started screeching: "Chak! Chak! Chak!"

The bird's racket made Sostratos' snores falter. He tried to wrap the himation around his head and sleep through the noise, but had no luck. When he muttered something unpleasant and sat up, Menedemos said, "Good day."

"Not too bad," Sostratos answered around a yawn. "Is our host awake?"

"I haven't heard anything stirring except for that jackdaw." Menedemos reached down and felt around under the bed till he found the chamber pot. He stood up to use it, then passed it to Sostratos—Kissidas' hospitality hadn't extended to one for each guest.

"Miserable noisy bird," Sostratos said. "If I could see it instead of just listening to it, I'd try to drown it in here." He set down the pot.

Menedemos shrugged on his tunic. "Let's find the kitchen and seen if we can get some bread and oil and olives, or maybe an onion. Kissidas' slaves will be up, whether he is himself or not. Then we can go back to the *Aphrodite*, get some sailors to haul things for us, and see what kind of luck we have in the agora."

"And what the Kaunians are selling," Sostratos said.

"And what the Kaunians are selling," Menedemos agreed. "Never can tell what you'll find in a place like this: things from the town, things from the rest of Karia—and, no matter what Kissidas says, things from the other end of the world. Ever since Alexander kicked the Persian Empire open for us Hellenes, we've come across all sorts of strange things we'd hardly known about before. Peafowl, for instance."

"They were nothing but trouble," Sostratos said.

"Not quite nothing—we turned 'em into silver." Menedemos waited to see what sort of argument his cousin would give him about that. When Sostratos didn't argue, Menedemos concluded he'd made his point. He went off toward Kissidas' kitchen in a good mood; he didn't win arguments from Sostratos every day.

Kissidas himself came into the kitchen just as Menedemos and Sostratos were finishing their breakfasts. "You boys are up early," he said as he tore a chunk from a loaf of last night's bread.

"We've got a lot to do today," Menedemos said. "The

sooner we get started, the sooner we'll get it done." He was always full of driving energy on the sea, less often on land—when he wasn't chasing some woman or other. But this morning he wished he could do everything at once. "Haven't you finished yet, Sostratos?"

Sostratos spat a last olive pit onto the rammed-earth floor. "I have now. I thought you were just my cousin and my captain, not my master."

"Shows what you know. Come on, let's get moving." He swept Sostratos along in his wake, as the *Aphrodite* brought her boat along in her wake with the tow rope. Over his shoulder, he called back to Kissidas: "We'll see you in the evening, best one. Wish us luck."

"I do, not that I think you'll need too much," the olive merchant answered. "Men who push as hard as you do make their own luck."

Menedemos hardly heard him; he was hustling Sostratos out the front door to Kissidas house. Only then did he hesitate. "Now—to find the harbor." Kaunos' streets did not run on a neat grid. In fact, they ran on no pattern known to geometry. This was an old town, unlike modern Rhodes, which had gone up only a century before, and whose streets went at right angles to one another.

"As long as we go east, we're fine," Sostratos said. "The shadows will tell us which way that is."

"Good enough." Menedemos laughed. "I usually steer by the sun out on the sea, not here on land. But you're right—it should work."

And it did. Menedemos wasn't so sure he'd be able to find Kissidas' house again, but the rising sun did lead him to the harbor and to the *Aphrodite*. A few sailors aboard the merchant galley were still snoring on the rowers' benches, leaning up against the planking of the ship's side. More were up and about but moving with the slow care of men who'd had too much wine the night before.

Diokles, predictably, was both awake and undamaged. "Hail, skipper," he boomed, making several men wince. "I was hoping you'd get here about now. Plenty of things to do today."

"That's right," Menedemos agreed. "Pick me six or eight men to haul jars of dye and perfume and pots of ink and a couple of these sacks of papyrus to the agora. Don't choose any of the fellows who stayed on the ship last night—they're entitled to their fun today."

"Right you are." The keleustes told off several sailors. They grumbled—they wouldn't have been free Hellenes if they hadn't—but they did as they were told. Leading their little procession, Menedemos and Sostratos headed back into Kaunos from the harbor district.

Menedemos had to ask how to get to the agora: no steering by the sun there. The first man he asked babbled at him in Karian, which he didn't understand. The next plainly followed Greek, but made a production of having to think things over till Menedemos handed him an obolos. Once he'd popped the little coin into his mouth, he gave quick, clear directions that also proved accurate. Menedemos silently thanked the gods; he'd known lots of quick, clear directions that had the sole flaw of not taking him where he needed to go.

The market square was still nearly empty when the men from the *Aphrodite* got there. That let them stake out a good spot, one that would give them shade for most of the day. They arranged the jars and pots and sacks the sailors had carried. Menedemos started crying his wares: "Perfume from Rhodian roses! Fine Phoenician crimson dye! Papyrus from the Nile! Fine ink, none better!"

A good many other people were shouting, too, for things like pots and figs—Kaunos was famous for its figs—and leather and wool cloth. *Those* shouts would have gone up in any city around the Inner Sea. Menedemos', for goods out of the ordinary, drew the curious and, he hoped, the slaves of the wealthy.

"Where's your crimson from?" a man asked. "Just saying 'Phoenician,' now, that doesn't mean a thing. Plenty of towns in Phoenicia, and every one of 'em has its own style of fixing up the shellfish."

"Byblos," Sostratos said. "Since Alexander sacked Tyre, everyone agrees that Byblian crimson is the best."

"Oh, I don't know about that," the Kaunian replied. "I've

always been partial to Sidon's dye, myself. But I might use Byblian on my wool, if I can get a halfway decent price for it. What do you want for one of your jars? They'll be a Rhodian kotyle apiece, won't they?"

"That's right," Sostratos replied. "About the size of a big drinking cup of wine. But you can get your wine for a few oboloi. Crimson dye is dearer—shellfish aren't so easy to come by as grapes."

"I know, I know." The wool merchant sounded impatient. "Tell me what you want for a jar. I'll tell you what a gods-detested thief you are, and we'll go from there."

Sostratos smiled. So did Menedemos; the Kaunian didn't believe in wasting time. "Just as you say, best one," Sostratos told him. "Thirty drakhmai the jar seems a fair price."

"Thirty?" the local howled. "You *are* a gods-detested thief! I expected you to say fifteen, and I'd've laughed at that. Ten would be too much, by Zeus Labraundeus." He spoke Doric Greek not much different from Menedemos' or Sostratos', but the god by whom he swore was Karian.

"Nice of you to stop by," Sostratos said pleasantly. The wool merchant made no motion to leave. The little crowd that had gathered leaned forward for the next move in the dicker. Sostratos merely waited. He was good at that, better than Menedemos, who was an impulsive plunger by temperament.

Looking like a man with a sour stomach, the Kaunian wool dealer said, "I suppose I might go up to twelve." Sostratos hardly seemed to hear him. As if every word hurt, the local added, "Or even thirteen."

"Well . . ." Sostratos plucked at his beard. Everyone waited. How much would he come down? Sometimes—often—Menedemos stuck his oar into the bargaining, too, but this didn't seem to be the moment. In tones of mild regret, Sostratos said, "I don't *suppose* my father would take a strap to me if I got twenty-eight drakhmai the jar." He didn't sound sure about that, though.

He didn't drive the wool merchant away, either. The spectators smiled and nudged one another: this would be a loud, long, entertaining haggle. One man whispered to the fellow beside him, offering a bet on what price the dye would finally bring.

Plainly, the dicker would tie things up for a while. Menedemos walked away, judging he had time for a quick look around the agora. He ate a fig candied in honey. He had to work to keep from exclaiming at how good it was. "Maybe we should talk," he told the man selling them. "I might try bringing a few of those to Rhodes, on the off chance some people would like them."

"Don't wait too long, my friend," the dealer answered. "They always go fast. I've already sold a lot."

"Let me see what else I might be interested in," Menedemos said. "This fellow next to you has . . . Are those really lion skins? And what's that one with the stripes?"

"That's from the Indian beast called a tiger," the man at the next stall said. "If I were to stretch the skin out, you would see it's even bigger than the ones from the lions. *They're* local. They were killing sheep up in the hills till a whole mob of men took after 'em with spears."

"Er—yes," Menedemos said. No lions on Rhodes. There never had been, not so far as anyone's memory reached. Here on the Anatolian mainland, though, it was a different story. He recalled the verses he'd recited on the sea; Homer had known the beasts well. They didn't live in Hellas these days, though some were still supposed to lurk in the back woods of Macedonia.

Menedemos was about to ask a price for the hides. Hellenes didn't wear furs—that was the mark of Thracians and Skythians and other barbarians—but images of Zeus and Herakles could be decked in lion skins . . . and, he supposed, in a tiger skin as well. Or maybe that would do for Dionysos, who was also said to come from India.

Before he put the question to the merchant, though, he noticed another item by the man's sandaled foot. "What exactly is *that*, and where did it come from?" he asked.

"I can answer the second question easier than the first," the fellow replied. "The fellow who sold it to me said he got it from a man who'd lived in Alexandria Eskhate."

"The *last* Alexandria?" Menedemos echoed. "Alexander

named towns for himself all over the east. Where's that one?"

"Way off near the edge of the world—in Sogdiana, on the Iaxartes River," the merchant said. "The Hellene who lived there got it from the Sakai who roam the plains to the north and east. Where the nomads found it, the man who sold it to me couldn't say. I guess the fellow who sold it to him didn't know, either."

"What *is* it?" Menedemos asked again. "What did it come from?" The merchant told him. His eyes widened. "You're joking."

"Looks like one, doesn't it?" the Kaunian said.

"I don't know. I've never seen one before," Menedemos answered. "I don't know anybody who has . . . or maybe I do." He glanced over toward Sostratos. His cousin looked to have just struck a bargain with the wool merchant. That meant he could come over and take a look. Menedemos whistled shrilly, then waved to draw his notice. "*Oë*, Sostratos!" he shouted. "Come here!"

SOSTRATOS WAS MORE than a little pleased with himself. He'd got the Kaunian wool merchant up to twenty-two drakhmai a jar for six jars of crimson dye. Anything over eighteen drakhmai the jar was profit, so he'd done pretty well. Now that the wool merchant had gone off to get the silver—*one mina, thirty-two drakhmai*, said the calculating part of Sostratos' mind that rarely rested—he wanted a moment in which he could relax and be proud of himself.

He wanted one, but he didn't get it. From halfway across the agora, Menedemos started waving and whistling and generally acting the fool. "*Oë*, Sostratos!" he called. "Come here!"

"What is it?" Sostratos shouted back. He doubted whether anything in Kaunos' market square was worth getting excited about.

His cousin, though, evidently disagreed with him. "Come here," his cousin repeated. "You've got to take a look at this."

"Take a look at *what*?" Sostratos asked irritably. Menedemos didn't answer. He just waved and called again. Muttering under his breath, Sostratos went over to see what besides a pretty girl could get his cousin in such an uproar.

When he got to the flimsy stall by which his cousin was standing, Menedemos pointed dramatically and said, "There!"

Sostratos stared. Staring didn't tell him what he needed to know, so he asked the question he had to ask: "What *is* that thing?"

"A gryphon's skull," Menedemos and the local merchant answered together. They might have come from the chorus in a revived tragedy of Euripides'.

"A gryphon's skull?" Sostratos echoed, as if he couldn't believe his ears. As a matter of fact, he couldn't. "But . . . I always thought—everyone always thought—gryphons weren't real. Herodotos puts them at the end of the world with the one-eyed Arimaspioi and other unlikelihoods."

"This skull comes from the end of the world," Menedemos said, and told Sostratos what the Kaunian had told him. Before Sostratos could say anything, his cousin added, "And if that's not a gryphon's skull, my dear, I'd like you to tell me what it is."

"I . . . don't know." Sostratos squatted beside the extraordinary skull—it was definitely the skull of some sort of beast, whether gryphon or not—for a closer look. After a moment, Menedemos crouched down beside him. "What *have* you come across here?" Sostratos asked his cousin.

"I already told you," Menedemos said. "You didn't want to believe me, that's all."

"Do you blame me?" Sostratos said. Menedemos only shrugged.

The skull itself said nothing at all, of course. It only lay on the muddy ground in the middle of Kaunos' agora and stared back at Sostratos out of large, empty eye sockets. The skull itself was impressively large, too: perhaps two cubits long, and almost a cubit and a half wide at the broadest point, though it narrowed at the front to a curved beak almost like that of an eagle. Growing astonishment and awe prickled through Sostratos; gryphons were supposed to have just that sort of beak.

Unlike an eagle's, though, this beak held teeth. Sostratos tilted the skull for a better look. He would have expected fangs to put a lion's to shame, but these flat-topped, square teeth looked more like a cow's or a goat's. "Isn't that interesting?"

Sostratos murmured. "No matter what we've heard, the gryphon may graze instead of killing."

"What makes you say that?" Menedemos asked.

"Its teeth," Sostratos answered, and explained his reasoning. Menedemos pursed his lips as he thought, then dipped his head in agreement.

"You're a clever fellow," the Kaunian merchant said. "That never would have occurred to me."

"A clever fellow, eh?" Sostratos tossed his head. "If I'm so clever, why did I never imagine . . . this?" He reached out and rested his palm on the skull's projecting, beaky snout. The feel of it surprised him anew; it was cooler and heavier, more solid, than he'd expected from old bone. "It might almost be stone under my fingers," he said, and glanced toward Menedemos. "You don't suppose some sculptor—"

"No." His cousin cut him off. "That's impossible, best one, and you know it as well as I do. Who could have imagined such a thing, let alone carved it? Those teeth are *teeth*. A man would break his heart and go blind trying to shape them. And the broken horn that sticks up and back from the skull? Don't be absurd."

Sostratos sighed. He would have loved to tell Menedemos he was wrong, but couldn't. "You have me, I'm afraid."

He straightened, picked up the skull—it weighed about a third of a talent, he guessed—and turned it all the way over, wondering if the underside would tell him anything the top hadn't. On closer inspection, he discovered the teeth weren't quite so much like a cow's as he'd first thought. But he still couldn't imagine the gryphon eating meat with them.

Menedemos pointed to some reddish dirt clinging to the bottom of the skull. "There. You see? It's not carved. It's been buried underground for a long time."

"Well, maybe." Sostratos tried to scrape off the dirt with his finger. It didn't want to be scraped. He broke a fingernail trying, in fact, and had to gnaw at it to get some sort of even edge. "It's not dirt. It's stone." He tried scraping, more cautiously, with his other index finger. A little of the stuff came away, but not much. "Soft, sandy stone, but stone, no doubt about it."

After reaching out himself and scraping a bit, Menedemos dipped his head. "You're right. How long do you suppose a skull would have to stay underground to have bits of stone stuck to it?"

"I couldn't begin to guess," Sostratos answered. "Herodotos says the Egyptians say their kings and priests go back 341 generations, which he makes out to be something over 11,000 years. Some good part of that time, anyway."

"Probably." Menedemos whistled softly. "Over 11,000 years? That's a long time. I don't suppose it's been even *one* thousand years since the Trojan War, has it? You know things like that."

Before Sostratos could tell him it hadn't been a thousand years, or even quite nine hundred, since the Trojan War, the Kaunian merchant said, "So what will you give me for this gryphon's skull?"

And, before Sostratos could even ask him how much he wanted, Menedemos laughed and said, "Oh, my dear fellow, that old bone is interesting to look at, but I don't think we want to buy it. What in the name of the gods is it good for, except maybe as the strangest decoration for an andron anyone ever saw? Now the lion skins you've got, and the one from the—tiger, did you call it?—those I might be interested in talking about with you."

"Menedemos," Sostratos said.

His cousin ignored him. Menedemos was turning into a haggler right in front of him. Examining the skins with a critical eye, he clicked his tongue between his teeth in dismay. "I'd pay more if it weren't for this poorly repaired hole here. Where a spear went in, I suppose?"

"Menedemos," Sostratos said again, rather louder. The next time, he would scream his cousin's name. He was sure of it.

But, for a wonder, Menedemos deigned to notice him. "Yes? What is it, best one? You wanted something?" He was the picture of slightly distracted good will.

Sostratos took him by the arm. "Walk with me for a moment, if you'd be so kind." He led his cousin out of earshot of the local before speaking in a low voice: "I want that skull."

"What?" As he'd thought it would, that got rid of Menedemos' distraction. "Why? What would you do with it?"

"Take it to Athens," Sostratos replied at once. "I'd want Theophrastos and the other philosophers at the Lykeion—and the ones at the Academy, too—to see it and study it and learn from it. Most philosophers have always thought the gryphon a mythical beast, like a centaur or a Cyclops. But *that*"—he didn't point back toward the skull, for fear of showing the merchant how much he wanted it—"proves it's as real as a horse. Don't you see how important that is?"

"Maybe," Menedemos said. "What I don't see is how we'll make any money from it."

To the crows with money, Sostratos started to say. But he didn't let the words out. His cousin understood silver much better than he understood the relentless drive of curiosity. And so Sostratos chose a different tack: "We might get the Lykeion and the Academy bidding against each other to see who would own it."

"Do you think so?" Menedemos quirked an interested eyebrow upward.

"Why not?" Sostratos said. "Do you suppose philosophers have any less desire for fame and any less desire to get a leg up on their rivals than ordinary men?"

"You would know better than I," Menedemos answered.

"My dear, you have no idea," Sostratos said. "Some of the things the men of the Academy did to us when I was in Athens—"

"And what did your side do to them?" his cousin asked shrewdly.

"Oh, this and that," Sostratos said in innocent tones. "But if you buy those hides—and I think you can make money from them—by all means get that skull, too."

"Well, I'll see what I can do," Menedemos replied. "But if he asks a couple of talents for it, the philosophers will have to do without, because I don't believe they'll come up with that kind of money. Now you go on back and tend to what we brought to the agora: we don't want to lose customers of our own. I'll take care of this fellow. Go on, now."

Reluctantly, Sostratos went. He wanted to stay and do the dickering himself. Menedemos, after all, didn't really care about the gryphon's skull. But, after a moment, Sostratos realized that gave his cousin an advantage. If he haggled himself, the merchant would see how much he wanted it, and would charge accordingly. What better shield against gouging than indifference?

To his surprise, the first Kaunian who came up to him was interested, not in dye or in perfume, but in papyrus and ink. In short order, Sostratos had sold him two round pots of ink and three twenty-sheet rolls of papyrus, and made fifteen drakhmai. "What will you do with it?" he asked the local.

"I aim to copy out all the city laws," the man replied. "As things are now, they're either carved in stone or written out on wooden tablets, and they're scattered all over Kaunos. If we have them all in one place, we can refer to them whenever we need to, and the papyrus won't take up nearly so much space."

"That sounds . . ." Sostratos cast about for a word, and found one that fit: "efficient. Very efficient indeed."

"It's a new world," the local said seriously. "If we don't change with the times, we'll go under." Looking pleased with himself, he carried his purchases out of the market square.

Sostratos cried the virtues of crimson dye and perfume and papyrus and ink—if he'd sold those to one man here, he might sell them to another. At the same time, he kept an eye on Menedemos and the man with the skins and the gryphon's skull. They both gestured with considerable animation; they were, to Sostratos' annoyance, too far away for him to hear what they were saying. Then a burly man came up and asked about his perfume, and he lost any sense of the dicker across the agora because he had to pay attention to the one at hand.

He soon recognized his customer as a brothelkeeper. "If the girls smell good, they'll get more trade, and they'll be able to charge more, too," the fellow said. "Of course, if you try and charge me too much for your rosewater here, I'll never make back the price, so you can't squeeze me too hard."

Sostratos felt like squeezing the local by the neck, for distracting him from the deal in which he was more interested. He ended up selling the perfume for less than he might have, both because he was distracted and because the brothelkeeper quibbled over oboloi with the dogged persistence of a man who struck a dozen bargains every afternoon. Sostratos didn't lose money on the deal, but he didn't make any to speak of, either.

At last, after what seemed like forever, Menedemos ambled back from the Kaunian merchant's stall. "Aristeidas, Teleutas, come on back to the ship with me. We need to get some silver, and then we need to pick up some things." He led the two sailors off toward the *Aphrodite* without telling Sostratos *which* things they would pick up and without giving him the chance to ask.

He did that on purpose, Sostratos thought with no small annoyance. He didn't mind Menedemos' always taking the lead, though he himself was older than his cousin. He didn't enjoy standing in front of men and shouting and gesturing to urge them on to pay higher prices, while Menedemos relished nothing more—except, perhaps, seducing their wives. *But when he gives orders deliberately intended to drive me mad . . .*

Kaunos wasn't a big city. Menedemos didn't need long to return to the agora, coins clinking in a leather sack he carried in his left hand. His right hand rested on the hilt of a sword he'd belted on. Aristeidas was similarly armed; Teleutas carried a belaying pin with the air of a man who knew what to do with it. It would have taken a large band of determined robbers to separate Menedemos from his money.

Along with the sailors, he strode over to the stall of the merchant with the hides—and the gryphon's skull. Sostratos watched anxiously and tried to listen, but got distracted again when a local came up and wanted to talk about the best way to make crimson dye fast to Koan silk. Normally, Sostratos would have been delighted to talk shop with the fellow. As things were, he'd never had a customer he wanted less. Even when the man bought a jar of dye, he had to make himself remember to take the money.

Here came Menedemos, carrying the striped tiger skin rolled up and tied with rope. At another time, that hide by itself would have been plenty to rouse Sostratos' always lively curiosity. Here came Aristeidas, with a rolled-up lion skin under each arm. And . . . here came Teleutas, lugging the gryphon's skull and looking put upon, as anyone who got stuck with the heaviest piece of the work would have.

Sostratos hurried over to Menedemos and kissed him on the cheek. "Thank you, O best one!" he exclaimed. Then, pragmatism returning, he asked, "What did you pay for it?"

"Thirty drakhmai," Menedemos answered. "Polluted whoreson wouldn't go any lower, not even when I asked him if he felt like waiting twelve years or so till another mad philosopher wandered into the agora here."

"He probably gave twenty-five to the Hellene he bought it from, and didn't want to part with it at a loss," Sostratos said.

"Exactly what I was thinking." His cousin grinned at him. "I notice you don't deny being a mad philosopher."

"I do love wisdom, or the chance to gain some," Sostratos said seriously. "As for mad . . ." He shrugged. "I'd rather call myself, mm, inquisitive."

Thoukydides had had some sharp things to say about men who called a thing by one name when it manifestly deserved another. But Sostratos honestly didn't think he was mad for knowledge the way, say, Sokrates had been. *Of course, what madman ever believes he is one?*

Teleutas said, "I've sailed up past Byzantion onto the Pontos Euxeinos, and I've seen gryphons painted on plates along that coast, and done up in jewelry. Up there, they make 'em out to be pretty. But any beast with a skull like this'd have to be the ugliest thing that ever hatched out of an egg."

"Now *there's* a question, my wisdom-loving cousin," Menedemos said. "Do gryphons hatch from eggs, or are they born alive?"

"It's a question with a simple answer, as far as I'm concerned," Sostratos replied. "I don't know."

"An honest answer, anyway," Menedemos said. "Come on, boys, back to the akatos again. We'll stow these prizes—and the skull—and then see what else we can get."

"Prizes—and the skull?" Sostratos echoed unhappily. "Why did you buy it if you didn't think we'd make anything from it?"

"Because, my dear, you'd have fussed and fumed this whole

sailing season if I'd left it sitting there on the ground. Thirty drakhmai isn't too high a price to pay for a summer's worth of peace and quiet," Menedemos answered. Sostratos' ears got hot. There were times when his cousin knew him much too well.

"OH, *That* Thing," Kissidas said when Menedemos and Sostratos went back to the Rhodian proxenos' house for supper that evening. "I've seen it in the agora. Everybody in Kaunos has seen it in the market square by now, I daresay. Why in the name of the gods did you want it?"

"Well . . ." Menedemos, usually so glib, found himself at a loss for words. "You see . . . That is . . ." *I bought it to keep Sostratos happy* didn't seem reason enough, not when he sat in the olive merchant's andron instead of bargaining in the market square.

Sostratos was glib enough here: "I want the philosophers in Athens to see it. It answers many questions about gryphons, starting with whether they're real or mythical beasts. I'd always thought they were the stuff of story myself, but I see I was wrong."

"Hard to have a real skull for a mythical beast," Kissidas said with a dry chuckle.

"Exactly so, best one," Sostratos agreed. He would have made a better merchant if everyday affairs roused the same passion in him as this oddity did. *Of course he needs oddities to interest him—he's odd himself,* Menedemos thought. His cousin went on, "At the same time, though, having a veritable gryphon's skull raises as many questions as it answers."

Those questions were for the moment forgotten when Kissidas' cook brought in a dogfish smothered with melted cheese and leeks to accompany his fresh-baked bread. Menedemos made sure he ate enough bread so as not to seem a shameless opsophagos, but the portion of dogfish set before him vanished with marvelous haste. To his relief, his host and his cousin ate their fish just as fast.

But, after Kissidas licked his fingers clean, he asked, "What sort of questions does the gryphon's skull raise? It just looks like ugly old bones to me."

To me, too, Menedemos thought. But Sostratos answered, "Well, for one thing, why would gryphons make good guards for the gold of the Skythians? They have—or this one has, at any rate—teeth that would be better for grazing than for ripping and tearing, as a lion might do."

Kissidas blinked. "I never would have thought to look at its teeth. Who would?"

"Sostratos is like that," Menedemos murmured.

He didn't think the olive merchant heard him. To his relief, he didn't think his cousin did, either. Sostratos went on, "And you're right to say it looks like old bones, but it doesn't feel like old bones. It feels like stone, and it has bits of stone stuck to it here and there. Why should gryphons have skulls made of stone when all other beasts have theirs made of bone?"

"All other beasts? I don't know about that," Kissidas said.

"Name another beast with a skull of stone," Sostratos challenged.

"Well, there's Hipparkhos, up in the fortress on the hill," the Rhodian proxenos said, deadpan.

Menedemos guffawed. "He's got you."

"So he has." Sostratos had the grace to chuckle. But then he got back to the business at hand: "You see why I want the philosophers to be able to examine it?"

"Old bones." Kissidas tossed his head. "You'll never make any silver with old bones."

"We didn't pay that much," Menedemos said, stretching a point. "And Sostratos hopes we can get a couple of the philosophical schools in Athens bidding against each other to see who gets to keep the gryphon's skull. So we may turn a profit yet." He didn't really believe it, but he would back his cousin against a near-stranger.

"For your sake, I hope your cousin is right." The proxenos didn't sound convinced, but he didn't sound as if he wanted an argument, either: "And I hope the rest of your business went well."

"Pretty well," Menedemos said. "We don't get the prices for perfume that we would if we were farther away from Rhodes, but we can't do anything about that. People here who want it badly can sail down to the polis and get it in the agora for the same price a Rhodian would pay."

"Pity we can't let the Lykeion and the Academy bid up the price of that tiger hide, too," Sostratos said wistfully.

"Well, we can't." Menedemos wanted to make sure his cousin had no doubts about that. "I'm sure we can get more for it somewhere else." Sostratos dipped his head, but didn't look happy. Menedemos went on, "Gods only know if we'll ever see another gryphon's skull, my dear, but you can be sure more tiger skins will make their way towards Hellas. They're beautiful, and they're bound to make money for the fellow selling them. You can't say either of those things about the skull."

"That's true." Sostratos sounded a little more cheerful.

One of the lamps in the andron burned out, making shadows swell and swoop and filling the room with the scent of hot olive oil. Menedemos expected Kissidas to call for a slave to refill it and light it again. Instead, the Rhodian proxenos put a hand in front of his mouth to hide a yawn. Voice still blurry, he said, "Your pardon, best ones, but I'm going to bed. It's been a busy day, and I have another one in front of me tomorrow." He picked up another clay lamp and handed it to Menedemos. "I'm sure you two can find your way to your own room tonight. Good night." Out he went, thriftily dousing torches on the way.

"Not the most subtle hint I've ever seen," Sostratos remarked, anger and amusement warring in his tone.

Anger triumphed in Menedemos, as it had in Akhilleus in the *Iliad*. Menedemos reckoned he had better reason for it than the hero of old. "He didn't much want us here in the first place," he growled. "Now he's treating us shabbily on purpose. Some proxenos he is."

"I don't know," Sostratos said. "He would have given us salt fish for opson were that so, not that lovely little shark. You can't blame him for being nervous about Antigonos' garrison in the fortress above the town."

"Who says I can't?" Menedemos returned. "We might as well go to bed now, though, unless you'd sooner sit in a dark andron here when this lamp goes out." He got to his feet. So did Sostratos.

They'd just left the andron when someone knocked on Kissidas' front door. "Who's that?" Sostratos said softly. "Whoever it is, I'll bet Kissidas wishes he'd go away. Good news doesn't come by night."

"It isn't our worry, and I'm not sorry it isn't." Menedemos headed back toward the cramped guest room they shared. They'd just undressed and lain down when a cry of anguish and alarm rent the nighttime stillness. Gladder than ever that it wasn't his worry, Menedemos blew out the lamp. Black night enfolded the room.

It didn't last long. Someone came rushing back toward the little chamber.

Torchlight sneaked under the bottom of the door. Kissidas knocked and called, "Open up, in the name of the gods!"

Menedemos got out of bed without bothering to put his chiton back on. He spoke to Sostratos: "Maybe it's our worry after all." Opening the door, he addressed the Rhodian proxenos in more normal tones: "Good heavens, what's happened?"

"I'll tell you what." Kissidas was practically hopping in agitation; the torch trembled in his hand. "Ptolemaios has brought an army and a fleet up to Phaselis, in eastern Lykia. The town fell to him a few days ago, and he's heading west—heading this way."

"*Oimoi!*" Menedemos whistled. Lykia, like most of Anatolia, was held by Antigonos. The summer before, Ptolemaios' general Leonides had struck at Alexander's one-eyed general in Kilikia, farther east along the southern Anatolian coast. Antigonos' son Demetrios promptly drove him away. But Ptolemaios, who ruled Cyprus as well as Egypt, didn't seem ready to give up the fight.

Kissidas wasn't worrying about the larger shape of the war between the marshals. His concern was more immediate, more personal. "When Hipparkhos hears about this, he's going to nail me to a cross," he moaned. "I give thanks to Zeus that the first man here with the news was a fellow who's bought my oil and olives for years."

From behind Menedemos, Sostratos said, "If Antigonos' captain here in Kaunos suspects the Rhodian proxenos of favoring Ptolemaios, he'll suspect a couple of real Rhodians even more."

"Just my thought." Kissidas eagerly dipped his head. "You have to get away—this very moment, if you can. And take me and mine with you." Awkwardly, he went to his knees and embraced Menedemos around the legs in supplication.

"Get *up,*" Menedemos told him. His wits worked furiously. His cousin and the olive merchant were right—to a point. "We can't flee in the night, not with half my crew in the taverns and the brothels here, not unless I want to leave them behind. This customer of yours—he won't go to the garrison commander with this word, will he?"

"No," Kissidas said. "He does not love Antigonos."

"All right, then. We'll sail at first light tomorrow. If you and yours are aboard when we leave, we'll take you down to Rhodes," Menedemos said. The proxenos gabbled out thanks. Sostratos made approving noises. Menedemos hardly heard either one of them. Only he knew how little he wanted to return to his home town.

SOSTRATOS STOOD ON THE *APHRODITE'S* tiny foredeck, peering into Kaunos. "Where is he?" he grumbled. Twilight was coming on, paling the waning crescent moon, Kronos' wandering star not far from it, and Zeus' bright wandering star now low in the west.

"I don't know where he is," Menedemos answered from the poop; Sostratos' voice must have carried better than he'd thought. His cousin continued, "I don't much care, either. If he's not here by the time the sun climbs up out of the sea, we're sailing anyhow. Furies take me if I'm going to risk my ship in this stupid war."

You risked it last year, in the war between Syracuse and Carthage, Sostratos thought. He'd reckoned Menedemos utterly mad, but his cousin had got away with it, and made a fat profit beside. Maybe Menedemos had learned his lesson. Maybe—more likely—he just saw no money in staying in Kaunos.

Aristeidas' arm shot out. "Someone's coming this way."

"Stand by to cast off!" Diokles rasped. "Rowers, be ready." If those were Hipparkhos' soldiers approaching the merchant galley rather than Kissidas and whatever companions he had with him, the *Aphrodite* could flee in a hurry.

Along with Aristeidas and everyone else aboard the akatos, Sostratos tried to make out who those shapes were. His eyes weren't bad, but the lookout's were better. "Whoever they are, they've got women with them," Aristeidas said. "See the long chitons?"

After a moment, Sostratos did. "Unless Antigonos has Amazon mercenaries, that'll be the proxenos and his family," he said. A couple of rowers chuckled. Once Sostratos had spoken, though, he wondered if that wasn't possible. With a gryphon's skull there among the *Aphrodite*'s cargo, what had seemed obvious myth suddenly looked like something else altogether.

Three men, three women, a little boy, a baby of indeterminate sex in one of the women's arms. One of the men, the biggest and squarest, was undoubtedly Kissidas. One of the women would be his wife. One might be a daughter. The other, almost without a doubt, would be a daughter-in-law; hardly any families reared two girls.

As the day got brighter and the women got closer, Sostratos saw they were veiled against the prying eyes of men not of their household. Kissidas called, "Thank you for waiting for us, my guest-friends."

"Come aboard, and quickly," Menedemos said from his station at the stern. "We've got no time to waste."

"You're probably right," Kissidas agreed with a sigh. "Chances are good a slave in one of our houses will have gone up the hill to Hipparkhos by now." He and his companions hurried along the quay toward the ship. As they boarded, the olive merchant introduced the males: "My son Hypermenes, my grandson Kissidas, my son-in-law Lykomedes son of Lykophron." He did his best to pretend the women weren't there.

Menedemos followed custom, too, doing his best not to look as if he was trying to see through those veils. *But he is*, Sostratos said. *He's bound to be. The more women cover up, the more he wants to know what they're hiding.* A lot of men among the Hellenes felt that way, but his cousin did so to a greater degree than most.

"Why don't you all go up to the foredeck?" Menedemos said; like Kissidas, he didn't acknowledge the women with any special words. The closest he came to it was a brief addition: "No one will bother you there."

"Thank you," Kissidas said.

Sostratos hastily descended from the foredeck and made his way back toward the stern as the Rhodian proxenos and his kinsfolk came forward. At least one of the women wore perfume; the sweet scent of roses made him whip his head around. But he couldn't even be sure which one it was.

"Cast off!" Diokles called, and the lines tying the *Aphrodite* to the pier thumped down into the akatos.

At almost the same moment, Aristeidas said, "I see more people coming down toward the harbor." Sostratos saw them, too. The horsehair plumes in their bronze helmets made them look taller and more fearsome than they really were.

"They aren't coming to invite us to symposion," Menedemos said with commendable calm. "Let's get out of here."

"Back oars!" Diokles said, and set the stroke with his mallet and bronze square. He also called it out: "Rhyppa*pai*! Rhyppa*pai*! Come on, you lugs! Put your backs into it!"

As if sliding through glue, the *Aphrodite* began easing away from the pier. Each stroke seemed to push her a bit faster than the one before, but she needed a little while to build up momentum. Kissidas' son—or maybe it was his son-in-law—spoke in a nervous tenor: "They're starting to run."

"Rhyppa*pai*! Rhyppa*pai*!" Diokles called.

"You, there!" someone shouted from the shore.

"Who, us?" Sostratos called as the *Aphrodite* eased another few cubits away from the pier.

"Yes, you!" That had to be a soldier; no one else could hope to put so much authority into a shout. "Are you the polluted Rhodians?" More soldiers trotted down to the end of the wharf. Most of them carried spears, which would do them no good, but a few had bows, and the merchant galley wasn't out of arrow range yet.

"Rhodians?" Sostratos answered. "Are you daft? We're the *Thetis*, out of Kos. Want to buy some silk?"

That made the fellow with the big voice pause for a moment to talk to one of his comrades. Then he started yelling again: "Liar! We know you've got that gods-detested Kissidas on board. Bring him back or you'll be sorry!"

"What?" Sostratos artfully cupped a hand to his ear. "Say that again. I couldn't hear you."

His performance might have won applause on the comic stage, but it failed to impress Antigonos' soldiers. They wasted no time in consultation now. One word came very clearly over the widening expanse of water: "Shoot!"

The handful of archers on the shore drew their bows and did their best. Sostratos thought the *Aphrodite* had got safely out of range. Indeed, most of the arrows splashed into the sea well short of the akatos. But one shaft, either shot with a superhuman tug on the bow or pushed along by a vagrant puff of breeze, thudded into the ship's planking a few cubits from Sostratos. *That could have killed me*, he thought with a sick dizziness he recognized only belatedly as fear.

Menedemos pulled in on one steering-oar tiller and out on the other till the *Aphrodite*'s bow swung toward the south. "Regular stroke!" Diokles commanded, and the rowers shifted from backing oars as smoothly as if they'd been working together for years. The archers kept on shooting, but now all their shafts fell short.

"Lower the sail from the yard," Menedemos called, and the sailors leaped to obey. The great linen square sail descended from the yard as the men released the brails that had tightly held it there. The sail wasn't a single piece of linen; for strength, it was sewn from many smaller squares. It also had light lines stretched horizontally across its front, perpendicular to the brails, giving it something of the appearance of a pavement made from square slabs of stone. The breeze blew from the north, as it usually did at this season of the year. As the sail filled with wind, the lines thrummed and the mast grunted in its socket as it leaned forward under the pull of the wind and got to work.

Sostratos ascended to the poop deck. Menedemos grinned at him. "You did a good job with those soldiers," he said. "You kept them confused till we were too far away for it to matter." He snickered. " 'Want to buy some silk?' "

"That was foolish of me." Sostratos was never satisfied with his own performance. "I should have said we came from Halikarnassos or Knidos. Antigonos holds all the mainland cities, but Kos belongs to Ptolemaios."

"Don't worry about it. It didn't matter," his cousin said.

A new and unpleasant thought occurred to Sostratos. "You don't suppose they'll send a trireme after us, do you?"

"I hope not!" Menedemos exclaimed, and spat into the bosom of his tunic to avert the evil omen. Sostratos was a modern man who prided himself on rationality, but he did the same thing. *It can't hurt*, he thought with a twinge of guilt.

"I didn't see any triremes in the harbor," Diokles said. Before that could do much to reassure Sostratos, the oarmaster went on, "I don't know how much it matters, though. A pentekonter or a hemiolia packed with soldiers could do for us nicely. Just depends on how bad that captain wants us."

He was right. Sostratos felt it at once. By Menedemos' dismayed expression, so did he. When Diokles spoke of matters pertaining to the sea, he almost always knew what he was talking about. Menedemos called, "*Oë*, Kissidas!"

"What is it?" the olive merchant asked.

"How bad does Hipparkhos want you dead? Will he throw some of his mercenaries into a ship and come after us?"

The blunt question made one of the women up on the foredeck begin to wail. But Kissidas tossed his head. "I don't think so. Now that I'm gone from Kaunos, he'll just go on about his business. He suspected me because I was Rhodian proxenos, not because I was myself, if you know what I mean."

He paused, then snarled a curse. "But I'll bet he steals my groves and my oil press, the son of a whore."

"If Ptolemaios really is coming west through Lykia, nobody who backs Antigonos will have long to enjoy them," Sostratos said.

"That's true." Kissidas brightened. He asked, "How long a sail is it to Rhodes? Do you know, I've never been to your polis, even though I've represented her in Kaunos for years. I've never been farther away than the edge of my groves."

"If the wind holds, we should be in the harbor in the early afternoon," Menedemos answered. "Even if the wind doesn't hold, we'll make it before nightfall. I'll put men at the oars to make sure we do, in case you're wrong and Hipparkhos does try to come after us."

The Rhodian proxenos—now, the exile—bowed. "From the bottom of my heart, I thank you for rescuing me and mine."

"My pleasure," Menedemos replied. Then mischief glinted in his eyes. In a voice only Sostratos and Diokles could hear, he murmured, "From the heart of my bottom, you're welcome."

Diokles guffawed. Sostratos snorted and gave his cousin a severe look. "You really have read too much Aristophanes for your own good."

"There's no such thing as too much Aristophanes," Menedemos said.

Before Sostratos could rise to that—and he would have, as surely as a tunny would rise to the anchovy impaled on a fisherman's hook—Kissidas called back to the poop in plaintive tones: "Excuse me, gentlemen, but does this boat always jerk and sway so?" He followed the question with a gulp audible all the way from the foredeck.

"He hasn't got any stomach at all, has he?" Menedemos muttered.

"No," Sostratos said. He sometimes got sick in what most sailors reckoned moderate seas, but this light pitching didn't bother him in the least. "Good thing it is only a day's journey." To a seasick man, of course, *only* was the wrong word; the voyage would seem to last forever.

His cousin must have been thinking along the same lines,

for he spoke up urgently: "If you have to heave, O best one, in the name of the gods lean out over the rail before you do."

"Good thing we've got a following breeze," Diokles said with wry amusement. "Otherwise, you'd have to explain the difference between leeward and windward—if he didn't find out by getting it blown back into his face."

Menedemos laughed the callous laugh of a man with a bronze stomach. "One lesson like that and you remember forever."

Well before noon, Kissidas and one of the women of his household bent over the rail, puking. From his post at the steering oars, Menedemos avidly stared forward. "Trying to see what she looks like without her veil?" Sostratos asked, his voice dry.

"Well, of course," his cousin answered. "How often do you get the chance to look at a respectable woman unveiled? Unwrapped, you might say?"

"*You* might," Sostratos said as another spasm of vomiting wracked the woman. "Tell me, though, my dear—if she came back here right now and wanted to give you a kiss, how would you like that?"

Menedemos started to say something, then checked himself. "Mm, maybe not right now." But he kept looking ahead. After a moment, he gave a dismissive shrug. "Besides, she's not very pretty. She must have brought a fat dowry."

The familiar bulk of the island of Rhodes swelled in the south, dead ahead. Sostratos said, "We *will* get in not long after noon."

"So we will," Menedemos replied.

Sostratos gave him a curious look. "Aren't you glad to be able to spend a couple of extra days at home?"

"No," Menedemos said. *Goodness*, Sostratos thought as his cousin steered the akatos south without another word and with his face as set and hard as iron. *His quarrel with his father must be worse than I thought.*

"*OÖP!*" DIOKLES CALLED, and the rowers rested at their oars. Sailors tossed lines to a couple of longshoremen, who made the *Aphrodite* fast to one of the quays in the great harbor of Rhodes.

"What are you doing here?" one of the longshoremen asked, looping the coarse flax rope round a post. "Nobody thought you'd be back till fall. Get in trouble up in Kaunos?" He leered at the merchant galley, and at Menedemos in particular.

"We had to get out in a hurry, all right," Menedemos said, and the longshoreman's leer got wider. *You haven't heard the news, then*, Menedemos thought. He smiled, too, but only to himself. After a suitably dramatic pause, he went on, "Ptolemaios has an army and a fleet operating in Lykia. He's taken Phaselis, and he's heading west—he'll probably take the whole country. Antigonos' garrison commander in Kaunos was going to seize the Rhodian proxenos there, and maybe us, too, so we grabbed Kissidas and his family and got away."

"Ptolemaios is in Lykia?" That wasn't just the one longshoreman; that was almost everyone within earshot, speaking as if in chorus. Heads swung to the northeast, as if men expected to see Ptolemaios from where they stood. An excited gabble rose.

"That will be all over the polis by sunset," Sostratos remarked.

"It should be. It's important," Menedemos said. "Now we ought to take Kissidas and his people to the Kaunian proxenos here. Do you know who handles Kaunos' affairs in Rhodes?"

"Isn't it that moneychanger named Hagesidamos?" Sostratos said. "He'll be easy to find—he'll have a table in the agora where foreigners can turn their silver into Rhodian money."

"And where he can turn a profit," Menedemos added. "Moneychangers never starve." He raised his voice: "Kissidas! *Oë*, Kissidas! Gather up your kin and come along with us. We'll take you to the Kaunian proxenos here. He'll make arrangements for all of you."

"Send the gangplank across to the pier," Kissidas said. "When I reach dry land again, I'll kiss the ground."

Menedemos gave the order. Bald head shining in the sun, Kissidas hurried up onto the quay, followed by his kinsfolk. He bustled down it to the end, stepped off onto the soil of Rhodes, and kept his promise. Sostratos took an obolos out of his mouth and gave it to a fellow standing on the wharf. "Go to my father's house, near the temple to Demeter in the north end of the city. Let him know we've returned, and that we'll see him soon. Menedemos' father lives next door. Tell him, too."

"Yes, tell my father we're home," Menedemos echoed with a singular lack of enthusiasm. Eager to put off the moment when he saw Philodemos again, he went on, "Let's go scare up old Hagesidamos." He started up the gangplank himself.

His cousin followed, but kept looking back over his shoulder. "Are you sure . . . things will be all right here?"

"I know you." Menedemos laughed in his face. "You don't mean 'things.' You mean your precious gryphon's skull. Answer me this, my dear: what thief would be mad enough to steal it?"

Sostratos' ears turned red. "I think the skull is worth something," he said with dignity. "I think the philosophers in Athens will agree with me, too."

"Anyone else?" Menedemos asked. Sostratos proved his basic honesty by tossing his head. Menedemos laughed again. It wasn't likely, and he knew it. He waved to Kissidas. "Come along with my cousin and me. We'll take you to the proxenos."

Having done that, though, he had little choice but to go home. His father waited for him in the courtyard. "I heard you were home," Philodemos said when he came in, "but I haven't heard why yet."

"I'll tell you," Menedemos said. He plunged into the tale, heading for the andron as he did. "—and so," he finished a little later, "I didn't see what else I could do except bring Kissidas and his family back here to Rhodes."

His father studied him. *He's looking through me, not at me*, Menedemos thought nervously. Somewhere outside the men's room, a woodpecker drummed on a tree trunk. The sudden noise made Menedemos start. "No need to jump, son," Philodemos said. "I don't see what else you could have done, either. If a man's made himself your guest-friend, you can't very well leave him behind to be harmed by his enemies."

Menedemos tried not to show how relieved he was. "My

thought exactly. He took us in even though he knew it might anger Antigonos' captain. And then this news of Ptolemaios . . ."

"Yes." Philodemos dipped his head. "That's part of the picture, too. If Ptolemaios is coming west across Lykia, it puts the war right on our doorstep. I wish it were farther away. If he and Antigonos start hammering away at each other next door to us, one of them or the other is bound to notice what fine harbors we have and what useful subjects we'd make."

"I wish I thought you were wrong, sir." Menedemos wished that for more reasons than one. Not only did he worry about his polis, he also worried about agreeing with his father. To keep from thinking about it, he changed the subject: "What sort of opson will Sikon have for us tonight?"

"I don't know," Philodemos replied. "He ran out to the market square as soon as that fellow from the harbor came here shouting that the *Aphrodite* had come in. He was muttering something as he went, something about why hadn't anyone told him." He rolled his eyes. "You know what cooks are like."

"Everybody knows what cooks are like," Menedemos said. Like any prosperous household's cook, Sikon was a slave. But, because he ruled the kitchen like a king, he often acted as if he were master of the whole house. Menedemos rose from his chair. "If you'll excuse me, Father, I think I'll go in there and find out what he's up to."

"Good luck." Even iron-willed Philodemos often lost his skirmishes with Sikon.

The cook was a middle-aged man, on the plump side—who would have wanted a man who didn't care for the meals he turned out? "Snooping, are you?" he said when Menedemos stuck his head in the door.

"I live here, every now and again," Menedemos said mildly. He didn't want to quarrel with the cook, either. A man who did that often regretted it in short order.

"Oh. It's you, young master." Sikon relaxed. "I thought it'd be your stepmother." He snorted, sounding amazingly like a bad-tempered donkey. Philodemos' second wife was ten years younger than her stepson. The cook went on, "You won't pitch a fit if I spend a couple of oboloi so the house has something better than sprats or salt fish for opson."

"Baukis takes the business of being a wife seriously." Menedemos didn't want to criticize the girl. What he wanted to do . . . Had she been another man's, any other man's, wife, he would have gone after her without hesitation. He knew himself well enough to be sure of that. But even he fought shy of adultery with his own father's new spouse.

"Seriously!" Sikon threw his hands in the air. "You'd think we'd all eat nothing but barley porridge for the next ten years if I buy something tasty. Can you talk some sense into her, young master? Your father doesn't want to do it; that's pretty plain. She just looks down her nose at me, the way free people do with slaves sometimes, but maybe she'd listen to you."

"Maybe," Menedemos said uncomfortably. He didn't want reasons to talk with Baukis; he wanted reasons to stay away from her. But Sikon had given him an opening to shift the subject, and he seized it: "What sort of tasty things did you find this afternoon?"

"Some nice shrimp—they were still wriggling when I got 'em," Sikon answered. "I'm going to glaze them with honey and oregano, the way your father likes. And a fellow there in the market had the first good eels I've seen this spring. What do you say to eel pie, baked with cabbage and mushrooms and silphium from Kyrene? And a cheesecake, to use up the rest of the honey I got for the glaze."

"What do I say? I say hurry up and cook, and quit wasting your time talking to me. Eels!" Menedemos had all he could do not to lick his chops like a hungry dog. He didn't ask what the seafood had cost. All he wanted to do was eat it.

And he did, along with his father in the andron. He supposed Sikon also sent some of the splendid supper to Baukis in the women's quarters. She would surely find out from Philodemos what the cook had bought; sharing the bounty might make her better inclined to him. If anything could, that would.

As he usually did, Menedemos woke before sunrise the next morning. He went to the kitchen for some barley rolls—leftovers from sitos at supper—and olive oil and wine for breakfast. Carrying them out to the courtyard, he sat down on a stone bench there and watched the sky get light. He would have done the same thing lying on the *Aphrodite*'s poop deck after a night spent at sea.

A couple of slaves dipped their heads to him as they ducked into the kitchen for their morning meal. They ate the same sort of breakfast he did; Philodemos wasn't the sort of master who gave them a precisely measured ration of flour every day and made sure they didn't sneak into the kitchen to supplement it. To make up for that generosity, he worked them hard.

When a laughing dove fluttered down into the courtyard, Menedemos tossed a small chunk of roll onto the ground in front of it. It walked over, head bobbing, examined the morsel, and ate it. They were very tame birds. Had Sikon tossed it crumbs, it would have been with a view toward netting it for a meal.

Someone came down the stairs and out into the courtyard. Tame or not, the dove took off, wings whirring. "Good day, Menedemos," Baukis said.

"Good day," Menedemos answered gravely.

"How are you?" his stepmother asked. The title, applied to a girl who couldn't have had more than sixteen years, was as absurd as Sikon's snort had made it. She was no great beauty, and even at sixteen had hardly more breasts than a boy.

"I'm well, thanks." Menedemos kept his tone formal. He knew what his father saw in her: dowry, family connection, the chance for another son or two. He was much less sure what he saw in Baukis himself. Maybe nothing but the chance to outrage his father in the greatest possible way. But maybe something more, too. Doing his best not to think about that, he asked, "And you?"

She thought before answering, "Well enough." She was no fool; the way she said even commonplace things showed that. *And so?* Menedemos jeered at himself. *Are you Sostratos, to look for what a woman has between her ears before you look for what she has between her legs?* Baukis went on, "I didn't expect to see you back in Rhodes so soon."

"I didn't expect to be in one of Antigonos' cities so close to where Ptolemaios started his campaign," Menedemos replied.

"This endless war is liable to be the death of trade," she said. "That would be bad for Rhodes, and especially bad for this family."

"True," Menedemos agreed. No, she was no fool; plenty of men who stood up and blathered in the Assembly couldn't see so clearly.

Her expression sharpened. "You surprised Sikon when you came home, too. Do you know how much he paid for last night's shrimp and eels?"

Menedemos tossed his head. "No. All I know is, they were delicious."

"Expensive, too," Baukis said. "If we make less money because of the war, how long can we afford such fancy opson?"

"Quite a while," Menedemos said in some alarm. However young she was, his father's second wife took her duties as household manager most seriously. She'd already had several rows with the cook. Menedemos went on, "We're still a long way from poor, you know."

"*Now* we are," Baukis answered. "But how long will we stay that way if we make less and spend more? I'd better have a word with Sikon. Sooner or later, he'll have to listen to me."

She strode off toward the kitchen. Menedemos' gaze followed her. She didn't have a boy's hips and backside, not at all. And, here inside the house, she didn't veil herself against the prying eyes of men. It was practically like seeing her naked all the time. Menedemos' manhood stirred.

Baukis came out of the kitchen with bread, wine, and an indignant expression on her face. "He's not in there yet," she complained. "He spends too much money, and he's lazy, too." She sat down on the bench, hardly more than a cubit away from Menedemos, and began to eat her breakfast.

Does she know what I feel? Menedemos wondered, as he had ever since realizing it himself the autumn before. He didn't think so, but . . . *Is she sitting there to tease me? Is she sitting there because she has something in mind, too?*

He had more than a little practice seducing other men's wives. Here, he didn't want to use what he knew. He wished he were aboard the *Aphrodite,* a steering-oar tiller in each hand, wave and wind and the chance of pirates all he had to worry about. None of them seemed so dangerous as the woman beside him.

Gulping down the last of his wine, he got to his feet and said, "I'm off. As long as I'm back in Rhodes, I have a couple of men I need to see."

"All right." Baukis went on eating. Menedemos' withdrawal felt uncomfortably like headlong retreat.

ONE OF THE advantages of being a free Hellene was having slaves to do the work one didn't care to do oneself. Sostratos took that for granted. His slave, a Karian named Arlissos, did not. "Is it much farther, boss?" he whined in almost unaccented Greek. "This polluted thing gets heavier every step I take."

Such illogical arguments were the wrong sort to use against Sostratos, who answered, "That's impossible," and for good measure added, "And, since no place inside the walls of Rhodes is more than about ten stadia from anywhere else inside the walls, you're not walking all that far."

"I bet it seems farther to me than it does to you," Arlissos said darkly.

Sostratos didn't deign to reply to that. He was just glad he'd had Arlissos drape the gryphon's skull in a square of sailcloth before taking it through the streets of Rhodes. Otherwise, people would have stopped him every plethron—more likely, every few cubits—and pestered him with questions.

Arlissos seemed more inclined to pester him with complaints: "And then, once we get where we're going, I'll have to lug it all the way back."

Not if I break it over your head, Sostratos thought. But he couldn't do that, no matter how tempting it might be. So far as he knew, this was the only gryphon's skull ever seen by Hellenes. He couldn't afford to have anything happen to it.

"You'll have plenty of time to rest and loaf when we get where we're going," he said. "In fact, if you slide back to the kitchen, you can probably wheedle the cook out of some wine, and maybe some figs or some nuts while you're at it."

The slave brightened, though he didn't seem to want to

show Sostratos he was any happier. "My arms are going to come out of their sockets," he grumbled.

"Oh, be quiet," Sostratos said, and then, "There's that little temple to Hephaistos, so it's only another couple of blocks."

They'd come into the western part of the city, most of the way from Sostratos' house to the gymnasion. But Sostratos didn't intend to strip off his clothes and run or wrestle. He exercised as little as he could get away with, not least because Menedemos easily outdid him when they went to the gymnasion together. Sostratos was larger than his cousin, but Menedemos was far quicker and more graceful.

"I . . . think this is the house," Sostratos said. He had trouble being sure; one blank housefront looked very much like another. *If I'm wrong,* he thought as he knocked on the door, *whoever answers can probably set me right.*

Somewhere inside the house, a dog started barking. Arlissos set down the gryphon's skull so he could stretch and show how put-upon he was. He'd just picked up the skull again when somebody said, "Yes? What is it?" through the door.

"Is this the house of Damonax son of Polydoros?" Sostratos asked.

"Yes. Who wants to know?" The door still didn't open.

Sostratos gave his own name, adding, "I've brought something your master may be interested in seeing."

"Wait," said the man on the other side of the door. Sostratos duly waited. So did Arlissos, who exuded silent reproach. After a bit, the door did swing open on the lengths of doweling that turned in holes in the floor and the lintel. "He'll see you," Damonax's slave reported. By his guttural accent and narrow, swarthy face, he was probably a Phoenician. "He's in the courtyard. Come with me."

"Hail, Sostratos," Damonax said when the doorman brought the newcomers into the courtyard. He was a handsome man about ten years older than Sostratos, his hairline beginning to recede at the temples. Pointing to the sailcloth-shrouded bundle Arlissos bore, he asked, "What have you got there?" Like Sostratos', his Doric Greek—the dialect spoken in Rhodes—had an Attic overlay; he'd studied at the Lykeion for several years, returning to his home polis the year after Sostratos arrived.

Like a conjurer performing at a symposion, Sostratos whipped away the square of sailcloth. "Behold!" he said. "A gryphon's skull!"

"Really? You're joking." Damonax got up off the bench where he'd been sitting and came over for a closer look. He tapped the skull with his fingernail. "No, by the dog of Egypt, I see you're not. Where on earth did you find it?"

"Kaunos," Sostratos answered, and explained how he and Menedemos had come by the skull. "I brought it here because you also studied under Theophrastos. What do you make of it?"

"I wish you could have brought that tiger skin you mentioned, too," Damonax said wistfully. "If going out to trade can lead to such marvels as this, the Hellenes who look down their noses at it may have to think again."

Most upper-class Hellenes looked down their noses at merchants. The life of a gentleman farmer was the ideal, with an overseer and slaves to do the actual work, giving the gentleman farmer himself the money and leisure he needed to live as he would, beholden to no one. Damonax wore two heavy gold rings; the clasps of his sandals were likewise golden. Roses scented the olive oil he rubbed into his skin. He lived the ideal.

Acknowledging that, envying it, Sostratos said, "Thank you, O best one."

"Thank *you* for letting me see this." Damonax pointed to the bench on which he'd been sitting, then spoke to Arlissos: "Why don't you put the skull down there, so your master and I can examine it as we please?"

"I'll gladly do that, sir." The Karian sighed with relief as he set down the skull.

To his own slave, Damonax said, "Bring us some wine, Phelles, and some olives, or whatever else you find in the kitchen." Nodding his head as barbarians often did to show agreement, the Phoenician hurried away. Damonax leaned close to the gryphon's skull and tapped it again. "It feels more like stone than bone," he remarked.

"I noticed the same thing," Sostratos answered. "I don't know what it means, except that the skull is old and was buried for a long time."

"Not just old," Arlissos muttered. "Heavy."

"Who was the philosopher," Damonax asked, "who found petrified seashells on the mountainside and realized the ocean must have covered it long ago?"

"I should know that." Sostratos thumped his forehead with the heel of his hand. "A pestilence! I *do* know that." He snapped his fingers, then suddenly grinned. "Xenophanes of Kolophon, that's who it was."

"*Euge!*" Damonax exclaimed. "Very well done indeed, in fact. I couldn't have come up with the name if you'd given me to Antigonos' nastiest torturer."

Phelles came back with a wooden tray on which he carried a bowl of olives and two cups of wine. He set them down on the bench by the gryphon's skull. Seeing no wine for himself, Arlissos took the tray from Phelles' startled hands. "Here, my friend," Sostratos' slave said, "let me carry this to the kitchen for you." Sostratos popped an olive into his mouth to hide a smile. If Arlissos didn't end up with a snack, he would be surprised.

Damonax pointed to the back-projecting horn. "Pity this bit seems broken off. I wonder what the beast would have looked like when it was alive."

"Not so pretty as gryphons are supposed to be, I suspect," Sostratos said. "And what do you make of its teeth?"

"I didn't pay any attention to them," Damonax confessed. As Sostratos had in the market square at Kaunos, the other Rhodian picked up the skull and turned it over for a closer look. When he put it down on the bench again, his face was thoughtful. "Doesn't have much in the way of fangs, does it?"

"I thought the same thing," Sostratos said. "How is it supposed to guard the gold at the edge of the world and fight off thieves?"

"With its claws, perhaps," Damonax suggested, and Sostratos dipped his head—that was a good idea, and it hadn't occurred to him. The older man looked from him to the gryphon's skull and back again. "Tell me, best one, now that you've got this remarkable thing here, what did you have in mind doing with it? Are you going to keep it at your house and tell stories about it the rest of your life?"

"No, by Zeus!" Sostratos exclaimed.

"Ah." Damonax looked wise. "Then you'll want to sell it, I expect." Try as he would, he couldn't keep a slightly dismissive tone from his voice. *No matter what he says, he really does look down on traders*, Sostratos realized. Smoothly, Damonax went on, "I could give you a good price for it myself, as a matter of fact."

So you can keep it here and tell your own stories about it, Sostratos thought. He tossed his head. "I was going to take it to Athens, to let the philosophers at the Lykeion and the Academy examine it."

As if he hadn't spoken, Damonax said, "How does two minai sound?"

"Two hundred drakhmai?" Sostratos tried hard not to show how startled he was. Menedemos, he was certain, would have sold the gryphon's skull on the spot, and spent the next year bragging about the profit he'd squeezed from worthless, ugly bones.

Damonax must have taken astonishment for rejection, for he said, "Well, if you won't take two, what about three?"

Part of Sostratos, the part that made him a pretty good merchant, wondered how high Damonax would go to buy the skull. The other part, the part that valued knowledge for its own sake, quailed in horror. *Gods be praised my family is well enough off that I don't* have *to sell it for the first decent offer that comes along*.

"You're very kind," he said, by which he meant, *You're very greedy*, "but I really do intend to take it to Athens. I'd be on my way there now if my ship hadn't had to bring the Rhodian proxenos and his kin here from Kaunos."

"Four minai?" Damonax said hopefully. Sostratos tossed his head again. Damonax sighed. "You're serious about going to Athens, aren't you?"

"Yes, of course I am," Sostratos replied.

"Isn't that interesting? And here I thought someone who traded things for money would trade *anything* for money."

Damonax didn't seem to think Sostratos might take that for an insult: the older man hadn't quite called him a whore, but he'd come close. Damonax continued, "You never did explain why you had to get the Rhodian proxenos out of Kaunos."

"Didn't I?" Thinking back, Sostratos realized he hadn't. He told the other man about Ptolemaios' descent on Lykia.

"Ah—that was news to me," Damonax said. "Are you sure you won't reconsider my offer? I wish you luck getting to Athens from here. As soon as the word spreads, the Aegean will be full of war galleys. How much will Ptolemaios and Antigonos' sailors care about a gryphon's skull?"

Sostratos grimaced. Ptolemaios' fleet was based on Kos, while Antigonos' navy sailed from ports on the Ionian islands farther north and on the mainland of Anatolia. Damonax was bound to be right: those ships *would* clash. Sostratos said, "We're free. We're autonomous. We're neutral. No one's ships have any business interfering with us."

"Certainly, that's how we Rhodians feel." Damonax was polite as the ideal landed gentleman, too. That didn't keep him from asking the next obvious question: "Do you think the marshals' captains, or the pirates they hire to do their scouting and raiding, will agree with us?"

"I can't answer that," Sostratos answered, in lieu of saying, *Not a chance they will.* But he went on, "The *Aphrodite* will try to get to Athens, though."

"You are a stiff-necked fellow, aren't you?" Damonax said. "Suppose I were to give you six minai for that skull?"

"I didn't bring it here to try to sell it to you." Sostratos raised his voice: "Arlissos! Where have you gone and disappeared to?"

When the Karian slave emerged, his cheeks were full as a dormouse's. "Are we leaving already?" he asked in disappointed tones around a mouthful of something or other.

"I'm afraid we must." Sostratos pointed to the gryphon's skull. "Wrap the sailcloth around that, and let's get's going." He wanted to get out of there as fast as he could. Damonax had shown even more interest in the skull than he'd expected, and not of the sort he'd looked for. If the gentleman farmer suddenly called out half a dozen hulking slaves . . . If that idea hadn't yet occurred to Damonax, Sostratos thought it wise to leave before it did.

"Are you sure I can't persuade you to let me take that skull off your hands?" Damonax said. "I offered a good price: six minai is a lot of money."

"I know, O best one," Sostratos answered. "But I want to take it to Athens. And who knows? I may do better there."

He didn't believe it for a moment. By Damonax's expression, neither did he. But the older man didn't try to keep Sostratos from leaving, and no burly slaves appeared to rape away the gryphon's skull. Once out in the street again, Sostratos breathed a long sigh of relief. He and Arlissos hadn't gone more than a few steps back toward his own house before the slave asked, "Did he really say he'd give you six hundred drakhmai for these miserable old bones?"

"Yes, that's what he said." Sostratos dipped his head.

"And you turned him *down*?" Arlissos sounded disbelieving. He sounded more than disbelieving; he sounded as if he'd just witnessed a prodigy. "By Zeus Labraundeus, master, I don't think you'd turn down six hundred drakhmai for *me*."

He might well have been right. Karian slaves were cheap and easy to come by in Rhodes, while the gryphon's skull was—and, Sostratos was convinced, would remain—unique. Instead of saying so straight out, Sostratos tried a joke: "Well, Arlissos, you have to understand: it eats a lot less than you do."

"Six hundred drakhmai," Arlissos said; Sostratos wondered if the slave had even heard him. "Six hundred drakhmai, and he said no." He looked down at the shrouded skull and spoke to it as if they were equals in more than price: "Hellenes are crazy, old bone, you know that?"

Sostratos indignantly started to deny it. Then he thought about what Menedemos would say if his cousin found out he'd turned down six minai for the gryphon's skull. Menedemos would be certain at least one Hellene was raving mad.

"NO," MENEDEMOS SAID impatiently when Sostratos began to pester him again. "We can't sail for Athens as soon as you want."

"But—" his cousin began.

"No," he repeated. "I want to get out of Rhodes, too, but we can't, not right now. Have you seen these new gemstones coming in from Egypt, the ones called emeralds?"

"I've heard of them. I haven't seen any yet," Sostratos replied.

"Well, my dear, you'd better, if you think you can pry me out of Rhodes before I pry some emeralds out of this roundship captain who has some," Menedemos declared.

"But the gryphon's skull—" Sostratos protested.

"No!" Menedemos tossed his head. His shadow tossed, too, and frightened a butterfly from a flower in the courtyard garden of Lysistratos' house. He watched it flitter away, then resumed: "The skull's been buried since before the Trojan War. We talked about that. Whether it gets to Athens now or next month or month after that doesn't matter so much. Whether I can get my hands on these emeralds does."

"That *is* logical," Sostratos admitted. Then, when Menedemos hoped that meant he would be reasonable, he added, "But I still don't like it."

"Too bad," Menedemos said heartlessly.

Too heartlessly: he put his cousin's back up. "What makes these emeralds so special?" Sostratos demanded.

"They're fine gems, that's what," Menedemos answered. "They're as fine as rubies, except they're green, not red. They're greener than green garnets; they're as green as . . . as . . ." He was stuck for a comparison till he plucked a leaf from one of the plants in the garden. "As this."

"That's my sister's mint, and she'd give you a piece of her mind if she saw you picking sprigs," Sostratos said.

"How immodest," Menedemos said. Except for her wedding, he hadn't seen Erinna unveiled since she was a little girl.

"She does speak her mind," Sostratos said, not without a certain pride. And she was probably up there in the women's quarters listening to every word said here in the courtyard. Women of good family might not get out much, but that didn't mean they had no way to find out—and to influence—what went on around them.

"Let's give her a chance to talk behind our backs, then,"

Menedemos said. "Till you've seen these stones, you have no idea why I'm in such an uproar about them. Thrasyllos has no idea I'm in such an uproar, you understand, and I'll thank you kindly not to give the game away."

"You know me better than that, I hope." Sostratos sounded affronted. "Thrasyllos is the man who has these emeralds?"

"That's right. He's just in to Rhodes from Alexandria with a round ship full of Egyptian wheat."

"Why has he got them, then?" Sostratos asked.

"He gets cagey about that," Menedemos answered. "I think one of his kinsmen works in the mine, somewhere out in the desert east of the Nile."

"So these may be . . . unofficial emeralds, then?"

"That thought did cross my mind, yes."

Sostratos' eyes narrowed craftily. "Lots of Hellenes from Egypt who can get Ptolemaios' ear come through Rhodes. If you have to, you might want to point that out to the marvelous Thrasyllos."

"You're a demon, aren't you?" Menedemos' voice rose in admiration. "I should have thought of that myself."

They left the house and headed down toward the harbor, a route Menedemos had taken ever since he was old enough to toddle along after his father. He didn't care to think about that now; he didn't like to think about anything having to do with Philodemos. But the journey was as familiar to him as any in the polis could be.

There stood Mnesipolis the smith, banging away at something while his fire sent smoke up into the sky. There was the usual crowd of gabbers and loungers outside the shop of Pythion the cobbler. Sostratos made the remark he usually made, too: "Sokrates taught outside a cobbler's shop just like this one. In Athens, they still show you the place that used to be Simon's."

"Pythion can teach you everything you want to know about shoes," Menedemos said.

"Can he teach me what's true and what's good and what's beautiful and why?"

"Certainly—about shoes."

"You're no help, and neither is Pythion."

"Yes he is, if the sole of my sandal is ripped—not that I wear sandals very often."

"What about your own soul?"

Instead of playing word games with his cousin, Menedemos picked a stone up out of the street and chucked it at a couple of scrawny dogs that were squabbling over some garbage by a wall. The stone hit the wall with a sharp crack. One of the dogs ran off. The other gulped down whatever they'd been fighting about. Then it, too, trotted away.

Agathippos' bakery was as smoky as Mnesipolis' smithy, but the sweet smell of baking bread made Menedemos forgive the smoke. A goggle-eyed gecko clung to the wall at Agathippos'. A crow tried to grab it, but it scurried into a crack in the mud brick and the bird flew away unhappy.

Down by the great harbor, every other building seemed to house a tavern. A man stood pissing against a wall by one of them; a drunk lay asleep in the street outside another. Sostratos clucked disapprovingly and said, "There is a man with no self-control."

"Can't argue with you," Menedemos said. "Getting a bellyful of wine is one thing. Getting blind-drunk in the morning?" He tossed his head. "No thanks."

Gulls and terns wheeled overhead, mewling and skrawking. A pelican, its wingspan as wide as a man was tall, flapped majestically by. Shorebirds skittered here and there with nervous little steps, now and then pausing to peck at bugs or small crabs.

Menedemos pointed ahead. "There's Thrasyllos' ship: the *Aura*."

" 'Fair Wind,' eh?" Sostratos' lip curled. "He ought to call her the 'Breaks Wind.' " Menedemos let out a yip of startled laughter. Sostratos went on, "How can the skipper of a ship that looks like *that* have any real jewels? He's probably trying to sell you green glass."

The ship wasn't much to look at. The eyes at the bow needed repainting, which gave her a sad, half blind appearance. The goose-head ornament on the round ship's sternpost hadn't been touched up any time lately, either. Her unpainted timber was gray with age. Even so, Menedemos said, "You'll see." He raised his voice: "*Oë*, Thrasyllos! You there?"

"Where else would I be?" The *Aura*'s captain came up on deck. He was a lean little man with a sailor's sun-darkened skin and a narrow, worried face. "Hail, Menedemos. Who's your friend?"

"My cousin," Menedemos answered, and introduced Sostratos. "He wanted to see your stones, too." That seemed better than saying, *He thinks you're a fraud.*

"Hail," Sostratos said politely, but his voice held no warmth at all.

"Well, come aboard, both of you." Thrasyllos didn't sound especially happy, either. He wasn't shy about explaining why, either: "The fewer people who know about this business, the better. Come on, come on. My crew's off getting drunk and getting laid. We can talk."

The *Aura* could probably carry ten times as much as the *Aphrodite*. Even so, Menedemos wouldn't have traded his akatos for the merchantman for anything in the world. The round ship lived up to her description, with a beam close to a third of her length. Even with a fair wind behind her, she would waddle along like a fat old man, and she'd be slower yet struggling to make headway against contrary breezes. "An amphora with a sail," Menedemos muttered as he strode down the gangplank.

"Amphorai have better lines than this floating hip-bath ever dreamt of," Sostratos answered, also in a low voice.

But Thrasyllos' big, ugly ship had certain advantages of its own. He had a much smaller crew than Menedemos needed on the *Aphrodite*, for he required no rowers, only men to handle the enormous square sail now brailed up against the yard. That kept his expenses down, and meant he could haul cargo that wouldn't have been profitable aboard the merchant galley.

Thrasyllos also enjoyed more comfort than Menedemos did. He had a real deckhouse on the poop, and could sleep in a bed even if the *Aura* had to spend a night at sea. Menedemos didn't mind occasionally wrapping himself in his himation and sleeping on the timbers, but he could see how other men might.

"Show my cousin these emeralds," he said as he came up to the round ship's captain.

"Let's go inside the deckhouse," Thrasyllos said nervously. "You never can tell who might be watching."

Menedemos was willing, but Sostratos tossed his head. "No. The light won't be any good in there. If I'm going to look at these stones, I want to be able to do a proper job of it."

"My cousin has a point," Menedemos said.

"Oh, all right." Thrasyllos didn't sound happy about it. He kept peering around the harbor, as if he expected Ptolemaios himself to emerge from behind a careened fishing boat. "Here." He reached into a leather sack with a drawstring mouth, took out a couple of stones, and set them in Menedemos' palm as if not trusting Sostratos to touch them.

"Let me see," Sostratos said. Menedemos handed him the emeralds; whether Thrasyllos did or not, he knew his cousin was almost painfully reliable.

He also knew, just at a glance, that Thrasyllos was showing his biggest and finest gems. One of them was wide as his fingernail, the other only a tiny bit smaller. Both had the astonishing deep rich green color that had drawn his eye when the captain from Egypt first showed him the stones.

"Interesting," Sostratos said, keeping his voice as neutral as he could make it. He was a merchant; he knew better than to show any sort of enthusiasm. But he couldn't help adding, "They are gemstones of a sort, no doubt about it."

"I said so," Menedemos told him.

"So you did." Sostratos gave him a measuring stare. "But you've been known to . . . How should I put it? To let your enthusiasm run away with you."

"At least I have enthusiasms. You're as cold-blooded as a frog." Were they alone, Menedemos might have had a good deal more than that to say. Sostratos wasn't the real opponent here, though. Thrasyllos was. And so Menedemos contented himself with adding, "You see why I'm interested in them."

"I can see why you might be, anyhow." Sostratos looked at Thrasyllos. "My cousin didn't tell me what you're asking for them."

Thrasyllos licked his lips. "A mina apiece," he said.

"A pound of silver?" Sostratos made a production of returning the emeralds. "I'm sorry, O marvelous one, but I have to tell you I think you're quite mad."

"*Brekekekex koax koax,*" Menedemos said softly—the noise of the chorus of frogs in Aristophanes' play. Sostratos ignored him, and Thrasyllos plainly had no idea what the nonsense words meant.

The captain of the *Aura* said, "You wouldn't talk like that if you know what my nephew went through to sneak these out of the mines. He stuck 'em up his arse, is what he did, then dosed himself with poppy juice so he wouldn't have to take a shit for a couple of days, till he was well away from there."

Sostratos unobtrusively rubbed the palm of his hand on his chiton. Menedemos fought down laughter. His cousin had always been a little on the prissy side. But Menedemos was using Sostratos as a weapon against Thrasyllos here, and so he said, "They are interesting, but your price is way out of line."

"Somebody will pay it," Thrasyllos said, but he sounded none too confident.

"Somebody will give your name to Ptolemaios, is what will happen," Menedemos said, and Thrasyllos flinched as if he'd hit him. Pressing his advantage, Menedemos went on, "He's not down in Alexandria—he's right over there in Lykia with a big fleet. You think you can outrun his war galleys in this wallowing scow? Good luck, best one."

"Menedemos and I now, we know how to keep quiet," Sostratos added, his tone suggesting they were the only people in the whole world who did. Menedemos dipped his head in solemn agreement.

Thrasyllos licked his lips again. His shoulders stiffened, though. Menedemos would have bet he was going to be stubborn. But one of the Rhodian dock loungers chose that moment to wave and call out, "*Oë*, Menedemos!"

"What is it, Moiragenes?" Menedemos asked impatiently.

The shabby, skinny man couldn't have played his part better had Menedemos paid him a mina of silver. "You hear the latest?" he said. "Ptolemaios just took Xanthos in Lykia away from old One-Eye, and they say he's going to move on Kaunos, too."

"No, as a matter of fact, I hadn't heard that," Menedemos answered, watching Thrasyllos much more closely than he seemed to. The news hit the merchant skipper like a twenty-mina rock flung from a catapult.

"How do you know it's true?" Sostratos asked Moiragenes. Menedemos wished his cousin hadn't chosen that moment to play the historian.

"Fellow who brought the news is called Euxenides of Phaselis," Moiragenes answered. "He got out of his home town two jumps ahead of Ptolemaios, got out of Xanthos one jump ahead of him, and he didn't want to try his luck at Kaunos, so he came here instead." He waved and went on down the pier to pass the news to someone else.

"Well, well," Menedemos said to Thrasyllos. "Isn't that interesting?"

"Ptolemaios won't come here," Thrasyllos said.

"Of course not," Menedemos said in soothing tones. "Gods be praised, Rhodes really is a free and autonomous polis. But sooner or later, you're going to have to sail away. Do you want to deal with traders whose grandfathers were in the business of buying and selling things, or will you take a chance on getting a little more from somebody who might cut your throat or might just blab instead?"

"To the crows with you," Thrasyllos whispered. "You're not a man. You're an evil spirit."

"All right. If you don't want to dicker . . ." Menedemos took a few steps toward the gangplank. Sostratos followed him.

He hadn't left the *Aura*'s deck before he heard the word he'd been hoping for: "Wait!" Thrasyllos croaked.

For dramatic effect, Menedemos did take a couple of steps up the gangplank before pausing. Even then, he asked Sostratos, "Do you think it's worth our while?"

"No," Sostratos said, and Menedemos could have kissed him. In lieu of that, he spent a little while taking his cousin around so he could stay and haggle with Thrasyllos. Sostratos did such a good job of acting reluctant, Menedemos wondered if he really was. No matter. Menedemos got his own way, as he was accustomed to doing.

"Well, if you won't pay a mina apiece, what will you pay?" Thrasyllos demanded when Menedemos and Sostratos finally came back to him.

"How many of those emeralds have you got to sell?" Menedemos asked in turn.

"Fourteen," Thrasyllos said. "How big an arsehole do you think my nephew has?"

"You'd know that better than I, O best one," Menedemos murmured. Sostratos almost succeeded in turning a guffaw into a cough. The joke, fortunately, went right by Thrasyllos. Menedemos said, "I haven't seen all fourteen of these stones yet, you know. I'm sure the ones I *have* seen are the best you've got, so the others are going to be worth less."

"No such thing," Thrasyllos said, but his show of indignation couldn't have sounded convincing even to himself, for he didn't push it.

"I'll give you . . . oh, two minai for the lot of 'em," Menedemos said. "Two pounds of silver free and clear for you—or one for you, one for your nephew, if you're in a generous mood."

"Two minai?" the captain of the *Aura* echoed. This time, his anger was altogether unfeigned. "You time-wasting, whip-worthy bastard, get off my ship, and take your kinsman with you. If I had a dog, I'd set him on you both."

"Well, what do you think they're worth?"

"I already told you: a mina apiece. Fourteen minai all told."

"And I already told you, I'm not going to pay that much. What would you take? I'm gambling, remember. These stones are new, so I don't know what I can resell them for."

"To the crows with you, pal—that's not my worry." Thrasyllos hesitated, then went on, "I wouldn't take a khalkos, not a single copper, less than twelve minai for the lot of them."

"Still too much. Still far too much," Menedemos said. He'd been afraid the round-ship captain wouldn't come down at all. That would have meant he'd have to go up first, and would have shown weakness, for he would have gone up—he wanted those stones. Now he could say, "I might give you three," and not worry: Thrasyllos had weakened first.

He got the emeralds for five minai, fifty drakhmai. "Thief," Thrasyllos ground out even as he clasped Menedemos' hand to seal the bargain.

"By no means," Menedemos said, though he was sure he would turn a handsome profit on the deal. "Ptolemaios won't hear about this even if he brings his whole fleet into the harbor here." That made Thrasyllos nervous all over again, as Menedemos had hoped it would. He turned to Sostratos. "Would you be so kind as to get the gentleman his silver while I wait here with him?" *I'll make sure he doesn't change his mind*, was what he meant.

Sostratos knew as much. He knew more than that, for as he dipped his head, he said, "If I get it, *your* father won't hear about it quite so soon."

"Maybe." Menedemos waved him away. Sostratos went, a grin on his face. Menedemos didn't like yielding him the last word, but liked squabbling with him in front of a stranger even less.

When Sostratos got back, he wore a sword on his hip and had a couple of burly slaves with him. Even in law-abiding Rhodes, carrying five and a half minai of silver was not to be taken lightly. "Here you are," Sostratos said, handing Thrasyllos the fat leather sack he'd brought. Menedemos held out his hand, and Thrasyllos gave him the much smaller sack with the emeralds.

Before leaving the *Aura*'s deck, Menedemos opened the sack, poured the stones into the palm of his hand, and counted them. "Don't you trust me?" Thrasyllos asked in aggrieved tones.

". . . twelve . . . thirteen . . . fourteen," Menedemos muttered. Then, having satisfied himself, he replied, "Of course I do, best one." *Now I trust you.* "Better to be safe, though."

"Safe?" the round-ship captain echoed. "I don't think I'll ever feel safe again. You'd better go now, before one of my sailors comes back and wonders who you are and what you're doing here."

"Just as you say," Menedemos answered. If this wasn't Thrasyllos' first smuggling venture, he would have been amazed. *I wonder if I could blackmail him into giving us the emeralds for nothing*, he thought. More than a little reluctantly, he tossed his head. He'd made a bargain. "Come on, Sostratos."

Thrasyllos dashed into the deckhouse with his silver, no doubt to stow it in the safest, most secret place he could find. As Menedemos and Sostratos went down the pier, Sostratos said, "You were thinking about squeezing him even harder, weren't you? I saw it in your eyes."

"Who, me?" Menedemos said in his most innocent tones. They both laughed.

When Menedemos got home, he found his father waiting for him in the courtyard. "Let's see those gemstones you just bought," Philodemos said.

So much for keeping things quiet, Menedemos thought. Sostratos must have told his father why he needed the money, and Uncle Lysistratos would have hotfooted it next door to give Philodemos the news. "Here you are, sir," Menedemos said, and handed his father the little sack he'd got from Thrasyllos.

As he had himself, Philodemos poured the emeralds out into the palm of his hand. Menedemos had brought them up close to his face for a better look. His father didn't. Philodemos held them out at arm's length. Even then, he grumbled; his sight had lengthened over the past few years. But at last he dipped his head. "You'll get some money from jewelers and rich men, sure enough. How much did you pay for the lot of 'em? Six minai?"

"Five and a half, Father," Menedemos answered.

"You could have done worse," Philodemos allowed: high praise, from him.

Inspiration smote Menedemos. He said, "Why don't you keep one of the stones, Father, and get it made into a ring or a bracelet for your new wife? She'd like that, I'd bet—it'd be something not many Rhodian women could match."

Only after the words were spoken did he pause to wonder what sort of inspiration that had been. But Philodemos, to his great relief, noticed nothing out of the ordinary. "Do you know, that's not a bad idea," his father said. "Women are fond of trinkets." He eyed Menedemos. "You know all about what women are fond of, don't you?"

That was just general sarcasm; Philodemos sounded about

as pleased as he ever did. "No man knows *all* about what women are fond of," Menedemos said with great conviction. "I may have found out a little something, though."

His father snorted. "Enough to get you into trouble from Halikarnassos to Taras." *Enough to get me into worse trouble right here at home, if I let it*, Menedemos thought. His father went on, "Here, pick a nice one for me," and held out his hand. "My eyes aren't up to such things these days."

"This one has a fine color," Menedemos said, holding up an emerald.

"So it does," Philodemos agreed. "I can see it better when you hold it than when it's in my own hand. Isn't that a sorry business? Old age is bitter, no doubt about it."

"Baukis will be happy, I think," Menedemos said. *Will she find out this was my idea and not my father's? I can't very well tell her, and half of me—the sensible half. I'm sure—doesn't want her to.*

Philodemos' thoughts were going down a different track. "What's a fourteenth part of five hundred and fifty drakhmai? I can't do that in my head."

"Neither can I," Menedemos said. "Sostratos probably could."

"Never mind; there's a counting board in the andron. I'll figure it out there." His father walked over to the men's chamber, where, sure enough, an abacus lay on a table. Philodemos flicked beads back and forth in their grooves. "Thirty-nine drakhmai—a couple of oboloi over, in fact. I'll have to move the silver from my own money to the business."

"Why bother?" Menedemos said.

"Because I'm buying it from the business, that's why," Philodemos said. "Because Lysistratos would bellow like a bull and roar like a lion if I didn't—and because he'd be right when he did. Never cheat the business, son, not if you want to stay in business."

"All right." Menedemos dipped his head. *Father is as stern with himself as he is with everybody else*, he thought. That made Philodemos more admirable, but hardly easier or more comfortable to live with.

His father pointed to the leather sack that held the rest of the emeralds. "Where do you think you can get the best price for those?"

"Well, Sostratos is wild to go to Athens on account of his gryphon's skull."

"*That* thing." Philodemos snorted once more, on a different note. "He ought to pay for it from *his* personal funds instead of sticking the business with the cost."

"He thinks he can get these two different schools of philosophy bidding against each other," Menedemos said.

His father snorted again. "Moonshine, nothing else but."

"I don't know," Menedemos said. "You never can tell with philosophers. Who can guess what they might want, and how much they'd pay for it?" He quoted from Aristophanes' *Clouds*:

" 'I walk the air and contemplate the sun. . . .
For never
Might I rightly discover the astronomical phenomena
If I didn't hang up my mind and mix up my
Subtle thought with the air it resembles.
But if I examined what's up above while I was down
on the ground
I'd never find anything. For the earth by force
Drags toward itself the juice of thought.
This same thing happens also with cresses.' "

He couldn't held smiling. He loved Aristophanes' absurdities.

"Cresses?" his father said. "What's he talking about, philosophy or salad?"

"Some of each, I think," Menedemos answered. "But Athens has some of the best jewelers in the world. I don't know what philosophers will pay for a stone skull, but I think jewelers will pay plenty for emeralds."

Philodemos pursed his lips. "You may be right," he said at last. "If you can *get* to Athens, that is."

Menedemos thumped his forehead with the heel of his hand. "*Oimoi!* That reminds me, Father." He passed on the news he'd got from Moiragenes at the harbor.

"Ptolemaios has Xanthos, you say?" Philodemos whistled.

"There's all of Lykia, near enough, stolen away from Antigonos just like that." He snapped his fingers.

"And Kaunos is next on the list," Menedemos said. "The fight between the marshals is so close now, we can see it from here."

"This is not good for Rhodes, not good at all," his father said. "The last thing we want is for the war to come to our door. The longer it stays close to us, the likelier someone will try to kick the door down."

That thought had occurred to Menedemos, too. He didn't like agreeing with his father. It didn't happen very often, so he seldom needed to worry about it. Here, though, he found himself saying, "I know. It's not easy staying a free and autonomous—a really free and really autonomous—polis these days. It puts me in mind of being a sprat in the middle of a school of hungry tunny, if you want to know the truth."

"I won't quarrel with you," Philodemos said: again, no small concession, coming from him. *When it comes to Rhodes, we can see eye to eye*, Menedemos thought. *When it comes to the two of us . . .*

He wished he hadn't suggested that his father mount the emerald and give it to Baukis. His father was liable to tell her he'd done so, as proof he wasn't worried about sharing an inheritance with any sons she might bear. And she might even take it that way, and be relieved.

Or she might think, *Menedemos gave me this lovely stone*. And if she thought that, what would she do then? And what would he?

SOSTRATOS HAD ALREADY CHECKED EVERYthing aboard the *Aphrodite* three different times. That didn't keep him from checking things once more. There was the gryphon's skull, securely wrapped in canvas and stowed near the poop. All they were waiting for was a few more sailors and some fresh water. "Then," Sostratos said, as if the old, old bone could understand, "people will try to figure out what to make of you."

From his station on the raised poop deck, Menedemos called, "Are you *talking* to that polluted thing? You need a hetaira to take your mind off what you're doing."

"Screwing isn't the answer to everything," Sostratos said with dignity.

"If it isn't, you tell me what is," his cousin retorted.

Before Sostratos could reply—and, very likely, before the argument could heat up—a man standing on the pier said, "Hail."

"Hail," Sostratos and Menedemos said together. Even as Menedemos asked, "What can we do for you?" Sostratos found himself disliking the newcomer on sight. The fellow was close to forty, medium-sized, handsome, well built, and carried himself like an athlete. *Jealous? Me?* Sostratos thought, and then, *Well, maybe a little*.

"I hear you're sailing north and west," the stranger said. "Will you be putting in at Miletos?" He had an odd accent, basically Doric but with a hissing, sneezy overlay. *He's spent a lot of time in Lykia*, Sostratos thought.

"Hadn't planned to," Sostratos said blandly, "but I might."

The man on the quay dipped his head. "It's like that, is it? What's your fare, then?"

Menedemos flicked Sostratos a glance. As toikharkhos, Sostratos had the job of charging as much as the passenger could bear to pay. Instead of answering directly, he asked a question of his own: "What's your name, O best one?"

"Me? I'm Euxenides of Phaselis," the stranger replied.

That made Menedemos blink. Sostratos smiled to himself. The fellow's accent and his bearing had made Sostratos think that was who he was. And Antigonos held Miletos. One of his officers might well want to go there. Sostratos enjoyed being right no less than any other man. He said, "Perhaps you should know: it's almost certain we *will* put in at Kos."

Kos was Ptolemaios' chief base in the Aegean. Euxenides

asked, "Are you saying you'd betray me there? That's not how neutrals should behave."

"No, nothing of the sort," Sostratos replied. "But you'd best remember, we'll have a big crew on board—all our rowers. They *will* go into the taverns, and they *will* gossip. I don't think anyone could stop them."

"And Ptolemaios' men *will* have ears around to hear such things," Euxenides finished for him. Sostratos dipped his head. Euxenides shrugged. "Chance I take. I'm not of a rank to make it likely that anyone much would have heard of me. How much for my passage? You still haven't said."

"To Miletos?" Sostratos plucked at his beard, considering. "Twenty drakhmai should do it."

"That's outrageous!" Euxenides exclaimed.

Most of the time, Sostratos would have asked half as much, and might have let himself be haggled down from there. Now he just shrugged and answered, "I have two questions for you, O marvelous one. First, when do you think another ship will sail from Rhodes to Miletos? And second, don't you think a trip to Miletos puts us in danger of ending up in the middle of a sea fight between Antigonos' ships and Ptolemaios'?"

Euxenides looked around the great harbor, as if hoping to find another ship on the point of sailing. There weren't more than a handful of akatoi in port, though, and he would have a long, slow journey on a round ship that had to tack its way up to Miletos against the prevailing northerly winds.

With a scowl, he said, "You're enjoying this, aren't you?"

"No one goes into business intending to lose money," Sostratos replied.

"Twenty drakhmai? *Pheu!*" Euxenides sounded thoroughly disgusted. But he said, "All right, twenty it is. When do you sail?"

"Soon, I hope," Sostratos said; as far as he was concerned, they'd already stayed in Rhodes much too long. He looked toward Menedemos. Being captain, his cousin had the last word in such things.

"Tomorrow, I hope," Menedemos said. "We'll share our water, but you do know you'll have to bring your own food and wine?"

"Oh, yes. I've traveled by sea a good many times before," Euxenides replied. "If we have to spend a night on the water, I expect I'll sleep on the foredeck."

I wonder if it still stinks of peafowl dung when you lie down on it, Sostratos thought. He didn't say that to Antigonos' officer. All he said, was, "That's right."

"I'll be here in the morning, then." Euxenides went off down the pier.

"Twenty drakhmai," Menedemos said. "That's more than I thought you'd squeeze out of him. *Euge!*"

"Thanks," Sostratos said. "He wants to get back to Antigonos, and probably to tell him everything he saw of Ptolemaios' fleet and his army."

"No doubt," Menedemos agreed. "He'll likely tell him everything he's seen of Rhodes, too."

"I hadn't thought of that." Sostratos' eyes went to the moles protecting the great harbor from the sea, and to the walls and towers fortifying them. "Maybe we shouldn't take him."

"I think it's all right," his cousin said. "Our works aren't exactly secret. Antigonos is bound to know about them about as well as our generals do."

That made more sense than Sostratos wanted to admit. "I don't much care for the side trip, though."

Menedemos laughed at him. "Of course you don't, my dear. It means you take a day or two longer to get to Athens. Believe me, nobody in Miletos will steal the gryphon's skull."

And Sostratos couldn't very well argue with that, either. Back before the Persians came, the polis was a hotbed of philosophy; Herodotos said Thales of Miletos had been the first man to predict an eclipse of the sun, an eclipse that also awed the warring Lydians and Medes to make peace with each other. Having seen an eclipse himself the year before, Sostratos understood how one might awe men into almost anything. But these past couple of hundred years, Miletos had been just another city.

Since he couldn't directly disagree, he shifted his ground: "Aren't you curious to see what the philosophers will make of the skull and what they'll be able to learn about gryphons from it?"

"Oh, a little," Menedemos answered. "What I'm really curious about, though, is how much they'll pay us, and *if* they'll pay us."

"The only way to find out is to get to Athens," Sostratos said. "Not Kos. Not Miletos. Athens."

"We're sailing tomorrow. Can you be patient that long?"

"I've been patient long enough. I want to *know*."

"You sound like me when I'm chasing a pretty girl."

"That's ridic—" Sostratos broke off. It wasn't ridiculous. It was, when you got down to it, a pretty fair comparison. He *did* chase knowledge as ardently as his cousin chased women. "Philosophy doesn't have a husband to shove a radish up my arse if he catches me in bed with her."

"Philosophy won't suck you off, either," Menedemos retorted. Sostratos' cheeks got hot. He couldn't even complain, not when he'd been crude first. Menedemos laughed and clapped him on the shoulder. "Don't you worry about a thing, my dear. We really do sail tomorrow."

"Tomorrow," Sostratos echoed dreamily.

"And believe me," his cousin added, "I'm as glad to be going as you are." Sostratos heard the truth in his voice. For the life of him, though, he couldn't figure out why it was there.

IF IT WOULDN'T have made people talk, Menedemos would have spent his last night in Rhodes wrapped in his himation on the *Aphrodite*'s poop deck. He would, indeed, have spent most of his nights thus. But someone might have figured out why he was doing so, and gossip with truth behind it was the last thing he wanted.

And so, when he went downstairs before dawn to head for Sostratos' house next door and then down to the harbor, he found Baukis already in the courtyard with some bread and a cup of wine from the kitchen. "Hail," he said. He couldn't ignore her. She would complain to his father—and she'd have reason—which would only touch off more trouble.

"Hail," she answered gravely. "A safe trip to you. Come back as soon as you can, and with plenty of silver."

"Thanks." Menedemos turned toward the kitchen himself.

"I'm going to get some breakfast, too, to eat on the way down to the ship."

She dipped her head. Everything she did, it seemed, was serious to the point of solemnity. *What would she be like, kindled and wanton?* Menedemos wondered. *Would she burn all the hotter because she's so quiet the rest of the time?* He all but fled into the kitchen, running from his own thoughts.

He would have stayed in there, too, hoping she would go back upstairs, but the *Aphrodite* wouldn't wait. And if he didn't go get Sostratos, Sostratos would come get him. Out he went, a chunk of bread in his hand.

Baukis remained, still busy with her own breakfast. "Be careful," she told Menedemos. "All the things we talked about before—they all look like they're coming true. And they're all bad for Rhodes, and they're all bad for trade."

"I know." Menedemos tore into the bread, eating as fast as he could. His mouth full, he went on, "But I'll come back. I have to. If I didn't, Father wouldn't have anyone to yell at."

Baukis drew in a sharp breath. Menedemos realized he hadn't criticized his father where she could hear before. When he'd complained about Philodemos, it had always been to Sostratos . . . till now. And complaining about a man to the man's wife was not the ideal way to enlist her sympathy.

She said, "He wants the most for you, from you. Anything less makes him angry."

And he picks the worst possible ways to try to get it, Menedemos thought. But he didn't say that to Baukis. He stuffed the last of the bread into his mouth, chewed quickly, and swallowed. It scraped down his throat like a boulder. "I'd better go," he said.

Baukis dipped her head. "Safe journey," she repeated. "Swift journey, too."

She got to her feet. He might have hugged her. She was his stepmother. *Oh, yes,* he jeered at himself. *And what would you do if Father came downstairs and saw that? You'd need to sail away and never come home.* He'd never had such attacks of nerves pursuing other men's wives in other towns. He headed for the doorway at something close to a run. Whenever he went away from Baukis, he felt as if he'd just been routed.

Getting out into the street was a relief. Getting out onto the open sea a thousand stadia from Rhodes would be a bigger one. He closed the door behind him, then turned to go next door and gather up Sostratos. He took a step—and almost ran into his cousin.

"Hail," Sostratos said. "You don't need to jump like that. I was just coming to get you."

"I was just going to get you," Menedemos answered. "I didn't hear your footsteps." That wasn't surprising; neither of them wore shoes. Menedemos went on, "Now that we've got each other, let's head down to the ship. What do you bet that Euxenides fellow will be waiting on the quay?"

"I have better things to do than waste my money," Sostratos said. "Have you got the emeralds?"

Menedemos tapped a little leather sack dangling from the belt that confined his tunic at the waist. "They're here, all but the one Father bought for his new wife." He kept his voice down, not wanting his words to travel back to Baukis; the stone was still at the jeweler's.

"Pity he decided to do that. It's one fewer we can sell." Sostratos spread his hands. "What can you do, though?"

"Not much," Menedemos answered. Sostratos didn't know he was the one who'd suggested giving the emerald to his father, and he wasn't about to tell him. "Come on. Let's go."

Mnesipolis was already banging away when they walked by the smithy. He waved, hammer in hand. They were as familiar to him as he was to them.

"Give him a limp and he'd make a good Hephaistos," Menedemos remarked.

"Why, so he would," Sostratos said. "There's a game: who of the people we know best matches the Olympians?" He eyed Menedemos. "Eh, wingfooted Hermes?"

Menedemos strutted with pride for a few paces. He *was* a formidable sprinter, even if he hadn't been quite fast enough to go to the Olympic Games to run for Rhodes. He hadn't thought of his chance remark as the start for a game, but was quick to fall in with it: "We've got Poseidon as keleustes."

"So we do," Sostratos said. "And Aristeidas will do for all-seeing Argos."

They went past Agathippos the banker's still playing the game. Menedemos said, "I know who gray-eyed Athene would be, too."

"Who?" Sostratos asked.

Menedemos pointed at him. "You."

"Me? Athana?" His cousin was so surprised, the goddess' name came out in a broad Doric drawl he hardly ever used. "You're out of your mind. I've got a beard, in case you hadn't noticed."

"It's the theater, my dear," Menedemos said airily. "Actors play all the female roles. With your face behind a mask, no one would care, for you've got the quick-darting mind the part needs."

"Thanks very much," Sostratos said, and kissed him on the cheek. "I don't think anyone has ever said anything kinder about me."

"I've never denied you have a clever mind, the cleverest I know," Menedemos replied. But if he gave Sostratos two undiluted compliments in a row, his cousin might die from the shock, so he added, "Now if you only had the good sense the gods gave a gecko . . ."

"You're a fine one to talk," Sostratos shot back. "You're the one who jumps out of second-story windows to get away from a husband home too soon."

"And you're the one who's been mooning over an old skull as if it were a young hetaira," Menedemos said. They chaffed each other all the way down to the harbor. Menedemos hurried down toward the *Aphrodite*. "Euxenides had better not keep us waiting. I want to get out on the open sea again."

"So do I. I want to sail for Athens." Sostratos pointed ahead. "Isn't that the man himself, already on the foredeck? You were right, up by our houses."

"Dip me in dung if it's not, and so I was," Menedemos said. "Good for him. I don't expect he got out of Phaselis and Xanthos by being late to his ship. And now he'll get out of Rhodes, too." He started up the pitch-smeared planks of the pier that led out to the akatos, calling, "Ahoy, the *Aphrodite*!"

Diokles gave answer in his raspy bass: "Ahoy, skipper! Passenger's already aboard."

"Yes, we saw him," Menedemos said. "Do we have all the rowers?"

"All but one," the oarmaster replied. "No sign of Teleutas yet."

Menedemos eyed the sun, which had just climbed up out of the sea. "We'll give him a little while—half an hour, maybe. If he's not here by then, we'll hire one of the harbor loungers, and many goodbyes to him. Rhodes has plenty of men who know how to pull an oar."

"That's how we got Teleutas a year ago," Sostratos said. "He's a funny one. He *will* work if you put him to it, but to him getting paid is the only part of the job that really matters."

"I still think he ran away in the market square in Kallipolis, too," Menedemos said. "He came back with more sailors so fast, I couldn't really call him on it, but I think he left us in the lurch. I wouldn't be sorry to see somebody else on his bench."

He walked down the gangplank and onto the *Aphrodite*'s poop deck. Standing between the steering oars, even with the ship still tethered to the pier, was in its own way almost as satisfying as lying between a woman's legs.

Fishing boats made their way out of the great harbor and onto the waters of the Aegean. Gulls followed them overhead like gleaners in the fields, knowing the pickings would be good. Menedemos drummed his fingers on the steering-oar tillers and gauged the creeping shadows. *If he doesn't get here soon. I* will *sail without him.*

Teleutas came up the pier and aboard the *Aphrodite* just before Menedemos set about replacing him. "By the dog of Egypt, where have you been?" Menedemos snapped.

The rower flinched. "Sorry, skipper," he said with a placating gesture. He kept his own voice low and soft. He also squinted, as if even the early-morning light was too bright to suit his eyes.

"You knew we were going out this morning," Menedemos said. "Why did you get drunk last night?"

"I didn't mean to," Teleutas answered. "It just sort of . . . happened." He gave Menedemos a sickly, ingratiating smile.

Menedemos wasn't about to let himself be appeased so

readily. "Go to your oar," he said. "I hope you hurt as much as you deserve all day long." That hangdog smile still on his face, Teleutas hurried off the raised poop deck and down into the waist of the merchant galley.

"Cast off!" Diokles called. Once the lines that had moored the *Aphrodite* to the quay were aboard, the keleustes smote his little bronze square. "Back oars! Rhyppa*pai*! Rhyppa*pai*!" The akatos slid away from the pier.

Once Menedemos had room to do so, he swung the ship about till her bow pointed out toward the mouth of the harbor. But he hadn't even passed out beyond the moles before he said, "I want everybody to do lookout duty on this voyage. It's not just pirates we have to be careful of—it's Antigonos' war fleet, and Ptolemaios', too. If you see anything, sing out. You may be saving all of our necks, including your own."

"We're Rhodians, and neutrals," Sostratos added. "That may help us in case of trouble, because neither side much wants to offend our polis. But some captains may not care about that. We'd rather not take the chance if we don't have to."

As it had a few days before, the motion of the waves changed as soon as the akatos left the sheltered waters of the great harbor. Menedemos smiled. He liked the livelier feel to the ship. Sostratos looked less happy. He would have preferred the sea as quiescent as the land. Menedemos glanced toward crapulent Teleutas. The rower had already gone a delicate green. *Too bad*, Menedemos thought. *It's his own foolish fault.*

"Rhyppa*pai*! Rhyppa*pai*!" *Clang! Clang!* Diokles beat out the stroke. Once they were outside the harbor, Diokles cut the rowing crew down to eight men on each side. He left Teleutas at his oar. The rower sent him a look of appeal. He ignored it.

Euxenides of Phaselis made his way back to the stair that led up to the poop. "May I come up?" he asked politely. Menedemos dipped his head, and Euxenides joined him and Diokles. The passenger said, "You've got a good crew here."

He spoke in tones of professional appraisal. "Thanks," Menedemos answered. "We're Rhodians, remember. We go to sea a lot." He pointed to the mouth of the naval harbor, which lay just northwest of the great harbor. A trireme was coming out, all three banks of oars manned, each stroke enviably smooth. Not lifting his hands from the steering oars, Menedemos pointed toward it with a thrust of his chin. "Most of my men have rowed in one of those, or else in a five."

"I hadn't thought of that," Euxenides said. "Now that I do, though, I see that you could put together a formidable little fleet."

"Little?" Menedemos said indignantly. But the indignation didn't last. Antigonos had all of Anatolia to draw upon, Ptolemaios the endless wealth of Egypt. Next to theirs, Rhodes' fleet would be small. *Too small?* Menedemos wondered. He hoped he'd never have to find out.

SOSTRATOS STOOD ON the *Aphrodite*'s little raised foredeck, peering north and west as if he expected to see Cape Sounion, the headland that announced one was coming up on Athens, appear over the horizon at any moment. Part of him did. Most of him, the rational part, knew perfectly well that Athens lay some days' journey from Rhodes, and that trading on the way would further delay the akatos' arrival. But the childlike part that never quite dies in any man insisted Cape Sounion would be there because he so badly wanted it to be there. And so he kept on looking.

The wind blew hard and steady out of the northeast—if anything, a little more out of the east than usual. The sailors had swung the yard from the starboard bow back toward the portside rear to take best advantage of it. The big square sail, full of the brisk breeze, pulled the *Aphrodite* along. Sostratos eyed the creamy wake thrown back from the ram and the cutwater. She was going about as fast as she could by sail alone.

Euxenides of Phaselis came up to stand not far from Sostratos. The leather sack that held his food and whatever meager belongings he owned lay on the foredeck. Like any sensible passenger, he kept an eye on it.

"Hail," he said.

"Hail," Sostratos echoed, a bit embarrassed; he probably should have spoken first. But his mind had been elsewhere.

Euxenides pointed. "What's that island there, off to the

right?" The way he said it proved to Sostratos that, even if he'd traveled by sea, he was not a naval officer.

"That's Syme," Sostratos answered. "We stopped there our first night out of Rhodes last year. But with the breeze so steady, we'll go farther today. I don't know whether Menedemos will make for Knidos"—he pointed, too, toward the end of the long finger of mainland north of Syme—"or whether he'll put in somewhere on Telos." He pointed again, this time toward the island dead ahead.

"I was in Knidos for a little while, three years ago I think it was, when Antigonos took Karia away from that traitor, Asandros," Euxenides said. "Telos I don't know at all. What's there?"

"Nothing much," Sostratos answered. "No polis. A few herders. A few farmers—not many, for it's not a well-watered island. But sometimes a quiet place where you can beach yourself and let your ship's timbers dry for a night is nothing to sneeze at."

Euxenides drummed his fingers on the rail. "I want to get to Miletos. I need to get to Miletos."

"I want to get to Athens," Sostratos said with a smile. "I need to get to Athens. And I will—eventually."

"Sometimes 'eventually' isn't fast enough," Euxenides said.

"Well, best one, you won't get from Rhodes to Miletos any faster than you will in the *Aphrodite*," Sostratos said.

"Yes, I found that out," Euxenides told him. He drummed his fingers some more. He might not be able to help it, but that didn't make him happy about it. He looked due north as avidly as Sostratos looked northwest.

As usual, most of the fishing boats whose crewmen saw the *Aphrodite* fled from her, fearing she was a pirate. That made the rowers laugh. It made Sostratos sad. Here close to Rhodes, even, men feared sea raiders. He feared sea raiders himself, as a matter of fact; he just knew he wasn't one of their number.

Menedemos held the merchant galley steady on a westerly course, and didn't swing north toward Knidos. Sostratos walked back to the stern. "You're going to put in on Telos?" he asked.

His cousin dipped his head. "That's right. We're not heavily laden, so I'll beach her for the night. It'll be good for the planking, and Telos is about as safe a place to put in as any under the sun."

"True enough," Sostratos said. "It hasn't got enough people to make up a decent-sized band of robbers."

"Just what I was thinking. And this splendid breeze is taking us straight there," Menedemos said. "Only drawback I can see is that it'll be a longer pull to Kos tomorrow, and the men will have to do more rowing. But we're still early in the season and getting the crew beaten in, so even that won't be so bad."

Diokles chuckled. "Easy for you to say, skipper. You're not one of the horn-handed bastards pulling an oar."

"I know how," Menedemos said. "Sostratos and I both know how, as a matter of fact. Our fathers made sure we do." He took his hands off the steering-oar tillers to show their palms. "And I've got calluses of my own."

Sostratos looked down at the palms of his own hands. They were fairly smooth and soft; he would blister if he ever had to do any rowing. The only real callus he had was one just above the first knuckle of the middle finger of his right hand: a callus showing where a pen or a stylus spent a lot of time. But Menedemos was right—he did know how.

The wind held. Telos drew near, the sun dropping down the sky towards it. The island was long and thin and curved, rather like a strigil lying in the water. Only a couple of fishing boats bobbed offshore; they were plenty to bring home opson for the inhabitants of the village near the north coast that was Telos' largest settlement.

A stretch of beach in front of the village was the most common spot for ships to put in, but Menedemos sailed past it. "Why did you do that?" Sostratos asked.

"Something one of the sailors told me while you were on the foredeck," his cousin answered. "Once we get past this rocky stretch here"—he waved at the forbidding coastline they were passing—"there's another good bit of beach, one where sea turtles come ashore to lay their eggs. They ought to make good eating. We can boil up a mess of them and have opson for the whole crew."

"Turtle eggs, eh?" Sostratos felt the lure of the exotic. "I've never tried them. Lead on, O best one." He patted his stomach. "It's been a long time since bread and wine back on Rhodes."

"Hasn't it just?" Menedemos agreed.

From the bow, Aristeidas pointed ahead and to port. "There's the beach, skipper!" the sharp-eyed sailor sang out.

"Good," Menedemos said, and then started calling out orders: "Brail the sail up to the yard! Rowers every other bench! Come on—move faster there. Do it as if you had pirates breathing down your neck."

To Sostratos, the men seemed to be moving quite fast enough, but Menedemos drove them like the commander of a trireme. The sailors didn't grumble. They knew they would have to be able to work together without thinking if they ever did need to flee pirates or fight them.

This length of beach was considerably shorter than the one near the village. Peering toward it, Sostratos exclaimed in excitement: "That fellow was right! I just saw a turtle crawling back into the sea."

Whistling, his cousin swung the ship so that her stern pointed toward the beach and her bow out to sea. A couple of men got into the boat she towed and rowed it ashore. "Back oars!" Diokles called. The rowers reversed their stroke. After the *Aphrodite* beached, pushing her into the sea again come morning would be easier bow-first.

Menedemos kept stealing glances back over his shoulder at the beach as the *Aphrodite* covered the last couple of plethra. Plovers scurrying along the sand took to the air when the merchant galley drew too close to suit them. "That's fine," Menedemos said, "just fine. Keep it going and—"

A grinding, scraping noise interrupted him. "What's that?" Sostratos asked at the same time as his cousin exclaimed in surprise and dismay. "Have we struck a rock?" It didn't feel like that, and the akatos still moved backwards through the water.

"*We* haven't," Menedemos answered. "But our starboard steering oar just did. Almost tore my arm out of the socket when it hit, too." Sure enough, the steering oar was torn out of the housing that secured it to the ship. And another crackle of splintering timber said the narrow length of the tiller hadn't come through undamaged, either.

The rock missed impaling the *Aphrodite*'s flank. A moment later, soft sand scrunched under her false keel as she beached herself as prettily as anyone could have wanted.

"Well, that's a nuisance," Sostratos said.

"It certainly is," Menedemos said. "I can guide the ship well enough with only one steering oar, but it's not something I want to do. If you've only got one and something goes wrong . . ."

He's a sensible and cautious seaman, Sostratos thought, *most of the time, anyway. Why doesn't his mind work the same way when he's on dry land?*

One more crackle and the steering oar fell away from the tiller and onto the sand, leaving Menedemos holding what was left of the tiller. With an oath, he threw it down onto the poop deck, narrowly missing Sostratos' toes. "What a miserable piece of luck," he said. "It was only a year old, and part of the best pair we ever had."

"You want to make repairs here, skipper, or go on up to Kos and have the shipwrights there do a proper job of it?" Diokles asked.

"I'm going to have to think about that," Menedemos answered. "For now, let's push her farther out of the water. I'll be able to take a better look at the damage then, too."

"Makes sense," the oarmaster agreed. He angled the gangplank down from the deck to the beach and descended. Sostratos and Menedemos followed. Sailors in the undecked waist of the ship simply scrambled over the side and dropped to the sand.

Sostratos, Menedemos, and Diokles added their weight and strength to those of the sailors. Sostratos' hands gripped the thin lead sheathing that helped hold shipworms at bay; his toes dug into the sand. Digit by digit, the *Aphrodite* moved up the beach.

Euxenides of Phaselis helped, too, and had plainly done such work before. After they'd shifted the ship far enough to suit Menedemos, the passenger asked, "Have you got woodworking tools aboard?"

"Of course we do," Sostratos answered. "If we end up in trouble, we may not find a kind-hearted nymph like Kalypso to lend us axe and adze and drill, as resourceful Odysseus did."

"I'm usually the one who quotes Homer," Menedemos said, "and you're usually the one who says I shouldn't, and that it doesn't fit. What have you got to say for yourself now?"

"Quoting him does fit here," Sostratos admitted. To keep from admitting any more, he turned back to Euxenides. "Are you a shipwright yourself, then?"

"No, no." The passenger tossed his head. "But I make and I serve catapults. I'm a good carpenter. If I can't repair that steering oar, I can certainly make you another to match it."

That wasn't Sostratos' choice to make. He glanced over to Menedemos. His cousin rubbed his chin. He didn't want to be beholden to Euxenides; Sostratos could see as much. "We've got men aboard who can do the same job," Menedemos said at last.

"No doubt," Euxenides answered, "but I can do it *right*."

"He has a point," Sostratos said. "There isn't much in the way of carpentry that's more complicated than what goes into catapults."

"That's right," Euxenides said. "No offense to your trade, captain, but shipbuilding is child's play beside it."

Menedemos grimaced. Sostratos turned away so his cousin wouldn't see him smile. More often than not—almost all the time, in fact—Menedemos did the pushing. Here, he was being pushed, and he liked it no better than anyone else did. "Let's talk about it in the morning," he said. "Nothing's going to happen till then anyhow."

"As you say, best one," Euxenides answered politely. Sostratos didn't think he could have phrased his own indecision as smoothly as Menedemos had done.

The *Aphrodite*'s crew had already realized they weren't going to get anything much in the way of repairs done before sunset. Some of them were gathering brush and driftwood for fires. Others went up and down the beach, thrusting spearshafts and sticks into the sand in search of sea-turtle nests. A couple of plethra away from the akatos, one of them stooped to dig with his hands, then whooped and waved. "Found some eggs!" he called.

Sostratos trotted over. "Let me have a look at those, Pasiphon, before you throw 'em in a pot," he said.

Pasiphon had pulled an oar on the *Aphrodite* the year before, and knew of Sostratos' ever-wakeful curiosity. "Sure thing," he said, and tossed Sostratos an egg as he might have thrown him a ball.

Awkwardly, and as much by luck as anything else, Sostratos caught it without breaking it. It turned out to differ in several ways from the birds' eggs he already knew. For one thing, it was round, not pointed at one end. *It can't very well roll out of an underground nest*, he thought, *but a round egg wouldn't be good up in a tree*. Creatures were surely shaped to suit the situation in which they found themselves. He hadn't imagined that extended to eggs, but saw no reason it shouldn't. The eggshell was leathery, not hard and brittle like that of a bird's egg. He wondered why; no explanation immediately occurred to him. The egg was also larger than any bird's egg he'd seen. That did make sense—sea turtles were large creatures themselves.

A little later, just as the sun quenched itself in the waters of the Aegean, another sailor found a nest. Like the first, it held a couple of dozen eggs. Everybody could have one, to go with the barley bread, cheese, olives, and wine the *Aphrodite* carried to keep her sailors fed.

Euxenides proved adept at more than carpentry. He twirled a fire drill and got a blaze going from scratch as fast as anyone Sostratos had ever seen. Searching for the lushest bushes, the sailors found a spring a stadion or so inland from the beach. They filled pots with fresh water and brought them back.

When Sostratos got his boiled egg, he discovered a couple of other differences between it and a bird's egg. The white didn't coagulate to nearly the same degree as a bird's egg would have. And the yolk was a deeper, richer orange than that of any bird's egg he'd ever seen; even by firelight, he was sure of that. The egg tasted fine, though.

Menedemos and Diokles told some men to serve as sentries through the night. "I don't think anyone on Telos will bother us," Menedemos said, "but I don't want to wake up with my throat cut and find out I was wrong."

Sostratos was immune to such duties. He found a spot not too far from one of the fires and curled up by it. The sand wasn't so soft as a proper bed, but made a better mattress than the planking of the poop deck. The thick wool of his himation held the night chill at bay. He stared up at the stars, but not for long.

WHEN MENEDEMOS WOKE in the predawn twilight, he needed a moment to remember that the *Aphrodite* wouldn't be leaving Telos as soon as her crew shoved her back into the Aegean. His yawn turned into a curse. "Miserable, polluted rock," he muttered, and got to his feet to go over and inspect the damage to the steering oar.

Most of the sailors were still snoring, but Menedemos found Euxenides of Phaselis already crouched by the oar examining it. "Hail," he said coolly.

"Oh. Hail," Euxenides answered. "I should be able to give you something that will serve you pretty well, if you don't mind my taking a few hours to make it. Forgive my saying so, but next to catapults this isn't very fancy work."

"That's what you think," Menedemos said. "If you don't get the shape of the blade exactly right, it won't cut the water the way it should. And if the weight isn't distributed the way it should be, it won't pivot properly, and the fellow steering the ship—me, I mean—will have to work a lot harder than he would otherwise."

"Yes, yes," Euxenides said impatiently, as to a child that kept pointing out the obvious. "I expect I can take care of all that. Only drawback of doing it right here is that I'll be working with green timber. But . . ." He raised an eyebrow. "I'll work for free, and the shipwrights on Kos surely won't."

He was right about that. And he sounded so certain he could do what he said he could, he won Menedemos over. "All right," Menedemos said. "We'll see what you come up with." If Euxenides proved more wind than work, his crewmen would be able to improvise something that would serve till they got to Kos.

But Euxenides quickly showed he knew what he was doing. After bread and wine for breakfast, he used one of the ship's hatchets to knock down a pine whose trunk was about the right size to shape into a steering oar. Once he'd lopped off the branches that grew from it, sailors dragged it to the beach with ropes. Using the sound steering oar as his model, Euxenides trimmed the trunk to the proper length with the hatchet, then set to work with the adze to give it the shape he wanted. Chips flew in all directions.

Perhaps halfway through the work, he looked up and remarked, "I may not be as resourceful as long-suffering Odysseus was, but by the gods I know what to do with a piece of wood."

"So you do, best one," Menedemos admitted. He made a tolerably good woodworker himself, good enough to recognize a master of the craft when he saw one. Euxenides shaped the pine with the same offhand brilliance a sculptor showed with marble. Watching him was an education.

Watching him kept Menedemos too interested to look out to sea. He jumped when somebody shouted, "Sail ho!" A pirate couldn't hope to do better than to descend on a merchant galley beached. How was he supposed to fight back?

"This is what happened to the Athenian fleet at the end of the Peloponnesian War," Sostratos said. "The Spartans caught them ashore at Aigospotamoi and had their way with them." Only after he'd finished was Menedemos sure their thoughts had gone in the same direction.

Then the cry of, "Sail ho!" changed to, "Sails ho!" Instead of getting ready to scramble back onto the *Aphrodite*, belt on his sword, and make what fight he could, Menedemos stared out to sea himself. He couldn't possibly hope to fight off more than one pirate ship.

The sound he made was halfway between a sigh of relief and an exhalation of awe. He wouldn't have to do any fighting. The fleet sailing west past the north coast of Telos cared no more about a beached akatos than Zeus cared about a flea on the skinny rump of a scavenger dog. Those weren't round ships out there, or even pirate pentekonters and hemioliai. They were war galleys, dozens of them: a fleet bigger and stronger all by itself than Rhodes could hope to put to sea. Triremes served as escorts for the bigger, beamier warships that formed the heart of the fleet. Were those monsters fours, fives, sixes? Did they carry even more than six rowers for each bank of oars? They were ten or fifteen stadia out to sea. Menedemos couldn't be sure.

"Whose fleet *is* that?" somebody asked—another good, relevant question.

Before Menedemos could reply, Euxenides of Phaselis said, "It has to be Ptolemaios'. If Antigonos had that many ships in these waters, they would be sailing toward battle with Ptolemaios over Lykia, not heading away from there."

Sostratos added, "They look as if they're making for Kos, too, and Kos is Ptolemaios' chief stronghold in the Aegean."

Menedemos dipped his head. "That all makes sense. For all we know, Ptolemaios is aboard one of those ships. They say he came up from Egypt himself this year, instead of giving the job to one of his admirals."

"He did," Euxenides said. Antigonos' officer coughed a couple of times. He turned toward Menedemos. "You've been saying you planned on stopping at Kos. If Ptolemaios' whole naval expedition is there, I don't think I want to visit the place, thank you very much. Can you put me ashore at Knidos instead? You can stop there before going on to Kos."

"Yes, I'll do that," Menedemos said at once. With Ptolemaios' whole great fleet and perhaps Ptolemaios himself at Kos city, he didn't want to get there with Antigonos' officer on board.

"I thank you." Euxenides drummed his fingers on the adze handle. "I shouldn't have to pay twenty drakhmai for the trip, either, not when I'm not going to Miletos."

Had Euxenides not gone to work on the new steering oar, Menedemos might have argued with him. But Sostratos, who was scrupulously fair, dipped his head in agreement with the officer's words. So Menedemos just said, "All right. I'll cut the price in half."

Euxenides looked . . . half pleased. "Ten drakhmai to Knidos is as outrageous as twenty drakhmai to Miletos." He paused. His nails clicked rhythmically on the axe handle. "It's no *more* outrageous, I suppose. A bargain, captain. Ten drakhmai."

He soon finished the steering oar and set to work repairing the pivot on which it would turn. He was as swift and deft there as he had been while turning a tree trunk into something useful. The sun had just swung past noon when he set the new steering oar in its place.

Menedemos went back aboard the *Aphrodite* to see how the new steering oar felt. The tiller seemed strange under his palm: it was a lopped-off branch from the tree that had made the steering oar, with the bark still on it. The new steering oar was a little heavier than the old one. *It would be*, he thought, *being made of green wood*. But the balance was everything it should have been, and the makeshift only had to last to Kos. Menedemos tossed his head. *No, to Knidos, if it turns out not to serve*.

He dipped his head to Euxenides of Phaselis. "Many thanks. It's plenty good enough."

Antigonos' officer seemed more embarrassed than pleased. "You're welcome, though I hate to take thanks for anything that simple. The joinery that goes into catapults . . ."

"Never mind," Menedemos said. "I believe you. You've made me believe you." He raised his voice and called out to the *Aphrodite*'s crew: "Come on, boys! Let's get her back into the water."

Half a dozen men shoved the merchant galley's boat back out into the Aegean. They made the boat fast to the *Aphrodite*'s bow with a line. The rest of the sailors, along with Menedemos, Sostratos, and Euxenides, stationed themselves along the length of the akatos' hull and at the stern.

"Ready?" Menedemos waited a heartbeat, then raised his voice to a shout: "*Push!*" He put his own shoulder against the lead plates that sheathed the ship and shoved with all his might. The men in the boat rowed with all their strength, pulling the *Aphrodite* while everyone else pushed.

She didn't move at the first try. Menedemos hadn't expected that she would. She was more heavily built than a war galley or a piratical pentekonter, and she still carried her cargo. Had she had more of it, Menedemos would have had the crew do some unloading before trying to refloat her—or he might not have beached her at all, but left her anchored offshore instead.

"Push!" he called again. His shoulder complained as he set it against the ship. His feet dug into the sand. His grunt was one of a chorus that rose from the straining men. Telos was a barren place, nowhere anybody could possibly want to be stranded.

Sand ground under the oak of the akatos' false keel. "She's stirring!" Sostratos gasped from his place a couple of men over from Menedemos.

"That she is," Menedemos agreed, also gasping. He paused for a couple of breaths, then managed a shout: "Put your backs into it, you lazy whoresons!" Something creaked in his own back as he shoved, but he didn't let that keep him from giving the work all he had in him.

Little by little and then, it seemed, all at once, the *Aphrodite* went into the Aegean. The sailors raised a cheer and waded out after the ship, scrambling aboard wet and naked and dripping. Menedemos took his place on the poop deck. His face wore a curious frown as he reached for the steering-oar tillers, one pale and sweat-stained, the other bark-brown.

Sostratos understood him perfectly. "Let's find out how that new one does now that it's really in the sea."

Menedemos dipped his head. "Just so." He called out to the crew: "Ten men on a side to the oars. Diokles, give us the stroke."

"Right you are, skipper," the oarmaster replied. He took out his mallet and square of bronze. "Come on, you lugs—pay attention to me. Rhyppa*pai*! Rhyppa*pai*!"

As the merchant galley slid forward over the blue, blue sea, Menedemos pulled and pushed on the steering oars, sending her now to the left, now to the right. He made sure to steer clear of the rock that had hurt the ship before. Sostratos asked, "How does she feel?"

"Fine," Menedemos answered. "A little odd, because the two steering oars don't weigh the same, and I can tell, but the makeshift does its job." He raised his voice: "Many, many thanks, Euxenides."

Antigonos' officer stood on the foredeck. He gave Menedemos half a bow. "I told you, you're welcome. I didn't want to stay on Telos any longer than I had to, either."

"I think a dead man would be bored on Telos," Sostratos said.

"I think you're right," Menedemos replied. He turned to Diokles. "Do you expect we'll make Knidos by nightfall?"

"If we don't, we'll be pretty close." The keleustes gauged the breeze, which blew straight into his face. "It'll be rowing all the way, though. If you want to go north during the sailing season, that's mostly how it is."

Menedemos dipped his head. "I know. If we were a round ship, we'd spend forever tacking back and forth, back and forth, sailing four or five stadia, maybe more, for every one we went forward." He paused. "Of course, if we were a round ship, we wouldn't have tried beaching ourselves, and we wouldn't have lost that steering oar." He eyed his cousin, who was peering ahead with a hand to his forehead to shield against sun glare. "What's chewing on you, Sostratos?"

"I was just wondering how big a fleet old One-Eye has in Knidos," Sostratos answered. "If it's big enough, it might have come out against Ptolemaios'. We don't want to wander into the middle of a sea fight."

"No, eh?" Menedemos said slyly. "Think what it would do for your history, if you ever get around to writing it."

Sostratos raised an eyebrow. "Wandering into the middle of a sea fight is one of the best ways I can think of to make sure I don't live long enough to write a history." Menedemos would have argued with him, but found no way to do it.

THE *APHRODITE* CAME into Knidos with the sun low in the northwest and the sky streaked with red and gold. Sostratos let out a sigh of relief. He didn't mind the discomfort of a night at sea; reaching port so late, he would probably sleep on the poop deck tonight anyhow. But out on the Aegean the merchant galley was hideously vulnerable to any storm that might blow up. Better, far better, to spend the night tied up at a Knidian quay.

Knidos was sort of a double city, like Syracuse in Sicily, though the offshore island that formed a part of it lay a little farther out in the sea than did Syracuse's Ortygia. Moles improved the harbor and connected the island to the mainland. Sostratos counted about twenty ship sheds, the sort in which war galleys stayed to keep their timbers dry when they weren't on campaign. *No wonder they didn't sally against Ptolemaios,* he thought. *He had to have twice that many ships, maybe three times as many.*

The passage of Ptolemaios' fleet hadn't gone unnoticed, and had, understandably, left Antigonos' garrison in Knidos nervous. No sooner had the *Aphrodite* found a berth than an officer in corselet and helmet came storming up the pier toward her. "What ship are you?" he barked. "Where are you from?"

"We're the *Aphrodite*, out of Rhodes," Sostratos answered soothingly. "We spent last night on Telos."

"Rhodes, eh?" the officer said. "Ptolemaios' catamites, are you?"

"We're a free and autonomous polis, and we're neutral," Sostratos said, knowing he had to hold his temper.

Antigonos' officer snorted. "Probably a pack of stinking spies."

"Hail, Aristarkhos," Euxenides of Phaselis said. "Haven't seen you for two or three years—not since we took back Karia."

"Euxenides?" the officer—Aristarkhos—said uncertainly. When the *Aphrodite*'s passenger dipped his head, Aristarkhos went on, "Zeus, Euxenides, what are you doing here?"

Getting us out of a nasty spot, went through Sostratos' mind. Euxenides answered, "Getting away from Ptolemaios, what else? I was in Phaselis when he took it, and in Xanthos when he took *it*. By now, he'll have Kaunos, too. The Rhodians here were taking me up to Miletos, but when Ptolemaios' fleet came by this morning I thought they'd do better to drop me off here. That way, I don't have to run the gauntlet heading north."

"Oh," Aristarkhos said. After the single syllable came out, a long silence followed. He looked as if he'd bitten off a big mouthful of bad fish. A large-souled man, or even an honest man, would have apologized. Aristarkhos plainly knew it, and as plainly couldn't bring himself to do it.

Sostratos prodded him a little: "You see, O marvelous one, we really are neutrals." Making sure Antigonos' officers understood that might be important for Rhodes.

"It . . . could be," Aristarkhos said after another pause. Sostratos decided not to push any further; that was too likely to make an enemy. Aristarkhos turned back to Euxenides: "So you saw Ptolemaios' fleet go by, too, did you?"

"I certainly did," Euxenides replied. "We were on the north coast of Telos. They couldn't have been more than fifteen or twenty stadia offshore as they went past. I counted fifty-five ships."

How professional of you, Sostratos thought. No matter how useful Euxenides had been, he couldn't warm to the man, who struck him as almost too competent to tolerate. Aristarkhos dipped his head. "That sounds about right." He frowned. "It must have been close to midday. Why were you still aground? Did you have trouble getting this ship back in the water?"

"It wasn't that," Euxenides said. "We needed some repairs."

"The steering oar and its housing," Menedemos said. "Hurt 'em on a rock backing the akatos onto the beach. I'll tell you this, best one"—he was more polite to Aristarkhos than Sostratos had been—"if Antigonos doesn't need Euxenides, he can come to Rhodes and make a good living for himself as a ship's carpenter."

"Euxenides the catapult man!" Aristarkhos exclaimed. Now his memory was fully jogged. "Not likely, Rhodian. Antigonos rewards men who are good at what they do, and Euxenides is one of the best." Euxenides gave back half a bow, acknowledging the compliment.

"I believe it," Menedemos said. Sostratos believed it, too. Whether he liked him or not, Euxenides was a consummate craftsman, an artist with adze and drill. If he was ignorant of anything having to do with woodworking, Sostratos couldn't imagine what it would be. He wondered if that made Euxenides also think he knew a great deal about matters in which he had less experience. He wouldn't have been surprised; that was the craftsman's besetting flaw, as Sokrates had pointed out in his *Apology*.

"I was worried about these Rhodians, too, but they treated

me as well as if I were one of Ptolemaios' men," Euxenides said, and Sostratos couldn't fault him for that. He went on, "They really did act as neutrals should, and I expect you'll show them every kindness here." That *expect* held the snap of command, and told Sostratos which of Antigonos' officers owned the higher rank.

"Just as you say," Aristarkhos answered, still sounding unhappy about it. "For now, though, come with me, why don't you? We'll send a messenger to Antigonos first thing in the morning. He'll be pleased to know you got away."

Euxenides picked up the leather sack that held his worldly goods. "Thank you for my passage," he said, waving first to Sostratos and then to Menedemos as he went up the gangplank to stand on the quay beside Aristarkhos.

"Thank you for your help on Telos," Menedemos replied. *Thank you for your help here*, Sostratos thought. Maybe jealousy *had* made him misjudge Euxenides. They could have made their own steering oar on the island, even if it wouldn't have been so perfect as the one the officer had turned out. But for Euxenides' acquaintance with Aristarkhos here in Knidos, though, things might have gone hard for them.

Aristarkhos asked, "What cargo are you carrying, Rhodians?"

"Perfume and purple dye," Menedemos answered.

"Papyrus and ink," Sostratos added. His cousin shot him a warning look. He realized he might have done better to keep quiet about the papyrus. It came from Egypt, Ptolemaios' stronghold. Reminding Antigonos' captain about it might cause trouble.

Aristarkhos only grunted. "Where are you bound?" he asked.

"Athens," Sostratos and Menedemos said together. Sostratos wondered if that admission were wise. For the past eight years, Demetrios of Phaleron had ruled Athens as Kassandros' puppet, and Kassandros was no friend to Antigonos, either.

But Aristarkhos merely grunted again, remarking, "With that cargo, you would be." He leaned forward, trying to see better as twilight thickened. "Will you stop at Kos on the way?"

Anther dangerous question. Lying might be safer, but also might be more dangerous. Sostratos decided to tell the truth, as calmly and reasonably as he could: "Of course we will, O best one. We are traders, and we are neutral. They make silk on Kos, and you can't get it anywhere else in the world. We'll buy some to take with us, and we'll sell crimson dye there."

"When I left Rhodes bound for Miletos, they warned me ahead of time they planned to put in at Kos," Euxenides said. "This was before we knew Ptolemaios' whole war fleet was heading that way."

"All right, fair enough," Aristarkhos said. His suspicions finally seemed to have dissolved. "Will you want to spend a day in the market square here before you go on?"

Sostratos and Menedemos looked at each other. Sostratos could think of nothing he wanted less. What he wanted was to get to Athens as fast as he could. But what he wanted and what was expedient were liable to be two different things. "Thank you," he said. "That's very kind."

He'd made the right choice. He saw that at once, by the way Aristarkhos relaxed. The officer turned to Euxenides, saying, "Come on, let's get you back to the barracks before it's too dark for us to see where we're going." They walked down the quay together.

"Just what I want—a day in Knidos' market square," Menedemos said. "It would take a special miracle from Zeus to make enough to pay the whole crew an extra day's wages." He reached up and set a hand on Sostratos' shoulder. "And I'm sure you're even happier about the layover than I am."

"Oh, of course." Sostratos' sounded even glummer than his cousin had. But then he brightened. "You never can tell what we might find, though. Who would have thought we'd come across the gryphon's skull in Kaunos?"

"Yes, who would?" Menedemos' tone suggested he would have been just as well pleased never to have set eyes on it. He sighed. "We couldn't even hope to find the Rhodian proxenos' house without a torchbearer now. Do you feel like going to an inn, or will the poop deck do for the night?"

"The poop deck is fine, as far as I'm concerned," Sostratos said. "Nothing but bugs and noise and thieves at an inn."

"Not *quite* nothing," his cousin observed.

"We've got wine here, and I'm not so mad for girls that I've got to have one the instant I come into a port," Sostratos replied.

"Well, I don't *have* to have one, either," Menedemos said in tones of affronted dignity. Sostratos smiled to himself. That gibe had gone home. Menedemos stripped off his chiton, crumpled it up, and set it on the deck to serve for a pillow. He wrapped himself in his himation and lay down. Sostratos did the same.

There was room on the deck for Diokles, too. But the keleustes perched on a rower's bench and leaned against the *Aphrodite*'s side planking, as he usually did when spending a night aboard ship. He'd got into the habit years earlier, when he still pulled an oar, and he'd never been able to get out of it.

Sostratos peered up into the night sky. Aphrodite's wandering star, brightest of them all, blazed in the west, following the sun down toward the horizon. That of Zeus, less brilliant but able to travel all around the heavenly sphere, shone low in the east. Distant music from the double flute and voices raised in song argued that more than a few people preferred revelry and wenching to this almost Lakedaimonian simplicity. *To the crows with them*, he thought, and fell asleep.

Menedemos was anything but enthusiastic about spending a day in Knidos' agora hawking the *Aphrodite*'s goods. "Not your fault," he said to Sostratos as they set up their little display of dye and perfume and papyrus and ink. "You couldn't afford to make that Aristarkhos angry at us. But even so . . ."

"Even so," Sostratos agreed mournfully. "I want to go on to Athens."

He sounded like a small boy who wanted a sweet and was about to throw a tantrum because his pedagogue wouldn't buy one for him. Menedemos chuckled. If there were thinking-brothels like the thinking-shop Aristophanes had given Sokrates in his *Clouds*, nothing would have kept Sostratos aboard the *Aphrodite* the night before. He'd practically boasted about not caring whether he got laid, but he would have been gone like a dart from a catapult if he'd seen a chance to argue about the whichness of what.

"We'll go through the motions," Menedemos said. "Then we can prowl the market square for a while, and then we'll head back to the ship."

"Fair enough." But Sostratos heaved a sigh. "We could be most of the way to Kos by now." He exaggerated, but not by a great deal; the island lay less than half a day's journey north and west of Knidos.

Local merchants started crying the virtues of their olives and onions and drinking cups and wool cloth. And, not too far away, a couple of bearded Phoenicians in ankle-length linen robes and brimless caps called out, "Balsam! Fine balsam! The finest incense and medicine the gods ever made!"

Hearing that, Sostratos perked up. "We ought to see what sort of bargain we can strike with them. A mina of balsam goes for two minai of silver."

"You're right," Menedemos said. "We'll have time to dicker, I expect. It won't move fast in a little town like this."

But they'd hardly begun singing the praises of their own goods before a man with the careful, forward-leaning walk of the shortsighted came up to them and said, "You'd be the Rhodians who got in last night?"

"That's right, best one," Menedemos answered. "What can we do for you?"

"Papyrus," the fellow answered. That surprised Menedemos. The man went on, "Aristarkhos said you had papyrus."

That surprised Menedemos even more. This fellow looked about as much like a soldier as a black Ethiopian looked like a fair-haired Kelt. "That's right," Menedemos repeated cautiously. "Who are you?"

"I'm Diodoros son of Diophantos," the nearsighted man said, leaning closer to Menedemos for a better look at him. Then he explained himself: "I'm Antigonos' paymaster hereabouts."

"Ah." Menedemos dipped his head. That made Diodoros a customer, all right. "Yes, best one, we do have papyrus. Quite a bit of it, as a matter of fact."

"Gods be praised!" Diodoros exclaimed. "My dear fellow,

do you have any idea how difficult it is to keep proper records when your commander is at war with Egypt? I've been writing on leather; on boards; even on potsherds, the way they did in the old days when they decided whom to ostracize." He spoke Attic Greek; Athens was the home of ostracism.

"We can probably help you," Menedemos said. Diodoros might be the paymaster, but he was too excited to make much of a bargainer. Menedemos asked Sostratos, "How much papyrus have we got left? I know you sold some in Kaunos."

"Oh, dear!" Diodoros sounded horrified at the thought of any of the stuff slipping through his fingers.

"We still have seventy-one rolls left," Sostratos answered; Menedemos had been sure he'd have the number at his fingertips. His cousin added, "We have some excellent ink, too." He pointed to one of the little round pots that held it.

Diodoros dipped his head. "Ink is all very well, but I can make my own at a pinch. I wish I could make my own papyrus. How much do you want per roll?"

How hard can I hit him? Menedemos wondered. It was a nice calculation. True, Diodoros was a paymaster, and knew how much things cost. But he'd also made it plain he badly needed what Menedemos had for sale. Still, if Menedemos asked too high a price, Antigonos' officer was liable to set soldiers on him and simply take what he wanted. Yes, a nice calculation indeed.

Menedemos made it between one breath and the next. "Six drakhmai," he replied. "You said it yourself, sir: there's a war on. Once I sell what we've got, who knows when I'll see more?"

"You're a Rhodian. Dealing with Egypt, that gives you an advantage," Diodoros said. He could remember business, at least to some degree. Sostratos chose that moment to take a roll of papyrus out of a sack and examine the smooth, creamy writing surface. Without saying a word, he smiled and put it back. Diodoros' eyes followed it as if it were a beautiful hetaira closing a door behind her. He sighed. "Necessity is the master of us all. I'll give you four drakhmai a roll for fifty rolls."

Even that was above the going rate. The dicker that followed didn't last long. They settled on five drakhmai, two oboloi per roll. After some thought, Diodoros decided to buy sixty rolls, not fifty. Menedemos felt like jumping for joy. As the paymaster went off to get the silver and a sailor hurried back to the ship for the requisite rolls of papyrus, he turned to Sostratos and said, "We made a profit here! Who would have believed it?"

"They were wild for papyrus in Syracuse last year, too, after the Carthaginian siege cut them off from it," Sostratos answered. "If you're going to keep records, you really can't do without it. More people are reading and writing these days, too. It's a good thing for us to carry."

"I can't tell you you're wrong," Menedemos said. "And Diodoros was right—we *do* have the inside track on bringing it out of Egypt. A round ship hauling grain could carry plenty for us to resell without even noticing the burden."

His cousin dipped his head. "True enough. And now, shall we see what those barbarians want for their balsam?"

"Certainly," Menedemos said. He and Sostratos walked over to the Phoenicians, one of whom was tall—almost as tall as Sostratos—and thin, the other short and even thinner. Menedemos bowed. "Hail." He named himself and his cousin.

"Hail," the shorter Phoenician replied. As he bowed, he touched his forehead, lips, and heart in turn. "I am Abibaalos son of Gisgon. Here with me, you see my brother, Abimilkios." He spoke good if guttural Greek, and even gave the foreign names endings a Hellene might have used. "How may we serve you, my masters?"

No free Hellene would have called another man *master*. As far as Menedemos was concerned, the Phoenicians carried flowery politeness too far. He said, "You have balsam, do you?"

"Ah, balsam! Indeed we do." Abibaalos bowed again. "We have the finest fragrant balsam from the garden of Engedi, clear and yellow as fine honey from Hymettos"—he really did know Hellenes well, to come up with that comparison—"burning with a sweet smoke, and also useful in medicines of all kinds, for epilepsy, for pain, as an antidote against deadly poisons, to warm the stomach and the liver, to heal inflamed eyes, to keep wounds from going bad, and to cure pleurisy and make a man's prong rise. It is effective, if the gods will."

That was a longer catalogue of virtues than Menedemos had bargained for, almost longer than the Catalogue of Ships in the *Iliad*. He said, "We might be interested in some, if the price is right."

Abimilkios spoke for the first time, in a hollow, rumbling bass: "The price is two of silver for one of balsam, by weight." His Greek was less fluent than his brother's, but he sounded more determined. And that was indeed the going rate for balsam.

"We are traders, too," Menedemos said.

Abibaalos and Abimilkios both smiled. Menedemos had seen that smile on Phoenicians before; it said Hellenes couldn't be traders, or at least not good ones. He leaned forward, responding to the silent challenge. He'd won some dickers from the men of the east. If he'd lost some, too, he chose not to dwell on those. Abibaalos said, "We heard you calling out your wares. You have perfume and dye and papyrus and ink, is it not so?"

"Only a little papyrus now," Sostratos answered. "We just sold most of it to an officer here."

"You would have got a good price for it, too, with Ptolemaios and Antigonos at war," Abibaalos remarked. He was no fool. He went on, "Crimson dye I can lay my hands on straight from the source. Perfume, now . . . These are the roses of Rhodes?"

Menedemos dipped his head. "Just so, best one. Even more fragrant than balsam."

"But less rare," Abimilkios put in.

"More people want perfume than balsam," Sostratos said.

"More people can afford it," Abibaalos replied. "In what size jars is the perfume?"

"Each one holds two kyathoi," Menedemos answered. The jars weren't very big.

"The standard size," Abibaalos said, nodding as barbarians often did. "One of those jars for each drakhma's weight of balsam, then."

"Outrageous!" Menedemos cried, though he wasn't particularly outraged. "We ought to get three drakhmai by weight, at least." After half an hour of insults and howls, he and his adversary settled on two drakhmai and one obolos' weight of balsam per jar of perfume.

"For a Hellene, you are not a bad bargainer," Abibaalos remarked as they clasped hands.

"From a Phoenician, that is high praise," Menedemos said. He and Abibaalos both smiled the same sort of smile, which meant they both thought they'd won the dicker.

SOSTRATOS ENJOYED WATCHING KOS RISE up out of the sea as the *Aphrodite* drew near; it was one of the most beautiful islands of all. It was famous for fruit of all kinds, and especially for its wines. A good many mulberry orchards, now springtime-bright with new leaves, grew within easy walking distance of the city of Kos. A little farther inland, on higher ground, stood the marble majesty of the Asklepeion.

As the akatos sailed past the healing god's shrine—easily visible from the south—Menedemos remarked, "All sorts of offerings in there from people the god cured."

"And I know just which one in particular you're thinking of, too," Sostratos said.

"Do you?" Menedemos sounded particularly innocent, which convinced Sostratos he was right.

"I certainly do," he said: "the Aphrodite rising from the sea that Apelles painted."

His cousin grinned, unabashed. "A painting of a beautiful girl—a beautiful goddess—with no clothes on is a lot more interesting than all those terracottas of knees or feet that people cured of sore joints or bunions give the god."

"It does make you wonder what Apelles was cured of, though," Sostratos said. "The clap, maybe?"

"Scoffer," Menedemos said. "His portrait of Antigonos is in the Asklepeion, too."

"So it is," Sostratos agreed. "Now if the whole Hellenic world could just be cured of not only old One-Eye but all the marching generals."

Menedemos laughed and clapped his hands. "Now *there's* a wish, my dear. Too much to hope for, though, I'm afraid." Sostratos dipped his head in agreement; he thought it was too much to hope for, too. And one thing a love for history had taught him was that poleis didn't need competing marshals to give them excuses to fight among themselves. The wars nowadays, however, were on a larger scale. Thoukydides, who'd reckoned the Peloponnesian War the greatest the Hellenes had ever waged, would have been horrified and amazed at the sheer scale of the fighting among Alexander's successors.

Several of Ptolemaios' fives patrolled the waters outside the harbor of the city of Kos. Sostratos would have been astonished had Ptolemaios not had ships ready to fight on the sea at all times. Kos looked northeast, toward Halikarnassos on the mainland only a little more than a hundred stadia—two or three hours' journey—away. Antigonos surely kept a fleet of his own there, and as surely had ships on patrol in front of his own harbor. Neither general would risk a surprise from the other.

One of those prowling galleys spotted the *Aphrodite* and came centipede-walking across the sea toward her, three banks of big oars rising and falling in the smooth unison that bespoke a well beaten-in crew. The five was fully decked, her oar-box also encased in timber to protect the rowers from missiles. She mounted a catapult near the bow. Its crew stood by to send darts farther than any archer could. Armored marines, the plumes on their helmets waving in the breeze, strode here and there across the planking.

"You couldn't pay me enough to wear a corselet aboard ship," Menedemos said. "One slip and splash!—right down to the bottom of the sea."

"A swimmer sometimes has a chance," Sostratos agreed.

Before his cousin could answer, an officer aboard the war

galley cupped his hands in front of his mouth and bellowed, "You, there! Heave to!"

Diokles looked a question to Menedemos, who dipped his head. "*Oöp!*" the keleustes called, and the rowers rested at their oars. The *Aphrodite* slid to a halt, bobbing in the light chop. Sostratos' stomach tried to complain. He ignored it.

Up came the five, a wooden cliff rising from the sea. She had twice the freeboard of the *Aphrodite*; her deck stood six or seven cubits above the sea. The officer peered down from the deck at the merchant galley. So did her marines, some armed with bows, some with javelins, some with thrusting-spears. "Who are you and where are you from?" the officer demanded.

"We're the *Aphrodite*, out of Rhodes," Sostratos answered.

That impressed Ptolemaios' officer less than he'd hoped it would. "All the stinking spies and pirates say they're Rhodians," the fellow said. "Whose ship is this?"

"My cousin's father's and my father's," Sostratos said. "Philodemos and Lysistratos."

By his accent, the officer wasn't a Rhodian. He turned and spoke in a low voice to some of the marines. One of them dipped his head. *Asking if they've ever heard of our fathers*, Sostratos thought. The answer the officer got must have satisfied him, for his next question was less hostile: "What are you carrying?"

"Crimson dye. Papyrus. Ink. Fine Rhodian perfume," Sostratos replied.

"Balsam from Engedi. A couple of lion skins. A tiger skin from far-off India," Menedemos added. He said not a word about the thirteen emeralds in the pouch on his belt. Sostratos would have been astonished if he had. Since they'd been smuggled out of Egypt, these servants of the master of Egypt were all too likely to confiscate them.

Sostratos hadn't said anything about the gryphon's skull, either. His reasons were different from the ones Menedemos likely had. He simply couldn't imagine a naval officer caring about old bones or being able to see that the skull might be valuable.

"A tiger skin?" the officer said. "You show me a tiger skin and I'll send you right on in to the harbor."

"Just as you say, O marvelous one," Menedemos replied. Sostratos wouldn't have used that sarcastic formula to a fellow aboard a war galley that could have crushed the *Aphrodite* like a man stamping on a mouse, but his cousin always liked to push things. Menedemos waved to him. "Show the gentleman the skin, Sostratos."

"Certainly," Sostratos said. Menedemos assumed he knew exactly where it was stowed, and Menedemos was right. He got out the large oiled-leather sack that protected the tiger skin from seawater and undid the rawhide lashing holding the sack closed. The rank odor of a not quite perfectly cured hide and, he supposed, of tiger itself wafted out.

A couple of sailors helped him spread out the great striped skin. The officer leaned forward, staring so hard he almost fell into the sea. The marines aboard the galley gaped, too. Finally, the officer blinked a couple of times and seemed to come back to himself. "I'm a man of my word," he said, and waved toward the harbor of Kos city a few stadia away. "Pass on."

"Rhyppa*pai*! Rhyppa*pai*!" Diokles called, beating out the stroke with his mallet and bronze square. As the rowers began to work, the oarmaster aboard the war galley also began his endless chant. Those three banks of sweeps bit into the Aegean. Ptolemaios' galley resumed its patrol, and the *Aphrodite* glided into the harbor.

Finding a place to tie up took a deal of time and a deal of shouting. The harbor was much smaller than that of Rhodes. It didn't have nearly enough shipsheds to accommodate all the triremes and bigger galleys from Ptolemaios' fleet; close to half of them had to moor at the quays like so many merchantmen. Because of that, space for real merchantmen was at a premium.

Menedemos almost rammed a round ship in his haste to seize a spot near the end of a pier. The round ship's sailors, who stood on deck ready to fend off the *Aphrodite* with poles, screamed curses at him. The akatos' rowers screamed back, louder and more foully. Since the *Aphrodite* had five or six times as many crewmen aboard, they shouted down the sailors on the other ship.

As had happened at Knidos, an officer came hurrying up to the end of the quay to question the men of the *Aphrodite* on where she was from, where she'd been, whither she was bound, and what she was carrying. Sostratos' patience frayed. "No one hounded us like this when we came here a year ago," he complained.

Ptolemaios' officer shrugged. "The war hadn't come to these parts a year ago, either."

That held some truth, but only some. As he had at Knidos, Sostratos said, "It's not *our* war. We Rhodians are free and autonomous and neutral."

"Kos is free and autonomous, too," the officer said. Sostratos almost laughed in his face. *Free to obey Ptolemaios*, he thought. *Autonomous as long as it does what he wants*. The fellow said nothing whatever about Koan neutrality.

Menedemos had been drumming his fingers on the mismatched steering-oar tillers for a while, too. Now he inquired, "Do we pass muster?"

"I suppose so," Ptolemaios' officer said grudgingly. Then, as the fellow aboard the war galley had done, he asked, "Have you really got a tiger skin aboard?"

"By the dog of Egypt, we do," Menedemos answered. "Do you want to show him, Sostratos?"

"Why not?" Sostratos said, thinking he shouldn't have bothered rolling up the skin and stuffing it back into its sack after displaying it to the naval officer. As he had out on the Aegean, he called on a couple of sailors to give him a hand. They soon had the skin stretched out.

Not only the officer but his retinue and the usual gaggle of portside loungers crowded up to the edge of the quay for a good look. *We ought to charge a khalkos or two for a peek, the way we did with the peafowl last year*. Sostratos thought. The officer stared and stared. "It's a . . . very big beast, isn't it?" he said at last.

Seeing the hide shown that way made it seem even bigger than it was. Sostratos gravely dipped his head even so. "Bigger and fiercer than a lion," he said. He had no idea whether a tiger really was fiercer than a lion. He did know this hide was bigger than either lion skin aboard the *Aphrodite*.

When he started to stow the skin in its sack once more, the officer sighed as if sorry to have to come back to the mundane world. "All right, Rhodians," he said. "Good trading here in Kos." He turned and walked back down the quay, his hangers-on following. Some of the loungers drifted away, too. Others crowded forward, hoping for something else new that might make interesting gossip.

They were disappointed. Perfume and balsam and papyrus and dye were much less interesting than tiger skins. Again, no one had said a word about emeralds—Sostratos hoped nobody would, not here—and the gryphon's skull remained in its wrappings. This wasn't the place to take it out.

"At least they're still willing to let us trade," Sostratos said.

"Once we talk them into it, yes," Menedemos said. "I wonder how much longer they will be, though. I don't know which is worse for people like us: pirates prowling as they please or war among the marshals."

Sostratos eyed his cousin in some surprise. Menedemos didn't usually think in such terms. Sostratos said, "They go together. If the marshals weren't warring, someone would put down the pirates. As things are, the marshals use them, and so they flourish."

"You're probably right." Menedemos waved around the crowded harbor. "Ptolemaios could put them down if he had a mind to. He's got the fleet for it right here. So could Antigonos, though his ships are more scattered. But who does the pirate-hunting around these parts? Our little Rhodes, that's who."

"If one of the marshals won, he might care more about proper rule for the lands he held." Sostratos sighed. "But they've been fighting among themselves ever since Alexander died, and even the truces they've made haven't been much more than breathing spells."

"No end in sight, either," Menedemos said. Sostratos wished he could have argued with his cousin, but he dipped his head in agreement instead.

* * *

WHITEWASH AND MARBLE and bright tile roofs against the lush green of springtime made Kos one of the prettier cities around the Aegean—indeed, around the whole of the Inner Sea. Menedemos hurried down the quay from the *Aphrodite*, Sostratos close behind. "I even remember how to find old Xenophanes' place," Menedemos said. "Two streets in, turn right, three streets over, and it's right across from the boy brothel."

Like Rhodes, Kos city was built on a sensible grid. It was an even newer town than Rhodes. The earlier polis on the island, Meropis, had lain in the far southwest, but an earthquake and a Spartan sack during the Peloponnesian War had put paid to it. The new polis looked forward to Anatolia, not back toward Hellas.

Going two streets up and three streets over produced no sign of the silk merchant's establishment—or of the boy brothel, either. Menedemos dug his toes into the dirt of the narrow street. "I'm *sure* that's how we got here," he muttered. "Remember? Last year we had to pay somebody an obolos to tell us the way."

"I remember," Sostratos said. "In fact, I remember the fellow saying *three* streets up and *two* streets over. If we go up one more street and back to our left . . ."

"I'm sure it was two up and three over." Menedemos looked around, then shrugged. "But it couldn't have been, could it?" He gave his cousin a glance half respectful, half rueful. "All right, my dear, we'll try it your way. I know you've got the same nose for details as a fox does for chickens."

One block farther up, one block back to the left, and there was the boy brothel, with the slaves lounging about in an anteroom open to the street, waiting for whoever might want them. Sostratos didn't say, *I told you so*. Menedemos wished he would have; he would have preferred it to the smug expression Sostratos wore.

The house across from the brothel was also familiar. Menedemos knocked on the door there. Before long, a plump Karian opened it. He smiled at them. "Well, if it isn't the gentlemen from Rhodes! Hail, both of you. Welcome. Come in." He spoke almost perfect Greek.

"Hail," Menedemos said, stepping forward as the Karian

slave stood aside to let him and Sostratos into the house.

"How are you, Pixodaros?" Sostratos asked. Menedemos smiled. His cousin *did* have the nose for details. He'd come up with the slave's name the year before, too. Menedemos had heard it and promptly forgotten it again. Sostratos went on, "And how's Xenophanes these days?"

Pixodaros' expressive black eyebrows leaped toward his hairline. "Haven't you heard—?" he began. But then he shook his head, proving he remained a barbarian no matter how long he'd lived among Hellenes. "No, of course you wouldn't have, for it happened a couple of months after the end of the sailing season. Xenophanes took sick with an inflammation of the lungs and died. He had no living children of his own, you know. In his will, he was kind enough to manumit me and leave me his business."

"I . . . see," Menedemos said slowly. Such things happened all the time. If his father, or Sostratos', had been childless . . . He didn't want to think about that. What he did think was, *I won't forget Pixodaros' name now.*

"Here we are." The slave—no, the freedman—led them to the parlor where they'd dickered with Xenophanes the year before. He waved them to stools. "Sit down, best ones." He called for a slave to bring wine. The year before, he'd done it himself. When the wine came, he splashed out a small libation. "My master had more than seventy years when he died. We'll be lucky if we match him."

"That's so." Menedemos poured a little wine onto the floor in Xenophanes' memory. So did Sostratos. Menedemos glanced over to his cousin. *Both our fathers are past fifty. How long will they live? How long will* we *live?* He shivered, as if he'd heard an owl hoot in daylight, and took a long pull at the wine. Again, Sostratos did the same thing. Maybe he was thinking along similar lines. Menedemos wouldn't have been surprised. Such thoughts fit his cousin better than him. *I'm not made for looking deep*, he thought, and drank again.

Presently, Pixodaros said, "And what is the news from the wider world?"

Menedemos laughed. "Living here on Kos, you'll know

more of it than we will, for Ptolemaios has been making most of it."

"So he has." Pixodaros didn't look delighted. A moment later, he explained why: "Even more drunken sailors than usual making a racket in the street at all hours of the day and night." He shrugged. "What can a peaceable man do?" Pointing to Menedemos, he went on, "You were heading far into the west last year. How did your journey fare? What is the news from those places?"

It was still early in the sailing season. No ship from Great Hellas was likely to have come into these waters yet. Menedemos told of the Romans' war against the Samnites, and the larger and more important war Syracuse was waging against Carthage. He spoke of the *Aphrodite*'s journey into besieged Syracuse with the grain fleet, and of Agathokles' escape from Syracuse and invasion of Africa.

"And there was the eclipse of the sun after we got into Syracuse," Sostratos added.

Pixodaros' eyes widened. "I have heard of them, but I have never seen one. They really do happen, then?"

"They really do," Sostratos said solemnly, "and they're even more awesome to see than you would think from the tales about them." Menedemos thought about that, then dipped his head in agreement.

"Well, well," Pixodaros said, and then again: "Well, well." He chuckled. "And I think I go traveling when I leave the city to check the fields and orchards that are mine now. You make me feel like a child in his cradle."

With a shrug, Menedemos said, "Some people do one thing, some another. I'm glad Xenophanes left his business in such good hands."

"Thank you." Xenophanes' freedman looked from Menedemos to Sostratos and back again. "The two of you didn't come to Kos just to chat."

"No," Sostratos said. "We do have a certain interest in your silk. We did well with it last year. We'd like to do well with it again."

"What are you carrying?" Pixodaros asked.

"We have more of the crimson dye of Byblos that Xenophanes always liked to use," Menedemos answered.

As Pixodaros dipped his head—he did it self-consciously, as if reminding himself to behave like a Hellene—Sostratos added, "And we also have fine Rhodian perfume. I remember you were interested in it last year, even though Xenophanes wasn't."

Menedemos hadn't remembered that. He'd kept Xenophanes' views in mind then, but not those of the man who'd been a slave then. Pixodaros dipped his head again. "Yes, I was. I still am—or I could be, if the price is right. We agree, more or less, on what silk is worth in terms of dye. But in terms of perfume?" He leaned forward on his stool, eager anticipation in his eyes. "We have a new dicker, my friends."

He called to his slave, who brought in more wine, and olives and onions to go with it. *A new dicker indeed*, Menedemos thought. *And this must be his first big one as a freedman. He wants to start things off the right way.* He filled his cup from the mixing bowl and bit into an onion. "When you buy our perfume, you know just what you're getting," he said. "Silk, now . . . I'd like to see what you want to sell us."

"It shall be as you say." Pixodaros clapped his hands. Looking a little harassed, the slave came back into the room. Pixodaros told him what he needed. The slave nodded and hurried away. He came back with a bolt of the rare fabric. Pixodaros held it up for his guests. "Top quality, O best ones, as you see. Xenophanes showed me everything he knew."

It did look very good. It was filmier than the gauziest linen; Menedemos could see Pixodaros through it. Yet it also shone and sparkled, as linen never did. Brothelkeepers paid high prices to deck their girls in the stuff. Hetairai bought it for themselves. And men eager for display or simply to have something few others in their polis did also set down their silver for silk—commonly in thicker grades.

"What *do* you weave it from?" Sostratos murmured.

He couldn't have expected an answer. It was only his curiosity talking. For a moment, though, Pixodaros' face went hard and hostile behind the transparent cloth. "That is the secret of Kos," he said. "The most I will ever say is that I was so surprised when I learned it, you could guess from the fall of Troy till now and you would never once come close."

"As may be," Sostratos said. "I don't need to know in order to want it." He turned to Menedemos. "Shall we get a hundred bolts, as we did last year?"

"That suits me well enough," Menedemos said. "We won't be going into the west this trip, but there's always a strong market for silk in Athens." He raised an eyebrow at Pixodaros. "You do have it?"

"Certainly." The Karian started to nod, then caught himself and dipped his head.

"All right, then," Sostratos said. "Shall we trade dye for half and perfume for the other half? Dye at the same rate we gave Xenophanes last year?"

"I thought the old man could have done a little better," Pixodaros replied, "but let it be as you say. Now, though, the perfume . . ."

"Top grade, just like your silk," Menedemos said. "An akatos can't afford to carry anything but the best. We make our money from quality. A round-ship captain with a load of olive oil in his hold can take along a little junk to peddle on the side, because it's not where most of his profit will come from. We don't dare sell junk. We always want the good and the beautiful." Sostratos stirred at that—the words came right to the edge of philosophy—but didn't speak.

"And how much do you want for one of your jars of perfume, as compared to the price for one of your jars of dye?" Pixodaros asked.

Menedemos smiled. "That's where the dickering comes in, wouldn't you say?" Pixodaros smiled, too. Oil and wheat might have something close to a fixed price, except in times of dearth, but luxuries? Luxuries brought what the seller could get, what the buyer could afford.

They drank. They ate. They haggled. Pixodaros flicked stones in the grooves of a counting-board. He didn't offer it to the Rhodians. Every so often, Sostratos would look up toward the ceiling, lips moving not quite silently, eyes far away. He was better than anyone else Menedemos had ever seen at working with numbers in his head. He was slower than Pixodaros with the advantage of the board, but he got right answers.

At last, as evening neared, Pixodaros held out his hand to Menedemos and Sostratos. "A bargain," he said, and Menedemos dipped his head. So did his cousin. Smiling, Pixodaros added, "Xenophanes used to complain about how hard a dicker the two of you gave him. I see he was right."

"It works both ways." Menedemos returned flattery for flattery.

Pixodaros beamed. "What would please you?" he asked. "Would you stay to supper here, or should I give you a guide to the Rhodian proxenos' house?"

"Perhaps we'd better see the proxenos," Sostratos answered. "He'll wonder if he's done something to offend unless we call on him. But would you be kind enough to send someone to the *Aphrodite* to let our men know where we'll be?" Menedemos might have been tempted to stay and see how the freedman's kitchen did, but Sostratos was formally correct, and he knew it.

So did Pixodaros, who dipped his head, playing the Hellene again. "As you wish, of course." He called for a couple of slaves. A year before, they would have been his fellows; now he owned them. Menedemos wondered what they thought of that. Did one of them hope to inherit the business, as Pixodaros had?

Whatever they thought, they obeyed. One headed down to the harbor. The other took Menedemos and Sostratos to the house of Kleiteles son of Ekdikos, the wineseller who looked out for Rhodian interests on Kos. Menedemos gave the slave an obolos and sent him back to his master. Kleiteles was a plump, happy man of about forty, who looked to enjoy having guests. "Pleased to see you, my friends," he said. "I heard you were in port, and told the cook to make sure we had plenty."

"Thank you very much," Menedemos and Sostratos said together.

"My pleasure, believe me," Kleiteles answered. "Don't just stand there in the front hall—come along to the andron with me. Come, come." He shooed them along as if they were children. He had practice at such things; in the courtyard, a boy of about eight and another perhaps five were playing in the fading light. "Run upstairs," Kleiteles told them. "You'll eat in the women's quarters tonight. I have company."

"Your sons?" Menedemos asked—they had the look of the Koan. Kleiteles dipped his head. "Promising lads," Menedemos remarked.

"You're too kind, best one." Kleiteles waved toward the andron. "Go on in, both of you. Use my home as your own."

A slave was lighting lamps and torches in the andron. In one corner of the room stood a wickerwork cage with a jackdaw inside. The gray and black bird hopped up and down a little ladder with a tiny bronze shield in its beak. Kleiteles laughed and tossed it some seeds. It dropped the shield with a clink and started pecking them up.

Such things always fascinated Sostratos. Sure enough, he asked, "How long did it take you to train the bird?"

"Less time than you'd think: only a couple of months," Kleiteles answered. "They're surprisingly clever—and, of course, the toy shield is shiny, and jackdaws like such things."

"How interesting," Sostratos said. Menedemos wondered if he would try to buy a jackdaw for himself when he got back to Rhodes.

They ate reclining on couches. With only three men in the andron, each had one to himself. The sitos was barley porridge flavored with onions and mushrooms and fennel. For opson, the cook brought in a casserole of shrimp and cheese and olives. If nothing was spectacular, everything was tasty.

And the wine, which came out after the supper dishes were cleared away, was very good indeed. Menedemos and Sostratos traded news with Kleiteles, who said, "Ah, so you saw Ptolemaios' fleet go by, did you? I don't know how long he'll stay here, but business will surely be fine for as long as that is. I've heard his wife is with him, and that she's with child."

"Hadn't heard that myself," Menedemos said. Sostratos tossed his head to show he hadn't heard it, either.

"I don't know it's true, mind you," Kleiteles said. "If Berenike is here, she doesn't do her own shopping in the agora." He chuckled.

So did Menedemos. But Sostratos said, "Oh, Berenike.

That's not Ptolemaios' wife; that's his concubine. He's married to Eurydike, old Antipatros' daughter." He kept track of such things as carefully as he kept track of the relative values of silk and perfume.

"Is he?" Kleiteles said in a slightly crestfallen voice. He'd had his news . . . oh, not quite turned false, but at least weakened. With a little thought, Menedemos might also have remembered to whom Ptolemaios was married. He didn't think he would have come out and said so, though. Relentless precision could make a man harder to get along with.

But the proxenos, fortunately, didn't seem much offended. After a few sips of wine, his smile came back like the sun returning from behind a small cloud. He called for a slave, spoke briefly to the man, and sent him away. The fellow returned a bit later, saying, "Everything is ready, master."

"Good, good. Go on off to bed, then—we won't need you any more tonight," Kleiteles said. The slave nodded and disappeared. Kleiteles turned to the Rhodians. "I know you've had a busy day. Your rooms are waiting for you."

"Thank you for your kindness," Menedemos said, and drained his cup. He wouldn't have minded drinking a bit longer, but he knew a hint when he heard one. Sostratos might not have, but did own wit enough to get to his feet when Menedemos did. He cast a last glance at the jackdaw as Kleiteles led them out of the andron and into the courtyard.

A couple of torches flickering there gave the wineseller enough light to lead the two cousins back to their rooms. "Have a pleasant evening," he said, "and I'll see you in the morning." Off he went, whistling a bawdy tune.

"Good night," Sostratos said, and went into one of the chambers.

"Good night," Menedemos replied, and went into the other.

The room held a stool, a small clay lamp perched on it, and a bed. The bed held a woman not far from Menedemos' age—one of Kleiteles' slaves, without a doubt. She smiled at him. "Hail," she said.

"Hail," Menedemos answered with a smile of his own. He wondered if Sostratos had company in his bedroom, too. Probably. Kleiteles was indeed a considerate host. "What's your name, sweetheart?"

"I'm called Eunoa," the woman answered.

"Well, Eunoa, get out of your chiton, and we'll go on from there." Menedemos pulled his own tunic off over his head. As soon as the woman was naked, too, he lay down on the bed beside her. He took her hand and set it on his manhood, while he kissed and caressed her breasts and rubbed her between the legs. As most women did, she'd singed off the hair there; her flesh was soft and very smooth.

Presently, Menedemos stood her up and had her lean forward against the bed. He poised himself behind her. He was about to thrust home when she looked back over her shoulder and said, "I wish I didn't have to worry about making a baby."

He could have ignored her. She was there to do as he wanted, not the other way around. But he shrugged and said, "Bend a little more, then," and, after spitting on himself to ease the way a little, went in at the other door. "There. Is that better?"

"I . . . suppose so," Eunoa answered. "It does hurt some, though."

"It was your choice," Menedemos said, not pausing to wonder whether she'd had a choice about coming to his bed. He went on. It didn't hurt him at all: on the contrary. After he finished, he patted her round bottom. "Here, dear, this is for you," he said, and gave her a couple of oboloi. "You don't need to tell Kleiteles you got them from me."

"Thank you," Eunoa said. "It wasn't so bad." The little silver coins evidently made it a good deal better.

Menedemos had thought they would. He lay down on the bed. "Sleep with me. We'll do it again in the morning, whichever way you like." He didn't say he would give her more money then, but he didn't say he wouldn't, either. She lay down willingly enough. The bed was narrow for two, but not if they snuggled together. His arms around the slave girl, Menedemos fell asleep.

SOSTRATOS WOKE UP when the woman Kleiteles had lent him for the night almost kicked him out of bed. He had to clutch at the frame to keep from landing on the floor. His sudden motion woke the slave up, too. They both needed a moment to remember what they were doing there lying side by side. Sostratos needed another moment to remember her name. "Good day, Thestylis," he said when he did.

"Good day, sir," she answered, sitting up and yawning. Her breasts sagged a little; her nipples were wide and dark. He guessed she'd borne a child before. Maybe it hadn't lived. When he reached out and idly stroked her, she said, "Just a minute, sir. Let me use the pot first, if you don't mind."

He wasn't sure he wanted her again till she said that. Then he decided it would be a nice way to start the day. "Go ahead," he told her. "And after you're done, I'll use it myself. And then . . ."

But he'd just set down the pot when brisk footsteps resounded out in the courtyard. Someone knocked first on his door, then on the one beside it it, the door to Menedemos' room. Thestylis let out a startled squeak. She plainly hadn't expected anyone to disturb them so early; the light leaking out through the shutters was predawn gray.

"Who's there?" Sostratos asked. His eye went to the little knife he carried, now lying on the floor. It was a tool much more than a weapon. He heard Menedemos asking the same question with the same undertone of worry. After Kaunos, who could be sure staying in a proxenos' house was safe?

"It's me, Kleiteles," came the answer. "You gentlemen need to get dressed right away and come out."

"Why?" Sostratos asked in some irritation. He looked back at Thestylis, who lay naked and waiting on the bed. Not getting the chance to dip his wick after he'd made up his mind that he was going to annoyed him.

But Kleiteles answered, "Because one of Ptolemaios' servants is standing here beside me. Ptolemaios wants to speak to you as fast as you can get to him."

Ice ran through Sostratos. *Zeus! Has he found out about the emeralds? How could he have found out about the emeralds? But what else would he want to talk about?* He had no idea. But he realized he was going to have to find out. Astonishment widened Thestylis' eyes.

As Sostratos put on his chiton, Menedemos spoke from the other room: "Ptolemaios wants to talk to *us*?" His cousin sounded unwontedly subdued. *Nothing like being discovered, or worrying that you've been discovered, to put the fear of the gods in you*, Sostratos thought. The fear, if not of the gods, then of a power greater than his own, was certainly in him.

"That's right," Kleiteles answered along with another man: presumably, Ptolemaios' servant. Sostratos touched the hilt of that little knife. Much good it would do him against one of the great marshals of the Hellenic world.

"I'll see you again," Sostratos told Thestylis, and hoped he meant it. He opened the door and stepped out into the courtyard. The fellow standing beside Kleiteles reminded him of Euxenides of Phaselis without looking like him: he was solidly made, erect, alert. *He looks like a soldier—that's what it is*, Sostratos thought.

"Hail," the stranger said. "I'm Alypetos son of Leon." Sostratos gave his own name. Menedemos came out. Alypetos went through introductions again, then gestured toward Kleiteles' doorway. "Come with me, best ones."

"Can you tell us why Ptolemaios wants to see us?" Sostratos asked as they went out onto the street.

"I can make some guesses," Alypetos answered, "but I might be wrong, and it's not my place to gab, anyhow."

Something else occurred to Sostratos: "We've just made a bargain with Pixodaros the silk merchant. He'll probably bring his cloth to the *Aphrodite* this morning, expecting to pick up dye and perfume in exchange for it. Can you send someone to his house, asking him to wait till we're back to look things over for ourselves?"

"I'll take care of it," Alypetos promised. He didn't sound as if Ptolemaios intended to do anything dreadful to Sostratos and Menedemos. That left Sostratos slightly reassured, but only slightly. *He wouldn't, would he? If he did, we might try to run away.*

Kos was waking up. Women with water jars gathered at a fountain, some of them pausing to chat before they took the water back to their homes. A farmer in from the countryside with a big basket of onions trudged toward the market square.

A stonecutter pounded away with mallet and chisel at a memorial stone. A little naked boy, pecker flapping as he ran, chased a mouse till it slipped into a crack in a wall and got away. The child burst into tears.

Like any house in a polis, the one where Ptolemaios was staying presented only a blank, whitewashed wall and a doorway to the world. Unlike any house Sostratos had seen, though, this one had a couple of hoplites in full panoply—crested helm, bronze corselet, greaves, shield, spear, sword on the hip—standing sentry in front of it.

"Hail," Alypetos said to them. "These are the Rhodians Ptolemaios wants to see."

"Hail," the sentries said together. Then one of them added something that sounded as if it ought to be Greek but made next to no sense to Sostratos. *They're Macedonians*, he realized. *Well, no surprise that Ptolemaios would use his countrymen for bodyguards*. Unless you were used to it, the dialect Macedonians spoke among themselves might almost have been another language.

Alypetos had no trouble following it. "He says to bring you right on in," he told Sostratos and Menedemos.

Inside, the house proved large and spacious, with a fountain and a bronze of Artemis with a bow in the courtyard. Alypetos ducked into the andron. Sostratos wondered whose home this was, and where he'd gone while Ptolemaios was using it. *Not a question to which you're likely to find an answer*, he thought.

Alypetos emerged. "He's eating breakfast," he said. "Plenty of bread and oil and wine for the two of you as well. Go on in."

"Thank you," Menedemos said. Sostratos dipped his head. Now he knew real relief. Ptolemaios, by all accounts, was not the sort of tyrant who broke bread with a man one moment and ordered him tortured the next.

"Go on. Go on." Alypetos shooed them toward the andron. Menedemos put a bold front on things and strode into it. Sostratos followed, content here to let his cousin take the lead.

Ptolemaios looked up from dipping a chunk of bread in a bowl of olive oil. "Ah, you must be the Rhodians," he said, speaking Attic Greek with a slight accent that put Sostratos in mind of the way the bodyguards outside the house talked (two more guards stood stolidly in the andron). "Hail, both of you. Have something to eat."

"Hail, sir," Menedemos said.

"Hail," Sostratos added. As he sat and reached for some bread, he studied the ruler of Egypt out of the corner of his eye. Ptolemaios was somewhere in his mid- to late fifties, but strong and vigorous for his years. Though his hair was gray, he had all of it; he wore it rather long, with locks falling over his ears. He had an engagingly ugly face, with a big nose and a jutting chin; a scar on one cheek; a wide, fleshy mouth; and alert, dark eyes under shaggy eyebrows. To Sostratos' way of thinking, he looked more like a peasant then a general.

A slave poured the Rhodians wine from the mixing bowl. Sounding apologetic, Ptolemaios said, "It's not very strong, I'm afraid. I don't care to start getting drunk first thing in the morning."

Macedonians had, and often lived up to, a reputation for drunkenness. But, sure enough, when Sostratos sipped, he discovered Ptolemaios didn't live up to it: the wine was cut three or four to one with water, a thin mix indeed. It was very good wine, though, and he said so.

"Thank you kindly." Ptolemaios' smile was engagingly ugly, too, for it showed a couple of broken teeth. *He's no youth*, Sostratos thought, *but he fought his way across Persia and into India with Alexander the Great*. More scars, old and white and puckered, seamed his arms.

The bread was good, too: of wheat flour, soft and fine. And the oil had a sharp green tang that said it was squeezed from the first olives picked in the fall. None of that surprised Sostratos. If the lord of Egypt couldn't afford the best, who could?

Ptolemaios let him and Menedemos eat and drink for a while. Then, after sipping from his own cup and setting it down, he said, "You boys are probably wondering why I sent for you this morning."

Sostratos dipped his head. His cousin said, "Yes, sir, we were."

"Well, I'd better tell you, then, hadn't I?" Ptolemaios chuckled. "You looked a little green around the gills when you came in here, but don't worry. You're not in trouble, leastways not with me. I was talking with an officer from the *Nike* last night, and he said you showed him a tiger skin. Is that right?"

"Yes, sir," Sostratos and Menedemos said together. Menedemos sounded enormously relieved; Sostratos supposed he did, too. Now they knew this had nothing to do with emeralds smuggled out of Egypt.

"Where on earth did you find one?" Ptolemaios asked.

"In the market square in Kaunos, sir," Sostratos answered.

"We got there a little sooner than you did," Menedemos added, risking a smile.

"Yes, the place is mine now," Ptolemaios agreed. "One of the fortresses above it surrendered to me; I had to storm the other one. But a tiger skin there? Really? Isn't that something?" He scratched his nose, then asked, "What did you have in mind doing with it?"

"Dionysos is supposed to have come from India, sir," Menedemos said. "We thought we might sell it to a shrine of his, for the cult statue to wear."

"Ah. Not a bad notion." Ptolemaios dipped his head. When he looked up again, his eyes were far away. "I hunted tigers a time or two in India. Formidable beasts—they make most lions seem like the little cats Egypt is full of beside 'em. Never thought to see a tiger hide this far west, though, and that's the truth."

"We were surprised, too," Sostratos said. "We might have been more surprised than you, in fact—we've never been to India, after all."

"That's true." Ptolemaios chuckled again. "The two of you wouldn't even have had hair on your balls yet when Alexander led us there." Sostratos had a sense of great deeds undone, a sense that the men of his own generation would always lag behind those of Ptolemaios' in glory. Before he could say anything—before he could even fully formulate the idea in his mind—the ruler of Egypt went on, "Would you boys sell that tiger skin to *me* instead of to a temple?"

Sostratos leaned forward in his chair. *So this isn't just a social call,* he thought. Menedemos sounded alert, too, as he answered, "We might, sir, as long as the price is right."

"Oh, yes. I understand that." Ptolemaios still looked more like a peasant than a general, but he looked like a very shrewd peasant indeed. "Well, what sort of price did you have in mind?"

"You said it yourself: it's a one-of-a-kind item," Menedemos said.

"Which means you're going to gouge me." Those shaggy eyebrows of Ptolemaios' came down and together in a frown. "The thing you need to remember is, this is something I'd like to have, not something I've got to have. You stick me too hard, I'll say, 'Nice meeting you,' and send you on your way. Now, let's try it again—what do you want for the skin?"

Sostratos did some rapid mental calculating. Menedemos had got the tiger hide along with the two lion skins and the gryphon's skull. Had he bought it by itself, it would have cost about . . . and that meant . . . "Eight minai, sir."

Ptolemaios tossed his head. "Nice meeting you," he said. "Have some more bread, have some more wine, and my man will take you back to your proxenos' house." He dipped another piece of bread in olive oil, then slowly and deliberately ate it. Only after he'd swallowed did he grudgingly add, "I might give you half that."

"Very nice meeting *you*, sir," Menedemos said. "We have to make a profit ourselves, you know."

One of the guards growled something in Macedonian that didn't sound pleasant. His hand slid toward the hilt of his sword. "Relax, Lysanias," Ptolemaios said in his clear Greek. "It's only a haggle, not a fight."

"Another question: whose minai are we talking about?" Sostratos asked.

Now Ptolemaios jabbed a thumb at his own chest. "Why, mine, of course."

"Fair enough." Sostratos dipped his head. "It does help to be clear in advance." It took five of Ptolemaios' drakhmai—or, multiplying a hundredfold, five of his minai—to make four of their Attic equivalent, the most commonly used weights among Hellenes. But, since the Rhodian drakhma was slightly lighter even than Ptolemaios', Sostratos couldn't complain.

And the ruler of Egypt didn't seem displeased at the question. "You're one of those fellows who likes to have everything just so, alpha-beta-gamma, aren't you? That's not a bad thing, especially in a young man. I suppose I could give you four minai, fifty drakhmai."

"I'm certain we'd do better somewhere else." Sostratos got to his feet. So did Menedemos. Sostratos turned to Alypetos. "If you'd be so kind as to guide us back to Kleiteles'?"

They'd taken a couple of steps out of the andron before Ptolemaios called after them: "Wait." He was smiling when they came back. "You like to play on the edge of the roof, too, don't you?"

Sostratos didn't. Menedemos, he knew, did. But his cousin said, "Sostratos is right. We'll do better than that in Athens, say." He sounded very sure of himself.

Ptolemaios' smile disappeared. "All right, then. You say you want eight minai, and you don't think four and a half are enough. Somewhere in between there is a number that will make you happy. Let's find out what it is."

He proceeded to do just that. Looking back on it later, Sostratos realized it was funny. Here he sat, facing what had to be the richest man in the world—and Ptolemaios haggled like a poor housewife trying to knock a couple of khalkoi off the price of a sack of barley. He gestured extravagantly. He shouted and stamped his feet. His eyebrows twitched. He cursed in Greek and then, when he was really angry—or trying to pretend he was really angry—in Macedonian. He came up in the dicker as if every extra drakhma were pulled out of his belly.

Sostratos did his best to bargain the same way. Menedemos backed him magnificently. Of course, as Ptolemaios had seen, Menedemos really did like taking chances, and didn't seem to worry that infuriating the ruler of Egypt might prove more dangerous than outraging a husband with a young, pretty wife.

The dicker stretched through the whole morning. At last, Sostratos said, "Well, best one, shall we split the difference?"

Ptolemaios counted on his fingers. He was good with numbers—*almost as good as I am*, Sostratos thought, without false modesty. "That would make what?—six minai, thirty-five drakhmai, right?"

"Yes, sir." Sostratos dipped his head.

"I'll tell you what else it would make," Ptolemaios grumbled. "It'd make you boys two of the biggest bandits left uncrucified." He raised a hairy caterpillar of an eyebrow. "I could take care of that, you know."

"So you could," Sostratos said evenly. "If you want to make Rhodes lean toward Antigonos, I can't think of a better way to go about it."

Ptolemaios grunted. "Just joking." Maybe he had been, maybe he hadn't. He went on, "This would have been easier if only you were fools. All right: six minai, thirty-five drakhmai. A bargain!"

"A bargain!" Sostratos agreed. He stuck out his hand. So did Menedemos. Ptolemaios clasped each of theirs in turn. His grip was hard and firm, the grip of a man who'd spent a lot of time with weapons in his hand. Sostratos said, "I'm sure I can get back to the harbor by myself. If you'd be so kind as to give me a man to guide me back here with the tiger skin . . ."

"Right." Ptolemaios pointed a blunt, short-nailed finger at the man who'd gone to Kleiteles' house for Sostratos and Menedemos. "Alypetos, see to that yourself."

"As you say, sir," Alypetos replied. He got to his feet. "Ready when you are, best one," he told Sostratos.

"Then let's go," Sostratos said. He wished Menedemos were getting the hide; he would have liked sitting around and chatting with Ptolemaios better. *It can't be helped*, he told himself. *And we've turned a nice profit, too.* But he still knew regrets as he started off toward the harbor. Chances for buying and selling came every day, but when would he next be able to talk with a man like the ruler of Egypt? Ever again? He had his doubts.

When he got to the *Aphrodite*, Diokles gave him a curious look. "There's been a lot going on this morning, hasn't there, young sir?" the oarmaster said.

"Oh, you might say so." Sostratos did his best to keep his tone casual.

By Diokles' expression, his best wasn't good enough. "First, Kleiteles' slave came, saying Ptolemaios had summoned your cousin and you. Then Pixodaros' slave showed up, saying he knew he'd have to wait with his silk on account of Ptolemaios. It was like Pixodaros wanted to get huffy about that but didn't have the nerve."

"I should hope not," Sostratos said; a Karian freedman wouldn't care to measure his privileges against those of Alexander's marshal. "Ptolemaios heard about our tiger skin from the officer who questioned us after the war galley made us heave to, and he's bought it."

"Ah. Is that what's been going on?" Diokles slowly dipped his head. "I did wonder, and I'm not lying. But that's good news, then, real good news."

"It certainly is. I'm going to take the skin now, and get our pay for it." Sostratos boarded the *Aphrodite*, found the leather sack with the right hide, and brought it back onto the quay. Alypetos didn't say anything, but looked about to burst from curiosity. Taking pity on him—and also realizing he might make a useful connection—Sostratos undid the rawhide lashing that held the sack closed and gave him a look at the tiger skin.

"Isn't that something?" Ptolemaios' man said softly. He reached out and stroked the fur. "And the beast is as big as a lion?"

"We have two lion skins aboard, too, and this one's bigger than either," Sostratos answered. "The tiger doesn't seem to have a mane, though, as lions do."

"Isn't that something?" Alypetos repeated. He needed a moment to gather himself. "Well, let's get on back. I can see why Ptolemaios would pay for a hide like that, indeed I can."

At the house the ruler of Egypt had taken for his own, more leather sacks, these fat with silver, lay waiting on a table in the andron. Ptolemaios had a couple of his men take the hide from the sack and spread it out so he could examine it. He sighed. "That's a tiger skin, sure enough. Been fifteen years since I last saw one of the beasts, but I'm not likely to forget."

"Have you a scale, sir, so I can weigh the coins?" Sostratos asked. "That would go much faster than counting them."

Menedemos looked horrified. Sostratos had almost got himself into trouble with a request like that the summer before in

Syracuse, and Ptolemaios was vastly more powerful than Agathokles of Syracuse even dreamt of being. But the marshal's tone was mild as he asked, "Don't trust me, eh?"

"I didn't say that, sir," Sostratos replied. "Anyone can make a mistake, or have servants who make a mistake—and I like to keep things straight."

"Yes, I've noticed that," Ptolemaios said. "Let's see what we can do." His men found a balance in the kitchen, but the weights weren't of the proper standard. "Count the drakhmai in one sack," he suggested, "and then weigh the others against it."

"Just as you say, sir," Sostratos agreed. The sack he checked held a hundred drakhmai. By the scale, so did the others—except for the odd one, which he also counted. "Thank you for your patience, sir. Everything is fine."

"Glad you approve." Ptolemaios' voice was dry. But he added, "If my men were as zealous in my service as you are in your own . . ."

I haven't got so many men in my service, Sostratos thought. *I have to do more for myself. Who will, if I don't?* But he wouldn't say that, not even to so good-natured a ruler as Ptolemaios had proved to be.

On the way back to the *Aphrodite*, Menedemos said, "I almost hit you when you wanted to start counting coins."

"I *do* like having things straight, and now I know they are," Sostratos answered. "What did Ptolemaios talk about while I was getting the tiger skin?"

"Oh, this and that," Menedemos answered, whereupon Sostratos wanted to hit him. He did his best to amplify: "Some about hunting in India, and the funny smells in the air there."

"Ah," Sostratos said. "That's interesting, but it doesn't seem too historical."

"Why should it?" his cousin asked.

In a way, Menedemos' question made perfect sense. Ptolemaios could talk about anything that crossed his mind, and he'd been thinking about tigers and distant India. In another way . . . "Because men will probably remember Ptolemaios a hundred years from now, the way we remember Lysandros the Spartan nowadays."

"Who?" Menedemos said. At first, Sostratos thought he was joking, and laughed. Then he realized his cousin meant it. He was very quiet all the way back to the merchant galley.

THAT EVENING, MENEDEMOS was all smiles for Kleiteles. "No, no, my dear fellow," he told the Rhodian proxenos at supper (it was barley bread, cheese, and fried sprats—good enough sitos, but not much of an opson). "He heard we had a tiger skin, and wanted to buy it from us. He did, too, and gave us a nice price."

"I'm glad to hear it," Kleiteles replied. "His garrison could have done worse than it has; I don't deny that. But people *have* disappeared. When you two got summoned that way, I feared the worst, and I won't tell you any different. He might almost have caught you in bed with his mistress. . . . Are you all right, best one?"

"Just swallowed wrong," answered Sostratos, who'd choked on a sprat and suffered a coughing fit. Menedemos sent his cousin a venomous look. Sostratos gave back an innocent smile—much *too* innocent for Menedemos' peace of mind.

"And your dealings with Pixodaros went well?" Kleiteles asked.

"Oh, yes." Menedemos dipped his head. "Pity old Xenophanes finally got ferried across the Styx, but the business seems in good hands."

"Pixodaros is a sharp fellow," Sostratos agreed.

"No doubt, but he's a foreigner," Kleiteles said. "Too many freedmen holding down businesses that used to belong to citizens. I'm glad I've got a couple of sons, and I burn incense to the gods every day to keep them safe." He sighed. "So many things can happen to children when they're growing up, and that's in time of peace. With the war heating up again . . ." He grimaced and sighed again.

"Incense can't hurt," Sostratos said gravely. Menedemos knew his cousin meant it probably wouldn't help, either, but the proxenos didn't take it that way. Sostratos went on, "We just got some fine balsam from a couple of Phoenicians in Knidos. I'd be pleased to give you a drakhma's weight of it tomorrow, to help repay your kindness to us."

"Thank you very much," Kleiteles said with a broad smile. "I've been burning myrrh; I'm sure the gods would fancy a fresh scent in their nostrils."

"Remind me in the morning, best one, before we go back to the *Aphrodite*, and I'll take care of it," Sostratos said. "I'm a little absentminded, I'm afraid." And so he was, but only in matters having to do with history or philosophy or birds or beasts—never in business. Menedemos dipped his head in unreserved approval. *The balsam was a nice touch. I should have thought of it myself.*

The Rhodian proxenos' slave brought in the wine. Kleiteles ordered a stronger mix than he had the night before. After a couple of cups, he sang a bawdy song in a strong, true baritone. It wasn't a regular symposion, but it came close. Kleiteles looked expectantly toward Menedemos.

Thinking of Xenophanes crossing the Styx gave Menedemos his inspiration. He quoted Kharon, the ferryman of the dead, from Aristophanes' *Frogs*:

" 'Who's off to a rest from evils and affairs?
Who's off to the Plain of Oblivion, or to take the fleece
from a donkey,
Or to Kerberos' crew, or to the crows, or to Tainaron?' "

He'd been to Cape Tainaron himself the year before. These days, instead of being nowhere to speak of, it was a hiring center for mercenaries. Menedemos rolled on with the *Frogs*, going through Dionysos' preposterous confrontation with the chorus of croakers.

Kleiteles laughed out loud. "That's good stuff," he said, raising his cup in salute to Menedemos—and perhaps to Dionysos, too. "*Koax, koax.*" He chuckled again, then swung his gaze toward Sostratos. "And what have you got for us, best one?"

Menedemos wondered if his cousin would lecture, as he often liked to do—perhaps about Lysandros the Spartan, who'd evidently been an important fellow a hundred years before. But Sostratos had something else in mind. "Me?" he said. "I'm going to talk about gryphons."

And he did, at some length: about the gold-guarding gryphons of the north and the one-eyed Arimaspioi who were supposed to steal their hoarded gold from them; about the way the nomadic Skythians and the Hellenic artists in their pay portrayed gryphons (*he's listened more to Teleutas than I thought*, went through Menedemos' mind); and about the way gryphons, if there were such things, really looked—all without mentioning that the *Aphrodite* carried a gryphon's skull along with its other cargo. Menedemos had heard the pieces of the talk before, but never all together. He was impressed almost in spite of himself. When Sostratos talked about something that interested him, he interested those hearing him, too.

He certainly interested Kleiteles. "*Euge!*" the proxenos exclaimed. "How do you go on about beasts you say are mythical as if you'd seen one just the other day?"

"Do I?" To Menedemos' ear, Sostratos sounded a little too bland to be convincing. But Kleiteles, who'd been drinking hard, wasn't a critical audience. He just dipped his head to show he thought Sostratos did. Menedemos' cousin smiled a small, secretive smile. "Homer was blind, they say. He never saw the things he sang about, but he's made others see them ever since."

"That's twice lately you've had praise for the poet," Menedemos said. Sostratos stuck out his tongue as far as it would go, as if he were a hideous Gorgon painted on a hoplite's shield. He and Menedemos both laughed.

So did Kleiteles, even if he didn't understand all of the joke the cousins shared. He'd drunk himself thoughtful, as he proved when he told Sostratos, "You have a gift for explaining things. Do you know your letters? You must, a clever fellow like you." When Sostratos didn't deny it, the Rhodian proxenos went on, "You ought to write down what you just said, so it doesn't get lost."

"Maybe I will, one day," Sostratos replied. "I've thought about it."

"You should." Kleiteles swigged from his cup. "Shall we have another round of songs and such?"

"If you've got the girls waiting in our bedrooms, I wouldn't mind going back there now," Menedemos said.

"I do." The proxenos laughed. "You two can screw yourselves silly with them. If I brought a house slave to bed, though, my wife would never let me hear the end of it. Come on." He picked up a lamp from a table. "I'll take you back there."

When Menedemos went into his chamber, he nodded to the slave on the bed. "Hail, Eunoa."

"Hail," she said. "We didn't get a chance to do it this morning." By that, she doubtless meant, *You didn't get the chance to give me anything this morning.* Menedemos dipped his head, thinking, *If she were a man, she'd be at Cape Tainaron now. She's mercenary enough.* She asked, "Did Ptolemaios really want to see you?"

"Yes," Menedemos said, and Eunoa looked impressed, and also proud, as if giving herself to someone who'd met the great man somehow made her more important. Slaves often basked in their masters' reflected glory; this seemed more of the same. Menedemos stripped off his tunic and lay down on the bed beside her.

As she had the night before, Eunoa fought shy of simply letting him take her. "I don't want to have a baby," she repeated.

Menedemos frowned. She was supposed to be there for his pleasure, not the other way round. But he humored her, sitting at the edge of the bed with his legs splayed wide. Eunoa scowled; she liked that less than giving him her backside. She finally squatted between his legs, though, and bent her head over his manhood. His fingers tangled in her hair, guiding her and urging her on.

Before long, she pulled back, coughing and choking a little. She found the chamber pot under the bed and spat into it. Sated and lazy, Menedemos gave her half a drakhma. He would have had to pay a good deal more for the same pleasure in a brothel. They stretched out on the bed side by side. Menedemos ran a hand along the sweet bare curve of her flank, then blew out the lamp. The room plunged into blackness. He fell asleep almost at once.

* * *

When the sharp knock woke Sostratos, he thought for a moment he was dreaming of what had happened the morning before. As he had then, he lay tangled with Kleiteles' slave, Thestylis. He and the woman both looked around in bleary surprise. Dawn was trickling in through the shutters.

Another knock sounded, this one next door. "Alypetos is here again," Kleiteles said, which convinced Sostratos he really was awake. "Ptolemaios wants to see both of you gentlemen, at once."

"But do I want to see Ptolemaios?" Sostratos muttered. He tossed his head in annoyance. That didn't matter. Even a free Hellene found limits to his freedom when he dealt with a Macedonian marshal. Sostratos patted Thestylis, saying, "Go back to sleep if you can. This has nothing to do with you." He threw on his tunic and went out into Kleiteles' courtyard.

Menedemos came out of the adjacent room at the same time. He too looked unhappy. "What is it now?" he demanded of Alypetos.

Ptolemaios' henchman only shrugged. "Come with me," he said.

Grumbling and yawning, Sostratos and Menedemos went. As they had the day before, they found Ptolemaios at breakfast. This morning, though, he offered them none, but fixed them with the sort of glare calculated to make them remember all their sins and fear punishment for every one. Sostratos did his best to show no expression at all. *Does he know about the emeralds?* he wondered nervously. His eyes flicked to Menedemos. His cousin, fortunately, was not a man to show guilt even if he felt it.

Ptolemaios thrust out his boulder of a chin and growled, "Why didn't you two tell me you had one of that one-eyed bastard's officers aboard your ship when you sailed into Knidos?"

He doubtless meant to intimidate them. But, since it had nothing to do with the gems, his blunt question came more as a relief than anything else. "Why should we have?" Sostratos answered. "Rhodes is free and autonomous and neutral. We can carry whoever pays our fare."

"He paid ten drakhmai, too," Menedemos added.

"Ten drakhmai, for passage from Rhodes to Knidos? You cheated him right and proper," Ptolemaios said. His anger seemed to evaporate; he might have donned it as a man dons a himation on a chilly morning and sheds it when the sun climbs higher. He eyed the two traders. "Free and neutral Rhodians, eh?"

"Yes, sir," Sostratos said stoutly.

"All right, then," Ptolemaios said. "If you did a service for Antigonos and made a profit, will you do one for me as well?"

"If we profit from it," Menedemos answered.

"You will," Ptolemaios said in a voice that brooked no contradiction. "I'll pay you a talent of silver—twenty minai in advance, to give you whatever money you'll need on the way, with the other forty waiting for you when you come back here to Kos."

"A talent?" Sostratos and Menedemos both whispered the words. Sixty minai, six thousand drakhmai—that was a lot of money. Slowly, Sostratos said, "You wouldn't offer us so much silver for just anything, sir. What have you got in mind?"

"You're a clever fellow, aren't you? I thought so before, by the way you haggled," Ptolemaios said. "Yes, you're right: I wouldn't pay so much for anything easy. You'll know that Antigonos' nephew Polemaios broke with his uncle last year and went over to Kassandros."

Menedemos dipped his head at the same time as Sostratos said, "Yes, we did know that."

"All right, then," Ptolemaios said briskly. "He's holed up in Khalkis these days, on the island of Euboia, and he's decided he doesn't like Kassandros any better than he liked his uncle. He was jealous of Antigonos' sons. I don't know what his quarrel with Kassandros is—I just know he has one. He'd make me a useful ally, I think."

He'd make you a useful tool, is what you mean, Sostratos thought. He wondered how wise the ruler of Egypt was. If Polemaios had fallen out with both Antigonos and Kassandros in a year's time, he was liable to turn in the hand of anyone who tried to wield him. But that was Ptolemaios' worry, not his. He said, "And you want us to go up to Khalkis?"

"And get him, and bring him back down here to me. That's right," Ptolemaios said. "He needs to slide out of the place without anyone's being the wiser—he hasn't got the fleet to just up and sail away."

"No, he wouldn't have the ships for that," Sostratos agreed. "He'd have to come past the coast of Attica on the way south. Athens isn't what it was in the days of Perikles, but it still has a decent navy, and Demetrios of Phaleron is Kassandros' creature."

"Exactly. I have officers who wouldn't see it that fast," Ptolemaios said. "Polemaios' soldiers can get out a few at a time in small craft once he's escaped. He'll lose some, but a lot of them will join him here. Polemaios himself is the man I really want. What do you say, Rhodians?"

Sostratos knew what he wanted to say. He wanted to say no to another delay in reaching Athens with the gryphon's skull. And this one would be all the more frustrating because the *Aphrodite* would go past the eastern coast of Attica on the way to and from Khalkis. But Ptolemaios had given him and Menedemos one big reason to say yes—or, looked at another way, six thousand little reasons.

That thought had hardly crossed his mind before Menedemos, who as captain of the akatos had the final word, gave it: "Sir, we say yes."

"Good. I thought you would, once I made sure you weren't really on Antigonos' side," Ptolemaios said. He snapped his fingers and called for a house slave. The man hurried away, returning with bread and oil and wine for Sostratos and Menedemos. *Aside from trying to put us in fear, as long as he was feeling us out about Euxenides, he didn't want to eat with us*, Sostratos realized.

"Sir, can we get a steering oar made before we sail?" Menedemos asked. "We're carrying one that's a makeshift, of green timber. It got us here, but . . ."

"I'll send a carpenter to your ship right away," Ptolemaios said. He ordered another slave off with the message. "Anything else I can do for you? I want Polemaios back here as soon as may be."

"The money," Sostratos said.

Ptolemaios smiled. "Ah, yes—the money. Don't you worry about that. It will reach your ship before the day is out."

Sostratos believed him. A lot of men, even those who had a great deal, would have lied about such a sum. Others would have haggled endlessly. Ptolemaios himself had haggled endlessly over the tiger skin. The skin, though, had been something he wanted, but not something he felt he had to have. Getting Antigonos' nephew here to Kos was different.

Something else occurred to Sostratos: "How will Polemaios know we're working for you, sir? How do we convince him we're not in his uncle's pay, or Kassandros'?"

"I said you were a clever fellow, didn't I?" Ptolemaios beamed at him. "I'll give you a letter and seal it with my eagle." He held out his right fist. On one thick finger he wore a gold signet ring whose design was an eagle like the ones on the reverse of his coins. "It'll come to your ship with the first installment of the money. Anything else?"

After glancing at Menedemos, Sostratos tossed his head. "No, sir. I think that's everything."

"Good enough, then." Ptolemaios was all business. "Would you care for anything else to eat or drink? No? Do you need Alypetos to take you back down to the harbor? No? Very good, very good. A pleasure talking to you."

The two Rhodians found themselves on the street in front of Ptolemaios' residence in a matter of moments. "A talent of silver!" Menedemos said softly.

"We'll earn it," Sostratos answered. "We're running the gauntlet for him."

"We can do it." Menedemos sounded confident—but then, he usually did. He went on, "What we need to do, though, is stop at Pixodaros' home on the way to the ship. We want to make sure we get the silk aboard before Ptolemaios' men finish their deliveries."

"Right," Sostratos said. "And we'd better hurry, too, because I don't think they'll waste much time."

"I don't, either," Menedemos said. As they headed toward the harbor, he went on, "Now, was it two streets up and three over from the seaside, or the other way round?"

"Three up and two over," Sostratos answered. "Why can't you remember something like that?"

"I don't know, my dear," Menedemos answered. "But I don't need to bother, not when I've got you around." It was praise, of a sort—about as much as Sostratos ever got from his cousin. They went down toward the sea together.

AS THE *APHRODITE* MADE HER WAY north and west, the rowers taking turns at the oars when the wind faltered, Menedemos waited for the trouble he was sure he would have. He'd guessed it would come before the end of their first day out of Kos, and his guess proved a good one. Not long after noon, Sostratos ascended to the poop deck. He peered off to starboard at the island of Kalymnos, then ahead toward the smaller, more distant island of Lebinthos, where they'd probably pass the night. He coughed a couple of times.

"I know what you're going to say," Menedemos told him. "The answer is no."

His cousin jerked in surprise. "How do you know what I'm going to ask you?"

"Because, O best one, you're transparent as air," Menedemos answered. "You're going to say something like, 'We could stop in Athens on the way up to Khalkis. It wouldn't take long, and we could get rid of the gryphon's skull.' Aren't you?"

Sostratos turned red as a roof tile. "Well, what if I am?" he muttered. His voice gained strength: "It's true."

"So it is," Menedemos said. "But we've got forty minai waiting for us in Kos. How much do you suppose that precious skull will bring?"

"If we're lucky, something on the order of six minai," Sostratos answered.

"Lucky? That'd take a miracle from the gods," Menedemos said. "Who'd be mad enough to pay such money for an old bone?"

What he meant was, *No one would pay such money for an old bone*. Sostratos understood him perfectly well, too. But he said, "You're not always as smart as you think you are. Damonax son of Polydoros offered me that much back on Rhodes."

Menedemos stared. "And you told him no? You must have told him no." Sostratos dipped his head. Still astonished, Menedemos asked, "But why? You can't think we'll get more than that in Athens."

"I don't," his cousin admitted. "But I took the skull to show it to him, not to sell. I don't want it gathering dust in a rich man's andron, or on display at drinking parties like Kleiteles' jackdaw with the little bronze shield. I want men who truly love wisdom to study it."

"You must," Menedemos said, and then, "I'm glad no mosquito bite ever gave *me* the itch for philosophy." He gathered himself. "But even if we got ten minai for the gryphon's skull, that'd only be a quarter part of forty. We can pick up Polemaios, bring him back to Kos, and then we can head for Athens. Am I right or am I wrong?"

With a longing sigh, Sostratos said, "Oh, you're right, I suppose. But that doesn't mean I have to like it." Scuffing his feet on the planking, he descended from the poop deck into the waist of the merchant galley.

"Did I hear right, skipper?" Diokles asked in a low voice. "Six minai of silver for that silly skull, and he turned it down? Who's crazier, that other fellow for saying he'd pay it, or your cousin for telling him no?"

"To the crows with me if I know," Menedemos answered, also quietly, and the oarmaster laughed. But Menedemos went on, "He really does chase philosophy the way I chase girls, doesn't he?" In an odd sort of way, the way he would have admired a boy who declined an expensive gift from a suitor he didn't fancy, he found himself admiring Sostratos for rejecting Damonax's enormous offer.

"You have more fun," Diokles said.

That made Menedemos chuckle. "Well, I think so, too," he said. "But if Sostratos doesn't, who am I to tell him he's wrong?"

Diokles grunted. "I can think of a good many hetairai who'd be happy if a fellow gave 'em half a dozen minai. Fact is, I can't think of any so grand that they wouldn't be." Menedemos only shrugged. Maybe Thaïs, who'd talked Alexander the Great into burning Persepolis. But maybe not, too.

The *Aphrodite* neared Lebinthos as the sun neared the Aegean Sea to the west. Menedemos steered the akatos toward a nice little harbor on the southern coast of the island. Both steering oars felt alike in his hands again; with seasoned timber at their disposal, Ptolemaios' carpenters hadn't needed long to replace the makeshift Euxenides of Phaselis had made. But even they'd praised it as they took it off the pivot.

"Aristeidas, go forward," Menedemos called. "If a pirate's lurking in that bay, you'd be the first to spot him."

"Not likely, skipper," Diokles said as Aristeidas went. "No water to speak of on Lebinthos. If it's got more than a family of fisherman living on it, I'd be amazed."

"So would I," Menedemos answered. "But I don't want any nasty surprises." The keleustes could hardly argue with that, and didn't.

But the small, sheltered bay was empty save for shore birds, which flew up in white-winged clouds as the *Aphrodite* beached herself. The beach seemed so deserted, Menedemos wondered if sea turtles laid their eggs here, too. *I'll send out some men to probe the sand with sticks*, he thought.

Sostratos came over to him. "Lebinthos," he said, pronouncing the name of the island like a man prodding his teeth with his tongue, feeling for a bit of food that might have got stuck there. And then, being the sort of fellow he was, he found what he was looking for: "Didn't Ikaros fly past this place on his way north from Crete?"

Menedemos looked up to the sky. Stars would be coming out very soon now. "I don't know," he answered. "If he did fly by, he probably took one look at it and pissed on it from up high."

"Scoffer." Sostratos laughed. He seemed to have forgotten

he was supposed to be angry at Menedemos, and Menedemos didn't remind him.

"It's true," Menedemos said. "Well, it could be true, anyhow. Maybe that's why this is such a blighted little place."

His cousin laughed again, but then turned serious. "If a few people did live on Lebinthos, they'd probably turn that into a myth to explain why more people couldn't."

That made a certain amount of sense. But being sensible didn't make Menedemos comfortable with it. "You called me a scoffer," he said. "I was just making a silly joke. You sound like you mean it."

"Don't you think that's how a lot of myths got started?" Sostratos asked. "As explanations for the way things are, I mean?"

"Maybe. I never worried about it much, though," Menedemos answered. The idea of asking *why* about a myth, as one might to a story of how a cart broke a wheel, made him nervous. "Myths are just myths, that's all."

"Do you really think so?" Sostratos said. Even at sunset and the beginning of twilight, his eyes gleamed. *Oh, dear*, Menedemos thought. *I've found an argument that interests him. Will I get any sleep tonight?* Sostratos went on, "How do you know that till you've examined them?"

Trying to head him off, Menedemos chuckled and said, "You sound like you come straight out of Sokrates' thinking-shop in the *Clouds*."

That didn't work. He should have known it wouldn't. Sostratos said, "You know what I think of Aristophanes for that."

They'd argued over the play before. With a small sigh, Menedemos dipped his head. "Yes, I do." He tried again, this time by pointing into the eastern sky: "There's Zeus' wandering star." He poked his cousin in the ribs with an elbow. "And what else could it possibly be *but* Zeus' wandering star?"

"I don't know," Sostratos admitted, "but we can't get close enough to examine it, so how can we be sure?" He sent Menedemos a sly look. "Maybe Ikaros could have given you a better answer."

"The same as he would have about the sun? Look what he got for flying too close to that." Menedemos mimed falling from a great height, then toppled onto the sand in lieu of splashing into the sea.

"You're impossible." But Sostratos was laughing in spite of himself.

A sailor with a pole in his hand came up to Menedemos and said, "Doesn't seem like there are any turtle eggs on this beach."

"Oh, well." Menedemos shrugged. "We've got enough bread and oil and olives and cheese for sitos and a sort of opson, and enough water to mix with the wine. For one night ashore here, that'll do well enough." Up the beach from the *Aphrodite*, the men fed bits of dry shrubs to a couple of fires they'd got going. Menedemos didn't think the night would be very cold, but fires always made a place more comfortable. And then someone with a bronze hook and a line hauled a fish out of the sea. Before long, it was cooking over one of those fires.

Back home on Rhodes, Menedemos would have turned up his nose at such a meager supper. Out on a trading journey, he ate with good appetite. He was spitting an olive pit onto the sand when Sostratos came up to him and asked, "Where will we head for tomorrow?"

"Naxos, I think," Menedemos answered. "I don't know whether we'll get there—that's got to be something like five hundred stadia—but we can put in there the next morning if we don't."

"Have we got enough water aboard for another day at sea?" he asked.

Menedemos dipped his head. "For one more day, yes. For two . . . I wouldn't want to push it. But we can fill up when we get into port there. Naxos is the best watered of the Kyklades."

"That's true," Sostratos agreed. "It's certainly not a dried-up husk like Lebinthos here."

With a shrug, Menedemos said, "If this place had a couple of springs, it would just be another pirates' roost. It's out in the sea by itself, but close enough to the other islands to hunt from. The way things are, though, the bastards can't linger here."

Sostratos sighed. "I suppose you're right, my dear. Too bad we have to worry about things like that."

"I didn't say it wasn't," Menedemos replied. "Now I'm going to finish eating and then go to sleep."

He wondered if he would have to be blunter than that; Sostratos didn't always take a hint. But his cousin said, "All right," and found his own place on the sand to lie down. Menedemos wrapped himself in his himation: the day's warmth was seeping out of the air faster than he'd expected. Next thing he knew, morning twilight brightened the eastern sky.

A BRISK BREEZE from out of the northeast sent the *Aphrodite* bounding across the waves. Even before noon, Sostratos said, "I think we will make Naxos by nightfall."

"If this wind holds, we will," Menedemos agreed. The wind tousled his hair—and Sostratos', too. It thrummed in the rigging and filled the sail. The rowers rested at their oars. A breeze like this pushed the merchant galley along as well as they could have.

Sostratos finally had his sea legs. The *Aphrodite*'s pitching and rolling had left him queasy at the start of the sailing season. Now he didn't even notice them till he realized he would have noticed them before. He wondered if that realization would bring back the queasiness, but it didn't. He was over it for another year.

Naxos crawled up over the western horizon, central mountain first and then the rest of the island. Its polis lay in the northwest, beyond the northernmost headland. The *Aphrodite* rounded the headland and dropped down toward the port with the sun at least an hour away from setting. Menedemos took his hands off the steering oars long enough to clap them together. "That's one of the nicest day's runs I've ever made," he said.

"*Euge*, O best one," Sostratos said agreeably. "And now here we are, in a place where all sorts of interesting things used to happen."

His cousin raised a quizzical eyebrow. " 'Used to happen'?" he echoed.

"I suppose everyone knows this is where Theseus abandoned Ariadne," Sostratos said, and Menedemos dipped his head. Sostratos went on, "This is also one of the places where the Hellenes first rebelled against the Persians. A generation later, the Naxians sent four ships to fight for Xerxes the Great King at Salamis—but they went over to the Hellenes instead. And a few years after *that*, the Athenians laid siege to Naxos and took it because it tried to secede from the Delian League. Nobody knew it then, but that was one of the first steps on the road that led to the Peloponnesian War."

Menedemos only grunted. He was intent on getting the *Aphrodite* a berth in Naxos' little harbor. Diokles gave Sostratos a curious look. "You don't mind my asking, young sir," he said, "but how do you know all that?"

With a shrug, Sostratos answered, "Well, you know about Theseus and Ariadne yourself, don't you?"

"I suppose I'd heard it," the keleustes said, "but I can't say I remembered it. And as for the rest . . ."

"That's in the writings of Herodotos and Thoukydides," Sostratos said. "I just put it all together, like a man making a table from the top and the legs."

Diokles scratched his head. "With a carpenter, you can see the pieces beforehand. The way you go on, it's like you're grabbing them out of the air."

"Sostratos collects funny facts the way a carpenter collects fancy pieces of wood," Menedemos said. "And a carpenter can only use a piece of wood in one table or chair, but Sostratos gets to use his facts over and over again." He grinned at Sostratos. It was a half mocking grin, or more than half, but the figure was so apt, Sostratos just grinned back.

If that disappointed Menedemos, he didn't show it. He went back to steering the merchant galley. A fishing boat that spotted the *Aphrodite* later than it should have lowered—all but dropped—its sail from the yard and did its best to get away from what it thought to be a pirate ship. Had the akatos really been a pentekonter, it would have run down the tubby little fishing boat inside a couple of stadia. Some of the rowers jeered at the fleeing fishermen.

"They're running now," Teleutas said, "but when they tell about it in a tavern tonight, they'll all be heroes." That made the *Aphrodite*'s crewmen laugh and send more jokes after the fishing boat. Sostratos laughed, too, but he eyed Teleutas thoughtfully. *He sounds like a man who knows what he's talking about*, went through his mind.

No sooner had the merchant galley tied up at a Naxian quay than an officer came up and started asking questions. Naxos favored Antigonos; it belonged to the Island League he'd started in the Kyklades a few years before. "Out of Kos, eh?" the officer said suspiciously. "What were you doing there?"

"Buying silk," Sostratos answered, doing his best to sound impatient rather than nervous. "We're bound for Athens. Always a good market for silk in Athens."

Athens was as much a thing of Kassandros' as Naxos was of Antigonos'; still, the lie seemed far better than saying they were going to Euboia to get Antigonos' unloved and unloving nephew. And the officer didn't pursue it. He had other things on his mind: nervously licking his lips, he asked, "Is it true? Has Ptolemaios really come to Kos?"

Sostratos dipped his head. "It's true." He made his voice deep and solemn.

"With a fleet? With a big fleet?"

"That's true, too." This time, Menedemos beat Sostratos to the punch. He, by contrast, sounded amused. With a big fleet, Ptolemaios could sweep the Island League off the face of the earth. Menedemos knew it. Sostratos knew it. The officer talking with them knew it, too. He looked very unhappy.

"Do you know what his plans are?" he asked after a pause.

"Oh, of course." Now Sostratos sounded sardonic. "Ptolemaios invited us to breakfast so we could talk things over." Sometimes—often—the truth served up with irony made the most effective lie.

Antigonos' officer turned red. "All right. All right," he said roughly. Sure enough, he didn't believe the truth, where doubtless he would have accepted any number of falsehoods. Sostratos wondered what Sokrates would have had to say had someone wondered about this while he was close by. Something worth hearing, the Rhodian was sure. The officer went on, "Will you trade here tomorrow?"

Now Sostratos hesitated. Ptolemaios would want Polemaios back on Kos as soon as possible. But Naxos was a big enough polis that passing up a chance to do business here would make people like this fellow wonder why. While Sostratos weighed advantages and risks, Menedemos cut through them as Alexander was supposed to have cut through the Gordian knot, saying, "We'll spend the morning here, anyhow, best one, while we fill our water jugs. After that . . . Well, we want to get to Athens as fast as we can."

As irony had, glibness satisfied the officer. He walked back down the pier. "Can we make Mykonos in half a day?" Sostratos asked.

"From here? I expect so," Menedemos answered. "And who knows? Maybe we really will sell some silk in the agora tomorrow."

"Maybe." Sostratos didn't believe it, but he didn't argue. They'd already been surprised a couple of times this sailing season. He did point north and ask, "If we leave tomorrow a bit after noon, are you *really* sure we can get up to Mykonos by sunset?" Haze-purple in the distance, the other island heaved itself over the sea-smooth horizon, with tiny, holy Delos and the altogether mundane Rheneia off to its left.

"I told you once that I think so," his cousin answered. With a grin, Menedemos went on, "Remember what a hard time we had last year convincing the people there that we weren't a pack of pirates?"

"I sure do," Sostratos said. "We almost had trouble with pirates ourselves in those waters. I could do without that."

"A lot of bald men on Mykonos." Menedemos ran a hand through his thick, dark hair. "I could do without that."

Laughing, Sostratos said, "Be careful, my dear, or your beauty will make me swoon. How can I possibly lie down on the poop deck beside you tonight and hope to go to sleep?"

That made Menedemos laugh, too. It also made him preen a little. He *was* a handsome man, and had had more than his share of suitors as a youth. For a while, a good many walls in Rhodes had had BEAUTIFUL MENEDEMOS and other such endearments scrawled on them. He'd basked in his popularity, too. Tall and plain and gawky, Sostratos had hidden jealousy behind a mask of indifference. Eventually, the mask became the thing itself, but it took a while.

With Aphrodite's wandering star already glowing in the

west, it was too late to go looking for the Rhodian proxenos here. They did sleep on the poop deck, with the stars and mosquitoes for company. In the morning, Menedemos sent a party of sailors into the polis with water jars. With a chuckle, he said, "You boys can surprise the women who gossip around whatever fountain you find."

"Now you've done it," Sostratos said, watching the rowers straighten up and start to primp. "We'll be lucky if they don't jump ship."

"They'd better not," his cousin said. "Anybody who's not aboard by noon gets left behind. That means they won't be able to get away from her husband or her father or her brothers." He spoke like a man with considerable experience in such matters. Sostratos knew he was.

More sailors carried silk and dye and balsam and perfume and papyrus and ink behind Sostratos and Menedemos as they made their way to the Naxian market square. Sostratos had to give a local an obolos for directions; Naxos was an old town, with streets running every which way. Men in the agora shouted about their garlic and cheeses, their barley and wool, their olives and olive oil, their raisins and the local wines. "Just another small-town market," Sostratos said.

Menedemos chuckled. "We'll take care of *that*, by the gods." As soon as they'd found a place that would stay shady all morning long and the sailors had set up the goods they'd brought along, he sang out, "Koan silk! Rhodian perfume! Crimson dye from Byblos! Balsam from Engedi, finest in the world!"

For a moment, everybody else in the market square stopped and gaped. Menedemos went right on crying his wares. He liked being the center of attention; he liked few things better, in fact. Having all the people within earshot crane their heads his way was sitos and opson and unwatered wine to him.

"Papyrus from Egypt!" Sostratos added for good measure. "It's been going fast—get it while we've still got some left. Best quality ink!"

"Silk! Perfume! Crimson! Balsam!"

Before long, they had quite a crowd around their little display: people eager to feel and to sniff and to gawk. The Naxians were Ionians, and dropped their rough breathings: " 'Ere, be careful! Get off my foot!" " 'E meant you!" "No, 'e didn't. 'E meant *you*!" "Watch where you put your 'ands, pal!" "You've got nutting wort' watching, lady."

People did plenty of looking, yes. They were less eager to part with their silver, though a physician did buy a couple of drakhmai's worth of balsam. "Good to see it here," he said gravely. "I find it very useful, but I seldom have a chance to buy any."

"You should get more, then," Sostratos said.

"So I should." The fellow smiled a sweet, sad smile. "Trouble is, I can't afford to. Necessity is master of us all." He took the little bit of balsam he had bought and went on his way.

Sostratos also sold a pot of ink, and Menedemos sold a couple of jars of perfume. But business was slow. When Aristeidas made his way into the market square to report that the water jars were filled, Sostratos and his cousin breathed identical sighs of relief.

Menedemos glanced at the sun. "Not quite noon yet, but close enough. Let's pack up and head back to the ship." Sostratos said not a word in protest.

Before long, the *Aphrodite* glided north over the waves. Diokles called out the stroke for the rowers. They were heading straight into the wind, so they went by oars alone, with the sail brailed up to the yard. Sostratos said, "We'll have an easier time bringing Polemaios back to Kos."

His cousin gave him an odd look. "As far as wind and weather go, yes," Menedemos said after a brief pause. Sostratos' ears burned. A lot of other things besides wind and weather might be involved.

AT PANORMOS ON the north coast of Mykonos, the *Aphrodite* got mistaken for a pirate ship again. That amused Menedemos and saddened him at the same time. He needed all his persuasive talent to keep the townsfolk there from either fleeing into the interior of the island or else attacking his ship. "Good thing we don't want anything more than an anchorage for the night," he told Sostratos after the locals calmed down.

"I know," his cousin answered. "I hope we don't run into any of the real sea-raiders as we head up towards Euboia."

"May it not come to pass!" Menedemos exclaimed, and spat into the bosom of his tunic to turn aside the evil omen. So did Sostratos. Menedemos smiled. For all of Sostratos' philosophy, he could act as superstitious as any other seaman.

Sostratos coughed and looked faintly embarrassed. Though he had a sailor's superstitions, he didn't wear them comfortably, as most sailors did. He seemed to be looking for a way to change the subject: "Another night aboard ship."

Panormos had no Rhodian proxenos. To Menedemos' way of thinking, the place barely counted as a polis. "We're probably better off here than we would be on dry land," he said.

"I should think so." Sostratos sent Menedemos a sly look. "No girls aboard the *Aphrodite*, though."

"Any girls in a backwater place like Panormos would likely be ugly anyhow," Menedemos replied. He spread out his himation on the poop deck, lay down on it and wrapped it around himself, and fell asleep.

When he woke up, Sostratos was snoring beside him. He got to his feet and pissed into the sea. The sky was lightening toward dawn. Diokles was awake, too. He looked back over his shoulder from the bench on which he'd been resting and waved to Menedemos, who dipped his head in return.

He let those sailors who could sleep till the sun followed rosy-fingered Aurora up over the horizon. Then the men who'd already wakened roused those who'd stayed asleep. They ate bread and oil and olives and onions. With Diokles beating out the stroke, they headed north and west toward Euboia.

A year before, the *Aphrodite* had sailed past Delos on her way toward Cape Tainaron. Now she left the sacred island and its ordinary neighbor behind, pushing up toward Tenos and Andros. The ship hadn't even come close to Tenos, one of the larger of the Kyklades, before Menedemos told Diokles, "Stop us for a bit."

"All right, skipper," the oarmaster said, and called out, "*Oöp!*" to the crew. The eight men on the oars on each side rested. They and the rest of the sailors looked back expectantly at Menedemos.

"Time to serve out weapons," he said. "I just don't like the way things feel. If we're ready for trouble, maybe we can hold it away from us."

"Probably not a bad idea," Diokles said. Men put on sword belts and leaned pikes and javelins by their benches or in other spots where they could grab them in a hurry. Menedemos set his bow and a full quiver of arrows on the poop deck behind him. He could string the bow and start shooting in the space of a couple of heartbeats.

"Aristeidas, go forward," he called. "I want the best lookout we've got up there." The sharp-eyed sailor waved and hurried to the foredeck. Menedemos dipped his head to Diokles. "All right. We can get going again."

"Rhyppa*pai*!" the keleustes sang out. "Rhyppa*pai*!" The oars bit into the blue water of the Aegean. The merchant galley slid forward again.

Sostratos came back to the raised poop. He had a sword on his hip and contrived to look foolish with it, like an actor in a role he hadn't rehearsed. "In Athens," he said, "they talk about nervous men who see every distant headland as a pirate ship."

Menedemos declined to get ruffled. "In Athens, from what I hear, they don't do much of anything *but* talk," he said. "Tell me, best one, how many islands in the Kyklades?"

"Some say twelve, others fifteen," his cousin answered.

"That's about what I've heard," Menedemos agreed. "But when they make that count, do they reckon in rocks like the one ahead?" He pointed to an islet just big enough to support a handful of bushes.

"Certainly not," Sostratos said, as if making a rejoinder in a philosophical discussion.

But this was property, not philosophy; freedom or slavery, not words. "Could pirates hide behind that nasty rock and come charging out when they see a merchantman go by?" Menedemos asked.

"Yes, without a doubt." Sostratos laughed. "I sound like one of Sokrates' foils, don't I?"

"I was thinking the same thing, as a matter of fact," Menedemos said. "You'd know better than I would, though—I'm sure of that. But it doesn't really matter. What matters is that you take my point."

Sostratos set a hand on his swordhilt. He still didn't look very warlike, but he said, "Would I be wearing this if I didn't?"

No hemiolia or pentekonter emerged from behind the rock. But another rock lay ahead, only fifteen or twenty stadia away. Beyond that one was the bulk of Tenos, whose jagged west coast offered raiders countless lairs. The polis of Tenos, like Panormos, hardly rated the name. It had no fleet to speak of, and didn't even try to keep pirates down. Andros, the next island to the north and west, might have been Tenos' twin. And a pirate ship based on Syros, off to the west toward Attica, might spot the *Aphrodite* coming by and dash out to try to seize her.

"It's not just Aristeidas up by the stempost," Menedemos said. "We all have to keep our eyes open, because we'll all pay for it if we don't."

"Well, certainly," Sostratos said.

Menedemos frowned. "You say 'certainly' now. A moment ago, you were talking about nervous Athenians and what they think they see."

"What if I was?" his cousin said. "You're neither nervous nor an Athenian, so what's that got to do with you?" After a moment's thought, Menedemos decided he meant it. *Maybe I was looking for an argument where there wasn't one to find*, he thought. *Maybe*. He still had trouble believing it. More likely, Sostratos was just finding smoother ways to get under his skin.

The akatos slid past the city of Tenos, the great temple to Poseidon a few stadia to the west, and the hills rising up behind. She found no trouble. A few fishing boats fled from her; Menedemos had grown used to that. They might spread the word that a pirate galley was brazenly cruising in the neighborhood. He shrugged. *The more ships that run from us, the fewer ships we have to run from.*

Having passed Tenos town, Menedemos looked up into the bright blue bowl of the sky and drummed his fingers on the steering-oar tillers. They both felt the same again, and he was still getting used to that. He drummed some more. He didn't think the merchant galley would get all the way up to Andros' polis by nightfall. That meant finding an anchorage somewhere short of the city. Plenty of promontories, without a doubt. Making sure he found one no raiders were already using . . . His fingers went up and down, up and down.

Sostratos pointed west toward the headland of Attica, clearly visible though misty with sea haze. Sighing, Menedemos' cousin said, "We could be heading there. We should be heading there."

"And we will be heading there, my dear," Menedemos said. "We have to pick up Polemaios and bring him back to Kos. Then we come back to Athens." He drummed on the steering-oar tillers yet again. "We get to come through the Kyklades twice. I could live without that."

Before Sostratos could answer, Aristeidas and several other sailors shouted, "Ship ho!" and "Ship to starboard!" and "Pirate coming at us!" Others added curses that would have sunk the hemiolia sprinting out from behind a spit of land if only the gods were listening.

"All men to the oars!" Menedemos called, and the crew scrambled to obey. As soon as every oar was manned, he turned to Diokles and barked, "Give us the stroke, keleustes—the best we can do."

"Right you are, skipper. . . . Rhyppa*pai*! Rhyppa*pai*!" The oarmaster struck urgent notes from the bronze square. The rowers, grunting with effort, pulled hard. And the *Aphrodite*, which had been ambling over the wine-dark Aegean, seemed to gather herself and then leap forward.

Since they'd been going against the wind, the sail was already brailed up to the yard. Menedemos glanced over toward the onrushing pirate ship. Her crew had taken down her mast and stowed it before sallying forth. And, however fast the akatos was going, the hemiolia, by the nature of things, had a better turn of speed. The *Aphrodite* needed to carry cargo as well as rowers, and was beamier than the lean predator knifing through the water propelled by its two banks of oars.

Menedemos' smile went wolfish. Relative speeds would have mattered more had he been trying to run away. But that wasn't what he intended. He yanked hard on the steering-oar tillers, swinging the *Aphrodite* straight toward the pirate ship.

"Going to ram, eh?" Sostratos said.

"If those bastards don't sheer off, I will," Menedemos answered. He'd played this game before. Pirate galleys weren't warships—they wouldn't strike home without counting the cost. They wanted easy victims, not fights. Show them you were ready to give them all they could handle and they weren't so likely to want anything to do with you.

That was the theory on which Menedemos operated, anyhow. It had worked for him more than once. This time . . . This time, his ship and the piratical hemiolia closed with each other at a truly frightening clip. The wind of the *Aphrodite*'s passage blew against his face and ruffled his hair. The hemiolia showed no signs of backing away. She swelled with each stroke of the merchant galley's oars, with each stroke of her own. She had archers on the foredeck, and a black-bearded ruffian at the steering oars bawling orders to his crew.

Archers . . . Menedemos said, "Sostratos, duck under me here, grab my bow and arrows, and go forward. You're a decent shot, and you're not rowing or steering."

"Certainly," his cousin answered, and did it. He fumbled a little as he strung the bow, but he was ready to shoot by the time he got to the *Aphrodite*'s foredeck. Menedemos knew he was a better archer than Sostratos, but he was also the akatos' best ship-handler, and that counted for more.

Only a couple of stadia separated the two galleys now: less every heartbeat. The rowers, gasping and drenched with sweat, couldn't see that, but Menedemos could. He bit his lip till he tasted blood. Had he outsmarted himself? The hemiolia carried more men than his akatos. If it came to that kind of fight, he would likely lose.

But if I ram, or if I can scrape my hull along her side and break half her oars . . . He'd done that to a Roman trireme the summer before—an astonishing victory for an akatos. But those Italians had been amateurs on the sea. By the way she was rowed, by the way she steered, the hemiolia had a solid crew. *Now, who's got more nerve?* Menedemos wondered. *Me, or that son of a whore over there?*

"They're shooting," Diokles said. The rhythm of mallet on bronze never faltered.

"I see 'em," Menedemos answered grimly. The arrows splashed into the sea, ahead of the *Aphrodite*'s ram. Archers always started too soon. Menedemos raised his voice to a shout: "Give 'em a couple, Sostratos! Show 'em we've got teeth, too."

His cousin waved, drew the bow back to his ear, and let fly. To Menedemos' astonished delight, one of the bowmen on the pirate ship clutched at his shoulder. His howl of pain came loud and clear across the water. Sostratos whooped joyfully and shot again. He had no luck that time, or none Menedemos could see.

And then, instead of going on to make a ramming attack against the *Aphrodite*, the hemiolia heeled sharply to starboard. The pirates' oarmaster screamed at his men, to get the last little bit of speed from them and make sure the merchant galley couldn't ram their ship. The black-bearded chieftain lifted a hand from the steering oars to shake a fist at Menedemos. Menedemos lifted his hand, too, to blow the pirates a kiss.

That hemiolia was faster than the *Aphrodite*. Even had Menedemos wanted to pursue the pirates, which he didn't, he couldn't have caught them. "Let the men ease off, Diokles," he said, thinking, *If I were the captain of a trireme, I* would *go after those bastards*. But even a trireme, as swift a naval vessel as there was, couldn't always keep up with a hemiolia. Menedemos scowled, wishing there were a ship that could scour swift pirate galleys from the seas.

But his scowl didn't last. The rowers raised a panting cheer. And Diokles said, "That was nicely done, skipper. Most of those abandoned catamites haven't got the stomach for a real fight."

"That's what I was counting on," Menedemos answered. "The son of a whore with the whiskers made me nervous, though. I wondered if he really did want to mix it up." He raised his voice so everyone on board could hear: "Let's have a cheer for Sostratos, who shot a pirate with his first arrow."

The rowers hadn't seen that, of course; they'd been looking

back toward the stern. The cheer they gave Menedemos' cousin was louder than the one he'd got himself; they had some of their wind back. Menedemos watched with amusement as Sostratos, still up on the foredeck, gave a wave the rowers also couldn't see and stammered out, "Thank you very much." *Even when he gets a chance to shine, he doesn't know what to do with it*, Menedemos thought.

Carrying the bow and quiver, Sostratos made his way back toward the stern. Menedemos greeted him with a line from the *Iliad*: "Hail, 'best of the Akhaioi in archery.' "

"I'm not, you know," Sostratos answered with his usual relentless honesty. "You're a better shot than I am, though not by a lot. And hitting anything when you're shooting at a moving target from a moving ship is as much a matter of luck as anything else."

Both those things were true. Neither of them mattered even an obolos' worth, not right now. Menedemos tossed his head. "You won't get out of it that easily, my dear. Like it or not, you're a hero."

He would have basked in the acclaim himself. What was a man worth, unless his fellows praised him? Not much, not as far as Menedemos was concerned. But Sostratos turned as red as a handsome youth importuned for the first time by an older man. Menedemos swallowed a sigh. There were times when his cousin took modesty much too far.

THE CHANNEL BETWEEN Andros and Euboia had an evil reputation, but its waters were calm enough when the *Aphrodite* crossed it. Once Euboia lay on the ship's right hand and the coastline of Attica on the left, Sostratos allowed himself the luxury of a sigh of relief. "We don't have to worry about that any more," he remarked.

Menedemos tossed his head. "Of course we do—unless you hadn't planned on going back?" As Sostratos' cheeks heated, his cousin let him down easy: "I'm not sorry to get to leeward of Euboia myself, I will say that."

"Nor I," Sostratos said. The long, narrow island lay like a shield to the northeast of Attica. "Khalkis tomorrow."

"I expect so," Menedemos answered, and began to quote from the *Iliad*'s Catalogue of Ships:

> " 'The Abantes, breathing fury, held Euboia—
> Khalkis and Eiretria and Hisitaia rich in grapes,
> Coastal Kerinthos and the steep city of Dion;
> They also held Karystos and dwelt in Styra.
> Their leader was Elephenor, descendant of Ares,
> The son of Khalkedon: lord of the great-hearted Abantes.
> Him the swift Abantes followed, with their hair long in back:
> Spearmen with ash spears ready
> To rend the corselets on the chests of their foes.
> Forty black ships followed him.' "

"Old cities," Sostratos murmured. But he looked west, toward Attica: toward the land to which he wished the *Aphrodite* were going. He pointed. "There's a place that's not so old, but it bears a name that will live as long as Troy: Marathon."

His cousin cared little for history, but even he knew what that meant. "Where the Athenians gave the Persians the first lesson on what it means to tangle with free Hellenes," he said.

Sostratos dipped his head. "That's right." And so it was, though things weren't quite so simple. Up till the battle at Marathon, the Persians had won their fights against the Hellenes with a monotonous regularity no one cared to remember these days. Sostratos asked, "Do you know the story of Pheidippides?"

"Oh, yes," his cousin said. "He's the fellow who ran from Marathon to Athens with news of the fight, gasped out, 'Rejoice! We conquer!'—and fell over dead."

"That's right," Sostratos said. "When I was in Athens, I went out to Marathon once, to see with my own eyes what the battlefield looks like. It was most of a day on the back of a mule—a long day's march for a hoplite. I don't wonder that Pheidippides dropped dead if he ran it all at once."

"What on earth made you want to go all that way?" Menedemos asked.

"I told you—to see it for myself," Sostratos answered.

"It's just a place," Menedemos said. "The battle happened a long time ago." They eyed each other in perfect mutual incomprehension. With an amused shrug, Menedemos went on, "Well, to each his own. I think I'll put in at Rhamnous, up past Marathon on the Attic side of the strait here. That's a better anchorage than I could get on the Euboian side."

"You're trying to drive me mad, aren't you, my dear?—either that or to tempt me to jump ship," Sostratos said. Menedemos laughed, and Sostratos *was* joking. He wouldn't snatch up the gryphon's skull, tuck it under his arm, and run like Pheidippides down to the Lykeion. *No, I won't*, he thought, *however much I want to*. Not quite changing the subject, he went on, "A little inland from the seaside village at Rhamnous, there's a temple to Nemesis, with the goddess' statue carved from a block of Parian marble the Persians had brought along for the victory monument they would set up in Athens. Some say Pheidias carved it, others his pupil Agorakritos."

"You've seen it?" his cousin asked.

"Oh, yes; on the trip to Marathon I stopped there, too. It's very fine work. She's wearing a crown ornamented with tiny Victories and with deer. In one hand, she holds a bowl carved with figures of Ethiopians in relief, in the other an apple branch."

"Ethiopians?" Menedemos said. "Why?"

"To the crows with me if I know," Sostratos replied. "A priest said it was because Okeanos is Nemesis' father and the Ethiopians live alongside Okeanos, but that seems like a stretch to me. It's just as likely Pheidias felt like carving Ethiopians, and so he did."

Rhamnous was a sleepy fishing village. The arrival of a merchant galley that looked a lot like a pirate ship created a small sensation. To explain the *Aphrodite*'s presence in those waters, Menedemos displayed some of the most transparent silk he'd got from Pixodaros and said, "We're bringing it up to Khalkis for Polemaios' favorite hetaira. If I told you how much he's paying, you'd never believe me."

"Let him waste his money," somebody said, to which there

was a general mutter of agreement. Sostratos hadn't expected anything else. Polemaios had broken with Kassandros, whose puppet ruled Athens and Attica. Demetrios of Phaleron was a popular leader, too; if he and Polemaios didn't get along, the people of Attica wouldn't have much use for Antigonos' nephew.

"A good story," Sostratos murmured to Menedemos. "No one will go hotfooting it back to Athens to let Demetrios know we're on our way up to Khalkis to see Polemaios."

"No, not for some silk," his cousin agreed, stowing the filmy fabric once more. "I wonder how fancy the hetairai in Khalkis are."

"Of course you do," Sostratos said. Menedemos clapped both hands over his chest and staggered, as if Sostratos had hit him with an arrow as he'd hit the pirate in the hemiolia. Sostratos laughed; he couldn't help himself. "You're impossible."

"Thank you," Menedemos said, which set them both laughing all over again.

Menedemos got the *Aphrodite* out of Rhamnous not long after sunrise; the akatos neared Khalkis not long after noon. A wooden bridge spanned the Euripos, the narrow channel separating Euboia from the mainland of Hellas. The fortress of Kanethos on the mainland protected the bridge, and was reckoned part of the city of Khalkis.

Putting in at Khalkis proved a good deal harder than getting to it had been. A strong current flowed south through the Euripos; the rowers had to pull hard to hold the merchant galley in place, let alone make headway against the rushing water. "You couldn't even get near this place from the south in an ordinary round ship," Menedemos said.

"Be patient, best one," Sostratos told him.

Sure enough, after something less than an hour, the current abruptly reversed itself and began flowing north. It almost carried the *Aphrodite* past Khalkis. Only some smart rowing let her ease her way alongside a pier. "By the dog of Egypt, I'd heard of that, but I wasn't sure I believed it," Menedemos said. He raised his voice to call out to the sailors: "Make sure she's securely moored. We don't want her swept away."

"Now you see it's true," Sostratos said as the men checked the lines and the knots. "The current in the Euripos changes direction six or seven times a day. Sometimes more—sometimes even twice that."

"Why would it do such a mad thing?" his cousin asked.

"I haven't the faintest idea, and I don't think anyone else has, either," Sostratos replied.

"One of your philosopher friends ought to look into it," Menedemos said. "Either it's something natural, in which case he'll figure it out, or it's a god putting his finger in there, in which case a philosopher won't do anybody much good."

"A cause could be natural without being easy to understand," Sostratos said.

His cousin didn't rise to the argument. Instead, Menedemos said, "Get that letter from Ptolemaios and come on. We've got to find Polemaios."

The winding streets of Khalkis were full of soldiers who followed Antigonos' rebellious nephew. They all had swords or spears. Quite a few of them had taken on too much wine. Ordinary Khalkidians mostly stayed indoors. Seeing how quarrelsome the soldiers were, Sostratos couldn't blame the locals. One of the soldiers, though, directed him and Menedemos to a house not far from the market square.

As at Ptolemaios' residence back on Kos, sentries stood guard in front of this one. One of them—an immense man, three or four digits taller even than Sostratos—rumbled, "Yes, he's here. Why should he want to see you people, though?"

"I have a letter for him." Sostratos showed it to the sentry. "He'll have some kind of answer to give us, I expect."

"Give me the letter," the big guard said. "I'll take it to him. You wait here." He held out his hand. That was, plainly, the best offer Sostratos would get. He handed the fellow the letter. The big man went into the house. The remaining guard set a hand on his swordhilt, as if expecting Sostratos and Menedemos to try to leap on him and beat him into submission.

Polemaios, Sostratos reflected, had burned two bridges in rapid succession. Maybe it was no wonder that his men seemed jumpy. Antigonos and Kassandros both wanted their commander dead. How could they be sure a couple of Rhodians weren't a couple of hired murderers? That was simple: they couldn't. And Polemaios himself had to feel more hunted than any of his soldiers.

That thought had hardly crossed his mind before the door opened again. Out came the bodyguard, followed by a man bigger still by a digit or two. "Hail," the newcomer said. "I'm Polemaios. You're the Rhodians, eh?"

"That's right," Sostratos said. He'd heard that Antigonos and his sons, Demetrios and Philippos, were big men; it evidently ran in the family. Demetrios was supposed to be very handsome. Polemaios wasn't. He had a broken nose and what looked to be a permanent worried expression. He was, Sostratos judged, getting close to forty.

"You'd better come in," he said now. "I think we've got some things to talk about." Like Ptolemaios, he spoke an Attic Greek with a faint undercurrent of his half barbarous northern homeland.

He'd been drinking wine in the andron. At his gesture, a slave poured cups for Sostratos and Menedemos, then left the room in a hurry. Polemaios picked up his cup and took a long pull. After pouring a small libation, Sostratos drank, too. The wine was sweet and thick and strong and quite unmixed with water. After a small sip, he set down the cup. He also shot Menedemos a warning glance—Polemaios seemed to live up to, or down to, stories about Macedonian drinking habits.

He didn't seem drunk, though, as he leaned toward the two Rhodians and said, "So Ptolemaios will take me in, will he?"

"That's right, sir," Sostratos said.

Something glinted in Polemaios' eyes. Maybe it was the wine. Maybe it was even fiercer. "He wants to use me," he said in tones that brooked no contradiction. "My uncle thought he'd use me. Kassandros thought *he'd* use me, too." Sostratos judged he was bound to be right about Ptolemaios, even if the word he chose for *use* was the one that described what a man did with a boy.

Menedemos spoke quickly: "Ptolemaios spoke to us of an alliance between the two of you." He sounded more solicitous than usual. Sostratos didn't need long to figure out why—if

Polemaios decided not to go back to Kos on the *Aphrodite*, that threw forty minai of silver into the sea.

"Only goes to show he knows how to tell lies, too," Antigonos' nephew said with a bitter laugh. "But I'll tell *you* something, Rhodians." His intent, solemn stare showed the effects of the neat wine. So did his being rash enough to jab his thumb at his chest and speak his mind to strangers: "I'm all done with being used. I'm no wide-arsed slave boy, not me. From now on, *I* do the using."

Ptolemaios wants this fellow around? Sostratos thought, doing his best to hold his face steady. *Me, I'd sooner pet a shark.*

His cousin still had his eye on the ruler of Egypt's fee. "O best one, *will* you sail with us?" he asked.

"Oh, yes," Polemaios replied. "Oh, yes, indeed. I'm squeezed here. I won't be squeezed . . . over there."

He'd paused there, quite noticeably. *What was he going to say till he changed it?* Sostratos wondered. *"I won't be squeezed, once I hold Egypt?" Something like that, or I miss my guess. And Ptolemaios* asked *him to come to Kos? The man must be raving mad.*

Menedemos' mind was elsewhere: on the practical details of getting Polemaios out of Khalkis and across the Aegean. "Come to our akatos a little before dawn," he told Antigonos' nephew. "We'll have you out past Attica before Demetrios of Phaleron is any the wiser, and you can make whatever arrangements suit you best to have your men follow you to Kos."

"Good enough," Polemaios rumbled. "You're a little chap, but you get things done."

Even with his passage worth a talent of silver, Polemaios was asking for trouble by calling Menedemos a little chap. Before Menedemos could lose his temper—or, at least, before he could show he'd lost it—Sostratos said, "We'll have you out past Attica provided the Euripos cooperates, that is. If the current is flowing north, we'll just have to wait till it turns around."

"A pestilence!" His cousin snapped his fingers in annoyance. "I'd forgotten that." He eyed Polemaios. "I don't suppose you'd like to go north around Euboia?"

Antigonos' nephew tossed his head. "Not likely! I'd be heading straight up toward Kassandros if I did, and I want to get away from him. I'd sooner wait till the Euripos turns around."

"All right," Menedemos said mildly—so mildly, Sostratos shot him a sharp look. Had he been thinking something like, *If Polemaios is worth a talent to Ptolemaios, how much is he worth to Kassandros?* No way to prove it.

Something else occurred to Sostratos. He spoke with as much diplomacy as he had in him: "You do know, sir, we'll be sailing through the Kyklades on our way back to Kos?"

"And through my gods-detested uncle's polluted Island League." Polemaios might have been harsh and crude, but he wasn't stupid. He went on, "Don't you worry about that. I won't travel under my right name." He looked from Sostratos to Menedemos and back again. "And I will bring some bodyguards with me."

"Of course, best one." The two Rhodians spoke together. If they hadn't promptly agreed to that, Sostratos doubted they would have got back to the *Aphrodite* alive.

As things were, Polemaios said, "I'll see you in the morning, early," and called for the slave. At his brusque gesture, the fellow led Sostratos and Menedemos out of the house and all but slammed the door in their faces.

Outside, the big bodyguard barked, "You find out what you needed to know?" Sostratos dipped his head. The guard said, "Why don't you get lost, then?" He set a hand on his swordhilt to let them know it wasn't a suggestion. They left in a hurry.

"What a charming fellow," Menedemos said once they were around a corner and out of earshot.

"Who?" Sostratos asked. "The man himself, or his comrade?" In a polis full of Polemaios' soldiers, he didn't name Antigonos' nephew.

"I had the man himself in mind," Menedemos answered. "But his comrade's just as delightful, isn't he?"

"Every bit." Sostratos walked on for a few paces, then turned to his cousin. "I wonder just how many friends the man himself will bring to the symposion."

He didn't mention bodyguards or the merchant galley, either, but Menedemos had no trouble following him. "What an interesting question," he said brightly. "Not so many that they get in the way of the slaves, I hope."

"So do I," Sostratos said. "This gets more and more complicated, doesn't it?"

His cousin flashed him a smile. "Well, my dear, have you ever heard of anything that didn't?"

MENEDEMOS HAD A knack for waking up whenever he told himself to do so, as if somewhere in the back of his mind there were a klepsydra like the one used to time speeches in the Athenian law courts. It was still dark when his eyes came open the next morning. A glance at the stars and the moon told him dawn wasn't far away, though. He peered into Khalkis. No sign of Polemaios yet.

Sostratos lay on his back on the poop deck, snoring like a stonecutter's saw working its way through a block of marble. Menedemos shook him. The snores rose in pitch but didn't stop. Menedemos gave another shake. His cousin's eyes opened. "What in the name of the—?" Sostratos spluttered.

"Good day," Menedemos said cheerfully. "We're waiting for a friend, remember?"

"Oh. That's right." Sostratos yawned till the hinges of his jaw creaked. "No sign of him yet?"

"You don't see him, do you?" Menedemos said. He paused to gauge the feel of the water under the *Aphrodite*. "I wish he'd get here, too, because the Euripos is going our way right now. If it switches back to the north, we'll be stuck here for hours."

"That's true," Sostratos said around another yawn, this one not quite so enormous. He got to his feet and, as Menedemos had done a moment before, stared into Khalkis. The town was dark and quiet. An owl hooted. A baby wailed. A dog barked—three individual, widely spaced sounds against the background of silence. "Where is he? I hope he hasn't changed his mind."

"He'd better not!" Menedemos exclaimed in horror: the elemental, entirely understandable horror of losing forty minai of silver.

"Cheer up," Sostratos said. "If he does, we can just drop down to Athens and go on about our business."

"You don't care about business. All you care about is that miserable old skull we got in Kaunos. I'm beginning to wish I'd never set eyes on the stinking thing. It won't make up for what Polemaios will cost us if he doesn't come—and nothing else will, either."

Instead of answering, Sostratos pointed into the sleeping polis. "What was that?"

"What was what?" Menedemos had been eyeing the gray starting to seep up into the eastern sky.

"Light, moving. Look—there it is again."

"You're right." Excitement filled Menedemos' voice. "That's torchlight on walls, sure as sure—we just can't see the torches themselves yet." And then, a moment later, as the men carrying them rounded a corner, he could: a dozen, at least. They flickered like bright stars on a cold night, and they were, without a doubt, heading for the *Aphrodite*.

From one of the rowers' benches, Diokles spoke up: "Looks like we're in business, skipper. And the current's flowing our way, too."

Menedemos smiled. "I might have known you'd be awake, too," he told the keleustes. "Let's get the men up and get ready to go."

They were waking sailors when feet thudded on the planks of the quay. "Ahoy, the *Aphrodite*!" Polemaios called. He towered over all the men with him except that one big bodyguard. He had ten soldiers in full hoplite's gear, plus a couple of torchbearers who were probably servants and, Menedemos saw with surprise, one woman, veiled against the prying eyes of men.

After a moment, the surprise evaporated. *He is of an age to have a wife*, Menedemos said to himself. Aloud, he answered, "Hail, best one. You're in good time, and the Euripos is with us."

"Then let's be off," Polemaios said. He spoke to his men in a low voice. They threw their torches into the sea. The torches hissed as they were quenched. Polemaios' followers came down the gangplank and into the *Aphrodite*. Antigonos' nephew followed them. As he stepped down onto the poop deck, he murmured, "Better glory than length of days."

Akhilleus might have said the same thing, camped by the beached ship on the windy plain of Troy. *And Alexander might have said the same thing, too,* Menedemos realized. *Polemaios is old enough to have gone east with him, if just barely.* Even fourteen years dead, Alexander still cast an enormous shadow across the Hellenic world.

"Cast off!" Menedemos called. A couple of his sailors scrambled up onto the pier, undid the lines securing the merchant galley, and came back down again. They stowed the gangplank as they did so. Menedemos glanced up the length of the ship. Polemaios had done a good job of herding his men—and the one woman—well forward, as much out of the rowers' way as possible. Menedemos caught Diokles' eye and dipped his head.

"Back oars!" the oarmaster bellowed, beating out the stroke with mallet and bronze. "Back *hard*, you lazy bastards! It's like getting away from a pier on a river."

It put Menedemos in mind of escaping the quay at Pompaia, on the Sarnos, the summer before. This was even more nerve-wracking, though, for the Euripos flowed harder than the river had—and because the channel between Euboia and the mainland had a couple of rocky islets right in the middle of it. Menedemos kept looking back over his shoulder as he handled the steering oars.

"Ready, boys?" Diokles called. The rowers' heads came up. To them, the world held nothing but their oars and the keleustes' voice. "Are you ready?" Diokles repeated. "Then . . . normal stroke!"

The men went from backing oars to pulling the *Aphrodite* forward as smoothly as if they'd been doing it for years. And, indeed, almost all of them *had* been doing it for years, aboard one ship or another. Menedemos pulled in on one steering oar and pushed out on the other, bringing the akatos' bow around so she aligned with the way the water was racing.

"Very neat," Sostratos said. "A little lucky, to have the Euripos flowing in the direction we needed, but very neat."

"The wind's with us, too," Menedemos said. "In a little

while, I'll have the men lower the sail from the yard. What with oars and wind and current, we'll be practically flying along."

"We still won't get clear of Euboia by nightfall," Sostratos said.

"Well, no," Menedemos admitted, "but we might make it all the way down to Karystos, at the south end of the island. No one could hope to get from there to Khalkis and back by the time we're away the next morning—or from there to Athens and back, either."

"Karystos," his cousin said musingly. "There's a marble quarry nearby, I know that. And there's something else about the place, too. Something . . ." He snapped his fingers in annoyance, unable to come up with it.

"They've got that strange stone there, the stuff that won't burn," Menedemos said. "They weave from it, and when the towels get dirty, they just toss 'em in the fire."

"Asbestos! That's right," Sostratos said. "Thank you. I was going to be worrying at that all day, like a dog with a bone. Now I don't have to. That stuff sells well, and it's not very bulky. We might do some business."

"We might," Menedemos said dubiously. "Nothing to make us late back to Kos, though, especially not in country Kassandros holds."

Sostratos looked forward, to where Polemaios was pointing something on the Euboian coast out to one of his henchmen. In a low voice, Menedemos' cousin said, "If Ptolemaios decides he wants anything to do with that fellow once he gets a good look at him, I'm a trouser-wearing Persian."

Menedemos knew *he* wouldn't have wanted anything to do with Polemaios. Nevertheless, he said, "My dear, that's not your worry, or mine either. Our job is to get him there and get paid for it, and that's what I intend to do."

Menedemos kept a wary eye on the coast himself as the *Aphrodite* made her way south, especially when the merchant galley neared one of the many headlands or little offshore islands. Lots of those little islands speckled the channel between Euboia and the mainland. Sheep or cattle grazed on some of them; others seemed just as the gods had made them.

A piratical pentekonter or hemiolia might have used any one of them for concealment before rushing out against a merchantman.

You're getting as nervous as that Athenian Sostratos was talking about, Menedemos thought. He wouldn't have fretted so much without such a valuable passenger aboard. Polemaios' bodyguards made the *Aphrodite* better able to fight off marauders than she would have been otherwise, but Menedemos didn't want to have to put that to the test.

As he had when Kissidas brought his kinsfolk aboard at Kaunos, he kept trying to get as many glimpses as he could of Polemaios' wife. He had little luck there; she stayed up on the foredeck, and the crowd of armored bodyguards did a good job of shielding her from his gaze. Even if he had got a clear look, it wouldn't have told him much, not when, like any respectable woman who had to leave her house, she kept on the veil that shielded her from the gaze of lustful men. He knew as much, but kept peering her way anyhow.

Presently, Polemaios came aft and ascended to the poop deck. Antigonos' nephew towered over Menedemos; he was one of the biggest men the Rhodian had ever seen. He wasn't lean and gawky like Sostratos, either, but massively built, broad in the shoulders and thick through the chest. He made a host in himself.

He was so massively made, in fact, that Menedemos lifted a hand from a steering-oar tiller, made a brushing motion with it, and said, "Excuse me, best one, but please step to one side or the other. I do need to be able to see straight ahead."

"Oh. Right." Polemaios didn't apologize. Menedemos would have been surprised if he'd ever apologized to anyone. But he did move, and had the sense to move to starboard rather than to port. If trouble suddenly boiled up, it was much more likely to come from Euboia, on Menedemos' left hand, than from the Attic mainland to his right. After a couple of minutes of silence, Antigonos' nephew asked, "How big a fleet did Ptolemaios bring to Kos?"

"Close to sixty ships," Menedemos answered.

For the first time in their brief acquaintance, Polemaios smiled. Even smiling, he remained formidable. "Plenty to give my dear uncle a kick in the balls," he said. "Not half what he deserves, either."

You say that now, Menedemos thought. *A couple of years ago, you were your dear uncle's right-hand man. I think he's not your dear uncle any more because he's got new right-hand men in his two sons*. He said none of that. Polemaios was not the sort of man who invited such opinions.

"Do you know who any of Ptolemaios' ship-captains are?" Antigonos' nephew asked.

Menedemos tossed his head. "Sorry, sir. I'm just a trader."

"You're not *just* a trader, or Ptolemaios wouldn't have sent you after me." Polemaios' gaze was as hard and bright and predatory as an eagle's. "Did you meet any of his commanders of marines?"

"Only one, and then only in a manner of speaking," Menedemos answered. "He was the fellow whose five stopped us on the way into the harbor at Kos. He asked the sort of questions you'd expect an officer to ask strangers."

"Ah." Polemaios leaned forward with a now-we're-getting-somewhere expression on his face. "What was his name? Did you bribe him to let you go on? How much silver did it take to get him to look the other way?"

"I never found out what his name was," Menedemos said in some exasperation. "And he never came aboard, so I couldn't very well bribe him."

Antigonos' nephew looked as if he believed not a word of that. "How did you get him to let you pass, then? Ptolemaios' officers are paid to be suspicious, just like any others. They wouldn't be much use to him if they weren't."

"How, O marvelous one?" Menedemos' patience began to slip. He didn't like being grilled like this aboard his own ship, especially when he saw no point to Polemaios' questions. "I showed him a tiger hide, that's how. After that, he let me alone and didn't bother me any more."

Polemaios didn't take the hint. He did shift the aim of his questions: "Where did you get a tiger hide? Have you ever been to India? You couldn't have gone with Alexander—you're not old enough."

Men who'd gone conquering with the great king of Macedonia were going to throw that in the younger generation's face as long as they lived. Menedemos had already heard it more often than he would have liked. He answered, "No, I haven't been to India. This hide came west. I bought it in the market square at Kaunos."

"Oh." Polemaios didn't bother hiding his disappointment. He turned away and went forward again. With a silent sigh of relief, Menedemos gave all his attention back to guiding the *Aphrodite* down the channel between Euboia and the mainland. Fishing boats fled back to Eiretria, the other prominent polis on the island, when they spotted the akatos and the armed and armored men aboard her. To Menedemos' relief, no war galleys came striding over the sea to investigate. *They must figure we're just another pirate, and not worth bothering about.* The thought saddened and angered him at the same time.

Dystos, south of Eiretria, lay inland, on the shore of a small, marshy lake. Its walls, shaped like some sort of polygon—*Sostratos would know its name: he's the one who cares for such things*, Menedemos thought—had ten or twelve towers to help hold foes at bay. They might not have done their job any too well; though the walls hadn't been breached, Dystos seemed half—more than half— abandoned.

Presently, Sostratos came back to the poop deck. Menedemos greeted him with a smile. "By the dog of Egypt, I'm glad of your company," he said.

"Are you?" His cousin raised an eyebrow. He set a hand on Menedemos' forehead, as if checking to see if he had a fever. "Do you feel well?"

Laughing, Menedemos said, "Better, anyhow." He lowered his voice: "You and Polemaios both ask lots of questions, but you're friendly about it, and he's fierce."

"What sort of questions was he giving you?" Sostratos said, also softly. "I *did* mean to ask you about that, as a matter of fact." Menedemos explained. When he finished, Sostratos let out an unmusical whistle. "Isn't that interesting? Do you know what he's doing?"

"Being nosy to not much purpose," Menedemos answered.

"Being nosy, yes, but I think he has a purpose." Sostratos

glanced forward to make sure Antigonos' nephew wasn't paying undue attention. "It sounds as though he's trying to find out whether Ptolemaios has any officers who can be corrupted."

Menedemos' whistle was even more discordant than Sostratos'. "I think you've fit that together like a mortise joining a couple of ship's timbers. That's *just* what he was doing, Furies take me if it's not." He whistled again. "He's a piece of work, that one."

" 'Many are the marvels—' " Sostratos began.

" '—and none is more marvelous than man.' " Menedemos finished the quotation from Sophokles for him. He dipped his head in agreement, too. "All the same, though, I've never seen anyone more eager to bite the hand that feeds him. You were clever to figure him out so fast." He sent Sostratos a curious glance. His cousin wasn't usually so sharp a judge of people.

"He's like someone from Thoukydides come to life," Sostratos said now: "a man who's practically nothing but plots and ambitions. An ordinary chap is much harder to make out, at least for me."

That's because you're not an ordinary chap yourself, Menedemos thought. More often than not, he would have twitted Sostratos about it. Now, when Sostratos had solved a puzzle that baffled him, he kept quiet. His cousin had earned a respite . . . for a little while.

AS THE *APHRODITE* MADE HER WAY south and east through the Kyklades toward Kos, Polemaios took to calling himself Alkimos of Epeiros. "He's a mercenary captain in my uncle's pay," he explained to Sostratos and Menedemos, "and a big, big man himself." He let more of his Macedonian accent come out; to an ordinary Hellene, it might well do for the speech of a man from another, equally barbarous, place.

He is shrewd, Sostratos thought reluctantly. Odds were, that ran in the family like height. Antigonos was outstandingly clever, and his sons, Demetrios and Philippos, also seemed able. And Polemaios had been one of Antigonos' leading officers till he chose to turn against his uncle. No one had ever said old One-Eye suffered fools gladly.

Whether a fool or not, though, Polemaios alarmed Sostratos. Ambition blazed from the man as light blazed from a bonfire. Would he be able to conceal it when he got to Kos? If he couldn't, how long would Ptolemaios take to notice it? The ruler of Egypt struck Sostratos as a very canny fellow.

Of course, Polemaios' soldiers would be following him to Kos. How many men did he have? Sostratos didn't know. How many did Ptolemaios have on the island? Sostratos didn't know that, either, though he could make a guess from the size of Ptolemaios' fleet. Would all of them stay loyal, or could Polemaios seduce them away from his near-namesake? An interesting question, sure enough.

To keep from drawing undue attention to the return, Menedemos chose a route different from the one he'd used going up to Khalkis. No one would be able to note how many days lay between his westbound and eastbound visits to a port and, as a result, make guesses about where he'd been. From Karystos, on the southern coast of Euboia, he took the *Aphrodite* due south across the rough strait and, aided by a brisk northerly breeze, made the island of Kythnos by nightfall.

Fig orchards and vines straggled across the sandy hills of Kythnos. Looking north and west, Sostratos could see Cape Sounion, the great rocky headland that marked Attica. He sighed. *I should be showing the gryphon's skull to Theophrastos*, he thought, *but instead I'm sailing away again. Where is the justice?*

Polemaios and his wife and bodyguards slept aboard the merchant galley. Antigonos' nephew took it in stride; he'd doubtless found worse places to lay his head on campaign. But, from Sostratos' place on the poop deck, he could hear the woman's shrill complaints at the other end of the shi

Polemaios sounded much less imperious with her than he did speaking to mere Rhodians.

With a soft chuckle—very soft, to make sure Polemaios didn't hear—Sostratos murmured to Menedemos: "Every hero has his weakness."

His cousin's snort of laughter seemed much too loud to him. "Agamemnon lord of men had his vanity, Akhilleus his anger—and his heel," Menedemos agreed. "Great Aias went mad." He reached out and tapped Sostratos on the shoulder. "But what of resourceful Odysseus? He was always right, or as near as makes no difference, and he came home safe where most of the others died."

"And he paid the price for always being right, too," Sostratos said after a little thought of his own. "He's a hero in the *Iliad* and the *Odyssey*, but the playwrights make him out to be a villain, too clever for his own good. Nobody likes a man who's right all the time."

"You would know, wouldn't you?" Menedemos said.

Sostratos grunted. That arrow hit too close to the center of the target for comfort. He *had* learned most people didn't take kindly to being corrected, even when they were wrong—often especially when they were wrong. He didn't do such things nearly so often as he had when he was younger. *And if I hadn't done them so often then, I might be happier now.*

He shifted on the planks of the poop deck, trying not only to get comfortable but also to escape his own thoughts. Like the Furies, they pursued him whether he wanted them to or not. But he could escape them, unlike the Kindly Ones, by falling headlong into sleep, and he did.

When he woke, it was to the sound of Menedemos cursing as if those Kindly Ones were hot on *his* trail. Yawning, Sostratos asked, "What's wrong?"

"Call yourself a seaman?" Menedemos snarled, which was most unfair: Sostratos was suddenly roused from sleep, and still flat on the deck besides. Upright and irate, Menedemos went on, "There's no polluted wind, that's what. None."

"Oh." Sostratos uncocooned himself from his himation and [illegible] his feet, too. He wasn't naked, as he would have been [illegible]ornings aboard ship; out of deference to Polemaios' wife, he'd left his chiton on. Menedemos was right: not a breath of breeze stirred his hair. "*Oimoi!* This isn't good. We'll have a hard time making Paros by sundown on oars alone."

"Isn't that the sad and sorry truth?" his cousin agreed. "And even if we do, the men will be worn to nubs and in a dreadful temper. To the crows with me if I blame 'em, either. Rowing all day is a hard way to make a drakhma and a half."

"I know." Sostratos set a consoling hand on Menedemos' shoulder. "Well, my dear, we got this job because we *can* go against the wind, or even without it. We could give the rowers a couple of days to roister in Kos once we get there."

"Not a bad notion." Menedemos dipped his head, then smiled a wicked smile. "There you go, being right again."

"I'm sorry. I'll try not to let it happen again," Sostratos said, and thought he came out of the exchange fairly well.

Menedemos had the pleasure of waking Diokles, who wasn't up quite so fast as usual. The oarmaster noted the calm as fast as the captain had. "The men'll have their work cut out for 'em today if things don't pick up," he said, and set about shaking sailors out of sleep. "We can't afford to waste time, then."

Polemaios and his bodyguards also roused. So did Polemaios' wife, who was no more happy about waking up aboard ship than she had been about the sleeping arrangements the *Aphrodite* offered. Barley rolls and raisins and olives for breakfast didn't seem to be to her taste, either, and she had some sharp things to say about the wine the akatos carried.

"It'll be hot work," Sostratos said. The sun was just climbing over the horizon, but, with the air so still, he could feel the furnace of noontime in his mind hours before it turned real. "Have we got enough water and wine to get us to Paros? We're carrying all those extra passengers."

"For one day, we'll be all right," Menedemos answered. Sostratos dipped his head; that was likely true. His cousin went on, "Besides, if I water the ship here, we lose that much traveling time, and we haven't got much to spare today."

Diokles put eight men at the oars on each side of the *Aphrodite*. At his orders, the oarblades bit into the sea. The galley glided out of Kythnos harbor, past the southern tip of the island, and then south and east toward Paros.

Navigating in the Kyklades was easy enough. A sailor rarely found himself out of sight of land. There was Seriphos, due south of Kythnos, and there due east lay Syros. A tiny islet between them gave a good course for Paros, and in the distance Sostratos could see clouds hovering about Mount Marpessos, Paros' central peak. Before long, the mountain itself came into view.

The sea seemed smooth as a polished piece of Parian marble. The oars rose and fell, rose and fell. Diokles gave the rowers shifts of about two hours, keeping them as fresh as he could. Polemaios' wife amused herself by complaining. His bodyguards prowled the ship like so many feral dogs on the prowl for something they could eat.

They were going to steal this and that. Sostratos knew as much. He couldn't keep his eye on all of them all the time. They couldn't steal too much, if only because they had nothing but their already-full sacks of personal goods in which to conceal their loot.

Not all of them seemed to realize that. One—the big fellow who'd been standing outside Polemaios' front door—bent down under an unoccupied rower's bench and came up holding the big leather sack that contained the gryphon's skull. Sostratos jerked as if stuck by a pin. "Put that down!" he yelped.

"Who's going to make me?" the guard demanded. His free hand went to the hilt of his sword. He hadn't doffed his armor aboard ship. Under the brim of his bronze helmet, his face twisted into a nasty grin. Sostratos wore only a wool tunic, and had nothing but a knife on his belt. He bit his lip in humiliation.

From the stern, Menedemos called, "Well, best one, if you want what you've got so much, why don't you see what it is?"

"I will." The Macedonian undid the lashing that held the sack closed. The gryphon's skull stared out at him from empty eye sockets. Now he was the one who yelped, in surprise and superstitious fear.

"Don't you dare drop that," Sostratos warned. This time, he managed to put a snap rather than a whine in his voice. "Put it back where you got it." Perhaps too startled not to, the bodyguard obeyed. He didn't close the sack, but that could wait.

Once the gryphon's skull was stowed under the bench once more, the fellow managed a question of his own: "What do you want with that horrible, ugly thing?"

Sostratos smiled his most sinister smile. "Before we got the commission to bring your master back to Kos, I was going to take it up to Thessalia, to sell it to one of the witches there." Northeastern Hellas was notorious for its witches. Sostratos didn't believe in witchcraft—not with the top part of his mind, anyhow—but to protect the precious gryphon's skull he grabbed any weapon that came to hand.

And this one worked. The big, fierce Macedonian went pale as milk. His fingers writhed in an apotropaic gesture. He said something in Macedonian that Sostratos couldn't understand. Once he got it out of his system, he switched to a dialect of Greek that made more sense: "I hope the witches turn you into a spider, you wide-arsed son of a whore."

Grinning, Sostratos said, "I love you, too, my dear." Behind the grin was a fright he wouldn't show. If the bodyguard got angry enough, or frightened enough, he would draw that sword, and Sostratos couldn't do much to fight back.

But the big man only shuddered and made another warding gesture before turning and stomping back up toward the foredeck. A couple of minutes later, Polemaios strode toward the stern. "Thessalian witchcraft?" he said.

How superstitious was he? Sostratos couldn't tell by the tone of the question. He just said, "That's right," and waited to see what happened next.

Polemaios grunted, ascended to the poop deck, and pissed into the sea. Then he too returned to his station on the foredeck. He and his bodyguard got into a shouting match. To Sostratos' frustration, it was in Macedonian. The bodyguard wasn't shy about saying whatever was on his mind, waving his hands in Polemaios' face and bunching them into fists. Polemaios showed no more restraint.

"A charming people, the Macedonians," Sostratos remarked in a low voice as he went up to stand near his cousin.

"Aren't they, though?" Menedemos rolled his eyes.

"And they rule almost the entire civilized world," Sostratos said mournfully. He drew himself up with more than a little pride. "But not Rhodes."

"Gods be praised!" Menedemos exclaimed, and Sostratos dipped his head.

"*OÖP!*" DIOKLES CALLED, and the *Aphrodite*'s weary rowers rested at their oars. Behind them, the setting sun streaked the Aegean with blood and fire. A couple of harbor men took the lines sailors tossed them and made the akatos fast to a quay in the polis of Paros. Up at the top of Mount Marpessos, the sunlight remained a good deal brighter than it was down here on the sea.

Menedemos clapped his hands together. "*Euge!*" he called to the merchant galley's crew. "Very well done! It's a long haul from Kythnos to here."

"Don't we know it!" somebody—Teleutas—said. Menedemos would have bet he'd be the one to speak up and carp, but he'd done as much as anybody else at the oars, and so he'd earned the right.

"Amorgos tomorrow," Menedemos said. "Then Kos, and a layover. You boys will have earned it."

"I'll say we will." Again, Teleutas took it on himself to speak for the rest of the sailors, and to make agreement sound halfway like a threat.

"We won't make Kos in one day from Amorgos, not unless we get a gale out of the west," Diokles remarked. "Not likely, although . . ." The oarmaster tasted the air, wetly smacking his lips a couple of times. "We'll have wind, I think. Tomorrow won't be a dead-calm day like this one."

"I think you're right," Menedemos said. The faintest ghost of a breeze brushed against his cheek, softer than a hetaira's hand. He looked north. A few clouds drifted across the sky; they didn't hang in place, as they had all through this long, hot day. "Be good to let the sail down."

"That'll be fine, sure enough," Diokles agreed. "Still and

all, though, even Amorgos'll be a push, because we will have to spend some time filling our water jars before we sail tomorrow. Can't let ourselves go dry."

"I know, I know." Menedemos consoled himself as best he could: "Paros has good water, not the brackish stuff we'd have got on Kythnos."

He stayed aboard the *Aphrodite* again that night. He didn't want to; he wanted to go into one of the harborside taverns, drink himself dizzy, and sleep with a serving girl or find a brothel. He hadn't had a girl since putting in at Kos. For a man in his mid-twenties, going without for several days felt like a hardship.

But somebody would ask, *Say, who's that big son of a whore with those soldiers?* Answering *Alkimos of Epeiros* might serve. On the other hand, it might not, and he might talk too much if he got drunk. He knew himself well enough to understand that. And so he wrapped himself in his himation on the poop deck, stared up at the stars for a little while, and fell asleep.

When he woke up, only the faintest hint of gray touched the jagged eastern horizon. He felt like cheering, for a brisk northerly breeze ruffled his hair. With sail and oars together, they had a much better chance of making Amorgos by nightfall. Then he took a deep breath, and frowned a little. The air felt damp, as if it was the harbinger of rain. He shrugged. It was late in the season for a downpour, but not impossibly so.

As soon as it got light enough for colors to start returning to the black and silver world of night, he started shaking sailors and sending them into Paros with the *Aphrodite*'s water jars. "How will we find a fountain?" Teleutas whined.

"Ask somebody," Menedemos said unsympathetically. "Here." He gave the grumbling sailor an obolos. "Now you can give something for an answer, and it's not even coming out of your own pay."

Teleutas, no doubt, liked lugging a hydria no more than anybody else. But Menedemos had quashed his objections before he could make them. He popped the obolos into his mouth and went off with his comrades. Menedemos imagined the surprise at a fountain when the sailors descended on women filling their water jars for the day's cooking and washing. Then he tossed his head. As at Naxos, a lot of ships put in at Paros. The local women would be used to such visits.

Sostratos pointed north. "I wonder if we'll get some rain," he said. "Some of those clouds look thicker and grayer than the usual run."

"I was thinking the same thing," Menedemos answered. "It would be a nuisance. Trying to figure out a course when we can't see more than a couple of stadia isn't easy. It'd slow us down, too, if the sail got soaked."

"The men might not mind, not after rowing all day in the hot sun," his cousin said. "Cool weather's more comfortable."

"At first, maybe," Menedemos said. "But it's easy to take a chill when you come off your stint at the oars, and to cramp up, too. Rain's no fun when you haven't any way to keep it off your head."

They left Paros almost as early as he'd hoped they would. As soon as they were out of the harbor, he ordered the sail lowered from the yard. The freshening breeze thrummed in the rigging. The mast creaked in its socket as that breeze filled the sail and pulled on it. The merchant galley ran before the wind till she slid through the channel between Paros and Oliaros, the smaller island to the southwest.

"I've heard there's a cave full of spikes of rock sticking up from the floor and down from the ceiling on Oliaros," Sostratos said. "That's the sort of thing I'd like to see."

"Why?" Menedemos asked. At his orders, the sailors swung the yard so that it stretched back from the port bow to take best advantage of the wind.

"Why?" Sostratos echoed. "It might be pretty. It would certainly be interesting. And they say some men Alexander the Great was after hid out there for a while."

"Do they?" Menedemos lifted his right hand off the steering-oar tiller to wag a forefinger at his cousin. "You're always going on about how 'they say' all sorts of things, and most of the time what 'they say' turns out to be nothing but a pack of nonsense. So why do you believe 'them' now?"

"There's supposed to be some writing inside the cave," Sostratos answered, "but I guess you're right—that doesn't have to mean anything. People could have written it in the years since Alexander died."

"Why would they?" Menedemos asked. "To draw visitors to these caves? If you ask me, anybody who wanted to go crawling through them would have to be daft." He gave Sostratos a meaningful look.

Having been on the receiving end of a lot of those looks, Sostratos ignored this one. "Maybe," he said, "though you'd need more than scratchings on a stalactite to get anyone to come to Oliaros. You'd need divinities born there, the way Delos has Apollo and Artemis."

Menedemos, who was much more conventionally religious than his cousin, bit down on that like a man unexpectedly biting down on an olive pit. By the way Sostratos said it, the god and goddess might not actually have been born on Delos, but the Delians might have claimed they were for no better reason than to draw people to the island and separate them from their silver. Menedemos didn't ask if he did mean that, for fear he would say yes. He did ask, "What other reason would somebody have for writing something that wasn't true?"

"Perhaps just for the sake of fame," Sostratos replied. "You know, like that madman who burned down the temple back before the Peloponnesian War. He did it just so he'd be remembered forever. Herodotos found out what his name was—and then didn't put it in his history."

"*Euge!*" Menedemos exclaimed. The more he thought about it, the more elegant he reckoned that revenge.

Several small islands lay south of Naxos, on the way to Amorgos. They were like Telos, over by Rhodes: they had villages, not poleis, and a few people scratched out a living in their hinterland. They drew steadily nearer as the *Aphrodite* glided east. So did the clouds the rising breeze brought down from the north.

Those clouds covered the sun. The day went from bright to gloomy. Before long, rain started pattering down, light at first but then increasing. A little rain made a sail perform better, holding more of the wind than the weave of the linen could by itself. More than a little, and the sail got heavy and saggy.

Menedemos could only try to wring as much advantage from what was going on as he could.

He'd known visibility would shrink in case of rain. The islands ahead disappeared in the veils of masking water falling from the sky. So did Ios, to the south of them, and so did Naxos itself. Menedemos sent sharp-eyed Aristeidas up onto the foredeck to look out for unexpected trouble. *In a while, I'll send a leadsman up there with him to take soundings, too,* he thought.

He hadn't got round to giving the order for that before he found himself in unexpected trouble of his own. Polemaios made his ponderous way back to the poop deck and stomped up to Menedemos. "How dare you place a man up there to spy on my wife?" he demanded.

"What?" For a moment, Menedemos had no idea what the Macedonian was talking about. Then he did, and wished he hadn't. "Best one, I sent Aristeidas up there to look for rocks and islands, not for women. Visibility's gone to the crows, what with this rain. I want to see something before I run into it, thank you very much."

"You should have spoken of this to me," Polemaios said, looking down his long, bent nose at Menedemos. "One of my guards could do the job perfectly well."

Menedemos tossed his head. "No. For one thing, Aristeidas has some of the sharpest eyes I've ever found in anyone. For another, he's a sailor. He knows what he's supposed to see on the water and what he's not. Your bodyguards are hoplites. They'd do fine on land, but not here. This isn't their place."

A slow flush rose from Polemaios' neck all the way to his hairline. Menedemos wondered how long it had been since anyone told him no. Antigonos' nephew set a hand on the hilt of his sword. "Little man, you'll do as I say," he growled. "Either that, or you'll feed the fish."

Before Menedemos could lose his temper, Sostratos spoke in calm, reasonable tones: "Consider, best one. By rejecting the best lookout in dirty weather, you endanger the ship, your wife, and yourself. Is that a choice a man who loves wisdom would make?"

Polemaios turned red all over again. He said, "I'm going to

tell that sharp-eyed son of a whore to keep his eyes on the sea and not on other men's wives," and stormed back toward the foredeck.

"Thank you," Menedemos said quietly.

"You're welcome," his cousin replied. "If Polemaios endangers the ship, he endangers me, too, you know." His shoulders shook; Menedemos realized he was fighting not to laugh out loud. "And if he's going to tell somebody not to look at another man's wife, he could do worse than to start with you."

Menedemos glowered at him in mock—well, mostly mock—rage. "Furies take you, I knew you were going to say that."

"Will you tell me I'm wrong?"

"I'll do worse than that. I'll tell you you're boring," Menedemos said. But Sostratos hadn't been wrong, and he knew it. He couldn't help looking at Polemaios' wife, not when he faced forward from the steering oars all day. And she hadn't thought to bring along a pot; she had to hang her bare backside over the rail when she needed to relieve herself, the same as any sailor. Menedemos hadn't stared. That would have been rude, and might well have brought Polemaios' wrath down on his head. Polemaios was the worst sort of jealous husband: the large, violent, dangerous sort. Menedemos had no trouble seeing as much. But he hadn't looked away. You never could tell.

Sostratos did know him pretty well, for he said, "Do you recognize the notion of *more trouble than it's worth?*"

"Occasionally," Menedemos said. "When I feel like it." He grinned. Sostratos spluttered. That made his grin wider.

They scudded on, under sail and oars together. The wind whipped up the surface of the sea. The *Aphrodite* rolled as wave after wave slapped the planks of her port side. Menedemos adjusted to the motion as automatically as he breathed, and with as little notice on his part. So did most of the merchant galley's crew. Sostratos looked a trifle pale under his seaman's tan, but even he shifted his weight as the ship shifted beneath him.

Polemaios' wife hung over the rail again, giving back whatever she'd eaten. Menedemos noticed that, too, but it didn't stir him—not even to much sympathy, for she'd shown herself a bad-tempered woman. Polemaios had the sense to get out of his corselet before leaning out beside her. Menedemos wouldn't have minded seeing him go straight into the sea, except that that would have meant forty minai going in with him.

Then Aristeidas sang out, "Land! Land dead ahead!"

Menedemos couldn't see it. The rain chose that moment to start coming down harder. But, as he'd told Polemaios, he had Aristeidas up on the foredeck precisely because the sailor's sight was keen. "Back oars!" he shouted to the rowers. "Brail up the sail!" he called to other sailors, who hauled on the lines with all their strength, bringing the great square sail up to the yard and spilling wind out of it. "Leadsman forward!" Menedemos added, kicking himself because he'd thought of doing that and then forgotten about it. He pulled one steering oar in and pushed the other out, swinging the *Aphrodite*'s bow away from the danger Aristeidas had seen.

As the ship came around, he did spy the little island—or maybe it was nothing more than a big rock: perhaps a plethron's worth of jaggedness jutting up above the waves. It would have been plenty to do in the merchant galley. No fresh water on it, of course, and nowhere to beach . . .

"Twelve cubits!" the leadsman called out, bringing up his line and tossing it into the sea again with a splash. He hauled it in again. "Ten cubits and a half!"

"Regular stroke!" Diokles bawled as soon as the akatos' bow pointed away from the islet. "Pull hard, you bastards! Rhyppa*pai*! Rhyppa*pai*!"

"Nine and a half cubits!" the leadsman yelled.

"Full crew to the oars," Menedemos ordered. The sailors scrambled to obey. More oars jutted from each side of the ship with every stroke, till all forty were manned. No one fouled anybody else. They'd been beaten in well enough to perform in smooth unison even in an emergency. A trierarch aboard a Rhodian war galley might have found something about which to complain. Menedemos couldn't.

"Eleven cubits!" the leadsman called, and then, "Fourteen cubits!"

"We're going to get away," Diokles said as the danger receded.

"Yes, it looks that way," Menedemos agreed. "By the dog of Egypt, though, I'm glad I'm in an akatos and not a wallowing round ship. I wouldn't want to try to claw away from there without oars."

"No, indeed, skipper." The keleustes' scowl mirrored Menedemos'. "That wouldn't be any fun at all. A round ship might have been able to swing away to southward if somebody spotted that polluted thing soon enough. Might, I say."

"I know." Menedemos dipped his head. But the other side of *might* was *might not*, as sure as the other side of the image of Apollo on a Rhodian drakhma was a rose.

Polemaios and the other passengers stayed up near the bow. Menedemos had hoped Antigonos' nephew might come back to the stern and apologize for complaining about Aristeidas' placement. The big Macedonian did no such thing. *Well, to the crows with him, then*, Menedemos thought as he brought the merchant galley back toward the west. *I know what an ass he made of himself, whether he does or not.*

TWO DAYS AFTER almost going aground in the Kyklades, the *Aphrodite* came back to Kos. Sostratos watched Polemaios staring north and east across the narrow channel that separated the island from Halikarnassos on the mainland of Anatolia. Had Antigonos' war galleys in Halikarnassos known who was aboard the *Aphrodite*, they surely would have swarmed out to try to seize the smaller ship. But, except for those on patrol in front of the city, they stayed quiet.

As Polemaios looked toward his uncle's stronghold, his great hands folded into fists. He growled something in Macedonian. Sostratos couldn't understand it, but didn't think it any sort of praise for Antigonos or his sons.

A couple of stadia outside the polis of Kos, a five flying banners with Ptolemaios' eagle on them came striding across the sea to challenge the *Aphrodite*. "What ship?" shouted an officer on the war galley's deck, cupping his hands in front of his mouth to make his voice carry farther.

"We're the *Aphrodite*, back from Khalkis on Euboia," Sostratos yelled in return, hoping Ptolemaios' men had been told to expect the akatos.

"And I," Polemaios cried in a great voice, "am Polemaios son of Polemaios, come to join in equal alliance against my polluted, accursed, gods-detested uncle with Ptolemaios son of Lagos."

Back on Khalkis, Polemaios had remembered he wouldn't be an equal partner in an alliance. Here, he traveled in a small merchant galley with a double handful of bodyguards along for protection. Ptolemaios had his whole great fleet and the army that went with it in and around Kos. The war galley approaching the *Aphrodite* could have smashed her to kindling with its great three-finned ram. The archers and catapult aboard the five could have plied the akatos with darts till she looked like a hedgehog. The marines from Ptolemaios' ship could have boarded and slaughtered every man on the merchant galley. All that being so, Sostratos doubted whether, in Polemaios' place, he would have dared claim equality with the ruler of Egypt.

But, for the time being, Antigonos' renegade nephew got away with it. "Welcome, welcome, thrice welcome, O best and most brilliant of men!" Ptolemaios' officer exclaimed, as if he were greeting Alexander the Great or a veritable demigod like Herakles. The fellow went on, "We had not looked for you for another few days." He waved to Sostratos, who'd spoken up first. "Congratulations on your fine sailing."

Sostratos, in turned, waved back to Menedemos at the steering oars. "My cousin's the captain. I'm just toikharkhos."

"*Euge!*" Ptolemaios' man called to Menedemos, who lifted a hand to acknowledge the praise. "Pass on into the harbor. Ptolemaios will be very pleased you've brought his ally to Kos." He said nothing about Polemaios' being an equal ally. Sostratos noticed that. He wondered whether Polemaios did.

The officer strode across the war galley's deck toward the stern. He spoke to another man, one who wore a crimson-dyed cloak fastened around his neck: the captain of the five, Sostratos judged. That worthy called out an order; Sostratos could hear his voice, but couldn't make out the words. Figuring out what it was didn't take long, though. The five's oarmaster began beating out the stroke. The warship's big oars bit into the sea. Two of its the banks had two men on each oar; only the thalamite rowers on the lowest level pulled alone. With so much muscle power propelling her, the five quickly built up speed and slid away from the *Aphrodite*.

"You boys heard him," Menedemos called to his own crew. "Let's take her on in to port. Keleustes, give us a lively stroke."

"Right you are, skipper," Diokles replied.

As it had been before, Kos harbor was packed as tight with ships as an amphora might be with olives. Masts reared skyward like a leafless forest. "There!" Sostratos exclaimed, pointing as he spotted an opening. Menedemos steered the akatos towards it. Sailors on ships already tied up to that quay shouted warnings and stood by with poles and sweeps, ready to fend her off. But Menedemos made her fit without scraping against the vessel to either side.

"Thanks for spying the space," he told Sostratos.

"You're the one who got us into it," Sostratos replied.

His cousin grinned. "Oh, I can always find a way to get it in." Sostratos made a face at him. Menedemos laughed.

An officer came hurrying up the pier toward the *Aphrodite*: the same one, Sostratos saw, who'd interrogated them on their previous arrival. The officer recognized them, too, saying, "You're back. And have you got Antigonos' nephew with you?"

"Zeus of the aegis!" Polemaios boomed. "Who d'you think I am, little man? Go tell your master I'm here."

"Yes, go tell him, by the gods," Menedemos echoed. Looking Sostratos' way, he spoke in a lower voice: "Tell him he owes us forty minai."

"Here's hoping he doesn't need reminding," Sostratos said.

"That's right. Here's hoping." Menedemos sounded worried. His next words explained why: "What can we do if he stiffs us now that we've delivered the goods?"

"To Ptolemaios himself? Nothing at all. We can't even go to law against him. As far as Egypt's concerned, he *is* the law." Sostratos had been thinking about that all the way back from Khalkis. "But we *can* make his name a stench in the nostrils of every Rhodian merchant we know, and everybody our fathers know. I don't think he'd like that. He needs Rhodes friendly."

Menedemos considered, then dipped his head. "Blackening a man's name isn't the worst weapon."

"No, it isn't," Sostratos agreed. "We go round and round about what Aristophanes did to Sokrates in the *Clouds*—and Sokrates didn't even deserve it."

"That's what we go round and round about: whether he deserved it or not, I mean." Menedemos held up a hand. "I don't want to start doing it now, thank you very much."

Since Sostratos didn't feel like taking up the argument just then, either, he turned away from his cousin. Ptolemaios' officer still stood on the pier, but a fellow in a plain chiton was hurrying back onto solid ground and into the city. Ptolemaios himself would soon know the *Aphrodite* had returned.

"We'll get paid," Sostratos murmured. "I really think we will. And then we can head back towards Athens and see what the philosophers there think of the gryphon's skull. We'll see what we get for it, too," he added hastily, forestalling Menedemos.

"So we will," Menedemos said. "And I'll be able to do some . . . other business in Athens, too." His eyes flicked toward the officer. Only the slight pause showed he meant the smuggled emeralds, and only someone who already knew he had them would understand what it showed.

Polemaios' wife started complaining when she and her man weren't immediately taken off the akatos and brought before Ptolemaios—or maybe she was complaining because Ptolemaios didn't come hotfooting down to the harbor to meet them. Antigonos' nephew did what he could to calm her down. Thinking, *I doubt he's had much practice playing peacemaker*, Sostratos hid a smile.

After half an hour, or perhaps a bit more, the officer's man returned in the company of a couple of dozen armed and armored hoplites. Sostratos and Menedemos exchanged a glance that said, *Ptolemaios isn't going to take any chances with his new ally*. The force—which looked like a guard of honor—was plenty to take care of Polemaios' bodyguards in case they proved troublesome. Now, Sostratos judged, they probably wouldn't.

The messenger said, "Ptolemaios is pleased to welcome another foe of the vicious tyrant, Antigonos, to Kos, and summons Polemaios son of Polemaios and his party to his residence. As a seeming afterthought, the fellow added, "Ptolemaios also summons the two Rhodians who brought Polemaios here so very promptly."

Oh, good, Sostratos thought. *He* is *going to pay us*. But that wasn't the only reason he was beaming. He would have paid a good deal to watch the meeting between the two Macedonians with similar names. Bribery, though, wouldn't have let him do it. Ptolemaios' generosity did. He and Menedemos went up the gangplank and onto the quay as Polemaios and his companions came back from the bow.

Once everyone had left the ship, Antigonos' nephew took the lead behind the messenger and Ptolemaios' officer. Menedemos, a proud and touchy man in his own right, seemed inclined to dispute Polemaios' place. Catching his cousin's eye, Sostratos tossed his head. Polemaios was the tunny here; the captain and toikharkhos of the *Aphrodite* were just a couple of sprats. To Sostratos' relief, Menedemos didn't push it, but hung back with him.

They all went up to Ptolemaios' residence, the ruler of Egypt's soldiers surrounding Polemaios' bodyguards, who in turn formed up around their master and his wife. After watching all those nodding horsehair plumes and all that gleaming bronze for a while, Sostratos glanced from his ordinary chiton to Menedemos' and back again. "We're underdressed," he murmured.

"I don't care," Menedemos answered; even more than Sostratos, he had a seaman's indifference to fancy clothes and abhorrence of armor. "We're not baking like a couple of loaves in the oven, either."

With the sun high and hot in the sky, Sostratos *was* sweating by the time the procession got to the house Ptolemaios was using as his own. The soldiers surely were baked by then. At the doorway, Polemaios got into an argument with Ptolemaios' officer, who refused to let any of his bodyguards into the house. The officer said, "If you think you need bodyguards when dealing with Ptolemaios, O best one, you shouldn't have come to Kos."

Polemaios fumed, but had to yield. *So much for that equal alliance*, Sostratos thought. Antigonos' nephew shifted his ground: "Will Ptolemaios at least have a slave girl waiting to take my wife to the women's quarters? By the nature of things, she's been out among men and under their eyes more than she should have since I left Khalkis."

"Certainly, sir. Let me go take care of that." By yielding at once on the smaller point, Ptolemaios' officer emphasized how unyielding he was on the larger. He disappeared into the house, returning a moment later to say, "A girl will be there waiting for your wife. Just come along with me." He started to turn back, then snapped his fingers, annoyed at himself. "And you Rhodians, you come along, too."

Sostratos and Menedemos made their way through the soldiers to get to the door. Ptolemaios' men simply stood aside. Polemaios' bodyguards glared. They were trained and paid to keep their master safe, and here they couldn't do their job. Even if they had been allowed into the residence, Ptolemaios' men would have preceded them and outnumbered them, but they didn't think in those terms. They didn't want to be on one side of a wall when Antigonos' nephew was on the other, and resented anyone who could go in while they couldn't.

When Sostratos walked along the entrance hall and into the courtyard, he got a glimpse of an unveiled slave woman taking Polemaios' wife to a stairway that would lead up to the women's chambers. Polemaios stood in the courtyard, looking after her.

Ptolemaios courteously waited in the andron till his new ally's wife was out of sight. Then he emerged, saying, "Hail, Polemaios. Welcome to Kos." He held out his hand.

Polemaios clasped it. Antigonos' nephew was more than a head taller than the lord of Egypt, and twenty years younger besides. Neither size nor youth mattered a khalkos' worth here. Ptolemaios, solid and blocky, was the stronger of the two.

He took that for granted, too, going on without giving Polemaios a chance to speak: "We'll strike some heavy blows against your uncle."

"I'll fuck his asshole instead of a sausage skin," Polemaios declared.

The gross obscenity staggered Sostratos. He hadn't dreamt even a Macedonian could come out with anything so crude. But Ptolemaios just chuckled. And so did Menedemos. Sostratos' horror must have shown on his face, for Menedemos leaned toward him and whispered, "That's Aristophanes."

"Is it?" Sostratos whispered back. Menedemos dipped his head. Sostratos eyed Polemaios with new respect. Not only had he quoted the comic poet—though what a line to choose!—but he'd been shrewd enough to guess that Ptolemaios would know he was quoting and wouldn't be disgusted.

"You'll have your chance," the ruler of Egypt said. "I can use every talented officer I can get my hands on, and as your men drift in I expect I'll get good service from them, too."

Antigonos' nephew looked as if he'd bitten into an unbaked quince. What Ptolemaios was talking about didn't sound like anything close to an equal alliance. Evidently it didn't sound like one to Polemaios, either; he said, "I thought we'd be partners in this."

"And so we will," Ptolemaios said easily. He reached up and clapped Polemaios on the back. "Come on into the andron, and we'll drink to everything we're going to do to Antigonos." He waved to Sostratos and Menedemos. "You boys come along, too. Don't you worry about a thing—I promise I haven't forgotten you."

In the andron, a slave poured wine for Ptolemaios and Polemaios, and then for the two Rhodians. Sostratos poured out a small libation. When he drank, his eyebrows rose. For one thing, the wine was strong: one to one, wine to water, or somewhere close to it. For another . . . "Very fine, sir," Sostratos said. "If this is Koan, I'd like to know from whom you got it. I wouldn't mind carrying some on the *Aphrodite*. We'd get a good price for it."

"It's better than that pitch-flavored vinegar you and your sailors drink, that's for sure," Polemaios said.

"It is a local wine, I think, but you'll have to ask my steward for the details." Ptolemaios waved a negligent hand. One corner of his mouth quirked upward in an engagingly wry smile. "Figuring out how to spend the silver you'll get from me, eh?"

"Yes, sir. Why not?" Sostratos said. Not getting the silver from Ptolemaios was one obvious reason why not. He didn't want to think about that.

"No reason at all, young fellow," Ptolemaios answered. "You're doing your job the best way you know how. Can't ask for more than that from a man. And you and your captain got this big fellow"—he pointed with his chin at Polemaios—"here in fine time, for which I thank you kindly. What did you think of them, Polemaios?"

"They both have tongues that flap too free. And *this* one"—Antigonos' nephew glowered at Menedemos—"will not keep his eyes to himself. But," he added reluctantly, "they do handle their ship well."

"Rhodians have that knack. Must come of their being islanders," Ptolemaios said. Two of his servitors came in, each carrying four good-sized leather sacks. When they set the sacks down in front of Sostratos, they clinked. Ptolemaios' eyes glinted. "Here is the balance of your fee. I suppose you'll want to count and weigh to make sure I haven't cheated you."

"No, sir," Sostratos answered. "If you're ready for me to do it, that's the best sign I don't need to."

"You see what I mean," Polemaios rumbled.

"Tending to one's business isn't insolence," Ptolemaios said. He pointed north and east, in the direction of Halikarnassos. "You and I have some business in common, some business with Antigonos."

"So we do," Antigonos' renegade nephew agreed. "But we'd do better not to talk about it where these fellows can listen." He pointed to Sostratos and Menedemos as if they were pieces of furniture, unable to understand anything.

That made Sostratos want to bristle, but he didn't show his anger. His cousin did, snapping, "You trusted us far enough to let us bring you here. What makes you think we've suddenly turned into Antigonos' spies since we found a berth in the harbor?"

Polemaios surged to his feet. "I've had everything I'm going to take from you, you pretty little catamite, and—"

"Enough!" Ptolemaios' deep, angry rasp effortlessly dominated every other voice in the room. "The Rhodian asked a fair enough question."

"He brought me here for pay." Polemaios pointed to the leather sacks full of coins. "If my uncle gives him silver, he'll sing for pay, too."

"What can he say? That you're here?" Ptolemaios shrugged. "Antigonos will know that by this time tomorrow. He'll have men here, the same as I do on the mainland. Some boat or other will sneak away from Kos and get over there with the news. Can't be helped."

Antigonos' nephew scowled. He was, plainly, not a man who liked disagreement or back talk. Being who he was, being part of his family, he wouldn't have heard much of it, and he would have been able to ignore more of what he did hear. But he couldn't ignore Ptolemaios, not here in the middle of the ruler of Egypt's stronghold.

"All right, then—fine," he said, not bothering to hide his disgust. "Tell them everything, why don't you?"

"I didn't say a word about telling them everything," Ptolemaios replied. "I did say you were silly to insult them for no good reason. I said it, and I still say it."

Could looks have killed, Ptolemaios would have been a dead man, with Sostratos and Menedemos lying lifeless on the floor beside him. Sostratos would have liked nothing better than hanging about and listening to the two prominent men wrangle: if that wasn't the raw stuff from which history was made, what was? But he didn't want Polemaios any angrier at his cousin and him than he was already, and he didn't want to make Ptolemaios angry by overstaying his welcome. Reluctantly, he said, "Menedemos and I had better get back to the *Aphrodite*."

"Good idea," Ptolemaios said. "You'll probably want an escort, too. I would, if I were walking through the streets with so much silver."

"Thank you, sir—yes," Sostratos said. "And if I might speak to your steward for a moment about the wine . . ."

"Certainly." Ptolemaios gave a couple of crisp orders. One

slave went outside, presumably to talk to some of the soldiers there. Another led the Rhodians out into the courtyard, where the steward met them. He was a plump, fussy little man named Kleonymos, and had the details of Koan winesellers at his fingertips. Sostratos found out what he needed to know, thanked the man, and left Ptolemaios' residence.

By the time he got back to the *Aphrodite,* he discovered that lugging twenty minai of silver through the streets of Kos had other drawbacks besides the risk of robbery. His arms felt a palm longer than they had been when he set out. Menedemos seemed no happier. The concentrated mass of the silver made it seem heavier than if he'd been carrying, say, a trussed piglet of like weight.

After the soldiers headed back toward Ptolemaios' residence, Menedemos said, "Well, I can certainly see why Antigonos' nephew makes himself loved wherever he goes, can't you?"

"Yes, he's a very charming fellow," Sostratos agreed. They could say what they wanted about Polemaios now: they didn't have him aboard the *Aphrodite* any more. Sostratos would have been just as well pleased never to have made his acquaintance, too.

But he'd made them a profit. Once aboard the akatos, they stowed the sacks of coins with the rest of their silver in the cramped space under the poop deck, where raiders—and any light-fingered sailors they happened to have in the crew—would have the hardest time stealing the money.

When they emerged once more, Sostratos said, "And now we can do what we should have done the last time we left Kos."

"What's that, O best one?" Menedemos asked innocently. "Drill the crew harder on getting away from pirates and fighting them off if we can't? No doubt you're right."

Sostratos, fortunately, wasn't holding one of those five-mina sacks of silver any more. Had he been, he might have tried to brain his cousin with it. As things were, the smile he gave Menedemos was as wolfish as he could make it. "That too, of course," he said, "as we go to Athens."

* * *

NO MATTER WHAT Menedemos' cousin wanted, the *Aphrodite* didn't immediately make for Athens. For one thing, Menedemos kept the promise he'd made to let the crew roister in the city of Kos for a couple of days to make up for the hard work they'd done rowing east from Kythnos in the calm. For another . . .

Menedemos eyed Sostratos with amusement as they walked through the streets of Kos. "This is your own fault, my dear," he said. "You've got no business twisting and moaning as if you were about to shit yourself, the way Dionysos does in the *Frogs*."

"Oh, to the crows with Aristophanes," Sostratos snarled. "And to the crows with Di—"

"You don't want to say that." Menedemos broke in before his cousin could curse the god of wine.

"You mean, you don't want me to say that." Sostratos understood him well enough.

"All right, I don't want you to say that. However you please. Just don't say it." Menedemos was a conventionally pious young man. He believed in the gods as much because his father did as for any other reason. Sostratos, he knew, had other notions. Most of the time, his cousin was polite enough to keep from throwing those notions in his face. When Sostratos started to slip, Menedemos wasn't shy about letting him know he didn't care for such remarks.

"Coming out!" a woman yelled from a second-story window, and emptied a chamber pot into the street below. The warning call let Menedemos and Sostratos skip to one side. A fellow leading a donkey wasn't so lucky; the stinking stuff splashed him. He shook his fist up at the window and shouted curses.

"You see?" Menedemos said as he and Sostratos walked on. "Aristophanes was as true to life as Euripides any day." His cousin didn't even rise to that, which showed what a truly evil mood he was in. "It's your own fault," Menedemos repeated. "If you hadn't asked Ptolemaios' steward about the wine we were drinking . . ."

"Oh, shut up," Sostratos said. But then, relenting a little, he pointed to a door. "I think that's the right house."

"Let's find out." Menedemos knocked.

"Who is?" The question, in accented Greek, came from within. The door didn't open.

"Is this the house of Nikomakhos son of Pleistarkhos, the wine merchant?" Menedemos asked.

"Who you?" The door still didn't open, but the voice on the other side seemed a little less hostile.

"Two Rhodian traders." Menedemos gave his name, and Sostratos'. "We'd like to talk to Nikomakhos about buying some wine."

"You wait." After that, Menedemos heard nothing. He started drumming his fingers on the outside of his thigh. Sostratos looked longingly back toward the harbor. If the door didn't open pretty soon, Menedemos saw he would have trouble persuading his cousin to hang around.

Just when Sostratos' grumbles were starting to turn into words, the door did open. The fellow standing there was a Hellene with a beard streaked with gray. He had a good-natured smile that showed a broken front tooth. " 'Ail, my friends. I'm Nikomakhos. 'Ow are you today?" Most people on Kos used a Doric dialect not far from that of Rhodes, but he spoke an Ionian Greek, dropping his rough breathings.

"Hail," Menedemos said, a little sourly. He introduced himself and Sostratos, then added, "Your surly slave there almost cost you some business."

"Ibanollis is a Karian as stubborn as Kerberos," Nikomakhos said with a sigh. " 'E's been in the 'ouse'old since my father's day. Sometimes you're stuck with a slave like that. But do come in, and we'll talk. I've 'eard of you, 'aven't I? You were running some kind of errand for Ptolemaios."

"That's right," Menedemos answered. "We just fetched Antigonos' nephew here from Euboia." Sostratos raised a finger to his lips as they followed Nikomakhos into the courtyard, but Menedemos shrugged and tossed his head. That Polemaios was here wouldn't stay secret, not when he'd tramped through the polis on his way to the ruler of Egypt's residence; Ptolemaios himself had known as much. Why not take credit for bringing him, then?

Nikomakhos whistled. "Old One-Eye over on the mainland

won't like that a bit. Of course, 'e won't like anything Ptolemaios 'as done to him this campaigning season. The andron's over this way." He turned left.

In the middle of the courtyard stood a bent, skinny old man with a bald head, a bushy white beard, and the angriest glare Menedemos had seen this side of an eagle—Ibanollis, without a doubt. The slave looked daggers at him and Sostratos. Menedemos wondered why he seemed so hateful. Did he think they would cheat his master? Or was he just angry because he'd had to answer the door? *Probably better not to know*, Menedemos thought. Sostratos didn't ask any questions, either.

A clean-shaven young man—younger than the two Rhodians—joined Nikomakhos in the andron. "This is my son, Pleistarkhos," the wine merchant said. "I'm teaching 'im the business, same as your fathers were doing with you not too long ago. Tell me what I can do for you, and I will if I can."

"We drank some of your wine at Ptolemaios'," Menedemos replied. "We liked it enough that Sostratos got your name from his steward. If we can make a deal, we'd like to buy some to take aboard our akatos."

"A merchant galley, eh? Then you'll want the best," Nikomakhos said. Menedemos dipped his head. In an aside to his son, Nikomakhos went on, "Akatoi can't carry much. They make money selling top-of-the-line goods to the folk 'oo can afford to buy them. There was one last year—remember?—came into the 'arbor with peacocks aboard, of all the crazy things. Bound for Italy, they were, to make the most they could."

"That was our ship, as a matter of fact," Sostratos said.

"Is that so?" Nikomakhos exclaimed. Both Rhodians dipped their heads. "And did you do well with 'em?" the wine merchant asked.

"We did splendidly." Menedemos would have boasted even if he were lying. That was how the game was played. He would have sounded sincere, too, every bit as sincere as he did while telling the truth.

"Well, good for you," the Koan said. "And now it's wine, is it?"

"Fine wine." Menedemos turned to Pleistarkhos. "Your father's right. We carry the best. Last year, we had Ariousian from Khios. It cost us a lot, but we made a profit from it. Everybody around the Inner Sea makes wine, but most of it's pretty nasty stuff. When you've got something that isn't, people will pay for it."

"Ariousian's first-rate," Nikomakhos agreed. "I'd like to say that what I make is just as good, but you'd call me a liar to my face. Still and all, though, I'm not ashamed of it." He eyed Menedemos. "You can't think it's too bad, either, or you wouldn't be 'ere."

Menedemos grinned at him. "I told you, it was Sostratos' idea."

"It's good wine," Sostratos said. "I'd like to get some—if we can afford it."

Nikomakhos' eyes glinted. "You're not poor men to begin with, or you wouldn't be in the trade you're in. And if you tell me Ptolemaios didn't pay you well to bring Antigonos' nephew 'ere, I'll be the one calling you a couple of liars."

"What you say may be true, my friend, but that doesn't mean we can throw our money away, either," Menedemos said. "We couldn't stay in business if we did. And even if I wanted to, my cousin would beat me." He pointed to Sostratos. "He doesn't look it, but he's terribly fierce."

Sostratos didn't look fierce. He did look annoyed. He didn't like being twitted. Menedemos didn't let that worry him, not when he was getting a dicker going. Pleistarkhos took Menedemos literally, and eyed Sostratos with a wary respect he hadn't shown before. Nikomakhos seemed more amused than anything else.

"Can't 'ave any beatings," he said. "Well, what do you suppose a fair price would be?" Then he raised a hand. "No, don't answer that. Why don't you taste some first?" He called for a slave—not the bad-tempered Ibanollis—and told him to bring back samples, and some bread and oil to go with them.

The wine was as sweet and strong as it had been in Ptolemaios' andron. It wasn't the magnificent golden Ariousian, but what was? After a few sips, Menedemos said, "I can see how you might get four or five drakhmai for an amphora."

"Four or five?" Pleistarkhos turned red. "That's an insult!"

His father tossed his head. "No it isn't, son. It's just an opening offer. 'E knows it's worth three times that much, but 'e can't come out and say so."

"It's a good wine," Sostratos said. "It's not worth three times what my cousin offered. If you think it is—good luck finding buyers at that price."

"We can do it," Pleistarkhos said.

"Maybe so, but we won't be among them," Menedemos said. "That's the kind of money we paid for the Ariousian last year. This is good, but it isn't that good."

They haggled for most of the morning. Nikomakhos came down to ten drakhmai the amphora; Menedemos and Sostratos went up as high as eight. And there they stuck. "I'm sorry, my friends, but I don't see 'ow I can sell for any less," Nikomakhos said.

Menedemos glanced at Sostratos. Unobtrusively, his cousin tossed his head. That fit in with Menedemos' view of things. "I'm sorry, too," he told the Koan. "I don't think we could show a profit if I went higher. If we were heading off to Italy again, I might take the chance, but not for the towns round the Aegean. If ten's really as low as you'll go . . ."

Very often, a threat like that would make the other side see things your way. This time, Nikomakhos sighed and said, "I'm afraid it is." He turned to his son. "Sometimes the best bargain is the one you don't make."

"That's true." Menedemos got to his feet. So did Sostratos. Menedemos dipped his head to Nikomakhos. "A pleasure to have met you, best one. We often come by Kos. Maybe we'll try again another time."

Ibanollis the Karian slave was still standing in the courtyard when Menedemos and Sostratos headed for the door. With his dour expression and forward-thrusting posture, he reminded Menedemos of a frowzy old stork perched on a rooftop. "Waste of time," he croaked to the Rhodians as they left. Had he stood on one leg, the resemblance would have been perfect.

"Lovely fellow," Menedemos remarked once they were out on the street.

"Isn't he just?" But Sostratos sounded embittered, not

amused. He explained why a moment later: "However charming he is, he was right. We did waste our time, and we could have been—"

"Twiddling our thumbs aboard the *Aphrodite*," Menedemos broke in. "You were going to say 'heading for Athens,' weren't you? But you're wrong. We couldn't have sailed this morning anyhow, not unless we wanted to break our promise to the crew, remember? And that was your idea, too."

"Oh," Sostratos said in a small voice. "That's right." He breathed a sigh of relief. "Good. I don't feel so bad now about getting Nikomakhos' name from Ptolemaios' steward."

They walked along toward the harbor. After a while, Menedemos said, "I've been thinking."

"*Euge*," Sostratos replied, his tone suggesting he was offering the praise because Menedemos didn't do it very often.

Refusing to rise to the bait, Menedemos went on, "I was thinking about the best way to get to Athens from here."

"Same route we used to pick up Polemaios, of course," Sostratos said, "though they'll probably be sick of seeing us in the Kyklades."

"That's what I was thinking about," Menedemos said. "Those are dangerous waters—we saw it for ourselves. And they're going to be more dangerous than usual. Polemaios' men, or some of them, will be heading this way. I don't want to run into them. The only real difference between mercenaries and pirates is that pirates have ships. When mercenaries take ship, they're liable to turn pirate, too."

"You *have* been thinking," Sostratos said. "That's well put."

"And, of course, on our way back, the cities of the Island League may have learned we smuggled Antigonos' nephew past them," Menedemos continued. "Since the league is Antigonos' creature . . ."

"They may not be any too happy with us," Sostratos finished for him. Menedemos dipped his head. His cousin scowled. "How do we get to Athens, then?"

"That's what I've been thinking about," Menedemos replied. "Suppose we go on up to Miletos and do some trading there."

"Suppose we don't," Sostratos said. "That's one of old One-

Eye's chief strongholds, and . . ." He broke off, looking foolish. "Oh, I see. Word of what we've done won't have got there yet."

Now Menedemos indulged himself with a sarcastic, "*Euge*."

His cousin's scowl returned. "I still don't like it."

Laughing, Menedemos said, "Of course you don't, my dear. It means one more pause before your precious gryphon's skull can be formally introduced to Athenian society. But consider: from Miletos, we can sail northwest to Ikaria, either stopping at Samos on the way or spending a night at sea, and then strike straight across the Aegean for the channel between Andros and Euboia instead of hopping from island to island. Traders hardly ever use that route, which means pirates don't, either. We could get almost to Attica without having anybody notice."

He watched Sostratos contemplate that. It wasn't what his cousin wanted; Menedemos knew as much. Most men, when thwarted in their desires, lashed out at whoever held them back. Menedemos had seen that, too. Sostratos' mouth twisted. But he didn't let loose whatever curses he was thinking. Instead, he said, "Well, I don't like to admit it, but that's likely best for the ship and best for business. Let it be as you say."

"I did think you would fuss more," Menedemos said.

Sostratos smiled a crooked smile. "I will if you like."

"Don't bother." Menedemos smiled, too. "I'm glad you're being so reasonable. I was just thinking that not many men would."

"Oh, I'll fight like a wild boar when I think I'm right, and I'll rip the guts out of the hunting dogs of illogic that nip my heels," Sostratos said. "But what's the point in getting hot and bothered when that would be wrong?"

"You might win anyhow. Some would say you had a better chance, in fact," Menedemos answered. "Look at what Bad Logic did to Good Logic in the *Clouds*."

"You keep coming back to that polluted play," Sostratos said. "You know it's not my favorite."

"But there's a lot of good stuff in it," Menedemos said. "By the time Bad Logic is done, Good Logic sees that practically all the Athenians are a pack of wide-arsed catamites."

"That's not true, though," Sostratos protested.

"It's what people think." Menedemos applied the clincher: "And it's funny."

"What people think to be true often influences what they do or say, and so becomes a truth of its own," Sostratos said thoughtfully. "I'll chase truth where it leads me, and it leads me there." He wagged a finger at Menedemos. "But I would never throw truth over the rail for the sake of getting a laugh."

"You're the soul of virtue." Menedemos could have spoken mockingly; his cousin did get tiresome at times. But Sostratos really did have a great many virtues, and Menedemos was more willing than usual to acknowledge them because his cousin wasn't fussing about heading up to Miletos.

Sostratos pointed. "There's the *Aphrodite*."

A couple of sailors aboard the merchant galley spotted their captain and toikharkhos and waved. Menedemos waved back. He also wiped his forehead with the back of his hand. "Hot and muggy," he grumbled.

"It is, isn't it?" Sostratos looked north. "Breeze is picking up a little bit, too, I think."

He spoke as if hoping Menedemos would tell him he was wrong. Menedemos, unfortunately, thought he was right. "I hope we don't get a blow," he said. "It would be late in the year for one, but I don't like the feel of the air."

"No. Neither do I," Sostratos said, and then, "We might have done better not to let the crew do its celebrating here."

Menedemos shrugged. "If it is a storm, we'd get it in Miletos, too. Just as well not to get it out in the middle of the Aegean, though." His feet went from the gravelly dirt of the street to the planks of the quay, hot under the sun but worn smooth by the passage of countless barefoot sailors.

When he and Sostratos came up to the *Aphrodite*, Aristeidas asked, "Will they bring some of this famous Koan wine aboard tomorrow?"

"Afraid not." Menedemos tossed his head. "Nikomakhos wouldn't come down far enough to make it worth our while to buy."

"Ah, too bad," the lookout said. A fair number of sailors had a lively interest in the business end of what the *Aphrodite* did; Aristeidas was one of them. Maybe he dreamt of owning a merchantman himself, or maybe of serving as captain aboard one and going on trading runs for the owner. The first was unlikely. The second was by no means impossible. Had things gone better for Diokles, he would have been doing that this sailing season. His time might—probably would—still come.

In his turn, Menedemos asked, "See anything interesting across the water at Halikarnassos?"

"No, skipper," Aristeidas answered. "Everything's quiet over there. Ptolemaios' war galleys go back and forth outside the harbor here, and you can see Antigonos', little as bugs, doing the same thing over there. They don't even move against each other."

"Just as well," Menedemos said. "I wouldn't want to sail out of here and end up in the middle of a sea fight."

"I should hope not," Aristeidas exclaimed.

In a low voice, Sostratos said, "Oh, you had warships in mind when you asked about Halikarnassos? I thought you were still worrying about the husband you outraged a couple of years ago."

"Funny," Menedemos said through clenched teeth. "Very funny." If he hadn't got out of Halikarnassos in a hurry, he might not have been able to get out at all; that husband had wanted his blood. But he made himself look northeast, toward the city on the mainland. "I'll get back there one of these days."

"Not under your right name, you won't," Sostratos said. "Not unless you come at the head of a fleet yourself."

He was probably right. No: he was almost certainly right. Menedemos knew as much. He didn't intend to admit it, though: "I could do it this year if I had to, I think. In a couple of years, that fellow won't even remember my name."

His cousin snorted. "He won't forget you till the day he dies. And even then, his ghost will want to haunt you."

"I doubt it." Now Menedemos spoke with more confidence. "He'll have another man, or more than one, to be angry at by then. If his wife bent over forward for me, she'll bend over forward for somebody else, too. Women are like that. And she'll probably get caught again. She's pretty, but she's not very smart."

As was Sostratos' way, he met that thoughtfully. "Character doesn't change much, true enough," he admitted. But then he pointed at Menedemos. "That holds for men as well as women. You in Taras last summer . . ."

"I didn't know Phyllis was that fellow's wife," Menedemos protested. "I thought she was just a serving girl."

"The first time you did, yes," Sostratos said. "But you went back for a second helping after you knew who she was. That's when you had to jump out the window."

"I got away with it," Menedemos said.

"And he set bully boys on you afterwards," his cousin said. "It'll be a long time before you can go back to Taras, too. In how many more cities around the Inner Sea will you make yourself unwelcome?"

He wanted to make Menedemos feel guilty. Menedemos refused to give him the satisfaction of showing guilt. "Unwelcome? What are you talking bout? The women in both towns made me about as welcome as a man can be."

"You can do business with women, sure enough," Sostratos said, "but you can't make a profit from them."

"You sound like my father," Menedemos said, an edge to his voice. Sostratos, for a wonder, took the hint. That proved he wasn't Philodemos: the older man never would have.

SOSTRATOS LOOKED UP AT THE EARLY morning sky and clicked his tongue between his teeth. It was after sunrise, but only twilight leaked through the thick gray clouds. "Do we really want to set out in this?" he asked Menedemos. The air felt even wetter than it had a couple of days before.

"It hasn't rained yet," his cousin answered. "Maybe it will hold off a while longer. Even if it doesn't, making Miletos is easy enough from here. And besides"—Menedemos lowered his voice—"paying the sailors for sitting idle eats into the money we make."

That struck a chord with the thrifty Sostratos. An akatos was expensive to operate, no doubt about it. The sailors earned about two minai of silver every three days—and, as Menedemos had said, earned their pay whether the *Aphrodite* sailed the Aegean or sat in port.

"You think it's safe to go, then?" Sostratos asked once more.

"We should be all right," Menedemos said. He turned to Diokles. "If you think I'm wrong, don't be shy."

"I wouldn't be, skipper—it's my neck we're talking about, you know," the oarmaster replied. "I expect we can make Miletos, too—and if the weather does turn really dirty, we can always swing around and run back here."

"I was thinking the same thing," Menedemos said. He raised an eyebrow at Sostratos. "Satisfied?"

"Certainly," Sostratos answered; he didn't want Menedemos reckoning him a wet blanket. "If we can do it, we should do it. And it puts us one day closer to Athens."

Menedemos laughed and clapped him on the shoulder. "I thought that might be somewhere in the back of your mind." He raised his voice to the sailors forward: "Cast off the mooring lines! Rowers to their places! No more swilling and screwing till the next port!"

The sailors had moved quicker. A good many of them had spent everything they'd made so far this season in their spree in the polis of Kos. Nobody was missing, though. Diokles had a better nose than a Kastorian hunting hound for sniffing men out of harborside taverns and brothels. "Come on, you lugs," the keleustes rasped now. "Time to sweat out the wine you've guzzled."

A couple of groans answered him. He didn't laugh. He'd done his share of drinking, too. The thick ropes thudded down into the waist of the *Aphrodite*. Sailors who weren't rowing coiled them and got them out of the way.

"Back oars!" Diokles called, and struck the bronze square with the mallet. "Rhyppa*pai*! Rhyppa*pai*!" Menedemos slid one steering-oar tiller in toward him, the other out, swinging the *Aphrodite* around till her bow pointed north. A round ship that had been lying at anchor a couple of plethra away from the pier sculled toward the spot the merchant galley had vacated. With Ptolemaios' fleet here, Kos' harbor remained badly overcrowded.

Just for a moment, the sun peeked through the dark clouds, highlighting the Karian headland north of Kos on which Halikarnassos and, farther west, the smaller town of Myndos lay. The yellow stubble of harvested grainfields and the grayish green leaves of olive groves seemed particularly bright against the gloomy background of the sky. Sostratos hoped that shaft of sunlight meant the weather would clear, but the clouds rolled in again, and color drained out of the landscape.

Menedemos took the *Aphrodite* up the channel between Myndos and the island of Kalymnos to the west. When the akatos came abreast of Myndos, Sostratos pointed toward the town and said, "Look! Antigonos has war galleys patrolling there, too."

"So would I, in his place," Menedemos answered. He blinked a couple of times, a comical expression.

"What's that about?" Sostratos asked.

"Raindrop just hit me in the eye," Menedemos said. He rubbed his nose. "There's another one."

A moment later, one hit Sostratos in the knee, another on the forearm, and a third gave him a wet kiss on the left ear. A couple of sailors exclaimed. "Here comes the storm, sure enough," Sostratos said.

The *Aphrodite*'s sail was already up against the yard, for she was heading straight into the wind. After those first few scattered drops, the rain came down hard, far harder than it had in the Kyklades. "Very late in the year for one like this," Menedemos said. Sostratos could hardly hear him; raindrops were drumming down on the planking of the poop deck and hissing into the sea.

"It is, isn't it?" Sostratos said. "I hope all the leather sacks are sound. Otherwise, we're liable to have some water-damaged silk."

"You look water-damaged yourself," Menedemos said. "It's dripping out of your beard."

"How can you tell, the way it's coming down out of the sky?" Sostratos replied.

Instead of answering directly, Menedemos raised his voice to a shout: "Aristeidas, go forward!" The sailor waved and hurried up to the foredeck. "Polemaios can't complain about him this time," Menedemos said.

"No," Sostratos agreed, "but how much good will he do with the rain coming down like this? I can hardly see him up there, and he's only—what?—thirty or thirty-five cubits away."

"He's the best set of eyes we've got," Menedemos said. "I can't do any more than that."

Sostratos dipped his head. "I wasn't arguing." He pulled off his chiton and threw it down onto the deck. In the warm rain, going naked was more comfortable than wet wool squelching against his skin. He looked back toward the *Aphrodite*'s boat, which she towed by a line tied to the sternpost. "I wonder if you'll need to put a man with a pot in there to bail."

"It *is* coming down, isn't it?" Menedemos said. An unspoken thought flashed between them: *I wonder if we'll need to start bailing out the ship.* Sostratos knew he hadn't expected weather this nasty, and his cousin couldn't have, either, or he wouldn't have set out from Kos. Menedemos quickly changed the subject: "Take the steering oars for a moment, would you? I want to get out of my tunic, too."

"Of course, my dear." Sostratos seized the steering-oar tillers with alacrity. Menedemos usually had charge of them all the way through the voyage. Sostratos didn't have to do any steering past holding the merchant galley on her course. Even so, the strength of the sea shot up his arms, informing his whole body. *It's like holding a conversation with Poseidon himself,* he thought.

Menedemos' soggy chiton splatted onto the planks of the deck beside his own. "That's better," his cousin said. "Thanks. I'll get back where I belong now."

"All right," Sostratos said, though his tone suggested it was anything but.

Laughing, Menedemos said, "You want to hang on for a while, do you? Well, I can't say that I blame you. It's like making love to the sea, isn't it?"

That wasn't the comparison Sostratos had thought of, but it wasn't a bad one. *And it suits my cousin, too*, he thought. "May I stay for a bit?" he asked.

"Why not?" Menedemos said, laughing still. But then he grew more serious: "Probably not the worst thing in the world for you to know what to do."

"I do *know*," Sostratos answered. "But there's a difference between knowing how to do something and having experience at it."

Before Menedemos could reply, Aristeidas let out a horrified cry for the foredeck: "Ship! By the gods, a ship off the port bow, and she's heading straight for us!"

Sostratos' head jerked to the left. Sure enough, wallowing through the curtain of rain and into sight came a great round ship, her sail down from the yard and full of wind as she ran before the breeze—straight for the *Aphrodite*. Sostratos knew what he had to do. He pulled one steering oar in as far as it would go, and pushed the other as far out, desperately swinging the akatos to starboard. That wasn't making love to the sea but wrestling with it, forcing it and the ship to obey his strength. And the sea fought back, pushing against the blades of the steering oars with a supple power that appalled him.

Had Menedemos snatched the steering-oar tillers from his hands, he would have yielded them on the instant. But his cousin, seeing that he'd done the right thing, said only, "Hold us on that turn no matter what." And Sostratos did, though he began to think he was wrestling a foe beyond his strength. "Pull hard, you bastards! *Pull!*" Menedemos screamed to the rowers, and then, to the men who weren't rowing, "Grab poles! Grab oars! Fend that fat sow off!" He cupped his hands and screamed louder still at the round ship: "Sheer off! Sheer off, you wide-arsed, tawny-turded chamber pot!"

A couple of naked sailors on the round ship were yelling, too. Sostratos could see their open mouths. They were so close, he could see that one of them had a couple of missing teeth. He couldn't hear a word they said, though. One of them ran back and snatched up a pole, too, to try to push the *Aphrodite* away. But the big, beamy ship lumbered on, right toward the merchant galley.

Right toward? At first, Sostratos had been sure she would simply trample the *Aphrodite* under her keel, as a war galley might have done. But his hard turn gave him hope. He had to turn his head farther to the left every moment to keep an eye on the round ship. Maybe she would slip past the akatos' stern. But she was close now, so close. . . .

"Port oars—in!" Diokles yelled, not wanting them broken and crushed by the round ship's hull. With only the starboard rowers working, the *Aphrodite* tried to slew back to port. Sostratos held her on course against the new pressure.

Poles probed out from each ship, trying to hold the other off. Sostratos felt two or three thud against the merchant galley's flank. With a far larger crew, the *Aphrodite* had more men straining to push away the round ship. Sailors on both ships cursed and called on the gods, sometimes both in the same breath.

They almost got their miracle. Had the rain been even a little lighter, had lynx-eyed Aristeidas spied the round ship even a handful of heartbeats sooner, the two vessels would have missed each other. But, with a grind of timbers, the round ship's side scraped against the *Aphrodite*'s stern. Sostratos jerked his arm off the port steering oar an instant before the other ship carried the oar away. Had he been late, he would have had the arm torn from its socket.

The round ship sailed on, as if without a care in the world. Sostratos shook himself, as if waking from a bad dream. But a dream wouldn't have left him naked on a pitching, rolling deck, both hands now on the tiller of the surviving steering oar.

"You did well there," Menedemos said quietly. "You did as well as anyone could. I'll take it now. Duck under the poop deck and see if we're taking on water. To the crows with me if that fat pig"—a word with a lewd double meaning—"didn't stave in some of our planking."

"All right," Sostratos said. "Why didn't you take the steering oars away from me? Maybe the round ship would have missed."

Menedemos tossed his head. "You had us going hard to starboard. That was the right thing to do, and I couldn't have done anything different. I didn't want the tillers without hands on 'em for even half a heartbeat there, so I just left you alone. Now go see how we're doing under here."

As Sostratos went past Diokles, the oarmaster clapped him on the back. That made him so proud, he all but flew down the steps from the poop deck to the waist of the ship: Diokles was not a man to show approval when it hadn't been earned.

Ducking under the poop deck, Sostratos found the one drawback to sending a tall man down there—he banged his head twice in quick succession on the underside of the deck timbers, the second time hard enough to see stars. He wished he had some of Menedemos' Aristophanic curses handy.

Then he found more reason to curse than a lump on the head, for his cousin had known whereof he spoke. The collision had staved in three or four of the timbers near the stern, cracking the tenons and breaking open the mortises that held them together. Seawater came through—not in a steady stream, but by surges, so the damage was close to the waterline but not below it.

Sostratos backed out from under the decking (and, not being the most graceful of men, hit his head once more for good measure). He went up onto the poop deck and gave Menedemos the news.

"I knew it," Menedemos said savagely. "And what do you bet we didn't do a thing to that stinking round ship? It'll have timbers as thick as its skipper's head. How much water's coming in?"

"It's not too bad," Sostratos answered. "It's leaking in spurts, not steadily."

"If we patch it with sailcloth and bail, do you think we can turn back and make Kos?"

"I suppose so," Sostratos said. "Myndos is a lot closer, though." He pointed east.

"I know it, my dear," Menedemos answered. "I'll go there if I have to. But I'd rather not. Damage like that takes a while to repair, and word *will* get to Myndos that we were the ones who brought Polemaios to Kos. If I have a choice, I'd sooner not be there when it does. If I don't"—he shrugged—"that's a different story, and I'll do what I have to do."

"Ah." Sostratos dipped his head. "That makes good sense.

As I say, it's not too bad. We got off easier than we might have. You might want to go under there and see for yourself."

"I suppose I'd better," Menedemos said. "All right, take the steering oars—uh, oar. Who would've thought we'd lose two on the same voyage? Long odds there, by the gods. Swing her around to southward to run with the wind. We'll make for Kos unless I decide we can't get there."

When Menedemos came back up onto the poop deck, he was rubbing the top of his head. Seeing that made Sostratos feel better about his own bumps. Menedemos said, "They're sprung, sure enough, but I think we can plug 'em. You're right—that's not too bad a leak. We'll make Kos easy as you please." He shouted commands, sending a couple of sailors under the poop deck with sailcloth to stuff up the sprung seams and ordering the sail lowered from the yard.

Sostratos peered forward. "What'll we do if we spot the round ship?"

"We ought to ram her," Menedemos growled. "See how she likes it, by the gods." In more thoughtful tones, he went on, "If we find out who she is, maybe we can go to law with her skipper or her owner."

"Maybe." Sostratos knew he sounded dubious. Going to law against anyone from another polis—and collecting a judgment if you won—was often a task to make Sisyphos' seem easy by comparison. Often, but perhaps not always. Sostratos brightened a little. "If she puts in at Kos, we could go straight to Ptolemaios."

"So we could." Menedemos smiled a predatory smile. "Hard to find a better connection than that, isn't it?"

Before Sostratos could answer, a sailor came out from under the poop deck and called to Menedemos: "Skipper, we've plugged up the sprung seams as best we can, but we're still taking on some water."

"How much is 'some'?" Menedemos demanded. He waved a hand. "Never mind—I'll see for myself. Sostratos, take the steering oar again and keep us on our course." As soon as Sostratos had hold of the tiller, his cousin disappeared under the deck once more. When he emerged, his expression was as gloomy as the weather. "Pestilence take it, I don't *want* to have to make for Myndos."

Diokles said, "Skipper, why not fother a square of sailcloth smeared with pitch over the damage? War galleys will do that when they're rammed—if they have the time before they're rammed again, I mean."

"Hold the sailcloth against the ship with ropes, you mean?" Menedemos said, and the oarmaster dipped his head. Menedemos looked thoughtful. "I've never tried that. You know how to go about it?"

"I sure do," Diokles answered. Some men would say as much regardless of whether it was true. Sostratos didn't think the keleustes was one of them.

Evidently his cousin didn't, either. "All right. Take charge of it," Menedemos said. "I'll learn from you along with the sailors."

"Right," Diokles said. "Getting pitch on the sailcloth will be a bastard in this rain, but what can you do?" As some of the sailors started that messy job, he ordered the sail brailed up again and took all but four rowers off the oars. "Hold her course steady," he told Sostratos. "We don't want much speed on her right now, on account of we'll bring the boat alongside, and it'll have to keep up."

"I understand," Sostratos said.

The oarmaster called to the crew: "Now, who can swim? We have anybody who's ever dived for sponges?" One naked sailor raised a hand. Diokles waved to him. "Good for you, Moskhion." He spoke quietly to Sostratos: "He'll be swimming under the hull. He ought to have something for it."

"Of course." Sostratos dipped his head and raised his voice: "Two days' pay bonus for you, Moskhion."

With a grin, Moskhion went down into the boat, along with the sailcloth to be fothered over the sprung seams and the lines to make it fast to the hull. He had a line tied around his own middle, too, and carried one tied to a belaying pin on the *Aphrodite*. A couple of rowers kept the boat alongside the akatos. Another pair of sailors wrestled the sailcloth against the damaged planks. Sostratos got all this from Diokles and Menedemos' comments. He wished his cousin would take back the surviving steering oar so he could see for himself, but no such luck.

Splash! Moskhion went into the sea. A surprisingly short time later, he scrambled over the starboard gunwale. He undid the line from his own waist and wrapped the one he'd carried round another belaying pin. Then he hurried over to the port side, got down into the boat again, hauled in his safety line, and tied it round himself again.

After four trips under the hull, he said, "That ought to do it."

"Let's see what we've got, then." Menedemos hurried down off the poop deck to go below and see what the fothering had done. Over his shoulder, he added, "You earned your three drakhmai, Moskhion."

"Wasn't as hard as sponge diving," the sailor said. "There, you go down so deep, your ears hurt and your chest feels like somebody piled rocks on it—and you carry a rock yourself, to sink faster. You keep that up, you're an old man before you're forty. I'm glad to pull an oar instead."

When Menedemos came out from under the decking, he looked pleased. "Down to just a trickle now. Thanks, Diokles—I wouldn't have thought of that trick. Two days' bonus for you, too. Remember it, Sostratos."

As Sostratos dipped his head, Diokles said, "Thank you kindly, skipper."

"I'll take the steering oar now," Menedemos said, and he did. He raised his voice to call out to the crew: "Eight men a side on the oars. And we'll lower the sail from the yard again now. The sooner we get back to Kos, the sooner we can get patched up and be on our way again."

"I'm beginning to wonder if the Fates *ever* intend to let me get to Athens," Sostratos said. "Here's one more delay, and not even one where we can turn a profit."

"This one's not our fault, by the gods," Menedemos said. He raised his voice again: "Two days' pay to whoever spots the ship that hit us. When we find out who she is, we *will* take it up with Ptolemaios."

That had the sailors avidly peering out to sea all the way back to Kos, but no one spied the round ship. Maybe the weather was too dirty, or maybe she'd been making for Kalymnos, not Kos. "Maybe she sank," Sostratos said as the *Aphrodite* neared the port from which she'd set out early in the morning.

"Too much to hope for," Menedemos said. "I don't see any of Ptolemaios' war galleys on patrol outside the harbor. They ought to be. The weather isn't too nasty to keep Antigonos from giving him a nasty surprise if he's so inclined."

When the akatos came into the harbor itself, Sostratos exclaimed in surprise: "Where did all the ships go? There's space at half the quays, where this morning everything was tight as a—"

"Pretty boy's backside," Menedemos finished for him. That wasn't what he'd been about to say, nor anything close to it, but it did carry a similar meaning.

A fellow who wore a broad-brimmed hat to keep the rain off his face came up the pier to see who the newcomers were. Sostratos asked him the same question: "What happened to all the ships?"

The man pointed north and east. "They're all over there by the mainland. Ptolemaios used the cover of the storm to mount an attack on Halikarnassos."

MENEDEMOS SCOWLED AT the Koan carpenter. "What do you mean, you can't do anything for the *Aphrodite*?" he demanded.

"What I said," the Koan answered. "I usually mean what I say. We're all too busy repairing Ptolemaios' warships and transports to have any time left over to deal with a merchant galley."

"Well, what am I supposed to do till you find the time?" Menedemos said. "Hang myself?"

"It's all the same to me," the carpenter told him. The fellow picked up his mallet and drove home a treenail, joining a tenon and the plank into which it was inserted. Then he reached for another peg.

Muttering, Menedemos walked away. It was either that or snatch the mallet out of the Koan's hand and brain him with it. But that wouldn't do any good, either: it wouldn't get the man to work for him, which was what he needed.

In the harbor of Halikarnassos, carpenters were probably just as busy repairing Antigonos' war galleys. That also did Menedemos no good. He looked northeast, toward the city on the Karian mainland. A plume of smoke marked any city at any time; smoke was a distinctive city smell, along with baking bread and the less pleasant odors of dung and unwashed humanity. But a great cloud of black smoke rose from Halikarnassos now. Did it come from inside the place, or had the defenders managed to fire a palisade Ptolemaios' men had run up? From this distance, Menedemos couldn't tell.

He hoped Halikarnassos fell, and fell quickly. His reasons were entirely selfish. If Ptolemaios' ships weren't constantly limping back to the harbor of Kos with sprung timbers or smashed stemposts or out-and-out holes from stones thrown by engines, the carpenters here wouldn't be working on them at all hours of the day—and, sometimes, by torchlight at night. They would have a chance to fix the *Aphrodite*.

But Ptolemaios had hoped to seize the town by surprise. That hadn't worked. Now his men had to settle down to besiege it, which could take a long time. *Troy took Agamemnon and Odysseus and the rest of the Akhaioi ten years*, Menedemos thought, and wished he hadn't.

Things would go faster than that nowadays. Homer's hexameters said nothing of catapults that flung javelins or stone balls weighing thirty minai or more. Homer's hexameters, as a matter of fact, said next to nothing about siege warfare itself, even though the *Iliad* was about the siege of Troy. *Alexander's army could probably have stormed Hektor's city in ten days, not ten years*. Menedemos paused to scratch his head at that thought. Agamemnon and Akhilleus and the Aiantes and Diomedes and the rest might have been heroes, some of them the sons of gods, but they hadn't known a lot of things modern soldiers took for granted.

Alexander had admired Akhilleus. He'd taken a copy of the *Iliad* with him on his campaigns in the trackless east. Had he ever realized his men could have thrashed the warriors who'd sailed the black ships to Troy? Menedemos doubted it.

The next thing that went through his mind was, *I can't tell Sostratos about this*. His cousin might shrug and say he'd thought of the same thing years before. If Sostratos hadn't thought of it, though, Menedemos knew he would get no peace till his cousin had squeezed the whey out of every single related possibility. Keeping quiet was a better bet.

His own thoughts returned to the *Aphrodite*. He didn't want to try making those repairs himself. He wasn't worried about the steering oar; he was confident the amateur carpenters aboard the akatos could fashion a substitute. But the planking at the stern had taken even more damage than he'd thought, with seams sprung, tenons cracked, and mortises broken open for several cubits' distance from the actual point of the collision. He wanted those planks repaired properly. If the merchant galley started taking on seawater halfway across the Aegean . . . He shuddered. Not all ships came home.

I need real carpenters. But I can't get them. So what do I do now? Only one thing I can do: I have to wait till I can get them. That was logical. It made Menedemos hate logic.

He stiffened when a pentekonter that might have come straight out of the Catalogue of Ships glided into the harbor. Such single-banked galleys were the only warships Homer had known. These days, though, they were pirate ships, not naval vessels. No pirate would have been mad enough to raid Kos harbor. And this ship peaceably tied up at a quay and started disgorging hoplites.

An officer rushed up the quay and took charge of the soldiers—or rather, tried to, for they eyed him with contempt veiled as thinly as the most transparent Koan silk might have done. Only after several minutes' talk—and only after the officer pointed back into the city of Kos, as if threatening to call for reinforcements—did the newcomers let him lead them away.

"More of Polemaios' men, I'd say," Sostratos remarked.

"I'd say you're right," Menedemos agreed. "They're slipping out of Khalkis a shipload at a time and heading this way."

His cousin pointed toward the smoke rising from Halikarnassos. "If I were Ptolemaios"—he pronounced the ruler of Egypt's name with care, so Menedemos couldn't doubt which Macedonian he meant—"I'd send Polemaios' men across to the siege . . . and wouldn't it be a shame if they got used up?"

Menedemos didn't need to think about that for very long

before dipping his head. "I'd do the same. But Ptolemaios doesn't seem to want to. He's just getting them out of the polis, making them encamp outside the walls. That doesn't seem safe enough to me."

"Nor to me," Sostratos said. "If he trusted Polemaios"—he named Antigonos' nephew carefully, too—"that would be one thing. But Polemaios turned on Antigonos, and then he turned on Kassandros, too. Ptolemaios would have to be feebleminded to think the man won't also turn on him the moment he sees a chance."

"Ptolemaios isn't feebleminded," Menedemos said. "He's one very sharp fellow."

"He certainly is." Now Sostratos dipped his head. "That's why I'm assuming he's got somebody keeping an eye on Polemaios and his soldiers. Remember how Polemaios tried to see if we knew which of Ptolemaios' officers would take a bribe?"

"That I do," Menedemos answered. "I thought we'd be out of Kos and across the Aegean before it could possibly matter. But the stinking collision put paid to that, the collision and the fight across the channel. That cistern-arsed scow—I hope it *did* sink in the storm."

"Maybe it did," Sostratos said. "No sign of it here, anyhow."

"Gods only know how long *we'll* be stuck here, though." Menedemos drummed his fingers on the outside of his thigh.

His cousin's voice was tart: "Believe me, my dear, I like it no better than you do. I want to be in Athens. I burn to be in Athens. As a matter of fact, I burn to be *anywhere* but here. We ought to start going to the agora and selling what we can. We'll make *something* that way."

"Not much," Menedemos said in dismay. "Ships from Rhodes put in here all the time. We won't get much of a price for perfume or ink—and how can we hope to sell the silk we just bought, except at a loss? Koans can buy direct from the folk who make it; they don't need to deal with middlemen."

"I understand that, believe me," his cousin replied. "But we have to pay the sailors no matter where we are or what we're doing, and that talent we got from Ptolemaios is melting away like the fat in a fire at a sacrifice to the gods."

Instead of drumming his fingers, Menedemos suddenly snapped them. "I know what would bring us some money—we've got those two lion skins. No lions on Kos. Somewhere in town, there'll be a temple to Zeus. Can't go wrong with a real lion-skin mantle for the god's image."

"True." Sostratos smiled. "And you're right—we ought to get a good price for at least one of the hides. Good idea."

"Thanks," Menedemos said. "Now if only I could come up with eight or ten more, we'd be fine."

"Pity that fellow back in Kaunos didn't have a leopard skin to go with the others," Sostratos said. "I know where the temple to Dionysos is."

"Yes, I remember going by it, too, on the way from Ptolemaios' residence down here to the harbor." Menedemos shrugged. "All we can do, though, is make the best of what we've got."

As often happened in a town of Hellenes, finding out where Zeus' temple was cost Menedemos an obolos. Knowledge was a commodity like any other, and seldom given away for nothing. After he'd paid out the little silver coin, he was annoyed to discover that the temple lay only a couple of blocks beyond the market square. It was a small building, but elegant, in the modern Corinthian style, with columns whose capitals looked like inverted bells and were ornamented with acanthus leaves.

"Pretty," said Sostratos, who was fond of modern architecture.

"If you like that sort of thing," Menedemos said. "It looks busy to me. I like the good old Doric order better—no bases to the columns, and plain capitals that just go on about the business of holding up the architrave and the frieze. These fancy Corinthian columns"—he made a face—"they look like a garden that wants pruning."

"There's a difference between *plain* and *too plain*, if you ask me," Sostratos said. "And Doric columns are squat. These Corinthian ones can be taller for the same thickness. They make the building more graceful."

"More likely to fall down in an earthquake, you mean," Menedemos said. Then he and Sostratos both spat into the bosom of their tunics to avert the evil omen. In the lands around the Inner Sea, temblors came too often even without invitation.

A young priest greeted them as they came up the steps and walked into the shrine. "Good day," he said. "Have you come to offer a sacrifice to the god?"

"No." Menedemos tossed his head, then pointed toward the life-sized marble cult image of the king of the gods. "As a matter of fact, we've come to adorn your statue there. Show him, Sostratos."

"I will." His cousin undid the lashing that closed the leather sack he carried. He drew out the lion skin. Menedemos helped him spread it on the floor.

"Oh, very good!" The priest clapped his hands. "I'd loved to see that draped over the god's shoulders. But I fear I'm not the one with whom you'll have to haggle. You'll need to talk with my father, Diogenes. I'm Diomedon, by the way."

"Pleased to meet you." After giving his own name, Menedemos went on, "As I said, this is my cousin, Sostratos. Where is your father? Can you fetch him?"

"He's sacrificing at the altar behind the temple," Diomedon replied. "As soon as he's finished, I'm sure he'd be pleased to talk with you. I hope you can make a bargain. Painting isn't enough to make the statue very impressive, I'm afraid."

Smiling, Menedemos said, "I think I'd sooner dicker with you than with your father."

"Of course." Diomedon smiled, too. "You can tell I'm a soft touch. You won't have such an easy time with him as you would with me."

"Why is your altar at the back of the sacred precinct, instead of in front or inside the temple?" Sostratos asked. "The other two arrangements are more common."

Diomedon dipped his head. "I know they are. When this temple was going up—it's almost sixty years ago now, when this whole polis was being built—one of the priests went to Zeus' oracle at Dodona, and placing it there was part of the advice the god gave."

"Can't argue with that," Menedemos said. Sostratos looked as if he wouldn't have minded arguing about it, but a glance from Menedemos kept him quiet. They were here to sell the priests a lion skin, after all. Annoying or angering them wouldn't make that any easier.

"Here comes my father," Diomedon said.

The man who walked into the temple through a doorway next to the cult image was a grizzled version of Diomedon himself. Not noticing his son or the two Rhodians inside, Diogenes turned back to the man who had offered the sacrifice and said, "The god was glad to receive your offering."

"I was glad to give it," the man replied. He was so tall, he had to duck his head to get through that doorway. Menedemos nudged his cousin. Sostratos hadn't needed any nudging: he'd recognized Polemaios, too.

"Father," Diomedon called, "these men want to sell the temple a fine lion skin to drape over the god's shoulders."

"Do they?" Diogenes said, and then, "What makes it such a fine skin?" Hearing that, Menedemos knew he'd have a harder dicker with the older priest than he would have with his son.

Polemaios came up through the naos in Diogenes' wake. "Ah, the Rhodians," he rumbled. "I might have known."

"Hail," Menedemos said politely.

"You know these men, sir?" Diogenes asked Antigonos' nephew.

"Oh, yes—a pair of whipworthy rascals, if ever there were any," Polemaios replied, a nasty grin on his face. But then, relenting slightly, he went on, "They're the captain and toikharkhos who brought me here from Khalkis. On the sea, they know their business."

"Why were you sacrificing here, best one?" Sostratos asked.

Polemaios' grin turned into a scowl. "On the land, they want to know everybody else's business," he growled, and strode out of the temple.

"A bad-tempered man," Diogenes remarked, which would do for an understatement till a bigger one came along. The priest gathered himself. "I'm Diogenes, as my son will likely have told you." He waited for Menedemos and Sostratos to give him their names, then said, "So you've got a lion skin, do you? Let's have a look."

As they'd done for the younger priest, Menedemos and Sostratos displayed the hide. "Isn't it splendid, Father?" Diomedon said.

"Right now, I don't know whether it is or not," Diogenes answered. "What I do know is, you probably just tacked an extra twenty drakhmai on to the asking price." His gaze, half annoyed, half amused, swung to Menedemos. "Didn't he?"

"Sir, I don't know what you're talking about," Menedemos said, as innocently as he could.

Diogenes snorted. "Oh, no, not much you don't." He bent toward the hide, then tossed his head. "If I'm going to see how *splendid* it is, I want a proper light. Bring it out by the god's altar."

Fat-wrapped thighbones smoked on that altar. The hot, metallic smell of blood still filled the air. Flies buzzed as a couple of temple attendants butchered Polemaios' sacrificial offering. It was a bullock: the Macedonian could afford the finest. Menedemos said, "Didn't he take any of the meat for himself?"

"No," Diogenes said. "He gave the whole beast. Would you and your cousin care for a couple of gobbets? We wouldn't want it to go to waste."

"Thanks. That's most generous of you." Like most Hellenes, Menedemos seldom ate meat, though he liked it very much. Smiling, he said, "You'll make me feel like one of the beef-munching heroes in the *Iliad*." He cast about for some appropriate lines, and found them: "This is Agamemnon talking, remember?—

'For you are first when hearing of my feast
When we Akhaioi prepare a feast for the elders.
Then you are happy to eat roast meat or drink
A cup of wine sweet as honey for as long as you like.
But now you would happily see ten lines of Akhaioi
Get ahead of you and fight with pitiless bronze.' "

Diogenes smiled. "You know the poet well."

"I should hope so," Menedemos said. "My cousin here can give you practically anything new and fancy"—Sostratos stirred at that, but kept quiet—"but Homer's good enough for me." He didn't mention how fond he was of the bawdy Aristophanes; Diogenes didn't strike him as a man who would laugh at jokes about shitting oneself.

The priest asked, "What do you want for your lion skin?"

"Four minai," Menedemos answered.

"I'll give you three," Diogenes said briskly. They settled at three minai, fifty drakhmai almost at once. Diogenes wagged a finger at the bemused Menedemos. "You were expecting a long, noisy haggle, weren't you?"

"Well . . . yes, best one, since you ask," Menedemos admitted.

"I don't like them," Diogenes said. "Nothing but a waste of time. We would have come to the same place in half an hour, so why not use that half hour for something else?"

"I agree," Sostratos said. "But only a few men do, and so we spend a lot of time dickering. Some people make a game of it, as if it were dice or knucklebones."

"Foolishness," the priest of Zeus declared. Menedemos dipped his head, but he didn't really think Diogenes was right. Had the priest made an opening offer of two minai and bargained hard, he might have got his hide for three minai instead of three and a half. He'd saved time and cost himself money. Which was more important? Menedemos knew his own opinion.

Diomedon went off to get the payment from the temple's treasury. When he came back with it, Sostratos quickly counted out the drakhmai. Diogenes said, "You're a careful man. This is a fine trait in one so young."

"Thank you, sir," Sostratos said. "Can I have that sack to carry the coins in?"

"Of course," Diogenes replied. "I'll wrap up the meat in some cloth, too, so you won't get blood on your chiton."

"You're very kind," Sostratos said.

Having done what they'd set out to do, Menedemos and Sostratos left the temple. A tavern stood only a few doors away. "Shall we get our meat roasted there?" Menedemos asked. He leered at his cousin. "If the barmaids are pretty, maybe they can roast our meat, too."

"I knew you were going to say that," Sostratos told him.

"You read the poet all the time, do you? Where does Homer use a line like that?"

"I didn't say Homer was the *only* thing I read," Menedemos answered. "If Diogenes wanted to take it that way, though"—he shrugged—"I wouldn't argue with him."

"He's not so careful as he thinks he is," Sostratos said in a low voice. "Plenty of Athenian owls and turtles from Aigina and other coins a lot heavier than Ptolemaios' standard in among the ones his son gave us. By weight, we made more than we did by price alone."

"Good," Menedemos said. "I was hoping that would happen. To some people, especially people who don't travel, one drakhma's the same as another. You can do pretty well for yourself if you know better." He strode into the tavern. Sostratos followed.

"How d'you do, friends?" the tavernkeeper said, his Doric drawl so strong that even Menedemos, who used a similar dialect himself, had to smile. The fellow pointed to the cloth in which Sostratos carried the meat. "If you boys ain't been sacrificin', I'm downright crazy. Want me to cook that there stuff up for you?"

"If you please," Menedemos answered. He looked around. The barmaids were plain. He sighed to himself.

"I'd be right glad to," the taverner said, and then, with hardly any drawl at all, he added, "Two oboloi."

Sostratos set the meat on the counter. He spat a couple of small coins into the palm of his hand and put them beside the cloth-covered gobbets. "Here you are."

"Thank you kindly." The taverner dropped the money into a cashbox. He unwrapped the meat and dipped his head. "That'll roast just as nice as you please. You don't want to eat it all by its lonesome, now do you? You'll want to wash it down with some wine, eh? You boys look like you fancy the best. I've got some fine Khian—can't get better this side of the gods' ambrosia, and that's a fact."

What that was, without a doubt, was a lie. In a tavern like this one, the proprietor would charge strangers and the naive three times as much for a local wine as he could hope to get if they knew what it really was. Menedemos tossed his head.

"Just a cup of your ordinary, if you please," he said.

"Same for me," Sostratos said.

"Whatever you like, friends," the taverner told them, and dipped out two cups of some of the nastiest wine Menedemos had ever drunk. It was, to begin with, shamelessly watered, but it would have tasted worse if it were stronger, as it was well on the way to becoming vinegar. He couldn't even throw it in the taverner's face and walk out, because the man had skewered the meat and set it over his fire. The savory smell helped make Menedemos forget the sour tang of the stuff in the cup.

"Don't leave it on the flames too long," Sostratos told the taverner. "The gods may like their portion burned black, but I don't."

"I reckon I know how to cook up a piece of meat, I do," the fellow said.

"He's going to get it too done," Sostratos grumbled. "I know he will."

"Even if he does, you're still ahead of the game," Menedemos answered. "It wasn't our sacrifice."

The tavernkeeper took the meat off the fire and put the chunks on a couple of plates, which he set in front of the Rhodians. "There you go, friends. Enjoy it, now."

Sostratos blew on his gobbet, then cut it with the knife he wore on his belt. "Gray clear through," he complained. "I like it pink."

Before Menedemos could answer, a skinny man tapped his elbow and said, "That's a big chunk of meat you've got there, O best one. Could you spare a bite for a hungry fellow?"

Meat from a sacrifice was supposed to be shared. Menedemos dipped his head. "Here you go, pal." He cut off a strip and gave it to the man.

Another customer came over to Sostratos and said, "If you don't fancy the way your meat's cooked, sir, I'll help you get rid of it."

That made Sostratos laugh. He said, "I'll bet you will." But, as Menedemos had, he gave some to the man. They both ended up serving out about half the meat they'd brought into the tavern. At last, Menedemos got to eat some. He sighed at the luxurious taste and feel of hot fat in his mouth. *If the warriors in front of Troy ate beef all the time, no wonder they were so strong*, he thought.

"More wine?" the tavernkeeper asked.

"No, thanks," Menedemos and Sostratos said together, in tones of such emphatic rejection that the tavernkeeper looked wounded. Menedemos only snorted. Either the fellow was playing for sympathy or he didn't know what slop he'd just served them. Neither possibility impressed the Rhodian, who turned to his cousin and pointed to the door. Sostratos dipped his head. They left.

As they headed toward the harbor, Sostratos said, "You weren't sharing out drakhmai the way we shared out the meat, were you?"

"No, by the gods." Menedemos held up the leather sack Diomedon had given him. "Unopened, unslit, unplundered, still a maiden."

"Very good." Sostratos made as if to applaud, then gestured for Menedemos to get the money out of sight. As Menedemos lowered the sack to his side once more, Sostratos went on, "I do wonder why Polemaios was sacrificing there."

"Of course you do, since he wouldn't say. It is an interesting question, isn't it?" Menedemos thought for a couple of paces, then suggested, "In thanks for getting here to Kos in one piece?"

"No. He *would* have said if it were something simple like that." Sostratos' reply was quick and certain. "And you saw him on the ship. You saw him when he met Ptolemaios, too. He wouldn't waste a bullock on anything like running away. He had that *done* to him. He's a man who wants to *do* things himself."

"Well . . . you're probably right," Menedemos said. "Which leads to the next question: what does he want to do, and to whom?"

"Sure enough," Sostratos agreed. "I'll tell you one thing, though."

"Only one?" Menedemos said.

His cousin ignored that, continuing, "Ptolemaios is a lot more interested in the answer than we are." Precise as usual, he checked himself: "Perhaps he's not more interested in it, but he's more concerned about it."

"You're right," Menedemos said. They went on down to the *Aphrodite* together.

SOSTRATOS SUCKED the flesh from the tail of a roasted prawn, then tossed the piece of shell on the floor of Kleiteles' andron. "Another lovely opson, best one," he told the Rhodian proxenos.

On the couch next to his, Menedemos dipped his head. "Your hospitality almost makes being stranded here worthwhile."

"You're very kind, my friends," the olive-oil merchant said. In the cage in the corner of the men's chamber, his trained jackdaw hopped up and down its ladder, carrying the toy shield in its beak.

Pointing to the gray-eyed bird, Sostratos said, "We feel caged ourselves. You're a Koan. You have connections here that we don't. Can you find us a ship's carpenter? He'd be well paid for his work, believe me."

"I do believe you," the proxenos said. "But I don't think it can be done, not till Ptolemaios takes Halikarnassos."

"You think the city will fall, then?" Sostratos said.

Kleiteles dipped his head. "Don't you? Antigonos hasn't even tried to relieve it. From what I hear, most of his army is away in the east, fighting what's-his-name—you know, the fellow who set himself up in Babylon last year."

"Seleukos," Sostratos said.

"That's the name," Kleiteles agreed.

"You can count on Sostratos to remember such things," Menedemos said. Sostratos couldn't tell whether his cousin meant that for a sneer or a compliment. He'd heard both from Menedemos' lips.

Kleiteles said, "Good thing somebody can keep all these generals straight. They say Antigonos sent his son Demetrios off to fight, uh, Seleukos. I bet he wishes he still had Polemaios on his side now."

"I don't know," Sostratos said. "You haven't met Polemaios, have you?" He waited for the proxenos to toss his head, then added, "I don't think he can be on anyone's side except his own."

Menedemos said, "Sostratos and I find all sorts of things to argue about, but he's dead right here. If Polemaios thinks you're in his way, he'll give you the fastest, hardest knee in the nuts you'd ever get from anybody."

"But Ptolemaios wanted him here, and wanted him here badly enough to send the two of you after him," Kleiteles said. "And more of Polemaios' men keep coming in from Euboia: another two shiploads of them today, in fact. Ptolemaios usually knows what he's doing."

"Usually," Sostratos agreed. "If he's not keeping an eye on what his new ally's up to, though, he's not as smart as everybody says he is. He—"

He fell silent, for a couple of slaves came in to clear away the supper dishes and clean up the mess on the floor. You never could tell who paid slaves to listen. Their entrance also startled the jackdaw. The shield fell out of its beak and clanked against the ladder in the cage. *"Chak!"* it cried, spreading its wings. *"Chaka-chaka-chack!"*

"It's all right, you stupid bird," Kleiteles said. The jackdaw calmed when the slaves went away, but screeched again when they came back with wine, water, a mixing bowl, and cups.

Sostratos imagined Polemaios as a bird in a cage, too, only he wouldn't be a jackdaw. He'd be a hawk of some kind, all beak and talons and glaring eyes. If anyone tried to loose him, would he do anything but fly straight at the hawker's face?

Kleiteles dipped out a little neat wine for his guests. Sostratos poured a libation to Dionysos and drank almost absently. Once the mixed wine—not too strong—started going around, he did his best to bring his mind back to the andron. He couldn't know what was going on inside Ptolemaios' residence and whatever house Antigonos' nephew was using. He couldn't know, but wished he could.

He suddenly noticed the Rhodian proxenos eyeing him. "The last time we drank together, you talked about gryphons as though you'd seen one just the other day," Kleiteles said. "What other strange things do you know?"

Menedemos snickered. "Now you've gone and done it," he said.

"And to the crows with *you*, my dear cousin," Sostratos said, which only made his dear cousin laugh out loud. He thought for a bit, then went on, "Herodotos says a Persian king sent some Phoenicians to sail all the way around Africa. He says they went so far south that, when they were sailing east around the bottom of it, they had the sun on their left hand."

"That's impossible," the proxenos exclaimed.

"I think so, too," Menedemos said, taking a pull at his wine. He pointed an accusing finger at Sostratos. "I'll bet you believe it."

"I don't know," Sostratos said. "If it happened at all, it happened a long time ago. And we all know how sailors like to make up stories. But that's such an odd thing to make up, you do have to wonder."

"Maybe *you* do," Menedemos said.

"It's impossible," Kleiteles repeated. "How could it be?"

"If the earth is a sphere, and not flat like most people say . . ." Sostratos tried to visualize it. He might have done better if he hadn't been drinking wine at the end of a long day. He shrugged and gave up. "I don't know."

Menedemos emptied his cup, set it on the table in front of him, and yawned. "Maybe it's that meat we ate," he said. "It can make you feel heavy."

"I told my slave women to go to your bedrooms," Kleiteles said. "If you're too sleepy to enjoy them, you can always send them back to the women's quarters."

"My dear fellow!" Menedemos exclaimed. "I didn't say we were dead." He turned to Sostratos. "Isn't that right?"

What Sostratos wanted to do was go to sleep. Admitting as much would make him look less virile than Menedemos. He didn't want Kleiteles thinking that of him. Even more to the point, he didn't want Menedemos thinking that of him. His cousin would never let him live it down. "I should hope it is!" he said, while he really hoped he sounded hearty enough to be convincing.

He must have, for the Rhodian proxenos chuckled indulgently and said, "Have fun, boys. When I was your age, I was that cockproud, too." He sighed; he was feeling the wine, even if it was well watered. "Can't get it up as often as I used to, worse luck."

"Onions," Menedemos said. "Eggs."

"Mussels and crab meat," Sostratos added.

"I've tried 'em." Kleiteles' shrug said the sovereign remedies had done no good.

"Pepper and nettle seed," Sostratos suggested.

The proxenos looked thoughtful. "That might be worth a go. It'd be bound to heat up my mouth and my stomach, so why not my vein, too?" He used a common nickname for the prong. Kleiteles glanced toward Sostratos and Menedemos. "Nettle seed is easy enough to come by, but pepper's foreign. I don't suppose you've got any in your akatos, do you?"

"I wish we did," Sostratos said. He looked at Menedemos. "Pepper, balsam—all sorts of interesting things come out of the east. We ought to think about that. Not this sailing season, of course," he added hastily. "Next one."

His cousin laughed. "You mean you don't want to sail off for Sidon and Byblos tomorrow morning? I can't imagine why."

"We are going to Athens," Sostratos said firmly. "If we ever find a carpenter, that is." He got to his feet. "And I am going to bed."

Kleiteles led Sostratos and Menedemos back to the guest rooms. "Good night," he said. He doused one of the torches burning in the courtyard in the fountain and carried the other one upstairs. Darkness abruptly descended. Sostratos had to grope for the latch.

To his relief, a lamp was burning inside. The proxenos' slave woman lay on the bed waiting for him. "Hail," she said, yawning. "You spent so long in the andron, I almost fell asleep."

Sostratos didn't want to apologize to a slave, but he didn't want a quarrel, either. Trying to avoid both, he asked, "How are you tonight, Thestylis?"

"Sleepy, like I told you," she answered. But she added, "It's nice that you remember my name," and smiled at him. The smile was probably mercenary. Still, he preferred it to a scowl.

"I don't think I'll forget you," he said. He remembered all

the women he'd bedded. He remembered all sorts of things, but Thestylis didn't need to know that.

Her smile softened. "What a sweet thing to say," she told him. "Nobody ever told me anything like that before. Most men, it's just, 'Take off your clothes and bend over,' and they never even find out what your name is, let alone remember it." The light from the lamp suddenly sparkled off tears in her eyes.

"Don't cry," Sostratos said.

"I didn't think somebody being kind could hurt so much," she mumbled, and buried her face in the cloth covering the mattress. A muffled sob rose.

"Don't cry," Sostratos repeated. He got down on the bed beside her and awkwardly patted her hair. Even as he did so, he wondered if her tears were a ploy to pry an extra obolos or two out of him. Anyone who dealt with slaves had to make such calculations. Slaves, he knew perfectly well, made calculations of their own about free men.

She sobbed again, and made as if to push him away. "Now see what you made me do," she said, as if her tears were his fault. Maybe, in a way, they were.

"If you want to go back up to the women's quarters tonight, that's all right," he said. Why not? He *was* tired, and she'd be there tomorrow. And so would he, because he still didn't know when a ship's carpenter would be able to work on the *Aphrodite*—or when Menedemos would get so fed up, he'd have some of the sailors make repairs that might at least carry the merchant galley to another, less crowded, polis.

Thestylis twisted. Now he could see her face, and the alarm on it. She tossed her head. "I don't dare do that," she said. "Who knows what Kleiteles would do to me?" More tears slid down her face, leaving bright tracks in the lamplight.

He leaned over and kissed her. If she'd pushed him away then, he would have lain down beside her and gone to sleep. But her arms went around him. His hand closed on her breast through the wool of her long chiton. She sighed, deep in her throat, and squeezed him tighter. Again, he wondered if she really meant it. But with his own excitement rising, he didn't much care. He reached under the hem of her tunic, his hand sliding up the smooth flesh of her thigh to the secret place between her legs. The flesh there was smooth, too; she'd singed away the hair with a lamp.

Before long, her tunic and his both lay on the floor. He kissed her breasts. She sighed again as her nipples grew stiff to his caresses. He grew stiff, too, and took her hand and set it on his manhood. She stroked him, easing his foreskin back.

"Here," he said. "Ride me like a racehorse."

"All right." She straddled him. He held his erection as she impaled herself on him. As she began to move, he squeezed her breasts and leaned up to tease their tips with his tongue. "Ah," she said softly, and moved faster.

At the end, she threw back her head and made a little mewling cry. By the way she squeezed him inside herself, he thought her pleasure real. His hands clutched her meaty backside as his seed shot into her.

She toppled down onto him, all warm and soft and sweaty, as he was sweaty, too. But then, even when he might have started a second round, she scrambled off, took the chamber pot out from under the bed, and squatted over it, her legs splayed wide apart. A wet plop and a muttered, "Well, that's most of it," said what she was doing.

"I'll give you half a drakhma," Sostratos said. "You don't need to tell Kleiteles you got it from me."

"Thank you, sir," Thestylis said, reaching for her tunic. "You *are* a kind man. Some people, you might as well be a piece of meat, for all they care about what you feel." It wasn't a complaint about men's treatment of women worthy of those Euripides had put in the mouths of his female characters, but sounded heartfelt even so.

"Don't put the chamber pot away," Sostratos said. After using it, he put on his chiton, too. Thestylis would be lying beside him if he wanted that second round in the morning. Meanwhile . . . Meanwhile, he yawned and lay down. No need to wrap himself in his himation on a warm summer night. "Blow out the lamp."

She did, then got into bed in the dark. Sostratos patted her, yawned again, and fell asleep.

* * *

Menedemos crouched under the *Aphrodite*'s poop deck, mournfully eyeing the sprung planks, the sailcloth stuffed between them, the broken tenons, the mortises that had turned into actual breaks in the timbers. He cursed the blundering round ship that had run into the akatos in the rain. He cursed Ptolemaios, too, for his siege of Halikarnassos, and for good measure cursed every carpenter in Kos.

When he came out from under the poop deck, he didn't duck far enough and, not for the first time, banged his head. That left him cursing life in general. With some sympathy, Sostratos said, "I've done that, too."

Well, of course you have, Menedemos thought sourly. *You're taller than I am, and clumsier, too.* He rubbed his head before speaking. That was probably just as well, for all that came out of his mouth was, "I know."

"What do you think?" Sostratos asked. "Have you changed your mind?"

"I only wish I had," Menedemos answered. "There's too much damage for me to want to risk the ship going anywhere very far, and too much for us to do the repairs ourselves. Resourceful Odysseus made a boat starting with nothing but logs, but we can't quite imitate him." He stroked his chin. "Maybe we could get up to Myndos. Maybe . . ."

Sostratos tossed his head. "I don't think that will do us any good. Halikarnassos is still holding out, but Ptolemaios' men just took Myndos."

"Which means the carpenters there will be busy working for him, same as the ones here." Menedemos rubbed his scalp again. The bump he'd got wasn't the only thing making his head ache.

"That's right," Sostratos said.

"When did you hear that about Myndos?" Menedemos asked. "It's news to me."

"Just now, as a matter of fact." His cousin pointed to a couple of men walking along the quay. "They were talking about it. If you hadn't been all muffled down below, you would have heard them, too."

With a sigh, Menedemos said, "Well, let's gather up our

perfumes and such and head for the market square. Maybe we'll do enough business to break even."

"Maybe." Sostratos didn't sound as if he believed it. For that matter, Menedemos didn't believe it, either. Sostratos put the best face on things he could: "The more we sell, the less we lose, even if we don't break even."

To Menedemos' surprise, they promptly sold four jars of perfume to a fellow with his right arm bandaged and in a sling. He had scarred shins, too, and a scar seaming his chin, and was missing the lobe of his left ear. "I've got to keep my hetaira sweet on me," he said. "You've got to give 'em presents, or they forget all about you, and how was I supposed to give her presents when I was sitting in a tent in front of Halikarnassos?"

"You weren't sitting in a tent all the time." Menedemos pointed to the soldier's wounded arm.

"No, and I'm almost not sorry I got hurt, you know what I mean?" the fellow said. Menedemos dipped his head, though he thought, *Whether you know it or not, you mean that hetaira's got her hooks into you deep.* He recognized the symptoms from experience. The soldier went on, "Now that I'm back here, at least she can't forget I'm alive."

Sostratos pointed to his arm, too. "How did it happen?"

"One of those things," the scarred man said with a shrug. "We tried scaling ladders. I was moving up towards one of 'em when I got shot. Might've been just as well, too, on account of I heard later they tipped that ladder over with a bunch of men on it. If I'd been near the top . . ." He grimaced. "It's a long fall."

"Have you got any idea how much longer the siege will take?" Menedemos asked.

"Not me, best one." The soldier tossed his head. "We're liable to still be at it by the time this heals"—he wiggled the fingers sticking out of the bandage—"and I've got to go back to work. That place has strong walls, and you might think old One-Eye's men in there were all citizens by the way they're fighting."

Menedemos grunted. That was exactly what he didn't want to hear. Ptolemaios' mercenary took the perfume and left the agora. He wasn't worried about the siege's going on forever; he just wanted to enjoy the holiday his wound had given him.

Menedemos wished he could take such a bright view of things himself.

A juggler strolled past, keeping a fountain of six or eight knives and cups and leather balls in the air. Someone tossed him a coin. He caught it and popped it into his mouth without missing a beat. Menedemos was fond of such shows. Most days, he would have thrown the fellow an obolos, too. Today, he let the juggler go by unrewarded. The man shot him a reproachful look. He stared stonily back. With news like that which he'd just got, he felt he needed to hang on to every bit of silver he had.

Sostratos said, "Not Myndos, then. Maybe Kalymnos. It's not much farther. Or we could go back to Knidos and use the wind instead of our rowers."

"I get more tempted with every day that goes by," Menedemos admitted. "We did make it back here from the middle of the strait between Kalymnos and the mainland. So I suppose we have a good chance of getting away with one more trip. But even so . . ." He scowled. "I don't like to take the chance."

"You're the captain," his cousin said. "I suppose I ought to be grateful you're more careful at sea than you are on land."

"Ha," Menedemos said in a hollow voice. Sostratos often twitted him harder than that. He raised his voice: "Perfume from fine Rhodian roses! Balsam from Engedi—makes a fine medicine or a wonderful incense. Best quality ink! Crimson dye!"

He and Sostratos sold some ink and some balsam by the time the sun sank toward the western horizon. They sold some more perfume, too, and a small-time silk merchant bought some of their dye. They didn't come close to making the mina and a half their crew cost them every day.

As they walked back toward the harbor, Sostratos said, "I hope we won't have to start selling the silk we bought from Pixodaros."

"We'd better not!" Menedemos said. "The only way we can unload it here where they make it is to sell at a loss. We've been over that road before."

"Don't remind me," Sostratos said. "But if we have to get silver to keep the sailors paid . . ." He kicked at the dirt.

"Nothing new here," Diokles said when they came aboard

the *Aphrodite*. But then the oarmaster tossed his head. "No, I take that back. One of Ptolemaios' fives limped back into the harbor a good cubit and a half lower in the water than she should have been."

Menedemos cursed. "One more thing to keep the stinking carpenters busy." He turned to Sostratos. "I wish we'd gone straight up to the proxenos' house. That's the kind of news I didn't want to hear."

"Can't be helped, my dear," his cousin answered. "It would have happened whether we heard about it or not."

That was true, but did little to console Menedemos. He took a couple of steps toward the gangplank to head back into the city with the last of the light when Diokles said, "Somebody's coming this way—coming in a hurry, too."

"By the dog of Egypt!" Sostratos exclaimed. "That's Polemaios!"

The big man trotted up the quay toward the akatos. He paused halfway there to look back over his shoulder, as if fearing pursuit. Seeing none, he hurried on. "Hail, Menedemos," he said, panting. "You must take me away from here, and quickly."

"What?" Menedemos said, startled. "Why?"

Antigonos' nephew scowled. "I'll tell you why. That whoremaster of a Ptolemaios thinks I've been spreading silver around to some of his officers, to turn 'em against him and towards me, that's why. . . . All lies, of course," he added after a couple of damning heartbeats.

"Of course," Menedemos said, not believing him for a moment.

"Will you get me out of this place?" Polemaios demanded. "By the gods, I'll pay my fare and more. Name your price. I'll meet it. I'll drown you in drakhmai, so long as you get me out of that old bastard's reach."

Ever so slightly, Sostratos tossed his head. Here, Menedemos didn't need his cousin's advice. He said, "I'm sorry, best one, but we're laid up ourselves. A polluted round ship rammed us, and we're still waiting for repairs. If we leave the harbor, we're liable to sink before we've gone even a stadion." That exaggerated things, but Polemaios wouldn't know it. With a wave, Menedemos went on, "Besides, you can see for yourself that most of my crew's not aboard. How could I hope to sail?"

Polemaios growled, deep in his chest, the sound a desperate hunted animal might make. He looked back toward the center of town again, then howled out a curse, for a squad of hoplites approached at a quick march. "Hide me!" he said, and then, "Too late. They've seen me." He yanked his sword from its scabbard.

The soldiers wore helmets and corselets, some of bronze, others of linen. They carried shields and long spears. They could have made quick work of the unarmored Macedonian. But their leader, an officer with a crimson-dyed crest nodding above his helm, politely dipped his head to Polemaios. "What point to fighting, most noble one?" he said. "Why don't you come along with us till this misunderstanding is sorted out?"

Menedemos thought Polemaios would make them kill him, but the big man grabbed hope like a drowning man seizing a spar. "Let it be as you say," he said, and sheathed the sword again. At a word from the officer, the ruler of Egypt's soldiers surrounded him.

Then the captain eyed Menedemos and Sostratos. "Why don't you Rhodians come along with us, too, so we can find out just what exactly was going on here?"

He phrased it as a request, but it was an order, and Menedemos knew it. He walked up the gangplank, Sostratos behind him. The truth lay on their side. But would Ptolemaios believe it?

PTOLEMAIOS LOOKED SEARCHINGLY FROM Sostratos to Menedemos and back again. Sostratos did his best to look back without flinching. He'd thought some flunky of Ptolemaios' would question them; he hadn't expected to be brought before the ruler of Egypt himself. "So," Ptolemaios rasped, "you say you weren't dickering over the price you wanted for getting him out of my reach?"

"That's right, sir," Sostratos answered. "Besides, even if we'd wanted to—which we didn't, as my cousin and I have told you over and over—we couldn't have gone anywhere with Polemaios."

A torch behind Ptolemaios' head crackled. The sun had set, but torches and lamps made the andron of the ruler of Egypt's residence almost as bright as day. Ptolemaios leaned forward, thrusting his blunt-featured, strong-chinned face toward the two Rhodians. "Why not?" he said.

"Because we've got sprung planking, that's why not," Menedemos exclaimed, his temper slipping. "If you don't believe us, ask any of your carpenters. We've been screaming at them for most of a month now, but they won't give us the time of day—they're too busy with your polluted ships to care a fig about ours."

Sostratos feared his cousin had spoken too boldly. Ptolemaios, though, only dipped his head, remarking, "You say what's on your mind, don't you?"

"Yes, sir," Menedemos answered. "If we could have got our ship repaired, we would have been long gone from here, and then you wouldn't be wondering if we were plotting with Antigonos' nephew."

"Suppose I ask my shipwrights if you've been coming by?" Ptolemaios said.

"By the dog of Egypt, go ahead," Menedemos burst out. Again, Sostratos wondered whether he should have used that particular oath to the ruler of Egypt. Menedemos went on, "Your men will tell you we've been in their hair like lice."

"Heh." Ptolemaios scratched reminiscently. "I've been lousy a time or two—more than a time or two. I hate those little bastards." He called for one of his men—a soldier, not a servitor—and spoke to him in a low voice. The fellow dipped his head. He hurried away. Ptolemaios went on, "We'll see if you're telling the truth."

If the Rhodians hadn't been, that would have alarmed them. As things were, Menedemos said only, "Fine."

"What's going to happen to Polemaios now?" Sostratos

asked, that being what was uppermost in *his* mind.

Ptolemaios scowled. "That son of a whore was trying to win over my officers with sweet talk and bribes. I took him in, a stray dog, and he used me so? I'll give him no bites at all, only a sip: he drinks hemlock tomorrow." He laid the full weight of his formidable stare on Sostratos. "And what do you think of that?"

"May I watch, sir?" Sostratos blurted.

"What?" Ptolemaios blinked. Whatever sort of answer he'd expected, that wasn't it. He stared more grimly than ever. "Why?"

Sostratos wished he'd thought more before speaking. He answered as best he could: "Because I studied at the Lykeion in Athens; and I've talked with men from the Academy, the school Platon founded; and I've read Platon's tale of how Sokrates died. I'd like to see it for myself, if I could."

"I've read the *Phaidon*, too," Ptolemaios said, which surprised Sostratos in turn; the ruler of Egypt looked like a warrior, not a man who'd studied philosophy. And Ptolemaios surprised him all over again by continuing, "That man wrote like a god."

"Y-yes," Sostratos stammered; his amazement came not because he disagreed but because bluff Ptolemaios was voicing such an opinion.

Going on in the same vein, the Macedonian marshal sighed and said, "I wish I would have met him. I was nineteen or twenty when he died, but I didn't get down to Athens till . . . later."

Till after the battle of Khaironeia, Sostratos realized he meant: *after Philip of Macedon crushed Athens as a power*. He eyed the ruler of Egypt. Khaironeia had been fought three years before he himself was born. So much had happened since—Alexander's astonishing career and the wars of his successors—that seeing a man who'd fought there seemed a surprise, too. *He's only a few years older than my father*, Sostratos reminded himself. But Ptolemaios had been so many places, done so much . . .

Ptolemaios' thoughts had traveled down a different road.

He shook a forefinger at Sostratos and said, "I warn you, it's not as neat as Platon tells it."

"Sir?" Lost in his own musings, Sostratos had dropped the thread of the conversation.

"Hemlock," Ptolemaios said. "Are you sure you want to see it?"

"Oh," Sostratos said, and then, after some thought, "Yes. Yes, I am. I'd . . . like to know what Sokrates went through."

"Ah," Ptolemaios said. "I can understand that. It may be foolishness, but I can understand it. All right, young fellow. I'm keeping Antigonos' nephew in the house next door to this one. You be here early tomorrow morning and you'll see what you want to see. But don't dawdle; my men won't wait. Bargain?"

"Bargain," Sostratos said at once. "Thank you, sir."

"Don't thank me, not till after you know what you talked yourself into." Ptolemaios turned to Menedemos. "What about you? Do you want to watch Polemaios die, too?"

Menedemos tossed his head. "Not me. What I want is a carpenter."

As if on cue, the man Ptolemaios had sent out came back into the andron. "Well?" the ruler of Egypt barked at him.

"Your Excellency," the man replied, "the shipwrights all say these Rhodians have been clinging to them like leeches in a swamp."

"Oh, they do, do they?" Ptolemaios rumbled. His messenger dipped his head. The marshal pointed at Menedemos. "You'll have your woodworker tomorrow. You can keep an eye on him instead of on Polemaios."

"Thank you very much," Menedemos said. "I think that's a better bargain."

"You and your cousin both want to see things for yourselves," Ptolemaios said. "You just want to see different things, that's all." He gestured toward the doorway of the andron. "Go on, get out of here. I've wasted too much time on you."

"May we beg a torch, to light our way back to the ship?" Sostratos asked.

"Take one from the courtyard." Ptolemaios gestured again,

even more imperiously than before. Sostratos retreated, his cousin on his heels.

Outside, a little twilight still lingered: enough, with the torch, to help the Rhodians find their way. As soon as they were well away from Ptolemaios' residence, Menedemos burst out, "Are you out of your mind?"

"What?" As Sostratos tossed his head, he stepped in something damp and nasty. He scrapped his foot in the dirt to clean it. "No, just curious. Ptolemaios understood that. He understood it better than I thought he would."

"He understood it wouldn't cost him anything to humor a zany," Menedemos said.

Sostratos tossed his head again. "No, I don't believe that's what he was thinking. He's read Platon himself. I never would have guessed that of a Macedonian, even if Aristoteles did teach Alexander."

His cousin walked along for a couple of paces before saying, "Well, maybe it worked out for the best. You did convince him we weren't plotting with Polemaios. And"—Menedemos did a couple of dance steps, his shadow swooping wildly in the torchlight—"we'll get the *Aphrodite* fixed up."

"That's good," Sostratos agreed. "That's very good. We'll finally be able to press on towards Athens."

"Toward Miletos first," Menedemos said as they started up the quay. Sostratos swallowed a sigh.

"Gods be praised!" Diokles said when they came aboard the merchant galley once more. "When the soldiers took you away, I didn't know what would happen next."

"As a matter of fact, neither did we," Sostratos said. "It's all right, though."

"It's better than all right," Menedemos added. "We get a carpenter tomorrow."

"*Euge!*" Diokles exclaimed. Then he asked, "What does Polemaios get?"

"Something to drink," Sostratos answered. "He won't be thirsty afterwards, either."

"Something to . . . ? Oh." The oarmaster didn't need long to figure that out. "Well, can't say I'm surprised. You play those games and lose, you pay."

"Just so," Sostratos said, and waited for Menedemos to tell Diokles and the handful of sailors aboard the merchant galley what he'd be doing in the morning.

But Menedemos said only, "Kleiteles will be wondering what happened to us. I'll have to send someone over there tomorrow and let him know. I wouldn't have minded another round or two with his slave woman, either." He shrugged. "Well, it'll be a hard deck tonight, not a soft bed and a wench. Can't be helped, I suppose." He lay down on the planking as calmly as if there were no such things as beds or women within a thousand stadia.

Diokles went forward to sleep sitting on a rower's bench and leaning against the planking, as he always did when aboard ship. Sostratos took off his chiton, folded it up for a pillow, and lay down beside Menedemos, wrapping a himation around himself for warmth. "Good night, my dear," he murmured.

"Good night," his cousin answered. "You'd better not sleep late tomorrow, or you'll miss your big chance."

He meant it sarcastically, which didn't mean he was wrong. Sostratos said, "You usually wake before I do. Give me a shake if I'm still sleeping."

"All right, though why you'd want to watch such a thing . . ." Menedemos said no more, but rolled onto his side with his back to Sostratos. In a few minutes, he was snoring. Sostratos stayed awake a little longer, but not much.

Next thing he knew, Menedemos' prodding hand was on his shoulder. The sun hadn't risen. Sostratos needed a moment to remember why his cousin was getting him up so early. When he did, he stopped the feeble complaints he'd been making and said, "Thank you. I know what needs doing now."

He gulped bread and cheese and wine, threw on his tunic, and hurried into the city of Kos. When he got to the street on which Ptolemaios was staying, he had no trouble figuring out which of the houses next door to the ruler of Egypt's residence held Antigonos' nephew. That one had more soldiers guarding it than did Ptolemaios' house itself. How many of Polemaios' men had come from Khalkis to Kos? Enough to leave Ptolemaios nervous, however calm things seemed at the moment.

Sostratos gave his name to one of the guards in front of the door. "Tell me who your father is, too," the fellow said. When Sostratos did, the soldier dipped his head. "All right, you are who you say you are." He rapped on the door. "Open up in there. That Rhodian's here."

The man who did open the door was another soldier, not a house slave. "Come along with me," he said briskly, and led Sostratos to the andron. The courtyard was also full of armed men. The soldiers in the andron were older, and looked to be of higher rank. *Ptolemaios' witnesses*, Sostratos thought. One chair among them remained empty. Sostratos' escort waved him into it. He tossed his head in bemusement as he sat down: the ruler of Egypt thought of everything.

Polemaios strode into the andron a few minutes later. He wasn't bound or fettered, and the soldiers flanking him looked very alert. A supper couch with a small table beside it waited for him. As he reclined on the couch, he glared at the men who'd come to see him die. "To the crows with all of you," he said harshly, and then, catching sight of Sostratos, "One more vulture waiting for my carrion, eh?"

Before Sostratos could find any words, a man brought in a plain earthenware cup and set it on the table. He started to slip out of the room. "Wait," Polemaios said. "Have I got enough here to pour out a libation before I drink?"

With a start, Sostratos recalled that Sokrates had asked the same question. His gaoler had said no. This fellow dipped his head. "Go on, if you care to. There's enough in there to do in an elephant."

"Taking no chances, eh?" Antigonos' nephew said, not without pride. He lifted the cup and spilled out a few drops, as if he were offering a little wine to Dionysos. Then he drank the poison down. As he lowered the cup, he made a horrible face. "Oh, by the gods, that's vile stuff. You'd never catch me drinking it more than once."

"*Euge!* Bravely done," murmured the officer sitting next to Sostratos. The Rhodian was inclined to agree. Polemaios might have earned every bit of what he was getting, but that didn't mean he wasn't dying well.

And he hadn't quite finished. He splashed some of the dregs

from the cup onto the floor of the andron, saying, "This for Ptolemaios the beautiful." He might have been playing kottabos and praising a pretty boy.

A couple of Ptolemaios' officers laughed out loud. Their master was a great many things, most of them praiseworthy, but hardly beautiful. *In his own blocky way*, Sostratos thought, *he must have made as unlovely a youth as I did.*

Polemaios glared at the fellow who'd fetched in the hemlock. "I don't feel anything," he said. "What do I do now?"

"Walk around till your legs get heavy, if you like," the man answered. "Then just lie down. It *will* work."

Antigonos' nephew muttered something nasty under his breath. He stumped around the andron. The soldiers watched him closely, their spears at the ready. He had nothing left to lose now. Who could guess what he might do? He caught them watching, and twisted his fingers into an obscene gesture.

Back and forth, back and forth strode Polemaios. The whole business took longer than Sostratos had thought it would. He'd got the impression from the *Phaidon* that Sokrates had died fairly fast. But Sokrates had been old, and of no more than average size. Polemaios was a huge bear of a man, and in the prime of life. Maybe that was why the drug needed longer to work on him.

Most of an hour had gone by before he grunted and said, "I can't feel my feet." He looked pale. Sweat beaded his forehead.

Sostratos looked around for the man who'd brought the deadly dose, but the fellow had left the andron. One of Ptolemaios' officers said, "You can probably lie down now."

"Right." Moving with some difficulty, Polemaios made his way over to the couch. As he eased himself down onto it, he said, "Before I came in here, that son of a whore told me the drug wouldn't hurt. One more lie."

"What does it feel like?" Sostratos asked.

"Drink some yourself and find out, you nosy bastard," Polemaios said. But then he went on, "Feels like my legs are on fire, and my belly, too. And I'm going to—" He leaned over the side of the couch and was noisily sick.

Besides the usual sharp stink of vomit, the air held an acrid tang Sostratos had never smelled before—the odor of hemlock, he realized. The officer sitting next to him waved to one of the soldiers and said, "Go fetch the man who brought the drug. Find out if puking it up will save Polemaios. If it does . . ." He slashed his thumb across his throat. The soldier hurried away.

But when the poisoner came back, he said, "No, it's too late now. He may take a little longer, but he's still a dead man. With hemlock, you need to heave it up right away to have any chance of coming through."

Polemaios vomited again half an hour later. He cursed Ptolemaios, and also all the men who were watching him die. Sostratos spat into the bosom of his chiton to turn aside the omen. He wasn't the only one, either.

"Cold," Antigonos' nephew moaned. "So cold. And it's getting dark." He paused, then tossed his head. "It can't be so late in the day already. The cursed drug must be stealing my sight." Despite the ravages the hemlock worked on his body, his mind stayed clear. Sostratos would have preferred delirium.

After a while, Polemaios fouled himself, adding one more stench to the air in the andron. The man who'd given him the hemlock came up to him and said, "I'm going to feel of you, to find out how far the drug has gone."

"Go ahead," Polemaios answered. "I can't feel any of myself down past my middle any more."

The poisoner probed at his groin and belly. "Your body's cold up to your navel. When it gets to your chest, that will be the end, because your heart will stop and you won't be able to breathe."

"I wish it would hurry up," the big Macedonian said. "I don't want to go on lying here smelling like Ptolemaios." Even as death advanced on him, he had the spirit to revile the man who was its author. But the ruler of Egypt had had the right of it, too: in the *Phaidon*, Platon had surely cleaned up the way Sokrates perished, not wanting to present his beloved teacher in an unflattering light.

Polemaios began fighting for air, each breath coming harder than the one before. "Furies take—all of you—and especially—Ptolemaios," he said, forcing the words out in little bursts. With ever increasing effort, he took a few more breaths, and then, after one last soft sigh, breathed no more.

The man who'd given him the drug took hold of his wrist, feeling for a pulse like a physician. When the fellow let go, Polemaios' arm flopped down limply. The poisoner dipped his head to his audience. "It's over, best ones."

"About time, too," grumbled the officer next to Sostratos. He got to his feet and stretched. "I really have to piss."

Another officer said, "Remember, we've got to mix his men in amongst our own so there aren't enough of 'em in any one place to give us trouble."

That struck Sostratos as a good idea, and very much the sort of thing Ptolemaios would think of. Yet another officer said, "As long as we pay 'em on time, they shouldn't cause too many problems. Mercenaries worry about what they get first and everything else afterwards." He added, "Let's get out of here. This place stinks."

Sostratos was glad to breathe fresh air out in the courtyard, too. His shadow puddled at his feet. It was close to noon. He hadn't realized he'd been in the andron so long. Several slaves went into the room. They came out carrying Polemaios' corpse. Sostratos wondered whether whoever owned this place knew it had just been used for an execution. Were the house his own, it wouldn't have been just a matter of making it ritually clean once more. Even after that, he wouldn't have cared to hold a symposion, say, in the chamber where a man had been put to death.

Fortunately, that wasn't his worry. He wouldn't see this place again, and he was glad of it. A soldier politely opened the door for him. When he stepped out into the street, a guard asked, "Did you find out what you wanted to know?"

How am I supposed to answer that? I was curious about how hemlock works, but did I really want *to watch a man die?* Finding no way to separate the one from the other, Sostratos sighed and said, "I suppose I did." He hurried away before the guard could find any other questions he didn't care to think about.

When he got back to the harbor, Menedemos hailed him

with, “It’s over, eh?” Sostratos dipped his head. His cousin went on, “How did he do?”

“As well as he could,” Sostratos answered. “Ptolemaios was right—it’s an uglier business than Platon made it out to be.” He could change the subject here, could and did: “How’s the *Aphrodite* doing?”

Before Menedemos could answer, the sound of a man pounding on something with a mallet came from under the poop deck. Sostratos’ cousin beamed. “That’s Nikagoras,” he said. “He got here just after you went into the polis, and he’s been banging away like Talos the bronze man ever since.” He raised his voice: “*Oë*, Nikagoras! Come out for a cup of wine and say hello to my cousin.”

More banging, and then someone—presumably Nikagoras—spoke from below: “Let me finish driving this treenail home. After that, I’m your man.” The banging resumed.

“He’s already joining the timbers, is he?” Sostratos was impressed. “He *does* know his business.”

“I heard that. I should hope I do,” Nikagoras said. After still more banging, he grunted. “There. That’ll hold the son of a whore.”

“Best part of it is, Ptolemaios is paying for him, too,” Menedemos said.

“That *is* good news,” Sostratos agreed. “Being laid up here has cost us too much already.” He lowered his voice: “Maybe he’s grateful we didn’t sail away with Antigonos’ nephew.”

“Maybe.” Menedemos also spoke quietly. “To the crows with me if [illegible] know where we would have taken him, though, even if we [illegible] wanted to take him anywhere.”

Sostratos dipped his head. “A point.” Polemaios had made enemies of all the Macedonian marshals except Lysimakhos up in Thrace and Seleukos in the distant east, and no doubt the only reason he hadn’t fallen foul of them, too, was that he hadn’t had much to do with them.

Nikagoras came up the stairs and onto the poop deck. He was in his early forties, naked as a sailor, with broad shoulders, powerful arms, and scarred, gnarled hands. “Hail,” he said to Sostratos, and wiped the back of one hand across his sweaty forehead.

"Hail," Sostratos said. "Sounds as though you're making good progress."

"Sure am," Nikagoras said. "Thanks," he told Menedemos, who'd given him the promised wine. He spilled a few drops onto the deck, drank, and then gave his attention back to Sostratos. "After all the battle damage I've repaired lately, this is almost like a holiday for me."

"I hadn't thought of it like that," Sostratos said.

"You would have if you were in my line of work," the carpenter told him. "Rams are bad enough. That's collision damage, too, like what you took, only worse, on account of a ram's going fast and the fins concentrate where it hits. But if you think that's rough, you ought to try patching up a ship that's had a couple-three thirty-mina stones smack into her right about at the waterline."

"Bad?" Sostratos asked.

"Worse," Nikagoras said. "Sometimes it seems like you end up taking out half the planks and replacing them. And naturally the captain's screaming at you that he's got to get back into the fight as fast as he can, and that everything'll be buggered forever if you don't get him fixed up right away. You want to drown big-mouthed bastards like that, by the gods—they think you're too cursed stupid to figure things out for yourself."

"I'm just glad you're finally here," Menedemos said. "It's taken a month of screaming at people to get a carpenter at all. Of course, the *Aphrodite*'s no warship."

"No, but you can fight if you have to. And," Nikagoras said shrewdly, "a lot of the time, being able to fight means you don't have to, doesn't it?"

"That's right," Sostratos said. "You're a man who sees how things work."

"I try," the carpenter said. "And that's a game I know myself. I haven't been in a brawl in close to twenty years now, on account of I look like I'm tough." He made a fist, then grinned. "Maybe I am, maybe I'm not. But nobody wants to find out the hard way."

"Fair enough," Sostratos said. Men seldom wanted to brawl with him, either, because he was well above average size. He knew perfectly well that he wasn't particularly tough, but that wasn't obvious from looking at him.

Nikagoras gulped the rest of the wine, wiped his mouth, and set down the cup. "Thank you kindly, best one. That hit the spot," he told Menedemos, and then disappeared under the poop deck once more. A moment later, he started banging away with the mallet again.

"A good man," Sostratos said. "I wonder if you could persuade him to go to sea."

His cousin laughed. "My dear, you're reading my mind. I asked him that very thing, but he said, 'I repair ships for a living. D'you think I'd be daft enough to want to travel on one when I know what all can happen to them?' "

"Hmm." Sostratos plucked at his beard. "What does that say about us?"

Menedemos laughed again. "Nothing good, I'm certain."

"COME ON, YOU lazy whoresons," Diokles called to the *Aphrodite*'s rowers. "Put your backs into it, and your arms, too. Do you still remember how to pull an oar? Rhyppa*pai*! Rhyppa*pai*!"

A couple of men groaned as they stroked. Listening to them, Menedemos could tell how much the unnatural layoff had cost them as a crew. "We'll have plenty of sore muscles tonight," he predicted as the *Aphrodite* glided out of Kos' harbor.

"That we will," the keleustes agreed. "Blistered hands, too, same as we do when we start out in the spring."

"If they'll rub oil on their hands as soon as they start getting raw, they won't blister so much," Sostratos said.

"Not a bad notion," Diokles agreed, smiting his bronze square to give the rowers their stroke. "I'd do that myself every now and again when I pulled an oar, and I did enough rowing to make my palms hard as horn."

Menedemos kept the merchant galley close to the coast of Kos. Across the channel, Ptolemaios' ships and soldiers still laid siege to Halikarnassos. Stopping up a harbor tight as a wine jar wasn't easy, though. Every so often, one or two of Antigonos' war galleys would slip out and sink or capture any ships they could catch. Menedemos didn't want to make things easy for them.

He glanced over to his cousin. "*Oë*, Sostratos, there's history going on, just a few stadia away."

"Well, so there is," Sostratos said. "But it's not going on very fast, is it? I don't think I'll miss much if I look northwest instead of northeast."

Look towards Athens, he meant. Menedemos said. "We're not there yet, and we're not going there yet, either. Why don't you look due north instead? That's where Miletos lies, near enough. We need the money we'll make there, too."

"I know," Sostratos said. "Every word you say is true. I understand that. But I have a hard time caring."

"You'd better not," Menedemos warned him. "When we trade there, we'll have to haggle extra hard, squeeze all the silver we can out of the merchants. If you're mooning over that miserable gryphon's skull, you won't do us any good."

"I know," Sostratos said again. But his gaze went back to the rower's bench under which the skull was stowed. A lover's gaze might have gone to his beloved in the same way. A lover's gaze would have been no more tender, either.

"Me, I'll be glad when we get to Athens, just so we're rid of the miserable, ugly thing," Menedemos said.

"Anything you can learn from is beautiful," his cousin said stiffly.

"When I want beauty, I'll find it in a girl's flesh, not a gryphon's bone," Menedemos said.

"There's beauty of the flesh, and then there's beauty of the mind," Sostratos said. "The gryphon's skull has none of the one, but thinking about it may lead those who love wisdom to the other."

After a few heartbeats, Menedemos tossed his head. "I'm afraid that's beyond me, my dear. Nothing you say can make that bone seem anything but ugly to me."

"Let it go, then," Sostratos said, somewhat to Menedemos' surprise: when his cousin felt philosophical, he was often inclined to lecture. A moment later, Sostratos explained himself: "I've got Platon and Sokrates on my mind, that's all."

"Why?" Menedemos asked. Before Sostratos could, he answered his own question: "Oh. Hemlock, of course."

"That's right," Sostratos said. "There's a good deal of talk about the relationship between physical beauty and real love in the *Symposion*."

"Is there? Well, that's more interesting than philosophy usually gets."

"Scoffer."

"Scoffer?" Menedemos assumed a hurt expression. "Now you've gone and got me interested, and you complain I'm scoffing. What does Sokrates have to say about it? Or should I ask, what does Platon have to say?"

"That's a good question," Sostratos said thoughtfully. "There's probably no one left alive who can say how much of what Platon put in Sokrates' mouth really belongs there, and how much comes from the younger man."

"Don't get sidetracked," Menedemos told him. "What *does* beauty have to do with real love? That's a lot more interesting than who wrote what."

"You were the one who brought it up, but never mind," Sostratos said. "If you follow the argument in the *Symposion*, not a great deal. Physical beauty leads you on toward beauty of the mind, and that's where real love lies."

"Sounds like an old man's argument to me," Menedemos said. "If your prick won't stand, you talk about the beauty of the mind so you don't have to fret yourself about it."

"You *are* a scoffer," Sostratos said, and then, "I just had a nasty thought."

"What's that?"

"Do we dare put in at Miletos? We spent all that time stuck in Kos when we hadn't planned to. By now, news that we brought Polemaios there will have spread all over the place. Antigonos' men may want to roast us over a slow fire."

"I know you. You're still looking for an excuse to head straight for Athens," Menedemos said. "That one won't do, though. Remember, Demetrios of Phaleron is Kassandros' puppet, and Kassandros won't be happy to find out Polemaios got loose, either." He suddenly grinned. "Besides, it's not a worry any more."

"Why not?" Sostratos asked.

"I'll tell you why not. Suppose they blame us for letting Polemaios get loose so he can plague his uncle. What do we say? We say, 'Well, O marvelous one, you don't need to lose any sleep about that, because we watched Polemaios die.' They won't be angry at us for that news—they'll be glad to hear it."

His cousin looked sheepish. "You're right. You're absolutely right, of course. I can't think of anybody who wouldn't be glad to hear Polemaios was dead."

"Neither can I," Menedemos said. "He made himself loved as much for his mind as for his beauty, didn't he?"

Sostratos started just to dip his head, but broke out laughing with the motion half done. "You're not just a scoffer, you're a dangerous scoffer. I think you'd make Sokrates choke on his wine."

"No, no—Sokrates choked down his hemlock, the same as Polemaios did," Menedemos replied.

He and Sostratos kept on chaffing each other as the *Aphrodite* sailed north and west through the strait between the Anatolian mainland and the island of Kalymnos. This time, the akatos had fine weather for the journey. One of Ptolemaios' war galleys came out from the newly captured town of Myndos to look her over, but turned back on recognizing what ship it was. "I remember you," an officer aboard the five called to Menedemos. "You're the fellow who brought what's-his-name—Antigonos' nephew—back to Kos."

"That's right," Menedemos answered, lifting a hand from the steering-oar tillers to wave to the war galley.

After the five swung away toward the east, Sostratos said, "You didn't tell him what's-his-name was dead."

"I certainly didn't," Menedemos said. "He would have wasted an hour of our time asking questions, and we haven't got an hour to spare, not if we want to make Miletos by sundown. You're not the only one who can be in a hurry to get where we're going, you know."

Not long after the war galley came out from the mainland, the *Aphrodite* passed a sponge boat most likely from Kalymnos, which had a lot of sponge divers. A trident in his right hand to free sponges from the ocean floor and a large stone clutched to his chest to make him sink quickly, a diver leaped off the stern of the boat and splashed into the blue water. He came up again a couple of minutes later, hanging on to black sponges of varying sizes. The other men on the boat took the sponges from him and hauled him aboard again. Naked and dripping, he waved to the *Aphrodite*.

From his station at an oar, Moskhion said, "This is what I was talking about when we fothered the sailcloth over the planks. Gods know I'd rather be here than over there doing that."

"I believe you," Menedemos said. As he had to the men on Ptolemaios' five, he did wave back. "He doesn't think we're pirates, anyhow. Either that or he knows there's nothing worth stealing on his boat."

"I wouldn't want his sponges, that's certain," Sostratos said. "They don't look like the ones you'd use in a fine bathhouse."

"Of course they don't," Moskhion said. "They haven't been cleaned and dried yet."

"Sponge diving is as hard a way to make a living as any other kind of fishing," Menedemos said.

"Harder," Moskhion said with conviction. "Believe me—harder."

"When you get right down to it, there's no easy way to make a living," Sostratos said.

"I'd rather be doing this than that," Menedemos said. Sostratos and Moskhion both dipped their heads in agreement. Menedemos went on, "Easy work, now—wouldn't you like to be a sophist and make speeches in the market square for money?"

"By the dog of Egypt, *I* would," Moskhion said.

"It can't be *that* easy," Sostratos said. "If it were, more men would be able to make a living at it. Most of the ones who try fail, you know. You need to be able to think on your feet, and people have to want to listen to you. Otherwise, you go hungry."

Menedemos hadn't thought about that. Sostratos had a way of reminding him of things he hadn't thought of. "Maybe you're right," Menedemos allowed. "It must be something like being an actor."

"Not so easy as acting, I'd say," his cousin answered. "A sophist hasn't got a mask to hide behind, the way an actor does."

A good-sized wave slapped the merchant galley's bow, and then another and another, making her pitch up and down. "And we're coming out into the Ikarian Sea," Menedemos said, "which means we haven't got any more islands to hide behind. We'll be bouncing like a toy boat in a little boy's hip bath all the way up to Miletos. This is one of the roughest stretches of the Aegean."

"I know." Sostratos gulped and looked faintly green. "I had my sea legs, but I may have lost them in the layover at Kos."

He wasn't the only one. A couple of sailors leaned out over the rail and heaved up their guts, too. Maybe they wouldn't have done it if they hadn't drunk deep in Kos the night before. But maybe, like Sostratos, they'd just spent too much time ashore.

To Menedemos' relief, the *Aphrodite* did make Miletos by nightfall. He wouldn't have cared to spend a night at sea in such rough waters, and a wind might have blown up to make things worse still. Tying up at a quay as the sun went down made him much happier about the world.

The Milesians who made the ship fast to the quay chattered away amongst themselves in the town's Ionic dialect. When one of Antigonos' officers strutted up to ask his questions, the harbor workers fell silent and flinched away like beaten children. A generation before, Miletos had tried to hold out Alexander's soldiers and been sacked for its effort. These days, the locals gave their occupiers no trouble.

"From Kos, eh?" the officer said. Menedemos hadn't dared lie about that, not when the akatos carried so much silk. Bristles rasped under the officer's fingers as he rubbed his chin in thought. At last, he asked, "While you were there, did you . . . hear anything about Antigonos' nephew joining forces with that ugly toad of a Ptolemaios?"

Oh, good, Menedemos thought. *He has no idea we're the ones who brought Polemaios to Kos. That makes things a lot easier.* Aloud, he answered, "Yes, Polemaios was there while we were. But your master doesn't have to worry about him any more."

"What? Why not?" the man demanded.

"Because he's dead," Menedemos replied. "He tried to bring some of Ptolemaios' officers over to his own cause. Ptolemaios caught him at it and made him drink hemlock. I'm sure the news is true—it was all over Kos when we left this morning." That seemed preferable to telling the officer Sostratos had watched Polemaios die. If the fellow believed him, he might—probably would—wonder how Sostratos had gained that privilege.

As things were, the officer's jaw dropped. "That's wonderful news, if it's so. Are you certain of it?"

"I didn't see his body," Menedemos answered truthfully, "but I don't see why Ptolemaios would lie about something like that. A lie would only make the soldiers who came along with Antigonos' nephew want to riot, don't you think?"

After a little thought, the officer dipped his head. When he grinned, a scar on one cheek that Menedemos hadn't noticed till then pulled the expression out of shape. "You're right, by the gods. This has to go straight to Antigonos. He's up by the Hellespont, setting things to rights there. You might want to stay in port here for a while; I wouldn't be surprised if he gave you a reward for the news."

Sostratos looked like a man who'd just taken a knife in the back. Menedemos spoke to the officer: "Best one, if I were sure of that, I *would* stay. But look at the size of my crew. I don't know that I can afford to linger just on the hope of a reward—I have to pay them any which way."

"That's a problem," Antigonos' man admitted. "You'll have to do what you think best, then."

Menedemos *was* tempted to linger. Old One-Eye might be very glad indeed to learn that his unpleasant nephew wouldn't bother him any more, with or without the help of Ptolemaios. But he'd meant what he said; the *Aphrodite*'s crew was expensive. If he waited half a month, he'd go through half a talent of silver.

Sounding like someone who'd just had a reprieve, Sostratos asked the officer, "What's the news here?"

"Not much right here," the fellow said, "though some from Hellas came in the other day."

"Tell us!" Menedemos spoke as quickly as his cousin.

"Well," the officer went on, with the smug smile of someone who knows something his listeners do not, "you may have heard tell of the youth called Herakles, Alexander's bastard son by Barsine."

"Oh, yes." Menedemos dipped his head. "The one who got out of Pergamon last year, and went across to Polyperkhon to help him drive Kassandros mad in Macedonia."

"That's right," Antigonos' officer said, at the same time as Sostratos spoke out of the side of his mouth: "This Herakles likely isn't Alexander's get at all, but a tool of Antigonos' against Kassandros."

"I know. Shut up," Menedemos hissed to him, before asking the officer, "What about this youth?"

"He's dead, that's what," the officer answered. "Dead as Polemaios, if what you say about *him* is true. Kassandros persuaded Polyperkhon that Alexander's kin were too dangerous to leave running around loose, and so—" He drew a finger across his throat. "They say Polyperkhon got land in Macedonia for it, and soldiers to help him fight down in the Peloponnesos."

"Kassandros doesn't want any folk of Alexander's blood left alive, because they weaken his hold on Macedonia," Sostratos said. "He's just a general; they could call themselves kings."

"That's true," Menedemos said. "Look how he got rid of Alexander's legitimate son, Alexandros, winter before last—and Roxane, the boy's mother, too."

"Sure enough, you can't trust Kassandros," Antigonos' officer declared. He started back up the quay. "I'm off to tell my superiors of *your* news. Like I say, you can be sure they'll be glad to hear it." He hurried away.

" 'You can't trust Kassandros,' " Sostratos echoed, irony in his voice. "You can't trust *any* of the Macedonian marshals, and they *all* want to see Alexander's kin dead."

"No doubt you're right," Menedemos said, "but it's still news. It hadn't got to Kos yet."

"I don't think there's even a bastard pretender from Alexander's line left alive now," Sostratos said.

"His sister Kleopatra's still up in Sardis, isn't she?" Menedemos asked.

"By the gods, you're right. I'd forgotten about Kleopatra." Sostratos looked annoyed at himself, as he often did when he forgot something like that. The smile following his annoyed expression wasn't one Menedemos would have wanted aimed at him. "I wonder how long *she'll* last," Sostratos added.

LIKE KAUNOS, MILETOS was an old city, one with streets wandering wherever they would. Sostratos had to pay out not one obolos but two to find his way to the market square in the middle of town. He feared he would need to pay for directions back to the harbor, too. He'd got so turned around, he had to keep looking at the sun to know which direction was which.

In the agora, hawkers cried the produce of the rich Anatolian countryside: onions and garlic and olives and raisins and wine. Potters and tinkers and leatherworkers and wool dealers added to the din. So did the fellow who walked through the square with a brazier shouting, "Fresh squid!"

Sostratos bought a couple of them. He burned his fingers and his mouth on the hot oily flesh, but didn't care: they were delicious. After he'd gulped them down, he started doing some shouting of his own: "Fine silk from Kos!"

Miletos being only a day's sail from the island, he hadn't expected too much in the way of business. He'd assumed most Milesians who wanted silk would have gone down to Kos and bought it for themselves. As soon as he opened his mouth, he saw he'd made a mistake, for he started selling the stuff as if it had never before appeared in this polis.

And that, it seemed, was not so far from the truth. "Thank you so much for fetching some at last," said a tailor who bought several bolts. "No one from Kos has been here for a while, and no one from our town wanted to go down there. You know how it is."

"Well, no, as a matter of fact," Sostratos said.

"Oh, but my dear fellow, you must," the tailor said. When Sostratos still looked blank, the fellow let out an exasperated sigh and condescended to explain: "If we go down to Kos or men from there come hither, what's likely to happen? Antigonos' officers will say we're spying for Ptolemaios, or else the other way round, that's what. Silk's all very fine, but it's not worth a visit to the torturer."

"I . . . see," Sostratos said in a small voice. And so he did, once the Milesian pointed it out to him. *This is what I get for living in a free and autonomous polis that really is both*, he thought. *Such things don't occur to me. These lands are subject to the marshals who rule them and if the marshals become enemies, so do the lands, no matter what most of the people want*. To someone from an independent democracy, the notion was absurd. But that made it no less real hereabouts.

Silver came clinking in from one customer after another. When Sostratos saw how eager the locals were to buy, he raised the price. That didn't keep him from running low on silk before noon. He sent a couple of sailors back to the *Aphrodite* to bring more to the market square.

Not long after they returned, Menedemos stopped by. He looked as happy and as sated as a fox in a henhouse. "You must have spent part of your morning in a brothel," Sostratos said. When his cousin tossed his head, alarm shot through him. "Don't tell me you found a friendly wife so quick. Remember, friendly wives have unfriendly husbands."

"No whores, no wives—no women at all," Menedemos answered. Seeing Sostratos' dubious expression, he went on, "I'll take oath by any god you care to name. No, I've been meeting . . . jewelers." He leaned forward and spoke the last word in a conspiratorial whisper.

"Jewelers?" Sostratos echoed. For a moment, he couldn't imagine why Menedemos might be interested in talking with them. Then he did, and felt foolish. "Oh. The emeralds." He also dropped his voice for the last word.

"That's right, Menedemos said. "This isn't Kos. I can sell them here without worrying about Ptolemaios. As a matter of fact, people here are all the more eager to buy just for the sake of giving Ptolemaios a black eye."

But if Ptolemaios ruled Miletos, they would—or some of them would—inform on you for smuggling, Sostratos thought—

the other side of the coin to his earlier reflections. Thinking of coins made him ask, "How much are you getting?"

"My dear, they're fighting with one another for the chance to get their hands on my little green stones," Menedemos said. "I sold two medium-good ones—not the finest, mind you—for ten minai."

"By the dog of Egypt!" Sostratos exclaimed—the right oath for gems coming out of Ptolemaios' realm. "That's almost twice what we paid for the lot of them."

"I know," Menedemos said happily. "And once the fellows who didn't buy take a look at the stones and decide they have to have some, too . . . We really may clear more than a talent from them."

"Who can buy from the jewelers at such prices, though?" Sostratos asked. "Are there that many rich Milesians?"

"I don't think so," his cousin answered. "But Antigonos has plenty of rich officers."

"Ah," Sostratos said. "That's true. And they'll have wives for whom they'll want rings or pendants—or else hetairai to whom they'll have to give presents."

Menedemos dipped his head. "You're beginning to understand."

At another time, his sarcastic tone would have irked Sostratos. His thoughts were elsewhere now. He wished he had a counting board, but managed well enough without one; along with his fine memory, he'd always had a knack for mental arithmetic. When he came out of his study, he found Menedemos looking at him oddly. He'd seen that particular expression on his cousin's face once or twice before. A little sheepishly, he asked, "How long was I away?"

"Not *very* long," Menedemos answered, "but I said something to you and you never heard me. What were you thinking about so hard?"

"Money," Sostratos said, a word that was enough to seize Menedemos' attention by itself. "If you can bring in a talent or so for those emeralds, and if I keep getting the prices I've been getting for the silk, we'll turn a profit on this run yet."

"And you would have flung me into the sea for wanting to

come here instead of making straight for Athens," Menedemos said.

"We might have done just as well for ourselves there," Sostratos said. "We probably would have with the emeralds: Athenian jewelers have Kassandros' officers to sell to, as the Milesians have Antigonos'. And there's the gryphon's skull."

"So there is." To Sostratos surprise, Menedemos chuckled and patted him on the back. "I'm all finished arguing about that with you. You want to take it over to a bunch of other men who'll stand around looking at it and thinking so hard, they can't even hear."

Sostratos kissed him on the cheek. "You *do* understand!" he exclaimed. Only later did he realize that his cousin's description of the philosophers of the Lykeion might have been imperfectly flattering.

Menedemos said, "I can't stay, my dear. I'm going to the ship, and then back to talk to some more jewelers. And who knows? One of them may turn out to have a pretty wife." He hurried off before Sostratos could even begin a gasp of horror.

Swallowing a sigh, Sostratos went back to calling out the virtues of the silk he was selling. *He did that on purpose*, he thought. *He wanted to make me jump, and he did*. But he also knew that, if one of the jewelers did turn out to be married to a women whose looks Menedemos liked, he might try to seduce her. *And if he does, we may have to head for Athens sooner than he wants*. Sostratos tossed his head. They were doing such good business here, they really needed to stay a while. And he wanted to be able to come back to Miletos next year or the year after.

A plump man wearing a chiton of snowy linen and sandals with gold buckles came up and waited to be noticed. "Hail," Sostratos said: the fellow looked prosperous enough to make him hope he was a customer. "Would you be interested in buying some silk?"

" 'Ail," the man replied, his accent not just Ionian but something else, something that told Sostratos he wasn't a Hellene. "Not for myself, no. But I 'ave come to tell you that my mistress may well be, if you 'ave what she wants."

"Your . . . mistress?" Sostratos hoped his startlement didn't show. Few Milesians dressed as well as this fellow; Sostratos had assumed he had money of his own. If he was someone's slave, how much money did his owner have?

"Yes, sir," the plump man said. "My mistress is Metrikhe, who is well known in Miletos. She might be interested in your silk, if you 'ave any fine enough. For . . . professional purposes, you understand."

"Yes," Sostratos said. *A hetaira. She has to be*, he thought. *And one of the very rich ones, if she can afford a slave like this*. "I'll be happy to show you what I've got here."

"Thank you, sir, but not to me." The plump man shook his head, again proving himself no Hellene. "If you would bring it to my mistress' house, though . . ."

Sostratos almost burst out laughing. *Menedemos will be sorry he's off talking to jewelers*, he thought. *If he were here, he'd do anything this side of bashing me with a rock to go himself.* "Yes, I'll come," he told the slave. "Let me find some bolts that might best suit her." As he gathered them up, he told the couple of sailors with him, "If anyone comes looking to buy, let him know I'll be back before too long."

"Right you are," one of them said. With a grin, he added, "Tough bit of work you've got ahead of you, sounds like."

"Doesn't it, though?" Sostratos answered, deadpan. He turned to the slave. "I'm ready. Take me to your mistress."

As in most poleis, the houses of the rich and poor lay side by side, and it wasn't easy to tell which was which from the outside: the rich hid their wealth behind their walls. When the slave stopped and said, " 'Ere we are," Sostratos saw that the house was whitewashed and had a very solid-looking door. Both suggested money; neither proved it.

Another slave opened the door when the fellow with Sostratos knocked. "Come with me, sir," he told Sostratos, and led him to the andron. Again, Sostratos held in amusement, thinking, *In a hetaira's house, is this still the men's chamber? And if it is, what exactly does that mean?*

The chairs and tables in the andron were well made. The courtyard at which Sostratos looked out also suggested quiet prosperity, with a colonnade around its outer edge, a neat flower garden surrounding a fountain, and a nearly life-sized statue of a goddess likelier to be Artemis than Aphrodite. Sostratos would have expected something gaudier and bawdier.

One of the slaves brought him wine and olives. The first taste of the wine made his eyebrows shoot up. He knew Ariousian, the finest vintage from Khios; the *Aphrodite* had carried it to Great Hellas the year before. If Metrikhe could afford it, she was more than prosperous. The tangy green olives were also very fine, plainly from the first picking.

Metrikhe gave Sostratos just long enough to refresh himself before coming to the andron. Maybe she had a slave keeping an eye on him; maybe she simply knew how long a man would need. At any rate, he'd just set down his empty cup when she paused in the doorway and said, " 'Ail. You are the silk-seller?"

"Hail. Yes, that's right." As Sostratos gave his name, he eyed Metrikhe. No one could have proved her a hetaira by the way she dressed. Indeed, she seemed the height of respectability. Over her long chiton, she wore a wrap of fine, soft wool; Miletos was famous for the quality of its khlaneis. She even veiled herself against his eyes. *How disappointing*, he thought.

What was in his mind must have shown on his face, for she chuckled. "Were you expecting to see me in something where you could see all of me?" she asked as she walked in and sat down. She moved with a dancer's grace.

Sostratos' ears heated. "I did . . . wonder," he mumbled, that seeming a safer word than *hope*.

"I can't say I'm surprised." Metrikhe tossed her head, a startlingly emphatic gesture. "But no. I don't show myself unless it's time to show myself. That makes it mean more when I do."

"Ah." Sostratos took the point at once. "I see. Each craft has its own mysteries. Plainly, you know yours."

"I 'ad better," she answered, and cocked his head to one side, studying him for a few heartbeats. "You're not a fool, are you?"

"I do try not to be." Sostratos smiled. "Of course, I understand that you want men to be fools around you, and I'm sure you know how to get just what you want." His cousin was far fonder of quoting Homer than he was, but a few lines from the *Odyssey* seemed to fit:

" 'They stood in the bright-tressed goddess' doorway
And listened to Kirke inside singing with her beautiful voice
While working at a great loom fit for a divinity, such as goddesses have
And turning out delicately woven work, pleasing and fine.' "

Metrikhe studied him again, this time, he thought, more sharply. An edge in her voice, she said, "I don't turn men into swine."

He didn't want to antagonize her. That might cost him a sale even before they started haggling. He picked his words with care: "I wouldn't think you'd need to. Isn't it true that a lot of men are swine before they stand in your doorway?"

"You *are* a man. 'Ow do you know these things?" She sounded half astonished, half suspicious.

How do *I know?* Sostratos wondered. He knew what happened to women when cities fell. In his student days in Athens, he'd gone to the theater for several revivals of Euripides, including *The Trojan Women*. And he worried about Menedemos whenever the *Aphrodite* came into a new port. How much of that could he tell a stranger? *None*, he decided. And so he simply shrugged and said, "Am I wrong?"

"No, by Zeus," the hetaira answered. "Be thankful you don't know 'ow right you are." Perhaps still taken aback by what he'd said, she dipped up a cup of wine for herself. She had to push aside the veils to drink. Sostratos didn't know what he'd expected—hard, dazzling beauty, most likely. He didn't find that; she was pretty, but not ravishing, and younger than he would have guessed from her voice: about his own age. She knew he was looking, of course. She smiled as she let the veiling drop back into place. "What do you think?"

He chose another line from the *Odyssey*. " 'Nausikaa, having loveliness from the gods . . .' " and then finished with his own invention, improvising the end of a hexameter: ". . . chose to look at silk."

Metrikhe clapped her hands. "*Euge!*"

"Not really," Sostratos said. "It's an anachronism, for they didn't know of silk in the days of the Trojan War. Homer never mentions it. But if *you* choose to look at silk, I'll be happy to show you what I have here."

"Please do," she said, and then, "You're an unusual man."

"I don't know what you're talking about," Sostratos answered. He didn't particularly expect her to notice the quiet irony in his voice, but she did, and dipped her head. He started opening leather sacks and taking out bolts of cloth. "Your slave said you wanted the thinnest I have."

"Yes," Metrikhe said. "Mysteries of the craft again—not that that's much of a mystery. . . . Can we go out into the courtyard? Seeing these in the sunlight's the best way to judge 'ow thin they are."

"Certainly," Sostratos said. "I wish most of the men I do business with had as good an idea of what they wanted."

"Thank you," Metrikhe replied. "And I wish most of the men 'oo come 'ere to do business—not *that* kind of business, but other sorts, the way you are—would *do* business with me, and not act as if all they care about is my little piggy." She used the obscenity as if it were the most natural thing in the world.

Out in the courtyard, Sostratos held up bolt after bolt of silk. Metrikhe waved for him to put some aside for later haggling; at others she simply tossed her head. After a while, he said, "That's the last one I have."

"All right," the hetaira answered. "What do you want for all the ones I can use?"

"For all those bolts together?" Sostratos looked up into the sky while numbers danced in his head. Before long, he named a price.

Metrikhe looked from the silk to him and back again. "I thought you would give me some round figure. You reckoned that to the very drakhma, didn't you?"

"Of course," he answered, honestly surprised. "Isn't that what you wanted me to do?"

"What you want and what you get often 'ave nothing to do with each other," she said. "If it weren't for what men want, I would have to be a washerwoman or a tavernkeeper or something of the sort. But what do they get from me they couldn't have from a three-obolos 'ore?" She snapped her fingers. "Illusion, that's all."

Sostratos smiled. "Should you tell me such things?"

"I wouldn't tell them to most men, but I think you can see them for yourself," Metrikhe said. "And I'll tell you something else: no matter 'ow carefully you figured your price, you're still a thief." She named one of her own, less than half as high.

"If I'm a thief, you're a joker," Sostratos replied. "I can't possibly make a profit on that, or anything close to it. You say you don't want to wash clothes or sell wine? That cuts both ways. I don't want to tan hides or make pots."

She stepped forward and set a hand on his arm. Till then, she'd acted like a well-bred woman and spoken like a well-educated man. Now, suddenly, she chose to remind him of what she really was, what she really did. Her flesh was warm and soft. Her voice was warm and soft, too: "Suppose I give you that very same price, and the rest of the afternoon in my bed? If you want illusion, I can give you the best."

"If my cousin were here, he might take you up on that," Sostratos said. "Please believe me, it's not that I'm not interested." That was true; her touch had startled him and stirred him at the same time. Even so, he went on, "You're lucky: you can make a living from illusion. I can't; I have to have silver."

"It's not always luck, believe me. Some of the men who visit here have illusions of their own," Metrikhe said. She went from wanton back to businesslike in the space of a sentence. "All right, then—silver and nothing but silver." She came up a little.

"You're speaking of Milesian drakhmai?" Sostratos asked.

Metrikhe dipped her head. "They're a little heavier than your Rhodian coins."

He'd known that. Somehow, he wasn't surprised she did, too. "Even so, you're still too low," he said, thinking, *When we do make a bargain, I won't find any heavy drakhmai here, the way I did at the temple in Kos.*

She said, "Let's go back into the andron and hash it out over more wine."

"Why not?" Sostratos said. "If you can afford to pay for the lovely Khian, you can afford to pay for my silk, too."

Metrikhe laughed. "You're as spiny as a hedgehog. Why didn't your cousin come here instead? He would have been easier to deal with."

"I'm sorry," said Sostratos, who wasn't sorry at all. "You're stuck with me."

When they did agree on a price, it was about as low as Sostratos was willing to go without abandoning the deal altogether. That didn't surprise him, either. And, when he went through the money she gave him, he found a few coins—only a few—from Rhodes and other poleis that coined to a lighter standard than Miletos. "I'll get you lions to take their places," Metrikhe said, and did replace them with Milesian money. As he'd expected, there were no owls or turtles or other heavy coins.

The drakhmai jingled sweetly as Sostratos put them back into the leather sack Metrikhe had given him. He tied the sack shut with a strip of rawhide. "Thank you for your hospitality and for your business," he told her, rising to go. "I hope to see you again one day." It could happen. Ships from his father and uncle's firm came into Miletos every year or two.

Metrikhe said, "Do you need to leave so soon?"

Sostratos frowned. "We're done here, aren't we? Or have you changed your mind about some of the silk you said you didn't want?"

"I wasn't talking about silk," she said, a hint—more than a hint—of exasperation in her voice.

His frown deepened. "Then what do you—?" He broke off because of one possibility that occurred to him. It would, he was sure, have occurred to Menedemos much sooner. "Do you mean *that*?" He was pleased his voice didn't rise to a startled squeak, as if he were still a youth.

"Certainly, I mean *that*," she answered, now sounding amused. "Why did you think I might mean anything else?"

Because those sorts of things happen to my cousin, not to me, Sostratos thought. *Because women don't usually find me very interesting*. He had just enough sense not to blurt that out to Metrikhe. Instead, he said, "Because you chose to dress like a woman of quality. Because you bargain like a man. Because I already turned you down when you, ah, didn't bargain like a man."

She laughed and waved that aside. "You didn't insult me. That was business on both sides, when I offered and when you said no. This wouldn't be business. I think this would be fun. You've treated me like a person, not like a slut. You don't know how unusual that is. And so . . ." She shrugged. "If you want to, of course."

"You really mean it," Sostratos said in slow wonder. Metrikhe dipped her head. He still had trouble believing it. In his youth, he'd had a couple of painful jokes played on him, painful enough to make him wince when he thought of them now, ten years later.

"Come on," Metrikhe said. "I'm doing this because *I* feel like it, not because I have to make one of my companions feel good. That's unusual, too, and I'm going to enjoy it."

Sostratos needed no more urging. He did bring along the silk she hadn't bought and the money she'd given him for what she had. If he left them here in the andron, he wasn't sure they would stay here till he got back.

Metrikhe didn't urge him to leave them behind. All she said was, "You don't take chances, do you?"

"I try not to," he answered.

"Well, good for you," she said. "My room is upstairs—it's the women's quarters, after all."

Her bed was wider, her mattress thicker and softer, than those Sostratos had used at Kleiteles' house back in Kos. As soon as she closed the bedroom door behind them, she took off her veil and set it on the cabinet by the wall. Her letting him see her face after concealing it through nearly the whole afternoon was almost like letting him see her altogether naked.

That soon followed. She neatly folded the khlanis and laid it beside the veil. Then, undoing her girdle, she got out of the long chiton and stood bare before him. "Praxiteles should have got a look at you," he said. "He never would have bothered modeling his Aphrodite on Phryne."

She blushed. He was delighted to follow the surge of color from her breasts all the way to her hairline. "I wish more men talked so sweetly," she said.

"If they don't, they're either blind or missing a chance," Sostratos told her, which made her flush all over again. *And I'm not even exaggerating very much*, he thought, pulling his own chiton off over his head. Metrikhe's shape was everything a man could ask for in a woman: slim waist, round hips, firm breasts of just the right size. A sculptor would have been pleased to use her for a model. *Most sculptors would be pleased to do quite a lot of things with her*, went through Sostratos' mind as he stepped forward and took her in his arms.

Her body molded itself against his. Her skin was so soft and smooth, he wondered if she oiled it. She tilted her face up to his. Seen from a distance of less than a palm, her eyes weren't brown, but dark, dark hazel, an intriguingly complex color. "I like tall men," she whispered.

"I like you," Sostratos answered. Metrikhe laughed and squeezed him. Her breath was sweet. When he kissed her, she tasted of wine.

They lay down on the bed. Sostratos' mouth went from hers to her cheeks, the lobes of her ears, her neck, her breasts. His hand wandered lower, down the curve of her belly to where her legs joined. They opened for him. He stroked her there while his tongue teased her nipples. She let out a soft sigh of pleasure. If it wasn't real, she was a better actor than any who went on the stage in Athens.

Before long, she began to stroke him, too, and then twisted, limber as an eel, and took him in her mouth. He enjoyed it for a little while before pulling away. "You don't need to play the Lesbian for me," he said: women from Lesbos were famous for giving men that particular pleasure.

Her smile was saucy. "Well, what *do* you want to do, then?" she asked archly.

"This," he said, and did it. Metrikhe sighed when he went into her. Having lain with the Rhodian proxenos' slave woman back in Kos a couple of nights before, he didn't feel the need to spend himself as fast as he could. He spun it out, enjoying the journey as well as the eventual destination. Metrikhe bucked against him like an unbroken colt. Her breathing came quick and short, till she threw back her head and a gasping moan broke from her.

Sostratos spent himself a few heartbeats later. In a throaty voice, Metrikhe said, "If we'd done that while we were bargaining, I'd 'ave paid you more for your silk, not less."

"Thank you," he told her, and gave her a kiss. "I don't suppose I'll get too many finer compliments."

She dipped her head; she was a merchant, too, in her own way, and knew what her words had meant. "You're welcome," she said. "And you're welcome 'ere any time, with silk or without."

That might have been a bigger compliment than the other. "Thank you," Sostratos said again. "For now, though, I'd better get back to the agora. Do I remember the turns rightly? First left, second right, fourth left, second right?"

She frowned. "That's not 'ow I keep track of the way. Let me think." After a moment, she dipped her head once more. "Yes, that will get you there."

"Good." Sostratos got off the bed and put his tunic back on. "Thank you for your business," he said, "and for everything else."

Metrikhe lay there smiling up at him, naked still. "Thank *you* for everything else," she said, "and for your business."

"We were—we are—bound for Athens," Sostratos said. "Now I hope we stay here for a while." Did he really mean that? Part of him did, at any rate, and he knew just which part. Which was more important in the general scheme of things, a woman or the gryphon's skull? *I can find women anywhere*, he thought. *There's only one gryphon's skull.* But the physical pleasure the hetaira had given him was less easy to surmount for the pleasures of the mind than Platon had made it out to be.

Realizing that made Sostratos leave Metrikhe's house faster than he would have otherwise. He made his way back to the agora, where he found Menedemos dickering over silk with a plump man who had the look of someone knowing himself to be important. After his cousin made the bargain—a better one than he'd got from Metrikhe himself—and sent the fellow on his way; he turned to Sostratos and said, "Well, my dear, I stopped back here for what I thought would be only a moment. It was just long enough to hear where you'd gone and to talk with that chap. *You* had a rugged bit of duty there, didn't you? Is she pretty?"

"As a matter of fact, yes," Sostratos answered.

"And did she give you half the price in trade?" Menedemos went on.

"Of course not. We need the silver." Sostratos held up the sack of coins. He told Menedemos what he'd sold and how much he'd got.

"Not the best bargain in the world, but passable, passable," his cousin said. "So you didn't get anything more from her than a smile and the money, eh?"

"I didn't say *that*," Sostratos replied, and had the satisfaction of seeing Menedemos look very jealous indeed.

"WE'RE ABOUT READY TO SAIL FOR Athens," Menedemos told Sostratos as they stood on the *Aphrodite*'s poop deck after several profitable days in Miletos.

"All right," his cousin said.

Menedemos laughed. " 'All right'? Is that the best you can manage? Before we got here, you would have been happy to skip this town and head straight for Cape Sounion, and you know it as well as I do."

"I still want to go," Sostratos said, sounding like a man doing his best not to sound annoyed. "You're making it seem as though I can't tear myself away from Metrikhe, and that isn't true."

"Well, maybe not." Menedemos laughed again. "You do come up for air every now and then—the way a dolphin does before it dives deep into the sea. Except you're diving deep into her—"

"Leave it alone, would you please?" Now Sostratos *did* sound annoyed.

Since irking his cousin was what Menedemos had had in mind, he did change the subject . . . in a way: "You've got to admit, we did the right thing coming here. Besides making you sleep like a dead man every night, we've unloaded most of the silk for a better price than we ever thought we'd get, and all but two of the emeralds. We'll show a profit when we get home. Our fathers won't have anything to complain about." Keeping his father from having anything to complain about was one of his main goals in life. Trouble was, Philodemos complained whether he had anything to complain about or not.

"You could have sold those last two stones," Sostratos said. "One of them's the best of the lot, isn't it?"

"Yes, it is—and I know I could have," Menedemos said. "But I kept thinking: if I'm getting these prices in Miletos, what would I get in Athens? This polis hasn't been anything special for a long time—"

"Since before the Persian Wars," Sostratos said.

"That's a long time," Menedemos said. *Somewhere close to two hundred years*, he thought. Before his cousin could tell him exactly how long—to the hour, as likely as not—he went on, "Let's save a couple, anyhow, for a really big polis, a really rich polis. Maybe we'll do better with them there."

"Maybe we will," Sostratos agreed. "We couldn't very well try selling them in Alexandria. It's the richest city in the world, but . . ."

"Yes. But," Menedemos said. "If we showed up with Egyptian emeralds in Ptolemaios' capital, people would wonder how we got them, and they'd take us apart trying to find out. I don't think I'd care to answer those kinds of questions."

"Neither do I," Sostratos said.

Menedemos pointed a finger at him. "Would your hetaira

want to buy one of the emeralds? I'd bet she's got the cash for it."

"I'm sure Metrikhe has the cash for it," his cousin answered. "I mentioned them to her the other day, as a matter of fact. She said, 'They sound very pretty. I'll have to see if one of my friends will buy some for me.' "

"Did she?" Menedemos laughed once more. "Sounds like she'd make a splendid merchant if she were a man—never use your own money when you can use someone else's instead."

"She would. I'm sure of it," Sostratos said. "And I don't think she'll be poor after her looks go, either. She'll use what she's got wisely."

"Oh, I don't know. How can you be so sure?" Menedemos said. "Look what she's doing with you—giving it away for nothing. If that's not bad business, I don't know what is."

Sostratos turned red. Menedemos grinned; he'd hoped that would embarrass his cousin. "If she wants to be foolish that particular way, I won't complain," Sostratos said.

"No, eh?" Menedemos said. Sostratos tossed his head. Menedemos' grin got wider, not least to hide his annoyance that Sostratos had had such luck here and he hadn't. He'd even hinted a couple of times that he would like to meet Metrikhe—in a purely social way, of course. But Sostratos had made a point of not inviting him along when he went calling. *Do you think I'd try to take your woman away? Would I do such a thing to my own cousin?* Menedemos knew himself well enough to answer that honestly: *if she were pretty enough. I might.*

"Exactly when were you planning to sail?" Sostratos asked.

"Day after tomorrow," Menedemos answered. "I was thinking we'd spend tomorrow in the agora, try to move as much as we can—silk, dye, perfume—"

"Balsam," Sostratos broke in. "We only have a little bit of balsam left. It's done well for us."

"It has, hasn't it?" Menedemos said. "I wish we'd bought more from those Phoenicians. Physicians and priests both snap it up. I hadn't expected quite so much demand."

"Neither had I," Sostratos said. "It's the perfect sort of thing for us to carry, though: it isn't bulky, and it's worth a lot. We ought to see if we can get more next year. We'd make money on it."

"Himilkon would probably be able to find some for us," Menedemos said. "All sorts of strange things come out of the east and end up in his warehouse. Peafowl, for instance."

"Don't remind me." Sostratos shuddered. He'd cared for the peafowl on the journey to Great Hellas the year before, and would likely spend the rest of his days trying to forget the experience. After a deep breath, he went on, "It might be worth our while to go east next spring and see if we can buy direct. Engedi, where the stuff comes from, is somewhere in Phoenicia, isn't it?"

"In it or near it," Menedemos said. "I'm pretty sure of that." He stroked his chin. "If we took a cargo along, so we could sell as well as buy—"

"Well, of course," Sostratos said.

"Yes, yes." Slowly, Menedemos dipped his head. "We've talked about this once or twice before, in an idle sort of way, but now I'm starting to catch fire, I truly am. We could save a fortune in the middlemen's fees the Phoenicians charge."

"We'll have to talk to Himilkon when we get back to Rhodes—see what he can tell us about the country and its customs," Sostratos said. "We'll have to hope it's not at war, too. If Ptolemaios decides to try to take it away from Antigonos, it's a good place to stay away from. We almost got stuck in their fight a couple of times this sailing season."

"We *did* get stuck at Kos," Menedemos said.

"So we did," Sostratos said. "But it *is* a good idea, I think. Not that many Hellenes go there. We could make quite a profit. And we can stop in the cities of Cyprus on the way there and back. I think we should have an easy time persuading our fathers."

Menedemos made a sour face, his enthusiasm suddenly half quenched. "*You* can say that. Uncle Lysistratos is a pretty easygoing fellow. But trying to talk *my* father into anything . . ." He tossed his head. "It's like trying to pound sense into a rock."

"I'm sure he says the same thing about you," his cousin remarked.

"What if he does?" Menedemos said. "*I'm* the one who's right." Sostratos didn't argue with him. Menedemos assumed that meant his cousin thought he was right. That it might mean Sostratos merely thought there was no point to arguing never crossed his mind.

The evening before they sailed, Diokles went through the brothels and taverns of Miletos, rounding up the *Aphrodite*'s crew. He made sure everybody was back aboard the merchant galley before she left the harbor. Menedemos clapped him on the back. "You go after them the way a hound goes after hares, and you dig them out wherever they hide."

"I know the spots," the oarmaster answered. "I'd better, by the gods. When I pulled an oar myself, I spent enough time drinking and screwing in them, and hoping my officers wouldn't grab me and haul me away."

Not long after sunrise the next morning, the *Aphrodite* left Miletos. Some of the sailors looked wan and unhappy, but some of them were bound to look wan and unhappy going out of any port. Sostratos stared west across the water at a destination he could see only in his mind's eye. "Athens," he murmured. "At last."

Menedemos gave him a quizzical look. "I've never seen anyone run so hard from a pretty girl, especially when nobody's running after you."

His cousin shrugged. "Metrikhe was pleasant, but she was only a hetaira."

"*Only*, eh?" Menedemos gave a skeptical snort. "I suppose that's why you made such a point of not introducing me to her."

Sostratos turned red. Menedemos hid a smile. Coughing a couple of times, Sostratos said, "I did find her first, you know." His voice got a little stronger, a little sharper: "And I don't see you introducing me to the women you meet at our stops."

"Well, my dear, you do get so tedious about meeting other men's wives," Menedemos said. Sostratos coughed again, this time as if he were choking. He soon found an excuse to go forward. Menedemos grinned and gave his attention to the steering oars.

Waves slapped the *Aphrodite*'s starboard side as she made her way west across the Ikarian Sea. The sail now bellied full, now lay limp in a fitful breeze from out of the north. Menedemos kept six, sometimes eight, men a side on the oars to push the akatos along even when the breeze fell. To the north and northwest, Samos and Ikaria and several smaller islands reared out of the water as if their central hills were the notched backs of mythical beasts.

Though the two were much of a size, Samos was an important place, Ikaria a backwater where nothing much ever happened. Here, Menedemos didn't need to ask his history-minded cousin why the neighboring islands differed so much. Samos had a good harbor. Ikaria didn't. As a result, it had no poleis, only a handful of villages and some herdsmen and their flocks. The world had passed it by, and the *Aphrodite* would do the same.

The akatos put in at Patmos, a small island south of Ikaria, for the night. Patmos had a decent harbor—it boasted several bays a ship might enter, in fact—but very little else. It was dry and rocky, baked brown as a bread crust by the sun. As the *Aphrodite*'s anchors splashed into the sea, Sostratos looked over the desolate terrain and said, "Now I understand."

"Understand what?" Menedemos asked.

"In the early days of the Peloponnesian War, a Spartan admiral named Alkidas was operating north of here, up near Ephesos," his cousin answered. "In those days, the Athenian fleet was much stronger than Sparta's. The Athenian commander—his name was Pakhes—found out the Spartans were around. He chased them as far as Patmos here, but then he turned back."

Menedemos scratched his head. "I'm still not following you, my dear."

"He took one look at this place and then went away," Sostratos said. "Wouldn't you?"

"Oh." Menedemos took another look at the island: at the rocks and the sand and the miserable little fishing village in front of which they were anchored. "A point. I wouldn't want to live out my days here, that's sure."

A few minutes later, just before the sun sank into the Aegean, a small boat put out from the village and made for the *Aphrodite*. As it drew near, one of the men inside called, " 'Oo are you? Where are you comin' from? Where are you 'eaded for?" His dialect was odd: half Ionic, half Doric, and thoroughly rustic.

After naming the merchant galley, Menedemos said, "We're out of Miletos, bound for Athens."

"Ah." The local dipped his head. "All them big places. Don't 'ave much truck with 'em 'ere." *I believe that*, Menedemos thought. *If you weren't a day's sail out of Miletos, no one would ever have anything to do with you.* The fellow in the boat asked, "What are you carryin'?"

Sostratos spoke up: "Koan silk. Crimson dye. Rhodian perfume. Papyrus and ink. Fine balsam from Engedi. A lion's skin." He didn't, Menedemos noted with amusement, mention the gryphon's skull. Was he afraid the people here might want to steal it? If he was, that had to be one of the more foolish fears Menedemos had ever heard of.

"Fancy stuff," the Patmian said. "I might've known. Thought you was a pirate when I first seen you."

Folk often made that mistake about the *Aphrodite*. Hearing of pirates got Menedemos' attention. "Have you seen any lately? Are they sailing in these waters?" he asked.

"Every now and again," the local answered, which might mean anything or nothing. He paused to spit into the sea, then asked a question of his own: "What d'you want for a jar o' your perfume? My woman'd take it right kindly if she got one."

"By the gods!" Menedemos muttered. "I never expected to do business here."

"Eight drakhmai," Sostratos told the Patmian, as calmly as if he were dickering in the market square in Rhodes.

Menedemos admired that calm. He also expected to see the local recoil in horror: a drakhma a day would keep a man and his family housed and fed, if not in fancy style. He looked toward the village again. Nothing here was fancy.

But the man just shrugged and said, "Deal, pal. I got the silver. Don't hardly got nothin' to spend it on, though. 'Ereabouts, we mostly just swap back and forth." He nudged the other man in the boat, who started to row toward shore. Over his shoulder, he called, "Be right back."

"Will he?" Menedemos wondered. "Or is he without an obolos to his name, and just trying to save face in front of us?"

Sostratos shrugged. "No way to tell. Either he'll come or he won't. If he does, I wonder what he'll use for money. They can't possibly mint coins here."

The boat beached itself a plethron or so from the *Aphrodite*. One of the men in it got out and went into a house close by the sea. The other man, the rower, sat in the boat, waiting. That made Menedemos begin to believe the first Patmian did have the money. And sure enough, as twilight began to deepen, he emerged from his house and trotted back to the boat. A moment later, it headed out toward the merchant galley.

"Can I come aboard?" the local called as it drew near.

"Come ahead," Menedemos answered. The boat pulled up alongside the akatos' waist. One of the sailors reached out and helped haul the Patmian into the ship. He walked back to the stern and up onto the poop deck.

"Hail," Sostratos said.

" 'Ail," the Patmian replied. "You got the perfume there? . . . That's not what you'd call a right big jar, is it?"

"It's the size we always sell," Sostratos said, which was true. "There's not a whole lot left after they boil down the roses and mix the scent with oil. It *will* last you a while—your wife won't need much to make herself smell sweet."

Menedemos wondered how true that was. The local hadn't bathed any time recently, which meant the odds were good his wife hadn't, either. True, this was a dry island, but even so. . . . There was no room to get upwind of the fellow, either. Menedemos did his best not to breathe.

With sudden decision, the Patmian dipped his head. "All right. I'll take it." He held out a couple of coins to Sostratos. Menedemos' cousin took them, hefted them, and handed the local the perfume. "Thank you kindly," the fellow said. He scrambled back into the boat. When he and his friend beached it this time, they pulled it well up out of the water and they both went into the village.

"What did he give you?" Menedemos asked.

"See for yourself." Sostratos set the coins on Menedemos' palm.

In the fading light, Menedemos held them up close to his face. "A tetradrakhm from Corinth," he said. "That's a pretty Pegasos on it. And another tetradrakhm from Aigina. Very nice—I'm always glad to get turtles, because they're so heavy."

"Notice anything unusual about this particular turtle?" Sostratos asked.

"I didn't." Menedemos looked more closely. "It's got a smooth shell."

"And flippers, not regular feet," his cousin agreed. "It's a sea turtle, not a tortoise. Aigina hasn't made them like that since the days of the Persian Wars. I wonder how this one ended up here."

"I wouldn't be surprised if this fellow's five-times-great-grandfather stole it from an Aiginetan, and it's been here ever since," Menedemos answered. "I'm just glad he's off my ship. Did you *smell* him?"

"I could hardly help it." Sostratos took back the coins. "However he got the silver, though, it doesn't stink."

"True." Now Menedemos was the one who looked west, towards Athens. "A couple of nights at sea coming up."

"I think that's a better bet than going through the Kyklades again," Sostratos said. "Too many pirates in those waters, and sooner or later we'd come across one who'd sooner fight than go the other way."

"That's what I think, too." Menedemos took off his chiton and threw it down on the poop deck. "Might as well go to sleep now."

When he woke the next morning and untangled himself from the folds of his himation, he exclaimed in low-voiced delight as he stood by the rail and pissed into the harbor of Patmos. The breeze came out of the northeast, strong and with a certain feel to it that made him think it would hold all day.

Every once in a while, such feelings let him down. More often than not, though, he gauged the wind rightly.

Diokles looked up from the rower's bench where he'd passed the night. "Kind of day that makes you want to get out to sea as fast as you can," he said.

"I was thinking the same thing," Menedemos said. The eastern sky was pink, but the sun wouldn't rise for some little while yet. He looked down at Sostratos, who still lay snoring on the poop deck, and stirred him with his foot.

His cousin gasped and sputtered and opened his eyes. "What was that for?" he asked indignantly, sitting up.

"What's the matter?" Menedemos was the picture of innocence. "Don't you want to go to Athens?"

"I want you to go to the crows." Sostratos got to his feet so quickly and fiercely, Menedemos wondered if he would have to fight his cousin. But then the angry glow faded from Sostratos' eyes. "That's a splendid wind, isn't it?"

"Feels good to me," Menedemos said. "The keleustes likes it, too. And I can't imagine anyone being sorry to get away from Patmos."

"All right." Sostratos walked naked to the rail, as Menedemos had moments before. When he turned back, he said, "Let's start getting the sailors up."

Diokles had already started waking the ones who hadn't roused by themselves. They ate bread and oil, drank watered wine, and had the anchors hauled up and stowed by the time the sun crawled above the horizon. They didn't even have to row out of the harbor. It faced west, and the breeze carried the *Aphrodite* away from it as soon as the sail came down from the yard.

Looking back over his shoulder, Menedemos watched Patmos recede behind him. Had he taken the akatos due west, he would have sailed through the Kyklades for the third time that sailing season. Instead, he used the steering oars to swing her somewhat to the north, so that she went up between Ikaria on his right hand and Mykonos on his left. Tenos lay northwest of Mykonos, Andros northwest of Tenos, Euboia northwest of Andros. Menedemos steered the *Aphrodite* on a course parallel to them but well to the east, out in the middle of the Aegean.

He didn't see another ship all day, which suited him fine.

"Late tomorrow or early the next day, we'll be able to slide through the channel between Andros and Euboia and make for Athens," he said.

"Good enough. Better than good enough, in fact," Sostratos said. "You had the right of it: not many ships out here in the middle of the sea."

"We don't guarantee getting through without any trouble this way," Menedemos said. "We do make our chances better, though. And we never get out of sight of land, the way you can sailing west to Great Hellas. So we always know where we are."

"Not easy to get out of sight of land in the Aegean," Sostratos said. "I'm not sure you could do it, not on a clear day."

"Up in the north, maybe," Menedemos said. "There's that broad reach from Lesbos to Skyros. Otherwise, though"—he tossed his head—"no, I wouldn't think so."

Some of the sailors baited lines with bits of bread and cheese and let them down into the sea. They caught a few sprats and a mackerel or two. And then, just when Menedemos was about to order the anchors dropped, Moskhion pulled in a gloriously plump red mullet. "He'll have friends tonight," Sostratos said.

"Won't he, though?" Menedemos agreed. The splendid fish made his mouth water. "I hope I'm Moskhion's friend tonight." As the captain of a merchant galley learned to do, he pitched his voice to carry.

Moskhion looked up from the mullet, an impish grin on his face. "Have we met, sir?" he asked, as bland as if he were a man with estates out to the horizon condescending to speak to a tanner.

Menedemos laughed as loudly as everyone else who heard the sailor. "You'll find out whether we've met," he growled, mock-fierce.

As the sun set, the men who'd caught fish grilled them over little braziers. The savory scent of the flesh filled the air. Moskhion did share the mullet as widely as he could, and sent small portions back to Menedemos, Sostratos, and Diokles. "That's only a bite," Sostratos said as he washed his down with a swallow of wine, "but it's a mighty tasty bite."

"It sure is," Menedemos agreed. "A bite of mullet's worth a bellyful of cheese any day." He knew a hungry man would say no such thing, but he enjoyed the luxury of a full belly. He ate an olive and spat the pit into the sea.

Diokles pointed into the southern sky, a little west of the meridian. "There's Zeus' wandering star," he said.

"Where?" Sostratos said, and then, "Ah. There. Now I see it. I wonder if it's true, as the Babylonians say, that the motions of the stars foretell everything we do."

"How can anyone know something like that?" Menedemos said. "Me, I want to think I do things because I want to do them, not because some star says I must."

"Yes, I want to believe the same thing," his cousin said. "But is it really true, or do I want to believe it because the stars say I should want to?"

Diokles grunted and refilled his wine cup. The oarmaster said, "That kind of talk makes my head ache."

"What do the Babylonians have to say about twins?" Menedemos asked. "They're born at the same time, and sometimes they're like each other, but other sets are as different as eggs and elephants. By the stars, they should all be just alike, shouldn't they?"

"That's true." Sostratos beamed at him. "Very logical, in fact. I wonder if any philosophers have ever thought about what that means. When we get to Athens, I hope I remember to ask."

Twilight deepened. More stars came out. Menedemos spotted Kronos' wandering star, dimmer and yellower than that of Zeus, not far above the eastern horizon. Pointing to it, he said, "I know what that star foretells: not long after I see it, I'll go to sleep."

"Amazing," Sostratos said. "I was born half a year before you, but it means the very same thing for me." They both laughed.

The *Aphrodite* rocked gently on the sea. Menedemos took the motion altogether for granted. It wasn't enough to bother his cousin, who was more sensitive to such things. They lay down side by side on the poop deck. Diokles went forward to sleep on a rower's bench.

When Menedemos woke, morning twilight had replaced that of the evening. He yawned and stretched and watches stars fade from the sky, as he'd watched them come out the night before. High up in the air, a gull screeched.

He got to his feet and tasted the wind, then dipped his head in satisfaction. It hadn't swung during the night, nor had it died. Up toward the bow, one early-rising sailor spoke to another: "Doesn't look like we'll have to pull too hard today."

"Good," the second sailor answered.

Sostratos stayed asleep till the men started hauling in the anchors. Then he looked about in bleary confusion. "Hail, slugabed," Menedemos said.

"Oh. Hail." Sostratos looked around some more, rubbed his eyes, and got to his feet. As he did, he wet a finger to test the wind. What he found brought a smile to his face and eagerness to his voice. "Do you think we'll be able to slide between Andros and Euboia this afternoon?"

"Maybe." Menedemos shook a stern finger at his cousin. "But even if we do, we've got another day's sail after that before we put in at Peiraieus."

"I know. I know." Sostratos waved impatiently. "But we're so close now, I can all but taste Athens."

Menedemos pursed his lips as if he were tasting, too. "Rocks and dirt and a little bit of hemlock, left over from Sokrates. Splash it with oil and it's not so bad."

"Splash you with oil and you're still an idiot," Sostratos said, doing his best not to splutter.

After a bow and a wave for his cousin, Menedemos raised his voice to call out to the sailors: "Eat your breakfast, lads, and then we'll be away. As long as the gods are kind enough to give us the breeze we need, we'd be fools and worse than fools if we didn't make the most of it."

Down came the sail from the yard. A gust of wind filled it almost at once. The mast creaked as it took up the strain. At Menedemos' shouted instructions, the men swung the yard from the starboard bow back to take best advantage of the breeze. The *Aphrodite* slid through the light chop, graceful as a tunny.

Flying fish sprang out of the water. So did dolphins, which leapt far higher and more gracefully. Menedemos tossed a barley roll into the Aegean. The merchant galley's boat had hardly passed it before a dolphin snapped it up. The sailors murmured in delighted approval. A couple of them clapped their hands. "Good for you, skipper," Diokles said. "There's good luck."

No less superstitious than any other seafaring man, Menedemos dipped his head. "Good luck for the dolphin, too," he said. "If it hadn't been in just the right spot, a sea bird would have got there first."

Sure enough, a small gull with a black head that had been swooping toward the roll pulled up with an angry screech: "*Ayeea!*" A moment later, a tern plunged into the sea. It came out with a fish in its beak.

"Between the dolphin and the bird, they've got sitos and opson," Menedemos said.

Instead of laughing at his little joke, Sostratos tossed his head. "For dolphins and terns, fish are sitos: they're what they have to have. When you gave them the barley roll, that was opson for them, even though it would be sitos for us."

Diokles clicked his tongue between his teeth. "Here I've been going to sea almost as long as you've been alive, young sir, and I never once thought of it like that. You've got an odd way of looking at the world—an interesting way," he hastened to add.

"A left-handed way," Menedemos said, which wasn't a compliment.

They didn't have the sea to themselves but for wild things that day. A few fishing boats were out on the wide water east of the Kyklades. When their crews saw the *Aphrodite* approaching, they lowered their sails and made for first Tenos and then, in the afternoon, Andros as fast as they could go. One of the crews cut a net free to be able to flee the faster.

"Poor frightened fools," Menedemos said. "That'll cost them a good bit of silver or a good bit of time to make good, and we didn't want anything to do with them."

"We ought to paint a legend on the side of the ship: I AM NOT A PIRATE," Sostratos said.

"And how long would it be before a pirate painted the same thing on his hemiolia?" Menedemos returned.

Sostratos screwed up his face and stuck out his tongue in a Gorgon's grimace. "That's a horrible thought."

"Are you telling me I'm wrong, though?" Menedemos asked. His cousin tossed his head. Menedemos' smile held slightly grudging approval. One thing Sostratos was, without a doubt: an honest man.

As the sun sank toward the rough horizon to the west, Sostratos pointed toward the channel between Andros and Cape Geraistos, the southernmost part of Euboia. "There it is. We can get through before nightfall."

"We can get through, yes," Menedemos said. "But we can't get very far past the channel if we go through now. When morning comes, we'd be sitting out in the open for anyone to spot. If we stay out here on the open Aegean till morning, though, we can dash between the islands and round Cape Sounion before nightfall tomorrow. How does that sound?"

Sostratos didn't look happy, but he didn't say no. He just sighed, made a pushing motion, and turned away. After a moment, Menedemos realized he was miming Sisyphos' eternal torment. Every time the wicked man got his boulder up near the top of the hill, it would slip away and roll to the bottom again.

"It's not so bad as that," Menedemos said.

"No, it isn't," Sostratos said. "It's worse."

Diokles spoke up: "Whether we go through now or in the morning, I'd serve out weapons first. You never can tell."

"That's a good idea," Menedemos said. "I wish it weren't, but it is." He rubbed his chin as he thought. "I do believe I'm going to bring us up a little farther north before we anchor for the night. That way, I can run straight before the wind in the morning, and we'll slide through as fast as may be."

"Very nice," the keleustes said. "You're right as can be—the sooner we're through there, the better."

The sun was just on the point of setting when Menedemos ordered the anchors into the sea. Sostratos still looked glum.

"Cheer up," Menedemos told him. "See? We're even aimed the right way now." Sure enough, he'd swung the *Aphrodite* around so her bow pointed southwest, straight toward the gap between the islands—and toward the mainland of Attica beyond.

His cousin sighed. "I know it, my dear. But it hasn't happened yet, and I'm not going to be content till it does."

Or even after that, Menedemos thought. The ideal world Sostratos built up in his mind sometimes made him have trouble accepting reality and its imperfections. Menedemos didn't twit him about it, though; the akatos was too crowded a place to make arguments worse.

Bread and olive oil, cheese and olives, rough red wine: a sailor's supper at sea. Not even a taste of mullet to savor tonight; the men hadn't caught anything much above sprat size. Menedemos shrugged. *I'll eat better when we get to Athens*, he thought.

"Another night on the planks," Sostratos said as they stretched out side by side on the poop deck. "I won't be sorry to sleep in a bed again."

There, Menedemos thought he could jab without making his cousin angry, and he did: "Back in Miletos, you weren't doing much in the way of sleeping when you ended up in that hetaira's bed."

Sostratos snorted. "You're a fine one to talk."

"Who, me?" Menedemos did his best to sound innocent. "I didn't do anything much in Miletos."

"No, not in Miletos," Sostratos said darkly.

Menedemos made some other protest, but only deep, heavy, even breathing answered him. Before very long, he fell asleep, too. He woke somewhere in the middle of the night, wondering why he had. Then he realized the *Aphrodite*'s motion had changed. The swells from out of the north remained, but the wind-driven chop had eased. He muttered something or other under his breath, wrapped his himation tighter around himself, and went back to sleep.

But when he woke the next morning, he wasn't surprised to find that the wind had died even though he hardly remembered rousing before. Catching his eye, Diokles mimed rowing motions. Menedemos dipped his head to the oarmaster.

"All I have to say is, it's a good thing we're not a round ship," Sostratos declared after Menedemos woke him and he realized they were becalmed. "If we were a round ship that had to lie here on the sea so close to Athens with no way to get any closer, I do believe I'd scream."

"I believe you'd scream, too," Menedemos said. His cousin gave him a dirty look. He went on, "But, since we go about as fast with oars as we do with the sail, you can save your screams till you need to throw them at your fellow philosophers."

"I'm not much of a philosopher," Sostratos said sadly. "I haven't got enough leisure."

"You're doing something useful, which is more than a lot of those windbags can say for themselves," Menedemos replied. His cousin looked shocked. Before Sostratos could rush to philosophy's defense, Menedemos added, "Eat your breakfast and then do one more useful thing: help me hand out weapons to the crew."

Like most merchant galleys—and, for that matter, like most pirate ships—the *Aphrodite* carried a motley assortment of arms: perhaps a dozen swords (Sostratos belted his on), a handful of peltasts' light shields, some javelins and pikes, hatchets, a couple of ripping hooks, iron crowbars, knives. Menedemos set his bow and a quiver of arrows where he could grab them in a hurry. *Or, more likely, where Sostratos or somebody else can get his hands on them*, he thought. *I'll be busy steering the ship.*

He shrugged. Odds were, this was nothing but a waste of time. Even if a pirate chieftain did make a run at the *Aphrodite*, a show of strength would probably make him choose a different victim. But if you didn't treat what might lie ahead as if it were real, you wouldn't be ready on the off chance it turned out so.

"Rhyppa*pai*! Rhyppa*pai*!" Diokles called, and beat out the stroke with his mallet and bronze square. As the channel between Arados and Euboia drew near, he looked back over his shoulder at Menedemos and asked, "Will you want to put a man at every oar for the dash through the strait?"

The oarmaster acted as if the *Aphrodite* might be sailing straight into danger. Menedemos didn't see how he could do anything less. He dipped his head. "Yes, let's," he said. "We haven't had to do much of that kind of thing this sailing season. Let's see how well they handle it."

"Good enough." Diokles ordered the rowers to the rowing benches. Menedemos sent Aristeidas up to the foredeck to keep an eye out for pirates as the akatos passed each promontory. *If we're going to do this, we'll do it the best way we know how*, he thought.

His own gaze kept swinging from north to south, from one island to the other, as the merchant galley sped down the channel. Diokles had hardly set a hotter pace when they were trying to escape the Roman trireme the summer before. *The men will be glad to ease off once we're through*, Menedemos thought. But then, just when he'd started to think they'd safely made the passage, Aristeidas pointed to port and shouted, "A ship! A ship!"

"A pestilence!" Menedemos exclaimed as the vessel emerged from the concealment of a headland on the northern coast of Andros and raced toward the *Aphrodite*.

"What do we do now?" Sostratos said. "Maybe we should have tried coming through yesterday afternoon."

"Bastard was probably lurking here then, too," Menedemos said. "There aren't many honest uses for a hemiolia, anyhow." The two-banked galley was short and lean and one of the swiftest things afloat. Her crew had already taken down the mast and stowed it abaft of the permanent rowing benches of the upper bank.

"Turn towards 'em and try and scare 'em off?" Diokles asked.

"That's what I'm going to do," Menedemos answered. "They can't have a crew much bigger than ours, so why would they want to mix it up?" He swung the *Aphrodite* into a tight turn toward the hemiolia. "Up the stroke, if you please."

"Right you are, skipper." The keleustes smote the bronze square more quickly still, shouting, "Come on, boys! Put your backs into it! Let's make that polluted vulture run for his nest!"

"I hope he *will* run," Sostratos said quietly.

"So do I," Menedemos answered. The hemiolia gave no sign of sheering off. Its rowers worked their oars at least as smoothly as those of the *Aphrodite*. The men whose benches had been taken up to give room to stow the mast and yard now stood by the gunwale, ready—or acting ready—to swarm aboard the merchant galley.

"Do you want me to take your bow, the way I did on the run up to Khalkis?" Sostratos asked.

"Yes, go ahead; duck under the tillers and do that," Menedemos told him. "Then go forward. Use your own judgment about when to start shooting. Aim for their officers if you see the chance."

"I understand." His cousin got the bow and the quiver, then hurried up between the two rows of panting, sweating rowers toward the foredeck. The men who powered the *Aphrodite* couldn't see what was going on, which was true of the rowers in every sea fight since before the Trojan War. As far as the ship went, the rowers were just tools. Menedemos and Diokles had to get the best use from them.

On came the hemiolia. "Doesn't look like those whoresons want to quit at all, does it?" the oarmaster said.

"No," Menedemos said unhappily. He *was* unhappy; he'd taken the *Aphrodite* closer to Andros than to Euboia because he'd worried more about pirates on the southern coast of the latter island. That meant this pirate ship hadn't had to go so far to close with the akatos. More unhappily still, Menedemos went on, "We couldn't very well have run away. A hemiolia will run down any other kind of ship on the sea."

Diokles didn't argue. That was so obviously true, no one could argue. Most pirates, though, didn't reckon a fight with the large crew of another galley likely to be profitable. If this captain proved an exception . . .

Menedemos picked a spot not far aft of the hemiolia's bow where he hoped to drive home his ram. The other skipper, the man handling the pirate ship's steering oars, would be picking his target on the *Aphrodite*. "Go on," Menedemos muttered. "Run for home, crows take you."

Aristeidas sang out: "They're shooting!"

Sure enough, arrows arced through the air toward the *Aphrodite*. The first shots splashed into the sea well short of the ship. Archers always started shooting too soon. No, almost always—Sostratos stood calmly on the small foredeck, a shaft nocked but the bow not yet drawn. If anyone could wait till he had the chance to make his missiles count, Menedemos' cousin was the man.

A shaft thudded into the stempost, a couple of cubits from Sostratos' head. That seemed to spur him into action. He thrust the bow forward on a stiff left arm, drew the string back to his ear as the Persians had taught Hellenes to do, and let fly. No one aboard the onrushing hemiolia fell, so Menedemos supposed he missed. He pulled another arrow from the quiver and shot again.

This time, Menedemos heard the howl of pain across the narrowing gap. "*Euge!*" he called. "Well shot!"

A moment later, one of the *Aphrodite*'s rowers let out a similar howl and clutched at his shoulder. He lost the stroke; his oar fouled that of the man behind him. The merchant galley tried to swerve. Menedemos worked the steering oars to keep it pointed at the pirate ship. "Clear that oar!" Diokles shouted. A couple of sailors who weren't rowing pulled it inboard.

More arrows struck the akatos' planking. The pirates had several archers, the *Aphrodite* only Sostratos. Several shafts whistled past him as they tried to bring him down. None bit. As coolly as if exercising at a gymnasion, he kept shooting back. Another pirate wailed. He fell into the sea with a splash.

"Oh, very well shot!" Menedemos exclaimed.

"They aren't pulling away," Diokles said.

"I see that," Menedemos answered. "Let's see if we can take out their portside oars and cripple them."

"Same trick we pulled on the trireme, eh?" After a moment's thought, the oarmaster dipped his head. "Worth a try. Safer than ramming, that's certain."

Another sailor on the *Aphrodite*—not a man pulling an oar—screeched and crumpled, clutching his leg. The hemiolia was terrifyingly close now, her oars rising and falling, rising and falling in smooth unison. Seeing how well the pirates rowed worried Menedemos. With a crew like that and a fast,

fast ship, their skipper could make plans of his own. If he swerved at the last instant . . .

"Portside oars—*in!*" Diokles bellowed. At the same time, the pirate ship's keleustes roared out an order of his own. And, at the same time as the *Aphrodite*'s portside rowers brought their oars inboard, so did the hemiolia's. Neither hull crushed the other ship's oars beneath it; neither set of rowers had arms broken and shoulders dislocated as oars flew out of control.

But the men who would have sat at the rear of the hemiolia's upper bank of oars had none to serve once the ship's mast was stowed. As the two ships passed close enough to spit from one to the other, several of them flung grappling hooks at the *Aphrodite*.

"Cut those lines! Cut them, by the gods!" Menedemos shouted.

Suddenly locked together in an embrace of anything but love, the two galleys pivoted around a common axis. The *Aphrodite*'s sailors frantically hacked at the ropes attached to the grapples, while the pirates hauled on those lines and drew the ships closer together yet.

With wild cries that hardly sounded like Greek at all, the first pirates leaped across three or four cubits of open water and onto the merchant galley.

SOSTRATOS SHOT ONE last arrow at the shouting men aboard the hemiolia, then set down Menedemos' bow, yanked his sword from the scabbard, and rushed to join the fight in the waist of the *Aphrodite*. "Dung-eating, temple-robbing whoresons!" he screamed, and swung the sword in an arc of iron at a pirate who was kicking a sailor in the face.

The blade bit between neck and shoulder. Blood spurted. It stank like hot iron. The pirate let out a horrible screech. He whirled toward Sostratos, who stabbed him in the belly. The fellow crumpled. Sostratos stepped on him to get at the next foe.

Madness in a very small space—that was how Sostratos remembered the fight afterwards. The *Aphrodite*'s crew by itself crowded the akatos. Having twice as many men aboard the ship meant, in essence, that no one had room for anything but seizing the closest foe and trying to kill him. Even telling who was friend and who foe wasn't easy; one of the *Aphrodite*'s sailors almost brained Sostratos with a belaying pin.

"*Aphrodite!*" he shouted over and over. "*Aphro*—oof!" A pirate who'd lost whatever weapon he carried punched him in the belly. He folded up, then made himself straighten, more by sheer force of will than anything else. *If I go down, they'll trample me to death*, he thought.

He grabbed at the nearest man to steady himself. It was another pirate: the fellow had a big gold hoop in each ear, wearing his wealth thus instead of in rings. Sostratos didn't have room to use his sword—hanging on to it was hard enough. But his left hand was free. He took hold of one of those rings and yanked with all his strength. The ring tore free. The pirate roared in pain. The earring remained on Sostratos' index finger.

Well, I just made a profit on the day, he thought: the first foolish thing that popped into his head. *Now I have to see if I live long enough to enjoy it*. That, unfortunately, made more sense.

When the press cleared a little, he traded sword strokes with another pirate. It was nothing like practice in the gymnasion. The *Aphrodite* pitched and rolled underfoot as the waves and the surge of men, now here, now there, made her rock. Sailors and pirates all around were pushing and shoving and shouting and cursing. Sostratos worried about a knife in the back almost as much as he did about the blade with which the fellow in front of him was trying to drink his life.

The pirate, who wore a crestless bronze helmet, a sword belt, and nothing else, had ferocity but no great skill. He beat Sostratos' sword aside when the Rhodian thrust at his chest. Sostratos' next blow, though, took him in the side of the head. That helm kept his skull unsplit, but he staggered even so. Sostratos sprang forward and pushed with all his strength. Arms flailing, the pirate went over the rail and fell into the Aegean.

Nimble as a mountain goat, another pirate leaped from the *Aphrodite* back to his own ship with a leather sack under his arm. He'd had all the fighting he wanted, but he'd managed to get away with some loot. Absurdly, that outraged Sostratos. "Come back here, you wide-arsed thief!" he yelled. The pirate paid no attention, and probably didn't even hear.

Then another pirate sprang back to the hemiolia, and another, and another, some with plunder, some without. "See, boys?" Menedemos roared in a great voice. "They can't lick us, and they cursed well know it. *Io* for the *Aphrodite*!"

"*Io!* The *Aphrodite*!" Sostratos' heart leaped as he took up the cry. He hadn't seen his cousin in the press of fighting, and hearing his voice was a great relief. Seeing the pirates beginning to flee the merchant galley was an even greater one.

Now the pirates were the ones who hacked and chopped at the lines tethering their ship to the akatos. Now they were the ones who pushed the hemiolia away from the *Aphrodite* with poles and oars. A couple of them retrieved the bows they'd left behind and started shooting into the merchant galley as the rest rowed away from a quarry that had proved tougher than they expected.

Sostratos rushed up to the *Aphrodite*'s foredeck, which had seen almost no fighting. Menedemos' bow and the quiver of arrows lay there undisturbed. Sostratos snatched them up again and shot back at the pirates. He was rewarded when their oarmaster screamed and crumpled with an arrow in his thigh. The Rhodian aimed a couple of shafts at the man handling the hemiolia's steering oars, who he thought was the captain. They went wide, though, and the man stayed at his station.

The hemiolia limped off. Not all its oars were manned, not any more. Sostratos wondered if Menedemos would order a pursuit. But his cousin was otherwise occupied: he stooped over a fallen pirate in the waist of the *Aphrodite*. The pirate raised a hand for mercy. Slowly and deliberately, Menedemos drove his sword into the man's body. Blood glistened on the blade as he straightened up. "Throw this carrion into the sea," he told the closest sailors, his voice cold as a Thracian winter.

That thrust hadn't killed the raider. He was still groaning and feebly writhing as the sailors lifted him and flung him over the side. *Splash!* The groans abruptly ceased.

Another pirate was already dead, his head smashed like a broken pot. The sailors threw his body out of the *Aphrodite*, too. Looking back toward the stern, Sostratos saw several men gathered around another body. One of them looked up and caught his eye. "It's Dorimakhos," the fellow said, and tossed his head to add without words that the sailor wouldn't be getting up again. "Took a javelin through the throat, poor beggar."

Menedemos made his way forward. Blood splashed his tunic and his hide, but he seemed hale. Looking down at himself, Sostratos found his own tunic similarly stained. He also found he had a cut on his calf he hadn't even noticed. Now that he knew it was there, it began to hurt.

"Hail," Menedemos said. "You fought well."

"We all did," Sostratos answered. "Otherwise, we wouldn't have driven them off. Are you all right?"

His cousin shrugged. "Scratches, bruises. I'll be fine in a couple of days. This was the worst I got." He held out his left hand, which bore a ragged, nasty wound.

"Is that a bite?" Sostratos asked. Menedemos dipped his head. "Pour wine on it," Sostratos told him. "That's the best thing I know to keep wounds from festering, and bites are liable to. I'm no Hippokrates, but I know that much."

"I wish we had Hippokrates aboard now, or any other physician we could get our hands on," Menedemos said. "You probably know more than most of us—and the men will think you do even if you don't. Come help sew 'em up and bandage 'em. We've got plenty of wine to splash on our hurts, anyhow."

Along with Menedemos and Diokles, Sostratos did what he could, suturing and bandaging arms and legs and scalps. He splashed on wine with a liberal hand. The sailors howled at the sting. The needle and thread he used were coarse ones made for sewing sailcloth, but they went through flesh well enough. "Hold still," he told Teleutas, who had a gash just below his knee.

"You try holding still with somebody stabbing you," Teleutas retorted.

"Do you want to keep bleeding?" Sostratos asked.

Teleutas tossed his head. "No, but I don't want to keep getting hurt, either."

Impatiently, Sostratos said, "You don't have that choice. You can bleed, or you can let me sew up this wound and then bandage it. I won't take long, and you'll stop getting hurt any more as soon as I'm done."

"All right. Go on," Teleutas said, but he jerked and cursed every time Sostratos drove the needle through his flesh. And he complained more when Sostratos wrapped sailcloth around the wound and made it fast with a sloppy knot: "Call that a bandage? I've seen real physicians bind up wounds, by the gods. They make a bandage worth looking at, all nice and neat and fancy. This? *Pheu!*" He screwed up his face as he made the disgusted noise.

"I'm so sorry," Sostratos said with icy irony. "If you like, I'll take it off, tear out the stitches, and start over."

"You try and touch that leg again, and I'll make you sorry for it," the sailor said. "I just want a proper job done."

"It's the best I can do," Sostratos told him. He knew Teleutas had a point. Real physicians made their bandages as neat and elaborate as they could, some to the point of showing off. He went on, "Just because it isn't neat doesn't mean it won't do the job."

"That's what you say." Teleutas pointed up to the yard. "If you were talking about the rigging, would you say the same thing? Not likely! You'd be screaming your head off to get all the lines shipshape."

Sostratos' ears burned. *So much for the men thinking I know more about doctoring than they do.* Of course, Teleutas complained and malingered at any excuse or none. Even so, Sostratos would have wished for a little more gratitude.

Another sailor did thank him, very politely, when he bandaged a stab wound in the man's belly. He sniffed the wound as he applied the bandage. It wasn't very wide, and wasn't bleeding nearly so much as Teleutas', but he did get a faint whiff of dung. He said nothing to the sailor, and held his face steady till he'd finished the job. Then he went looking for Menedemos.

"Why so grim?" his cousin asked as he dealt with a wound much like Teleutas'. The sailor he was helping didn't snarl at him or criticize his inartistic bandages; the man just seemed glad to have the cut dealt with.

But Sostratos, though he noticed that, had too much on his mind really to envy Menedemos' luck. He said, "I'm afraid Rhodippos is going to die."

"*Oimoi!*" Menedemos exclaimed in dismay. "Why do you say so? He didn't seem that badly hurt. I saw him."

"His gut's pierced," Sostratos answered. "Such men almost always die of fever. Remember that sailor last summer, after the Roman archer shot him from their trireme as we went past?"

Menedemos drummed his fingers on his right thigh. His hands were bloody. Looking down, Sostratos saw his own were, too. Voice troubled, his cousin said, "Yes, I do. Well, here's hoping you're wrong, that's all."

"Here's hoping indeed," Sostratos said. "I'm *not* a physician—if you don't believe me, ask Teleutas. But I do remember what I've seen and what I've heard."

"I know," Menedemos said. "You remember everything, as far as I can tell."

"I wish I did," Sostratos said.

"If you don't, you come closer than anyone else I know," Menedemos said. "I know we're lucky to have come off even as well as we did, but all the same. . . ." He clicked his tongue between his teeth. "We've got a lot of men hurt."

"Most of them should get better," Sostratos said.

"Gods grant it be so," Menedemos said. "If it *is* so, I'll give Asklepios a sheep at his temple on Kos if we put in there on the way home, or back on Rhodes if we don't." He glanced up toward the heavens, as if hoping to catch sight of the god of healing listening.

Sostratos wasn't sure a sacrifice would do any good, but he wasn't sure it wouldn't, either. *Even Sokrates, when he was dying, remembered he owed Asklepios a cock*, he thought.

"At least the whoresons didn't try to wreck our rigging, the way they would have if we were a round ship," Menedemos said: maybe that glance heavenward had in fact been aimed at the yard.

"Not much point to it with a galley," Sostratos said. "We

can still row perfectly well, and we could even if the sail came down. Of course," he added, "they might not have thought of that. One often doesn't think of everything in the middle of a fight."

A sailor limped up to them with the broken shaft of an arrow sticking out of his calf. "Will you draw this polluted thing for me?" he said through clenched teeth. "I tried pulling it out, but it hurt too cursed much for me to do the job myself."

"A good thing you stopped," Sostratos said. "The point's barbed; you would have hurt yourself worse if you'd kept on." He bent and felt the wound.

"Well, how will you get it out, then?" the man asked after a yelp of pain.

"We'll have to push it through," Sostratos answered, "either that or cut down to the point. Where it is, I think pushing it through is a better bet—it's only a digit or two from coming out already."

The sailor looked fearfully to Menedemos. The captain of the *Aphrodite* dipped his head. "My cousin's likely right, Alkiphron," he said. "Here—sit down on a bench and stretch out your leg. He'll hold it and I'll push the arrow through and bandage it up. It'll be over before you know it." To Sostratos, he added a quick, low-voiced aside: "Make sure you hang on tight."

"I will," Sostratos promised as Alkiphron eased himself down to a rower's bench. He bent beside the sailor and grasped his leg above and below the wound. "Try to keep as still as you can," he told him.

"I'll do that," Alkiphron said.

Menedemos took hold of the protruding shaft. Alkiphron gasped and tensed. Menedemos gave him a broad, friendly smile. "Are you ready?" he asked. Before the wounded man could answer—and before he could tense himself any more—Menedemos pushed the arrow through.

Alkiphron shrieked. He tried to jerk his leg away. Sostratos couldn't quite stop the motion, but kept it small. The blood-smeared bronze point burst through the sailor's skin. "There," Sostratos said soothingly as Menedemos drew the shaft out after it. "Now it's over."

"You took it like a hero," Menedemos added, wrapping several thicknesses of sailcloth around the wound. He had a knack for saying things that made men feel better. *It's probably the knack that makes him such a fine seducer*, Sostratos thought. Whatever it was, he wished he had more of it himself.

He also noted that Menedemos' bandage was no neater than the ones he'd made himself. Alkiphron didn't seem inclined to be critical. He watched the bandage start to turn red. "That . . . hurt like fire," he said. "But you're right—it's better now. Thank you both."

"Glad to do it," Menedemos said. "I hope it heals clean."

"It should, too," Sostratos told the sailor. "It's bleeding freely, and that helps."

"Take a cup of wine, Alkiphron," Menedemos said. "That will help build your blood up again." Sostratos frowned. From what he remembered, Hippokrates and his fellows would have prescribed differently. But Alkiphron looked so pleased at Menedemos' suggestion, Sostratos held his peace. And Menedemos remarked, "I wouldn't mind a cup of wine myself."

Sostratos thought it over, not that he needed long. "Good idea," he said. "Splendid idea, in fact. If you put it to the Assembly, it would carry in a flash."

Neither he nor Menedemos bothered watering the wine they dipped from an amphora, either. As Menedemos sipped, he said, "I don't do this every day"; he had to know they were being immoderate as well as Sostratos did.

Sostratos replied, "Well, my dear, we don't fight off a pirate ship every day, either."

"No, we don't, and a good thing, too," Menedemos said. "Most of those abandoned catamites have better sense than to tangle with a ship like ours. And I'm going to make sure our boys do plenty of wineshop bragging, too. Let the word get around: the *Aphrodite*'s a hedgehog, too prickly to quarrel with."

"That's good. That's very good," Sostratos said. After a couple of swigs of strong neat wine, it certainly seemed good.

Menedemos drained his cup and filled it again. Catching sight of Sostratos' expression, he grinned. "Don't worry—I still know where Attica lies."

"You'd better," Sostratos told him.

"What I wish I knew," his cousin said, "is how to keep pirates from coming after merchants in the first place. It's not just that no one patrols the sea hard enough, though we Rhodians do what we can. But a pirate in a hemiolia can show his heels to any ship afloat; even a trireme can't always catch a hemiolia. Honest men ought to be able to beat the bastards at their own game."

"You've said that before," Sostratos remarked. "What's the answer?"

"To the crows with me if I know. If it were easy, somebody would have thought of it a long time ago, wouldn't you say? But there's got to be one somewhere."

Sostratos started to ask him why there had to be one, but checked himself. He didn't want to argue, not now. All he wanted to do was take a moment to be glad he remained alive and free and unmaimed. A little wine sloshed out of his cup. He laughed in embarrassment. "I'm not pouring a libation. My hand is shaking."

"That's a sign you need more wine," Menedemos said, refilling the cup before Sostratos could protest. His cousin went on, "It's all right to shake a little now, when everything's over. I've done that myself—you start thinking about what might have been. But you did fine when you needed to."

"I didn't have time to be afraid then." Sostratos took a pull at the wine and decided not to complain about Menedemos' giving him more.

Menedemos' mind was already moving on to other things: "We'll have to put poor Dorimakhos' body in the boat. You know how the men feel about having a corpse on board ship. And when we do get in to Attica, we'll have to pay a priest to purify the boat—and the *Aphrodite*."

"One more thing to take care of." But Sostratos didn't argue about that, either. The blood spilled aboard the akatos, the deaths she'd seen, left her ritually polluted. After his time in the Lykeion, Sostratos wasn't sure he still believed in such pollutions. But he was sure the sailors, superstitious to a man, did. Cleansing the ship would put them at ease, and so it needed doing.

"I wonder how much the gods-detested pirates managed to steal when they went back aboard their ship," Menedemos said.

"We'd better find out," Sostratos replied. "We can't sell what we haven't got any more."

"You tend to that," Menedemos said. "You know where everything's supposed to be."

"Right," Sostratos said tightly. Every once in a while, he wished he didn't have such a retentive memory. He also wished his cousin didn't take that memory so much for granted. Neither wish seemed likely to come true here.

Menedemos, for a wonder, noticed his glower and asked, "Is something wrong?"

"Never mind," Sostratos answered. He was as he was, just as Menedemos was as *he* was. And his cousin did have plenty of other things to do. Sostratos clicked his tongue between his teeth as he ducked under the poop deck. Being as he was, he found himself taking the other fellow's point of view, which made staying annoyed harder.

He hadn't seen any of the pirates get down under there, but the silver was the first and most important thing he needed to check. A glance told him all the leather sacks were where they had been before the hemiolia dashed out from behind the headland on Andros. He breathed a sigh of relief. After all they'd sold on Miletos, losing their money would have been a dreadful blow.

He came out with care, and felt a certain amount of pride at not banging his head. *What next?* he wondered. The answer wasn't long in coming: *the balsam.* It was literally more precious than silver. He knew under which bench it was stowed. When he squatted there, he found it undisturbed.

Now that I've made sure of the money and the balsam, he thought, *Menedemos can't blame me if I check the gryphon's skull.* He knew exactly where it was (*of course I know exactly where it is,* went through his mind): port side, stowed under the ninth rower's bench. He hurried forward and stooped as he had to make sure the balsam was where it belonged.

The gryphon's skull wasn't there.

Sostratos straightened. His first, automatic, assumption was that he'd counted benches wrong. He counted them again. This was the ninth. He bent again. Still no trace of the big leather sack that had held the skull. He looked under the eighth, and also under the tenth, on the off chance—the preposterous, ridiculous, utterly unlikely off chance—he'd miscounted benches when stowing the skull. No sign of it under either bench, only what he recalled putting in those places.

Desperation clanging inside his mind, he checked the starboard benches. *Maybe you put it over there after all.* But he hadn't. The gryphon's skull was gone.

Wild-eyed, Sostratos stared out to sea. The hemiolia was long vanished. With it went a skull that had come from the edge of the world; a skull that, by an accident of fate, had found the perfect owner; a skull that now, by a more malign accident of fate, would never reach the men who might have wrung sense from its strangeness. Gone. Gone with a filthy pirate who surely couldn't write his name, who cared nothing for knowledge, who'd chosen theft and robbery in place of honest work. Gone. Gone forever, past hope of returning.

Sostratos burst into tears.

"What's the matter, young sir?" Diokles asked. "What did the thieving whoresons get?"

"The gryphon's skull," Sostratos choked out.

"Oh. That thing." The oarmaster visibly cast about for something to say. At last, brightening, he found it: "Don't fret too much. It wouldn't've brought in all that much cash anyways."

"Cash?" The word tasted like vomit in Sostratos' mouth. He cursed as foully as he knew how—not with Menedemos' Aristophanic brio, perhaps, but with far more real anger, real hatred, behind the foul language.

Sailors shied away from him. They'd never seen him in such a transport of temper. He'd never known himself in such a fury, either. He would gladly have crucified every pirate ever born and set fire to every forest from which the shipwrights shaped the timbers of their hemioliai and pentekonters.

From the stern, Menedemos called, "What's gone missing?"

He had to say it again: "The gryphon's skull."

"Oh," his cousin said. "Is that all?"

"All?" Sostratos howled. More curses burst from him. Still hot as iron in the forge, he finished, "They could have taken anything else on this ship—*anything*, do you hear me? But no! One of those gods-detested rogues had to steal the single, solitary thing we carried that will—would—matter a hundred years from now."

Menedemos came forward and set a hand on his shoulder. "Cheer up, my dear. It's not so bad as that."

"No. It's worse," Sostratos said.

His cousin tossed his head. "Not really. Just think: right this very minute, you're probably having your revenge."

"My what?" Sostratos gaped, as if Menedemos had suddenly started speaking Phoenician. "What are you talking about?"

"I'll tell you what," Menedemos answered. "Suppose you're a pirate. Your captain decides to go after an akatos for a change. 'It'll be a tough fight, sure enough,' he says, 'but think how rich we'll be once we take her.' You manage to board the *Aphrodite*. Her sailors are all fighting like lions. Somebody stabs you in the leg. Somebody else cuts off half your ear."

He paused. "Go on," Sostratos said, in spite of himself.

Grinning, Menedemos did: "Pretty soon, even Antigonos the One-Eyed can see you aren't going to win this scrap. You grab whatever you can—whatever's under that bench there—and you hop back aboard your hemiolia. You have to get away from those fighting madmen on the merchant galley, so you pull your oar till you're ready to drop dead. Somebody slaps a bandage on your ear and sews up your leg. And then, finally, you say, 'All right, let's see what's in this sack. It's big and heavy—it's got to have something worthwhile inside.' And you open it—and there's the gryphon's skull looking back at you, as ugly as it was in the market square in Kaunos. What would you do then?"

Slowly, Sostratos smiled. That *was* vengeance, of a sort.

But Diokles said, "Me, I'd fling the polluted thing straight into the sea."

That struck Sostratos as horribly likely. In his mind's eye, he could see the pirate staring at the skull. He could hear the fellow cursing, hear his mates laughing. And he could see the blue waters of the Aegean closing over the gryphon's skull forevermore.

"Think of the knowledge wasted!" he cried.

"Think of the look on that bastard's face when he opens the sack," Menedemos said.

It was the only consolation Sostratos had. It wasn't enough, wasn't anywhere close to enough. "Better I should have sold the skull to Damonax," he said bitterly. "What if it sat in his house? Maybe his son or his grandson would have taken it to Athens. Now it's gone."

"I'm sorry," Menedemos said, though he still seemed more amused than anything else. He pointed west, toward the distant mainland of Attica. "We still might get to Cape Sounion by sundown."

"I don't care," Sostratos said. "What difference does it make now?" He'd hoped his name might live forever. *Sostratos the Rhodian, discoverer of* . . . He tossed his head. What had he discovered? Thanks to the pirate, nothing at all.

MENEDEMOS BROUGHT THE *APHRODITE* into the little harbor of the village of Sounion, which lay just to the east of the southernmost tip of the cape. He pointed inland, towards a small but handsome temple, asking, "Who is worshiped there?"

"That's one of Poseidon's shrines, I think," Sostratos answered. "Athena's is the bigger one farther up the isthmus."

"Ah. Thanks," Menedemos said. "I haven't stopped here before, so I didn't remember, if I ever knew. Sounion . . ." He snapped his fingers, then dipped his head, recalling some lines from the *Odyssey*:

" 'But when we reached holy Sounion, the headland of
Athens

There Phoibos Apollo the steersman of Menelaos
Slew, assailing him with shafts that brought painless death.
He held the steering-oar of the racing ship in his hands:
Phrontis Onetor's son, who was best of the race of men
At steering a ship whenever storm winds rushed.' "

"Not storm winds now, gods be praised," his cousin said. "You did a good job steering the *Aphrodite*, though, to get us here before nightfall."

"Thanks," Menedemos said. "Do you suppose we could get a priest to purify the ship now, or will we have to wait here till morning?" He answered his own question: "Morning, of course, so we can get Dorimakhos' body off the ship and set him in his grave." He lowered his voice: "And you were right, worse luck—Rhodippos has a fever I don't like, enough to put him half out of his head."

"I know." Sostratos sorrowfully clicked his tongue between his teeth. "I wish such things didn't happen with belly wounds, but they do." He ground out, "I wish I'd shot the bastard who stole the gryphon's skull right in the belly. I want him dead."

He was usually among the most gentle of men. Menedemos regarded him with more than a little curiosity. "I don't think you'd sound so savage if someone stole half our silver."

"Maybe I wouldn't," Sostratos said. "We can always get more silver one way or another. Where will we come by another gryphon's skull?"

"For all you know, there'll be another one in the marketplace at Kaunos next year," Menedemos answered. "Who knows what will come out of the trackless east these days?"

"Maybe." But Sostratos didn't sound as if he believed it. On reflection, Menedemos couldn't blame his cousin. The gryphon's skull wasn't obviously valuable, and was large and heavy and bulky. How many merchants would carry such a thing across ten thousand stadia and more on the off chance someone in the west might want it? Not many—that one had still surprised Menedemos.

He said, "Now that we haven't got it any more, do you still want to go on to Athens?"

"I don't know," Sostratos answered. "Right now, I'm so tired and so angry and so disgusted, I know I can't think straight. Ask me again in the morning, and maybe I'll be able to tell you something that makes sense."

"Fair enough," Menedemos said. "Let's have some more wine now. It's been a long time since the fight."

They were on their second cup when someone on shore pushed a boat into the water and rowed out toward the merchant galley; no one had bothered to build quays here, and the *Aphrodite* lay at anchor a couple of plethra from the beach. "What ship are you?" a man called from the boat.

"The *Aphrodite*, out of Rhodes," Menedemos answered. "We were bound for Athens, but pirates came after us between Euboia and Andros. We fought them off, and here we are."

"Fought 'em off, you say?" The fellow in the boat sounded dubious. "What's your cargo?"

He thinks we're *pirates*, Menedemos realized. When a galley came into an out-of-the-way harbor like this one, the locals often started jumping to conclusions. "We've got Koan silk aboard, and crimson dye from Byblos," Menedemos said, "and perfume from Rhodes, and fine ink, and some papyrus from Egypt—though we're almost sold out of that—and a splendid lion skin from Kaunos on the Anatolian mainland, and the world's best balsam from Phoenicia."

"World's best, eh?" The man in the boat laughed. "You sound like a tradesman, all right."

"And we've got news," Sostratos added.

"News?" With the one word, Menedemos' cousin had done a better job of snaring the man in the rowboat than he had himself with his whole long list of what the *Aphrodite* carried. "Tell it, man!" the local exclaimed.

"Polemaios Polemaios' son is dead," Sostratos said. "When he went to Kos, he tried to raise a rebellion against Ptolemaios, and the lord of Egypt made him drink hemlock. We were there when it happened." As usual, he said nothing about taking Polemaios to Kos, or about watching Antigonos' nephew die.

What he did say was plenty. "Polemaios dead?" the Sounian

echoed. "You're sure?" Menedemos and Sostratos solemnly dipped their heads. "That *is* news!" the man said, and started rowing back to shore as fast as he could go.

"We could have just told him that, and he wouldn't have worried about anything else," Menedemos said. He yawned. After the desperate day, those two cups of wine were hitting him hard. As the stars shone down on the merchant galley, he stretched out on the poop deck and dove into sleep like a dolphin diving into the sea.

However worn he was, he did not pass a restful night. Rhodippos woke him—woke the whole crew—two or three times with cries of rage and dread as the wounded, feverish sailor battled demons only he could see. By the time the sun followed rosy-fingered dawn up out of the sea to the east, the man was moaning almost continuously.

Menedemos pulled the stopper from a fresh amphora of wine. "Last night this made me sleepy," he said as he dipped some out. "Now I hope it'll wake me up." He added water to the wine and drank.

"Get me some, too, please," Sostratos said. "Poor fellow," he added around a yawn. "It's not his fault."

"Fault doesn't matter." Menedemos was yawning, too. His head felt filled with sand. Most of the sailors were awake, too, though a couple snored on despite Rhodippos' ravings. Menedemos envied them their exhaustion.

Sostratos said, "We need to see about one burial—two soon—and about getting the ship cleansed of pollution." Menedemos envied him, too, for being able to concentrate on what they had to do when he was as weary as everyone else.

Despite Dorimakhos' corpse, they used the akatos' boat to go ashore. For an obolos, an old man pointed them toward the burial ground outside Sounion, and toward the gravedigger's house. "You'll be the Rhodians," that worthy said when they knocked on his door. Gossip, as usual, had wasted no time. "You lost someone in your fight with the pirates?"

"We lost one man, and we're losing another," Menedemos answered.

"Will you stay here till he dies?" the gravedigger asked. Menedemos and Sostratos looked at each other. Sostratos sighed and shrugged. Menedemos dipped his head. So did the gravedigger. "Three drakhmai, then, for two graves," he said.

Sostratos gave him three Rhodian coins. He took them without a nurmur, though they were lighter than Athenian owls. Menedemos asked, "Who's the chief priest at Poseidon's temple here? We'd like him to purify our ship."

"That would be Theagenes," the gravedigger replied.

As the two Rhodians walked toward the temple, Menedemos asked, "Where do we go from here?"

His cousin looked at him. "Why, back to the ship, I would think."

Menedemos made an exasperated noise. "No. What I mean is, where does the *Aphrodite* go from here?—and you know it, too."

"Well, what if I do?" Sostratos walked along for several paces, his bare feet kicking up dust from a dirt path that hadn't seen rain since spring. Then, suddenly he stopped and sighed and shrugged. "I'd hoped I would change my mind with some sleep, but I haven't. Without the gryphon's skull, I don't much care where we go. What difference does it make now?"

"It makes a lot of difference," Menedemos answered. "It makes a difference in what we end up selling, and for how much."

Sostratos shrugged again. "We'll show some profit this sailing season. We won't show a really big one, the way we did coming back from Great Hellas after the peafowl and that mad dash down to Syracuse loaded with grain."

"That wasn't mad. That was brilliant," Menedemos said. It had been his idea.

"It turned out to be brilliant, because we got away with it. That doesn't mean it wasn't mad," Sostratos said, relentlessly precise as usual. A fly lit on Menedemos' hand. He brushed it away. Back among the trees, a cuckoo called. Sostratos continued, "Without the gryphon's skull, whether we go to Athens or not doesn't matter to me. It's just another polis now, as far as I'm concerned."

"You really do mean that," Menedemos said. His cousin dipped his head. He looked as sad as a man whose child had just died. Trying to cheer him up, Menedemos asked,

"Couldn't you—I don't know—tell your philosopher friends about the gryphon's skull?"

He didn't know whether he'd cheered Sostratos, but saw he had amused him. "Kind of you to think of such things, my dear, but it wouldn't do," Sostratos said. "It would be like . . ." He paused a moment in thought, then grinned and pointed at Menedemos. "Like you bragging about some woman you've had, where nobody else has seen her or knows whether you're telling the truth."

"Don't you listen to the sailors?" Menedemos said. "Men talk like that all the time."

"Of course they do. I'm not saying they don't," Sostratos answered. "But the point is, half the time the people who listen to them think, *By the gods, what a liar he is!* If I can't hold up the skull to show the men of the Lykeion and the Academy, why should they believe me?"

"Because they know you?" Menedemos suggested. "I'd be likelier to believe you bragging about a woman than I would most people I can think of. I'm still jealous about that hetaira back in Miletos, and you didn't even brag about her."

"Men know about women. They know what they're like—as much as men can hope to, anyhow," Sostratos said, and Menedemos laughed. His cousin went on, "But suppose men had only known boys up till now. Think about that."

"I like women better," Menedemos said. "They enjoy it, too, and boys usually don't."

"Never mind that," Sostratos said impatiently. "Suppose all we'd known were boys, and somebody started talking about what a woman was like. Would you believe him if he didn't have a woman there with him to prove what he was saying?"

Menedemos thought about it. "No, I don't suppose I would," he admitted.

"All right, then. That's what I'd be up against, talking about the gryphon's skull without being able to show it." Sostratos let out another sigh, a lover pining for a lost love. "It's over now. Nothing to be done about it. Let's find this Theagenes and get the ship purified."

The priest was pruning a fig tree in a little orchard by the temple when the Rhodians came up to him. "Hail," Menedemos called.

"Hail," Theagenes answered over his shoulder. "Just a moment, and I'll be right with you." A smooth-barked branch thudded to the ground. Theagenes grunted in satisfaction and lowered his saw. He turned toward Menedemos and Sostratos. He was a short man, shorter than Menedemos, but with wiry muscles shifting under his skin as he moved. "There. That's better. Now, what can I do for the two of you? You'll be from the ship that got in last night?"

"That's right." Menedemos gave his name and Sostratos'. "If you heard that, you probably heard we fought off pirates, too. We had a man killed, and another who looks sure to die of his wounds."

Theagenes dipped his head. "I did hear that, yes. You'll want me to purify the vessel?"

"If you please," Menedemos said. "And we'd like to sacrifice here as a thanks offering for driving those whoresons away." Sostratos stirred at that. Menedemos had been sure he would; he hated expense. But it needed doing.

"Good enough." The priest hesitated, then went on, "This wounded man, if he dies after I finish the job . . ."

"You'd have to do it over again," Sostratos said.

"That's what I meant, yes," Theagenes agreed. "A death is a death. As far as the ritual goes, how it happens doesn't matter."

"We'll move him to the boat," Menedemos said. He'd done that with the dying sailor after the clash with the Roman trireme the year before. "Purifying that will be less work for you—and if you can't come for some reason, well, we can buy another boat."

"I understand," Theagenes said. "Let me get my lustration bowl, and then I'll come to the harbor with you." He went into the temple.

When he came out again, Sostratos stirred. "How long has this temple had that bowl?" he whispered to Menedemos.

"What do you—? Oh." Menedemos saw what his cousin meant. The bowl had an image of Poseidon in it. The god was done in black against a red background. That style had been replaced by red figures on a black background about the time of the Persian Wars. How many black-figure bowls still survived? Menedemos said, "They're very careful of it."

"I should think so," his cousin answered.

The two Rhodians and the priest walked back toward the seashore. When Theagenes got a good look at the *Aphrodite*, he said, "Your ship is too beamy to make a proper pirate, but I can see how people might think at first glance she was one."

"We've had it happen, yes," Menedemos said. "As far as I'm concerned, Poseidon or someone ought to sweep all pirates off the sea."

"I wish that might happen myself," Theagenes said. "The world would be a better place."

Menedemos waved to the rowers waiting for his return. The men waved back. They took him and Sostratos and Theagenes out to the *Aphrodite*. Dorimakhos' body lay, wrapped in bloodstained sailcloth, at the stern of the boat. As Theagenes neared the akatos, he filled that ancient bowl with seawater. He handed it to Menedemos before scrambling from the boat to the ship.

What would he do if I dropped it? Menedemos wondered. But he didn't: he just gave it back to Theagenes. The priest looked at the dark stains on the *Aphrodite*'s planking. "You did have a hard fight here," he remarked.

"It would have been harder still if we'd lost it," Sostratos said.

"Of course," Theagenes said. He went up and down the ship, sprinkling the water from the bowl over the planks and murmuring prayers in a low voice. As he came up onto the poop deck, he remarked, "The sea purifies anything it touches."

"I suppose that's why, in the *Iliad*, Talthybios the herald threw the boar Agamemnon sacrificed when he finally apologized to Akhilleus into the sea," Menedemos said.

"Just so." Theagenes sounded pleased. "The carcass of the boar carried the burden of Agamemnon's oath. It should not have been eaten by men. The sea was the path of its travel to earth, sun, and the Furies." The priest beamed at Menedemos. "I see you are a man who thinks on such things."

"Well . . ." Menedemos was no more modest than he had to be, but he couldn't take that kind of praise with Sostratos standing beside him. He said, "My cousin leans more toward philosophy than I do."

"I don't particularly lean toward philosophy myself," Theagenes said. "I think we ought to do as the gods want us to do, not make up fine-sounding excuses to do as we please."

Sostratos raised an eyebrow at that. Before he could start the sort of argument that had made Sokrates a candidate for hemlock, Menedemos said, "We do thank you for purifying the ship." He gave Sostratos a look that said, *Please don't.*

To his relief, Sostratos didn't. Theagenes said, "I am pleased to hear such words from you, young man. A man who loves the gods will be loved by them." He went down into the waist of the ship and splashed a little seawater on Rhodippos. The wounded man, lost in a fever dream, moaned and muttered to himself. Theagenes sighed. "I fear you're right about him. Death reaches toward him even as we watch."

"I wish something could be done about wounds like his, whether by gods or healers," Sostratos said—no, he wouldn't casually let it drop after all.

"Asklepios has been known to work miracles," the priest said.

"So he has," Sostratos agreed. "If he did it more often, though, they wouldn't be miracles, and a lot more men would have longer lives."

The priest sent him a sour stare. Menedemos felt like a man standing between two armies just before they shouted the paean and charged each other. Doing his best to change the subject, he said, "Come on, boys, let's get Rhodippos into the boat. We'll give him the best care we can there."

Rhodippos howled piteously as several sailors lowered him into the boat. He kept on howling even after they rigged an awning of sailcloth to keep the sun off him. "The kindest thing we could do for him would be to cut his throat," Sostratos said.

"He doesn't know what's happening to him," Menedemos said. "It's a small mercy, but a mercy."

"And the gods may yet choose to preserve his life," Theagenes added.

Menedemos didn't believe that, not for a moment. And, in his zeal to keep his cousin and the priest from squabbling, he'd been too clever for his own good. With Rhodippos in the boat, how was Theagenes to get back to Sounion? Menedemos hadn't the heart to take the wounded man out of there again. The sailors hailed a rowboat from the shore. He gave the fellow in it a couple of oboloi to row the priest home.

Once Theagenes was out of earshot—or nearly so—Sostratos sniffed and said, "He may be holy, but he isn't what you'd call bright."

Theagenes' back got very straight. No, he hadn't been quite out of earshot; Menedemos hadn't thought so. "He probably thinks you're bright, but not very holy."

"I don't care what he thinks," Sostratos said. "And if you think—"

"I think the ship is ritually clean again," Menedemos broke in. "And I think that's good. Don't you?" He gave Sostratos a hard look, as if to say he'd better.

"Oh, yes," his cousin admitted. "I try not to be superstitious, but I don't succeed so well as I'd like. I don't think you can be a sailor without being superstitious."

"I believe in luck and the gods. If you want to say that makes me superstitious, go ahead," Menedemos said, and wondered how big an argument he'd get. To his surprise, he got none at all. Sostratos hadn't heard him; his cousin was watching a flock of seabirds flapping past. Menedemos laughed. "And how do the omens look?"

Sostratos did hear that. "I wasn't watching them for the sake of omens," he said. "I just don't think I've ever seen those particular petrels before."

"Oh," Menedemos said, crestfallen. Many another man might have been lying when he made such a claim. Sostratos? Menedemos tossed his head. He believed his cousin implicitly.

RHODIPPOS DIED THREE days later. The crew of the *Aphrodite*, acting for his family, buried him in the grave the local gravedigger had excavated. Theagenes came out to the merchant galley once more, this time to cleanse the boat. He gave Sostratos a sour look. Sostratos pretended not to see it.

In the meanwhile, a round ship from the island of Aigina put in at Sounion. After talking with its captain, Menedemos declared, "Now I know where we're bound next."

"What? To Aigina?" Sostratos asked. His cousin dipped his head. Sostratos threw his hands in the air. "Why? Everything they make there is cheap junk. Aiginetan goods are a joke all over the Aegean. What have they got that would be worth our while to carry?"

"They've got silver," Menedemos said. "Lots and lots of lovely turtles. And they have a temple to Artemis they're talking about prettying up. Artemis is a huntress. Wouldn't her image look fine in a lion skin?"

"Ah." After some thought, Sostratos said, "You might convince them of that. You might even have a better chance than at Athens, I suppose. More hides come in to Athens than to Aigina, I'm sure."

Menedemos kissed him on the cheek. "Exactly what I was thinking, my dear. And it's only a day's journey from here." He pointed west. "You can see the island, poking its nose up over the horizon."

"Islands have noses?" Sostratos said. "I don't think any philosopher ever suspected that." Menedemos made a face at him. But his own whimsy didn't last long. With a sigh, he went on, "I wish we were heading to Peiraieus instead. Without the gryphon's skull, though, what's the point?"

"Not much." No, Menedemos wasn't heartbroken at the loss of the ancient bones. "We'll see how we do somewhere else."

Winds in the Saronic Gulf were fitful the next day; the rowers spent a good deal of time at the oars. But they seemed glad enough to row. Maybe they were eager to escape Sounion, where two of their comrades would lie forever. That wasn't anything Sostratos could ask, but it wouldn't have surprised him.

With a circumference of perhaps 180 stadia, Aigina wasn't a big island. These days, it also wasn't an important island, though that hadn't always been true. When the *Aphrodite* made for the polis, which lay on the western side of the island,

Sostratos said, "This place would be a lot better off if it hadn't gone over to Dareios before Marathon."

"It got what it deserved afterwards, eh?" Menedemos said.

"If you want to call it that," Sostratos replied. "The Athenians dispossessed the Aiginetans and planted their own colonists here. Then, after the Peloponnesian War, the Spartans threw those people out and brought back the original Aiginetans and their descendants."

"So who's left nowadays?" Menedemos asked.

"Aiginetans," Sostratos said. "They're a mongrel lot, I suppose, but that's true of a lot of Hellenes these days. If a polis loses a war . . ." He clicked his tongue between his teeth; he didn't like to think of such things. But he refused to shy away from them: "Remember, Rhodes had a Macedonian garrison when we were youths."

His cousin looked as if he would have been happier forgetting. "It's our job to make sure that never happens again."

"So it is," Sostratos said. *If we can*, he added, but only to himself. He might think words of evil omen, but he would do his best not to speak them aloud.

Whatever their ultimate origins, the modern Aiginetans spoke a dialect halfway between Attic and Doric. It sounded odd to Sostratos. Menedemos, though, said, "They talk almost the same way you do."

"They do not!" Sostratos said indignantly.

"They do so," Menedemos said. "They sound like people who started out speaking Doric but went to school in Athens."

"Most of them sound as though they've never been to school at all," Sostratos retorted. He was proud of the Atticisms in his own speech; they showed him to be a man of culture. To his ear, the Aiginetans didn't sound cultured at all. He and his cousin might have been the asses in Aisop's fable, except that they were dithering over dialects rather than bales of hay.

"All right. All right. Let it go." Menedemos, having planted his barb, was content to ease up. "We made it past the rocks. Now that we're in the harbor, we'll sell the lion skin and make the trip worthwhile."

"Rocks?" Sostratos said.

Before Menedemos could answer, Diokles spoke up: "Didn't you notice how careful-like your cousin was steering, young sir? The approach to this harbor's as nasty as any in Hellas, but he handled it pretty as you please."

Menedemos looked smug. Praise from a seaman as accomplished as the oarmaster would have left anyone feeling smug. *And I didn't even pay attention to what he was doing*, Sostratos thought ruefully.

The next morning, the two cousins took their tawny hide up to the temple of Artemis, which stood close by those of Apollo and Aphrodite. Menedemos peered into the one dedicated to Apollo. "We might try here if we have bad luck with Artemis' priest," he said. "The Apollo is naked—carved from wood, looks like, and old as the hills."

That made Sostratos look, too. "I wonder just how old that statue is," he said. "People have been making images of marble or bronze for a long time now." Menedemos only shrugged, and with reason. They had no better way of learning the statue's age than they'd had of finding out how old the gryphon's skull was. Sostratos grimaced, wishing he hadn't thought of that comparison. He couldn't see Attica from here; the higher ground of the north of Aigina shielded the mainland from his eye, which was more than a small relief.

The marble statue of Artemis was draped, but only in a carved tunic that didn't even reach the goddess' knees. "Why, she'd catch her death of cold if she didn't don our skin for a cloak," Menedemos said.

Sostratos looked around. "Where's the priest?" he asked, seeing no one in the sacred precinct. He got no answer, either.

Before long, an Aiginetan ambled in. "Are you the priest?" Menedemos asked him.

He tossed his head. "Not me. Nikodromos is probably still in town. He's a man who likes to sleep late, he is."

"What shall we do till he gets here?" Sostratos asked in annoyance. "Grow moss?"

"You might as well, pal," the local replied. "He isn't going to get here till he gets here, if you know what I mean."

Sostratos grunted. The Aiginetan had a point. Another man came into the temple. He wasn't Nikodromos, either. He was somebody else looking for the priest. "Lazy, sour bastard's probably still home snoring," he said. Nikodromos' habits were evidently well known. He would never have made a seaman—but then, he hadn't tried. As a priest, he could sleep late if he wanted to.

"Maybe we ought to find his house in town and throw rocks at the shutters," Menedemos said a little later.

Just when Sostratos was starting to think that sounded like a pretty good idea, Nikodromos strolled into the temple with a self-satisfied expression on his face. Both Aiginetans promptly started dunning him for money they said he owed them. What followed wasn't quite a screaming row, but wasn't far from one, either.

In a low voice, Sostratos said, "If we do sell him the hide, let's make sure we see the silver before we hand it over."

Menedemos dipped his head. "I've heard ideas I liked a lot less."

After half an hour or so, Nikodromos' creditors threw their hands in the air and left. He hadn't promised them a thing. In an abstract way, Sostratos admired him. In the real world with which he had to deal, he wondered if this image of Artemis really needed to be draped with a lion skin after all.

"Hail," the priest said, coming up to the two Rhodians. "And what do you want today? You've been patient as can be while those idiots spouted their lies."

He didn't seem too sour to Sostratos, but then, Sostratos hadn't been trying to get money out of him. His foxy features did not inspire confidence, though. Neither did his squabbles with a pair of Aiginetans unconnected to each other. Nonetheless, after naming himself and Sostratos, Menedemos said, "We've got a splendid Karian lion skin here, with which you can adorn the statue of the Maiden."

"Do you indeed?" Nikodromos' eyes widened slightly. *Excitement or art?* Sostratos wondered. He would have bet on art. Those eyes were a light brown that in certain lights seemed tinged with amber: as foxy as the rest of him, or maybe even more so. He went on, "Let me see it, best ones. By all means, let me see it."

Menedemos and Sostratos spread out the skin on the temple

floor. Then Sostratos, with a happy inspiration, picked it up and draped it over the marble Artemis' shoulders. "See how fine she'd look?" he said.

"Not bad," Nikodromos said—small praise, but praise. "That skin might remind people of what a great huntress she is, true. But, of course, one question remains: how much do you want for it?"

"Five minai," Menedemos said. Sostratos hid a smile behind his hand. If his cousin would get cheated, he aimed to get cheated out of a lot of money.

Nikodromos coughed. "My dear fellow, you can't be serious."

Menedemos smiled his most charming smile. "I'll make it six if you like. Not so many lions left in Europe these days, you know."

"And so you think you can charge whatever you please when you bring one here?" the priest said.

"Not quite," Sostratos told him. "But no one ever said we had to sell our goods at a loss, either."

"Five minai is out of the question," Nikodromos said. "I might pay two."

"You might indeed," Menedemos said pleasantly. "But not to us. As my cousin said, we need to make money to stay in business."

"Well, two minai and a half, then," Nikodromos said.

"Come on, Menedemos," Sostratos said. "Let's head back to the ship. Plenty of other temples, plenty of other poleis."

They made as if to begin rolling up the lion skin and putting it back into its leather sack. Sostratos watched Nikodromos out of the corner of his eye. If the priest let them leave, then he did, that was all. But they hadn't got very far before Nikodromos said, "Wait. I might go to three."

"We might talk a little more, in that case," Menedemos said.

Nikodromos would have failed as a trader for more reasons than sleeping late. He kept coming up and up, and didn't draw the line till the price had gone to four minai, twenty drakhmai, though he grumbled and whined every step of the way. He did his best to make it seem as if he were doing the Rhodians a favor by dealing with them at all.

"Four minai, twenty." Sostratos looked from him to Menedemos and back again. "Bargain?"

"Bargain." His cousin and the priest spoke at the same time.

"Good enough." As far as Sostratos was concerned, it was better than good enough. They hadn't got nearly such a fine price for the other hide back on Kos. *Nice, solid profit*, he thought.

And then Nikodromos said, "Let me take the hide back to town, and I'll bring you your money right away."

A lot of people had made requests like that over the years. More often than not, Sostratos and Menedemos, like most traders, said yes. Most people were honest. Sostratos wasn't so sure about Nikodromos. He saw his cousin wasn't, either. Smiling, Menedemos tossed his head. "You can bring the money here and then we'll give you the hide, or else we'll come down to Aigina with you."

Nikodromos sent him a sour stare. "You're afraid I'll cheat you. That is an insult."

"Best one, we just stood here watching a couple of your own people trying to get money out of you," Sostratos answered. "If they have trouble prying their silver loose, why wouldn't we? We're just a couple of foreigners to you. Better not to take chances."

"I told you, the silver they want isn't theirs at all," the priest said, making a fine show of indignation. "They're nothing but a couple of temple robbers."

With a shrug, Sostratos said, "I don't know anything about your quarrels, any more than you know about the quarrels back on Rhodes. All I know is, you'll have the hide when we have the money."

He wondered if that would queer the deal. *If it does, too bad*, he thought. *That would mean this rogue never intended to pay us in the first place*. The Aiginetans who'd tried to squeeze silver out of Nikodromos had certainly sounded as if they had a right to it.

"Those abandoned rascals blacken my name," Nikodromos complained.

"Easiest way to prove that, sir, is to give us the price you agreed to," Menedemos said. "As soon as we have the turtles, we'll sing your praises at every stop we make."

"Of course, we won't do anything of the sort if you go back on the bargain," Sostratos added. Sometimes—often, in fact—knaves acted like honest men if the choice was having their knavery published to the world.

Knave or not, Nikodromos let out a loud, exasperated sigh. "Come along, then, both of you," he said. "You'll get your money. Bring the hide. Let there be no doubt that I am a man who keeps the agreements he makes."

"Let's go," Menedemos said.

When they got to Nikodromos' house, Sostratos wondered whether the priest would be able to pay them at all, for no slave opened the door to let them in: Nikodromos had to do it himself. Was a man without a slave likely to be a man who had more than four minai of silver in his home? It struck Sostratos as unlikely.

He relaxed a little when he saw a woman tending a flower garden in the courtyard. A maidservant might not answer the door, but at least Nikodromos had some help. Then the priest snapped, "Go back to the women's quarters, Asine. I have traders with me."

"Yes, my husband," the woman said, and hurried away, though she did look back over her shoulder at the Rhodians.

"She wasn't expecting company," Nikodromos said apologetically.

"It's all right, best one," Sostratos said, though what he was thinking was, *Just you and your wife? How do you get anything done? You might as well be peasants, or even barbarians.*

"Quite all right," Menedemos echoed. His tone was all it should have been. Even so, Sostratos disliked the way his eyes slid toward the stairway to the second floor, the stairway up which Asine had gone.

You barely got a look at her, Sostratos thought. *She barely got a look at you. Why do I think—why do I know—you want to lie with her if you can? Why? You're my cousin, that's why. I've seen you around women too many times by now. I've seen you land in trouble too many times by now, too.*

Trying not to think about what might be—what all too

likely was—going through Menedemos' mind, Sostratos asked Nikodromos, "Shall we wait here while you get the money?"

"Oh, I suppose you can step into the andron," Nikodromos said grudgingly. "I won't be long."

In a proper household, a slave would have offered them wine and olives or raisins. Here, they simply sat in the men's room and waited. "Well, what do you think?" Menedemos asked, almost without moving his lips. "Is he lying to us, or is he the greatest miser since Midas?"

"I don't know," Sostratos answered. "But I'm guessing he's a cheapskate. Would he have had the gall to bring us here if he couldn't pay us?"

"We'll find out," Menedemos said. "His wife's pretty. Did you notice?"

"No, and I wish you wouldn't have, either," Sostratos said. His cousin made a face at him.

Before they could start arguing in earnest, Menedemos let out a sharp hiss. Sostratos fell silent; he'd seen Nikodromos coming, too. The priest carried a leather sack. When he set it down on a table in the andron, it clinked. "Here you are," he said. "Four minai, twenty drakhmai. Go ahead and count it. You'll see all is as it should be."

With some men, that invitation to count would have told Sostratos he didn't have to. With one so mean as Nikodromos, he did anyhow. When he'd finished, he looked up and told the priest, "I'm afraid you're still six drakhmai short, O marvelous one."

He'd laid the silver coins in neat rows and stacks; Nikodromos could hardly challenge his assertion. In a low, furious voice, the Aiginetan said, "I'll get them," and hurried away.

"Shameless," Sostratos said.

"Are you surprised?" Menedemos kept looking toward those stairs. Sostratos noticed that with as much resignation as alarm: up till now, Menedemos hadn't eyed anyone else's wife with desire on this trading run. Sostratos had started to wonder if his cousin were off his feed.

Before he could warn Menedemos, Nikodromos and Asine started yelling at each other. Sostratos couldn't make out the words, but they both sounded furious. "Charming couple," Sostratos murmured.

Menedemos grinned. "Aren't they just? Still, though . . . Oh, wait, here comes the priest back again."

What had he been about to say? *Maybe I don't want to know*, Sostratos thought. Nikodromos stormed into the andron, his scowl black as moonless midnight. He slapped down half a dozen drakhmai. "There," he snarled. "Are you satisfied now?"

"Perfectly so, best one," Sostratos answered. "It is what we agreed to, after all."

"To the crows with—" Nikodromos began, but he caught himself. Trying to sound civil, he said, "The Huntress will be glad to have the lion-skin cloak."

"Of course she will." Menedemos sounded as smooth—and as greasy—as olive oil. Sostratos' suspicions flared; he'd heard that particular conspiratorial tone before. Sure enough, Menedemos went on, "Would you be interested in some fine Rhodian perfume, sir? Or even"—he lowered his voice almost to a whisper—"in emeralds? I've got a couple of fine ones, straight from Egypt."

"Now why would I want anything like that?" Nikodromos kept the growl in his voice, but leaned toward Menedemos even so.

"You never can tell what will sweeten up a woman," Menedemos remarked, for all the world as if he hadn't heard—as if the neighbors hadn't heard—the priest and his wife quarreling a moment before.

Nikodromos grunted. "That's true, I suppose."

"For that matter," Menedemos added, as if just remembering, "I also have some Koan silk, which is not the sort of stuff every lady in Aigina would be wearing."

"*Do* you?" Nikodromos said. Menedemos gravely dipped his head.

Sostratos sat there putting the coins back in their sack and doing his best not to laugh out loud. Nikodromos thought Menedemos was interested in helping him make up with his wife after their fight, and in making some money doing that. Sostratos knew better. Oh, his cousin wouldn't mind making money off Nikodromos. But what Menedemos really wanted was Asine. If he sold Nikodromos perfume or jewels or silk, he would use his visits here to make himself known to her—even if she stayed in the women's quarters while he was around—and to scout out the ground and see what his chances were.

"Maybe you should bring some of these things by, give me a chance to look at them," Nikodromos said. "Not today: I should take the hide up to the temple now, and I'll be sacrificing through the afternoon. Tomorrow morning, not too early?"

"Tomorrow morning," Nikodromos agreed. "I'll see you then."

Nikodromos had hardly closed the door behind them when Sostratos wagged a forefinger under his cousin's nose. "I know what you've got in mind," he said.

"My dear, I haven't the faintest idea what you're talking about." But Menedemos' eyes danced. He couldn't make that sound convincing no matter how hard he tried. "Why aren't you swelling up like a toad and telling me what a bad character I am?"

Sostratos had been wondering about that himself. He gave the most honest answer he could: "If anyone ever had it coming, that petty thief of a Nikodromos does."

"Well, well," Menedemos said, and then again, "Well, well." He walked on for a few paces before adding, "There's no guarantee, you know."

"Don't put yourself in danger," Sostratos said. "Nikodromos isn't worth it."

His cousin chuckled. "Of course he isn't. Asine, now, Asine just may be. I'll have to see how it goes, that's all." He tapped Sostratos on the chest with his finger. "One thing, though."

"What's that?" Sostratos asked with sinking heart.

"However the other turns out, I expect I'll make a profit from that polluted priest," Menedemos said.

"Huzzah," Sostratos said in hollow tones. Menedemos laughed out loud.

MENEDEMOS RUBBED HIS chin. He'd taken care to shave before coming up from the harbor to Nikodromos' house. He'd done a good job; his skin felt almost as smooth as it had when he was a beardless boy. He had on the cleaner of his tunics, too. Nikodromos would interpret all that as being no less than his own due—he had plenty of self-importance. How Asine would interpret it, if she would interpret it at all . . .

"I'll find out," Menedemos murmured, and rapped on the priest's door.

Nikodromos opened it himself. With what he'd spent on the lion skin, he'd shown he had plenty of money, but he was too mean to buy a slave to make life easier for himself and his wife. "Hail," he said now. "Where's your cousin?"

"In the market square, selling to whoever will buy," Menedemos answered easily. "You, though, best one, you're a special customer, so I'm here to show you these goods with no one else's eyes on them."

As he'd thought it would, that tickled Nikodromos' vanity. "Come in, come in," the priest said. He even went so far as to add, "Go on into the andron, and I'll bring you some wine."

That wasn't what Menedemos had in mind. "The courtyard might be better, most noble one," he said. It would certainly be better for him, because Asine would be able to see and hear him. But he had a plausible explanation, and trotted it out: "You'll want to examine the silk and the jewels by sunlight."

"So I will," Nikodromos said. "I don't aim to let anyone cheat me."

"Nor should you," Menedemos said, ignoring the threat in the other man's words. As he came out into the courtyard, he paused to admire the garden: "What splendid plants! How wonderfully green they are, even in the middle of the dry season. They're perfectly pruned, too."

With a shrug, Nikodromos said, "I haven't the time to worry about such trifles. My wife tends them."

"They're lovely." Menedemos left it at that; he knew better than to give a woman direct praise in her husband's hearing. His eyes couldn't help slipping to the stairway, and to the rooms above it. What would Asine be doing in there? Spinning? Weaving? No, probably not—he would have heard the loom. Surely, though, she would be listening to—maybe even watching—what went on down below. He said, "Here is the perfume. Smell it. It's from the very best Rhodian roses."

"Fripperies," Nikodromos muttered. But he drew out the stopper and sniffed. In spite of himself, one eyebrow rose. "That's very sweet." He rallied. "I'd bet the price is enough to sour anybody, though."

"Not at all." Instead of naming it, Menedemos went on, "Let me show you the Koan silk. Any woman who wore a silk tunic would be the envy of all her neighbors. Wool? Linen?" He tossed his head. "They don't compare."

"In price, either." Yes, the priest had a one-track mind.

"Wool and linen are fine for everyday wear," Menedemos said. "But your wife will want something special, won't she, when she goes out into the streets on a festival day? After all, women don't get out of the house much, so they like to make the most of it when they do. And she can wear this Rhodian scent and these emeralds and be the envy of every other woman in Aigina."

"Let's see these so-called emeralds," Nikodromos said. "I wouldn't be surprised if you were trying to sell me a couple of lumps of glass."

"By the dog of Egypt, I am not," Menedemos said indignantly, fishing them from the pouch he wore on his belt. "They come from Ptolemaios' land, as I said. People in Miletos were happy enough to buy them; I made more than a talent on the dozen or so I sold there. My father and my uncle have been traders since before I was born. Their ships go all around the Inner Sea. If I cheat, I ruin the firm's reputation, and we can't afford that. Here, O marvelous one—see for yourself."

The two emeralds he had left were the ones he'd intended to take to Athens, including the largest and finest stone he'd bought from the Egyptian round-ship captain. No one, not even Nikodromos, could claim they were glass after seeing their deep, rich color and waxy luster. The priest sighed as he handed them back. "You'll want too much," he predicted, tacitly admitting they were genuine.

"I want what they're worth." Pitching his voice to carry up to the women's quarters, Menedemos asked, "Doesn't your wife deserve the best?"

Nikodromos waved his hands and shook his head like a man

trying to drive away bees. "Let me see this silk you were gabbling about," he said.

"Nothing like it for making a lovely woman lovelier," Menedemos said, again—he hoped—as much to Asine as to her husband. "This is a particularly fine bolt here. Look." He unrolled it and held it up in the sunlight. "You can practically see through it."

"That's indecent," Nikodromos exclaimed.

"Only if the woman who's wearing it isn't worth looking at," Menedemos said with a wink, as one man of the world to another. "My dear fellow, you simply wouldn't believe how much silk my cousin sold to the fanciest hetaira in Miletos."

"I don't want my woman looking like a hetaira," Nikodromos said, but his voice lost force with each succeeding word. Why wouldn't a man want his wife to look as desirable as she could?

"You need another sniff of the perfume." Menedemos pulled the stopper from the little jar again. "Here. Sweeter than honey, isn't it?"

By the way the priest screwed up his face, he wanted to deny it, but he couldn't. "What . . . what will you want for all this?" he asked at last, sounding almost fearful.

"For the emeralds, nine minai apiece," Menedemos answered. "Two minai for the silk, and twenty drakhmai for the perfume." All the prices were outrageously high. He knew that. With a little luck, Nikodromos wouldn't. He'd certainly overpaid for the lion skin.

He bawled like a branded calf now. "Outrageous," he spluttered. "Absurd. Downright criminal, if you want to know the truth."

Menedemos shrugged. "If you're not interested, I'm sure someone else will want to deck his wife out in style. Goods like these don't come to Aigina every day, you know, or every year, either." That was true enough. Back in the old days that fascinated Sostratos so much, Aigina had been an important polis. Not any more. It was a backwater now, completely overshadowed by Athens. The *Aphrodite* never would have put in here if not for the pirates.

The real question was, just how much silver did Nikodromos have? Menedemos tossed his head. No, the *real* question was, how much would he spend? If he wouldn't lay out any on a slave, would he spend any for his wife? If he didn't intend to spend any, had he invited Menedemos back for no better reason than to waste his time? That might make Asine unhappy, and Menedemos had already heard she wasn't shy about letting her husband know how she felt.

Licking his lips, Nikodromos said, "I will give you five minai for one of the emeralds, one mina for the silk, and ten drakhmai for the perfume."

"Only one emerald?" Menedemos said, using three words to imply the priest was surely the meanest man in the world.

"I can't afford them both," Nikodromos said. Something in his voice told Menedemos he was lying about that. *It will tell his wife the same thing*, the Rhodian thought cheerfully. Nikodromos, meanwhile, gathered himself for a peevish outburst: "And I get to choose which stone, do you hear me?"

"Of course." Menedemos spoke as if humoring a madman. Then his own voice hardened: "But you won't choose either unless you come closer to meeting my price." He almost said, *unless you meet my price*, but that would have given Nikodromos no haggling room at all.

"You think you can sail into Aigina with your fancy goods and cheat people out of their shoes because we don't see such things very often," the priest grumbled. Since that was exactly what Menedemos thought, he denied it with special vigor. He'd made his initial demands so high, even Nikodromos' first counteroffers guaranteed him no small profit. And he didn't intend to settle for those first counteroffers.

Once, during the dicker that followed, Menedemos wondered if he'd pushed too hard. Nikodromos stamped his foot and shouted, "No, by the gods! Not another drakhma! Take your trash and get out of my house!"

"As you wish, best one," Menedemos said coldly. A moment later, a crash came from upstairs: someone had dropped—or hurled—a pot. *Sure enough, we're playing to an audience*, Menedemos thought. He pretended not to notice the noise or the way Nikodromos flinched, but gathered up the silk and the perfume and started for the door.

"Wait!" Nikodromos said unhappily. "Maybe we could talk a little more."

"Maybe." Menedemos did his best to sound as if he were doing the priest a favor. "If you're ready to be more reasonable."

"You're the one who's not being reasonable." But Nikodromos nervously looked up toward the women's quarters, as if expecting another pot to shatter at any moment. A proverb crossed Menedemos' mind: *even Herakles can't fight two at once*. Nikodromos might have held his own against Menedemos. Against Menedemos and his own wife, he had no chance.

"Are we agreed, then?" Menedemos asked not too much later.

"I suppose so." The priest gnawed at a fingernail. "Seven minai, fifty drakhmai for the emerald. One mina, sixty drakhmai for the silk. And twelve drakhmai for the perfume." He gave the Rhodian a triumphant smirk at that last price.

Menedemos smiled back, as if acknowledging that Nikodromos had beaten him down there. He didn't tell Nikodromos he'd purposely gone easy on the small haggle because he'd done so well on the larger ones. Let Nikodromos keep his tiny triumph, if it made him happy. Counting on his fingers, Menedemos said, "That makes . . . let me see . . . nine minai, twenty-two drakhmai altogether. If you'll fetch the silver, you may choose whichever emerald you like."

"Wait here," Nikodromos said gloomily. "I'll be back." A hunted look on his face, he scurried into the house. Menedemos cocked his head toward the women's quarters. To his disappointment, Asine kept quiet. But she'd already made her presence felt.

When the priest came back with a fresh leather sack, Menedemos said, "If you don't mind, I'm going to take this into the andron."

"I made one small mistake, and now everyone thinks I'm a thief," Nikodromos said, more glumly than ever.

Of course. What else would you expect? Menedemos thought. He didn't say that out loud, though he was tempted. What he did say, was, "Not at all. I'm like my cousin, though: I want to have things straight."

When he'd counted up the coins and put them into glittering rows and stacks in the andron, he found that Nikodromos' payment was four drakhmai over. He picked up four turtles and handed them to the priest without a word: he was convinced the Aiginetan had put them there to test his honesty. "Er—thank you," Nikodromos said, a faintly embarrassed expression on his face.

"You're welcome," Menedemos answered. "I don't want more than my due, just what you said you'd pay." That wasn't strictly true, but Nikodromos couldn't know it wasn't. A show of virtue made the best shield. "I'm sure your wife will enjoy everything you've bought for her." He raised his voice a little to say that, hoping it would carry up to the women's quarters.

"I want her to," Nikodromos said. "I want to get my money's worth. And now, if we have no more business . . ."

That was barely polite enough to be a hint; in a moment, he'd be shouting, *Get out of my house!* Menedemos scooped the coins back into the sack, captured a couple that fell on the floor and tried to roll away, and headed out the door in a hurry. Nikodromos all but slammed it behind him. As Menedemos went, he started whistling a Persian love song whose tune Alexander the Great's men had brought back to Hellas.

While he whistled, he looked up to the second floor, to what he thought were the windows of the women's quarters. If one of those shutters opened, he would see what happened next. If not, he would go back to the *Aphrodite* knowing he'd pried plenty of silver out of Nikodromos.

A shutter had to open pretty soon. He couldn't stand outside the house whistling for very long, or Nikodromos would figure out why he was doing it. Fleeing an angry husband after a seduction was part of the game. Fleeing before a seduction was nothing but an embarrassment.

Menedemos abruptly stopped whistling, for a shutter *did* open. The woman who looked down at him wasn't beautiful, but she was . . . *prettier than Nikodromos deserves*, Menedemos thought. "Hail, sweetheart," he said in a low voice. "Your husband's bought you some very nice things." If Asine was more faithful than the priest deserved, that remained safe enough.

When her eyes flashed, he knew he had a chance. "What if he did?" she answered, nothing but scorn in her vice. "I listened to you shaming him into doing it. What would it be like to be with a man who cared about what I wanted without having someone else remind him he ought to?"

Menedemos grinned. He'd hoped she would feel something like that. Had he been married to Nikodromos, he was sure he would have. He couldn't have asked for a better opening. He said, "Dear, if you want to find out, tell me when he won't be home."

Asine couldn't very well misunderstand that. She couldn't, and she didn't. "He's going up to the temple tomorrow morning," she said, "He'll be there most of the day."

"Well, well. Isn't that interesting?" Menedemos said. "So if I were to knock on the front door, there'd be only a poor lone woman in the house?" He winked.

Asine didn't. She looked furious. "He's too stingy to buy me a slave," she snapped. "It's a wonder you got him to do this. You must be able to talk anyone into doing anything." Her expression changed: now she was paying attention to Menedemos, not raging at her husband. "Who knows what you'll be able to talk me into doing?"

"We'll find out tomor—" Menedemos broke off, for she closed the shutter in a hurry. Maybe Nikodromos was coming up the stairs to show her what he'd bought.

When Menedemos went back to the *Aphrodite*, Sostratos greeted him with, "How did it go?" By way of reply, Menedemos handed his cousin the leather sack. Sostratos hefted it and whistled softly. "There must be nine or ten minai of silver in here—and that's Aiginetan minai, too, which means they're heavier than ours."

"Nine and a quarter," Menedemos answered. He eyed Sostratos with reluctant respect. His cousin could be fussy as a broody hen, but he knew what he knew. "How did you figure that out so fast?"

"My first guess was in Rhodian weight, because that's what I'm most used to," Sostratos said. "I know what part of an Aiginetan mina a Rhodian mina is, so I converted from one to the other in my head before I spoke." He made it sound as if it were nothing out of the ordinary. And so it wasn't—for him. After a moment, he added, "You squeezed him pretty hard, then. *Euge*."

"Thanks," Menedemos said.

"The money isn't really what I meant, though," Sostratos said. "How did the other go?"

Menedemos needed a moment to understand him. When he did, he blinked. Sostratos wasn't in the habit of asking about his pursuits of other men's wives, except to try to talk him out of them. "You *really* must dislike Nikodromos," Menedemos murmured. His cousin dipped his head. Menedemos said, "He's going up to the temple to sacrifice tomorrow. I'm going back to his house."

"*Euge*," Sostratos said again. "Wear a sword, though."

"A sword?" Menedemos tossed his head. "I intend to use my spear."

Sostratos snorted. "I know what you intend. I don't know what Nikodromos and the woman have in mind. He may come back to the house when you don't expect him to—remember the window you jumped out of in Taras last summer? Or the woman may be playing a different game from the one you think she is. Wear a sword."

When Menedemos saw Asine, he saw what he wanted. When Sostratos thought about her, he saw trouble. If that didn't sum up the differences between them, Menedemos didn't know what did. But he hadn't seen that trouble himself, and he couldn't deny it might be real. "All right," he said. "I'll wear one. I'll swagger through the streets like a bandit or a barbarian."

"Good," his cousin said.

When morning came, Menedemos couldn't go into town as early as he would have liked. Nikodromos liked to sleep late, and knocking on the door before the priest left didn't strike him as a good idea. He made himself wait till the sun stood well above the eastern horizon before leaving the harbor and heading into Aigina. The bronze scabbard of his sword bumped against his left hipbone at every step. A couple of Aiginetans gave him odd looks, but no one seemed inclined to ask too many questions of an armed man.

He knocked on Nikodromos' door. As soon as he did, his

hand fell to the hilt of the sword. If Asine was playing games of the sort Sostratos imagined . . .

She opened the door. "Come in," she said. "Quick. Don't hang around for the neighbors to see."

She sounded practiced at deceit. *Maybe I'm not the first one who's come in while her husband's away*, Menedemos thought. But if she was so practiced . . . "Should you be wearing that perfume?" he asked. "Nikodromos is liable to notice it."

"He'll think I put it on for him. He thinks everything's for him." Asine didn't try to hide her scorn.

"Ah," Menedemos said politely; that fit what he'd seen of the priest. He smiled at Asine. "When he has such a pretty wife, I can understand why he feels that way."

She studied him as he was studying her. "You're smooth, aren't you?" she said. "How many times have you done this?"

"Often enough to know that's a question better left unanswered." Menedemos wagged a finger at her. "It's better left unasked, too."

He watched her think it over. She dipped her head. "You're probably right. So . . ." She took a step toward him.

He put his arms around her. She was only a couple of digits shorter than he was. She hardly needed to tilt her face up at all to let her mouth meet his. Her breath was sweet. She was somewhere not far from twenty: too young to have had much trouble with her teeth. The kiss went on for a long time.

When Asine at last drew back, amusement danced in her eyes. "I will say I haven't kissed a man who shaves before. It's . . . different."

For a moment, Menedemos' mind worked as precisely as Sostratos' so often did. *Just because you'll say it doesn't mean it's true*. "Is it better or worse?" he asked, and then went on before she could answer: "Why don't we try it again, so you have a better idea?"

They did. Her body molded itself to his. Her breasts were soft and firm. He stroked her hair with one hand; the other cupped a buttock. Before long, he was firm himself, though far from soft. Asine rubbed herself against him. "Sweet," she murmured.

He kissed the side of her neck and nibbled at her earlobe.

His thumb and forefinger teased her nipple through the thin linen of her tunic. Her head fell back. She sighed softly. He took her hand and guided it to his manhood. Her fingers closed on him. She squeezed, not too hard. After a little while, he pulled away. He'd been at sea for a while. He didn't want to spend himself too soon.

"Come on, then," she said. "Let's go up to my bedroom."

They were walking through the courtyard when he said, "Wait." Asine stopped, raising an eyebrow. Menedemos said, "Why not right here?"

"In the sunshine?" Both eyebrows rose this time. "You *are* shameless."

"You make me that way." Menedemos untied the girdle that bound her tunic at the waist, then pulled the tunic off over her head. When she was naked, he bent his head to kiss her breasts. Her nipples were wider and darker than he'd expected; faint pale lines marked her belly. "You've borne a child," he said in surprise.

Her face clouded. "I've borne two. Neither lived past its second birthday. Maybe your seed will be stronger than Nikodromos'."

"I hope so, if that's what you want." His hand slid down toward the joining of her legs. She spread them a little to make it easier for him to stroke her. After a while, he said, "Bend forward." Asine did, resting the palms of her hands on a stone bench. She looked back over her shoulder as Menedemos took off his own chiton and poised himself behind her.

"Oh," she said softly when he went into her. He held her by the waist—his skin sun-darkened, hers almost white—as he thrust home again and again, pausing every now and then to spin out the pleasure for him and for her. She shook her head. Her dark hair flew back and forth. She gasped and shuddered and let out a little muffled cry. At the same time, she squeezed him from within, so that he couldn't hold back another instant. He drove deep, the world utterly forgotten in his moment of joy.

He patted her backside. She started to pull away and straighten up. "Don't," he said, beginning once more: he *had* been at sea for a while.

Asine looked back at him again. "Well, well," she said. "No wonder you've been able to do this before."

"No wonder at all," he said, so smugly that she laughed. He kept on with what he was doing. He didn't have to pause this time to keep from spending too soon; despite his boast, he began to wonder if he would be able to spend at all. But, panting, he managed, and brought Asine with him, too. No sooner had he finished than he flopped out of her. A third round wouldn't come soon, which meant it likely wouldn't come at all.

He and Asine both dressed in a hurry. Now that they'd done what they'd set out to do, they were warier with each other than they had been. *Maybe it's just that we aren't blind with lust any more*, Menedemos thought as he put his sword belt on again. "You didn't need that," Asine told him.

"Never can tell who might get home at the wrong time," Menedemos answered. He didn't mention that he'd worried Asine might be helping her husband play a game of their own.

She tossed her head. "He'll be out there all day. He cares about that more than he cares about me. He cares about everything more than he cares about me. Maybe if my son had lived . . ." Asine tossed her head again. "I don't think so. He would have cared about the boy, but not about me."

"I'm sorry," Menedemos said.

"Are you? Why?" Her laughter was barbed as an arrow point. "You got what you wanted. What do you care now?"

How many men *had* come through the door while Nikodromos went to the temple? Menedemos almost found himself sympathizing with the priest, the last thing he would have expected. Nettled, he said, "I wasn't the only one."

"No," Asine said. "You gave me what I needed. You couldn't possibly give me what I want."

What would that be? Menedemos wondered. The answer took shape in his mind almost at once. *A couple of slaves, a better place among the families of Aigina*. Sure enough, these sweaty couplings couldn't give her that. She could get it only from her husband—and he didn't much care whether she had it or not.

Menedemos said, "The silk and the emerald will help some."

"A little," Asine said—she was one of those people who,

no matter what they had, always wanted more. Menedemos understood that well enough; he was the same way himself. "You'd better go," she told him.

"Yes, you're right." He wondered if coming here in the first place had been worthwhile. He supposed so. He hadn't been looking for anything more than a morning's pleasure. It had never felt so empty afterwards, though.

Asine gave him a kiss as she unlatched the door. "Will you remember me after you sail away?" she asked.

"I'll never forget you," he answered. It could have been a pretty compliment, a polite fib, but he heard the raw truth in his voice. Asine must have heard it, too, for she smiled, pleased with herself. She'd taken it for praise, then. As a last favor, Menedemos didn't tell her otherwise.

A couple of naked little boys, one perhaps eight, the other six, were playing with a toy oxcart in the dusty street. They looked up as Menedemos came out of Nikodromos' house—looked up and started to giggle. His ears burned. He hurried off toward the market square.

Sostratos waved to him as he came over to the little display the men of the *Aphrodite* had set up. "Glad you're back," he called, and then, "Well?"

"Very well, thanks. And you?"

His cousin rolled his eyes. A couple of the sailors who'd fetched and carried for Sostratos guffawed. A third looked blank. One of the others leaned close to mutter something to him. Menedemos couldn't hear what it was, but saw the obscene gesture accompanying it. The third sailor laughed, getting it at last.

"All right," Sostratos said. "You didn't get held for ransom, you didn't get murdered—"

"Not that I noticed, no," Menedemos agreed.

"Interrupt all you please," Sostratos told him. "I'm still going to ask the questions that need asking. For instance, can we stay in Aigina without worrying about getting knifed whenever we show our faces away from the *Aphrodite*?"

That was indeed a question worth asking. Menedemos thought about the two giggling little boys. They probably weren't the only neighbors to have noticed his coming to Nikodromos' house when the priest wasn't home. That meant . . . Menedemos tossed his head. "Maybe not."

"*Another* place we can't visit again any time soon," Sostratos said with a sigh. "Seems as though there's one every voyage, doesn't it?"

"This isn't like Halikarnassos or Taras," Menedemos said. "I think I'm just one in a long line of men Nikodromos hates."

"Ah. Like that, is it?"

"Afraid so." Menedemos didn't feel like dwelling on what he'd done, so he asked, "How are things going here?"

Sostratos shrugged. "I've sold some silk and some crimson dye with it and a few jars of perfume, but people aren't rushing up to buy. Probably about time to have Diokles start pulling sailors out of the taverns and whorehouses, wouldn't you say?"

"Time to leave Aigina, you mean," Menedemos said, and Sostratos dipped his head.

Menedemos thought it over. After a moment, he did the same. He said, "We might not do badly to head back to Rhodes. It's a little early in the season, but only a little, and we've gone through most of what we set out with."

"Do you know, my dear, I was thinking the very same thing not an hour ago," Sostratos said. "Strikes me as a good idea. We'll show a solid profit if we do. But if we cruise around for another month without accomplishing much, maybe not. And I don't mind getting home early at all."

"Neither do I," Menedemos said. *What a liar I am*, he thought.

AS THE *APHRODITE* GLIDED EAST THROUGH the Saronic Gulf, away from Aigina, Sostratos mournfully peered north toward the mainland of Attica. There were Athens' two chief ports, Peiraieus and Phaleron, seeming almost close enough to touch. There on the higher ground inland lay Athens itself, the magnificent buildings of the akropolis tiny but perfect in the distance. Pointing to port, he burst out, "A pestilence take those pirates! We should be there now."

"We'll get there yet," Menedemos said soothingly.

"But not with the gryphon's skull." Sostratos scowled at his cousin, though it wasn't Menedemos' fault. But he couldn't get the picture out of his mind: the pirate, maybe—he hoped—wounded, undoing the leather lashing that held the sack closed, staring in horrified dismay at the skull that stared blindly back, and then, cursing, flinging it into the sea while all his thieving comrades laughed.

"Can't be helped. We were lucky to get away with our freedom and most of our goods," Menedemos said.

He was right again; Sostratos knew as much. But his cool indifference grated. "So much knowledge *wasted*!" Sostratos said.

"A lot, a little—how can you tell?" Menedemos remained indifferent. "You can't even tell for sure whether your philosophical friends would have cared a tenth as much about the skull as you did."

Sostratos bit down on that like a man biting down on a big piece of grit in a chunk of bread, and counted himself lucky not to break a mental tooth. He *didn't* know what the philosophers of the Lykeion and the Academy would have made of the gryphon's skull. He never would know now. He gave back the best answer he could: "Damonax was interested in it."

"Damonax didn't care about studying it—he wanted it for a decoration," Menedemos said. "That says something nasty about his taste, but it doesn't say anything about what a real philosopher would think of it."

Stubbornly, Sostratos said, "Aristoteles wrote books about animals and the parts that make them up. His successor Theophrastos, whom I studied under, is doing the same thing with plants. He would have wanted to see the gryphon's skull."

"Why? Would he think it grew on a tree like a pine cone?"

"You're impossible!" Sostratos said, but he laughed in spite of himself.

Maybe that was what his cousin had had in mind. Little by

little, Athens receded behind the *Aphrodite*. Sostratos found things with which to busy himself about the ship instead of mooning over the city like a lover over his lost beloved. Eventually, he looked up and saw that it lay far astern. *I* will *come back*, he thought, *even if it is without the gryphon's skull.*

For now, though, mundane business: he asked Menedemos, "Are you going to put in at Sounion again tonight?"

"That's right. Why?" His cousin gave him a suspicious look. "Do you plan on jumping ship and heading back to Athens even without your precious toy?"

"No, no, no." Sostratos tossed his head. Having taken so many barbs, Sostratos gave one back: "I was just thinking how handy it was that there are still a few places around the Inner Sea where you haven't outraged any husbands."

"Heh," Menedemos said: one syllable's worth of laughter. But he'd never been a man who could dish it out without taking it. After a moment, he lifted one hand from the steering-oar tillers and waved to Sostratos. "All right, my dear, you got me that time."

Sounion, as far as Sostratos was concerned, remained as unprepossessing as it had been the last time the *Aphrodite* put in there, a few days earlier. Now, at least, the ship didn't need to be cleansed of pollution (*unless adultery counts*, he thought), and they had no dead or dying aboard. The setting sun sent gold and orange and crimson ripples across the sea as the akatos' anchors splashed down into the water.

A boat rowed out from the hamlet toward the merchant galley. Sostratos had seen the man at the oars before, but not his passenger, a dapper fellow who looked out of place in Sounion. The dapper man hailed the ship: "Ahoy, there! Who are you, and where are you bound?"

"We're the *Aphrodite*, out of Rhodes, and we're heading home," Sostratos replied.

"Told you so," said the man at the oars in the small boat.

The dapper man ignored him. "Will you take a passenger to Kos?" he called.

"That depends," Sostratos said.

"Ah, yes." The dapper man dipped his head and grinned. "It always does, doesn't it? Well, what's your fare?"

Sostratos considered. This fellow plainly didn't belong here, which meant that, for one reason or another, he had some urgent need to go east. And so the only question was, how much to charge him? Sostratos thought of Euxenides of Phaselis, and how how much they'd squeezed out of him for a much shorter trip. Bracing himself for either a scream of fury or a furious haggle, he named the most outrageous price he could think of: "Fifty drakhmai."

But the dapper man in the boat didn't scream. He didn't even blink. He just dipped his head and said, "Done. You sail in the morning, don't you?"

Behind Sostratos, Menedemos muttered, "By the dog of Egypt!" Sostratos couldn't tell whether that was praise for him or astonishment that the dapper fellow—the new passenger, he was now—hadn't screamed blue murder. Some of both, maybe. As for Sostratos himself, he had the feeling he could have asked for a whole mina, not just a half, and he would have got the same instant agreement.

He had to make himself remember the man's question. "That's right," he said. "You pay half then, half when we get there."

"I know how it's done," the dapper man said impatiently. "I'll have my own food and wine, too."

"All right." Sostratos knew he sounded a little dazed, but couldn't help it. He had to make himself come out with one more question: "And, ah, your name is . . . ?"

"You can call me Dionysios son of Herakleitos," the man answered. "I'll be aboard early enough to suit you, I promise." He spoke to the local at the oars, who took him back to Sounion.

Sostratos stared after him. "Well, well," Menedemos said. "Isn't that interesting?"

"I wonder what he's running from," Sostratos said. "Nothing right here in town, surely, or he'd have asked to spend the night on the foredeck. Something back in Athens, I suppose. He looks like an Athenian—sounds like one, too."

"*I* wonder who he is," Menedemos said.

"Dionysios son of Herakl—" Sostratos began.

His cousin tossed his head. "He said we could call him that.

He didn't say it was his name." Sostratos thumped his forehead with the heel of his hand. He prided himself on noticing such things, but he'd missed that one. Menedemos went on, "He strung a couple of the most ordinary names in the world together, is what he did. He might have been Odysseus telling Polyphemos the Cyclops to call him Nobody."

"Trust you to haul Homer into it somehow," Sostratos said, but he had to admit the comparison was apt. And then his own wits, stunned since Dionysios so casually agreed to that ridiculous fare, started to work again. "He wants to go to Kos."

"He said so," Menedemos agreed. After a moment, he snapped his fingers. "And staying on Kos—"

"Is Ptolemaios," Sostratos finished for him, not wanting to hear his own thought hijacked. "I wonder if he's some sort of envoy from Demetrios of Phaleron here in Attica, or from Kassandros, or if he's one of Ptolemaios' spies."

"I'd bet on the last," Menedemos said. "Ptolemaios has all the money in the world, so why should his spies have to quarrel about fares?"

"That makes sense," Sostratos said. "Of course, just because it makes sense doesn't have to mean it's true. I'll tell you something else." He waited for Menedemos to raise a questioning eyebrow, then continued, "Whatever he is, we won't find out from him."

"Well, my dear, if you think I'm going to argue about *that*, you're mad as a maenad," Menedemos said.

Dionysios son of Herakleitos—or whatever his real name was—proved as good as his word. He hailed the *Aphrodite* so early the next morning, some of her sailors were still asleep. Carrying a leather sack big enough to hold food and wine and the few belongings a traveling man needed, he scrambled up from the local's rowboat into the low waist of the merchant galley.

"Hail," he said as Sostratos came up to him.

"Good day," Sostratos replied.

"I doubt it," Dionysios replied. "It's going to be beastly hot. I hope you don't expect a man to bring his own water along with everything else."

"No," Sostratos said. "Water we share, especially on a hot

day—and I think you're right: this will be one. My eyes feel drier than they should, and the sun's not even over the horizon." He held out his hand. "Now, if you'd be so kind, the first part of the fare."

"Certainly." Dionysios reached into the sack for a smaller leather wallet. He took coins from it and gave them to Sostratos one by one. "Here you are, best one: twenty-five drakhmai."

The coins had an eagle on one side and a blunt-featured man's profile on the other. "These are Ptolemaios' drakhmai!" Sostratos said in dismay—they were far lighter than the Attic owls he'd expected.

"You never said in whose currency you wanted to be paid," Dionysios pointed out.

"Have we got a problem?" Menedemos called from the stern. After Sostratos explained, his cousin asked, "Well, what do we do about that? Shall we send him back to shore unless he comes up with the proper weight of silver?"

"Where's the justice in that?" Dionysios demanded. "I'm not cheating you out of anything I promised to give."

"So what?" Menedemos said. "If you don't pay us what we want, you can wait for another ship." That made the dapper man unhappy, try as he would to hide it.

But Sostratos reluctantly tossed his head—that gibe about justice struck home. "He's right, Menedemos. It's my own fault, for not saying we wanted it in Attic money." He took advantage of exchange rates whenever he could; it wasn't often that anyone got the better of him, but it had happened here.

"You're too soft for your own good," Menedemos grumbled.

Dionysios son of Herakleitos gave Sostratos a bow. "What you are, my dear fellow, is a *kalos k'agathos*."

"A gentleman? Me? I don't know about that," Sostratos said, more flattered than he was willing to show. "I do know I expect people who deal with me to be honest, so I'd better give what I hope to get."

"And if that doesn't make you a *kalos k'agathos*, to the crows with me if I know what would," Dionysios said.

The sun, a ball of molten bronze, rose over the little island of Helena, where Helen had paused on her way home to Sparta after the Trojan War. Almost at once, the air began to quiver and dance, as it would above hot metal in a smithy. Those first few harsh beams seemed to scorch the hillsides back of Sounion. They'd been sere and dry and brown before; Sostratos knew as much. But he could almost watch the last moisture baking out of them now. He marveled that he couldn't watch the sea steam and retreat, as water would in a pot left over the fire too long.

"*Papai!*" he exclaimed. "I hope we have some wind. Rowing in this will be worse than it was the last time we went through the Kyklades."

Dionysios rummaged in his sack again. This time, he pulled out a broad-brimmed hat, which he set on his head. "I don't care to cook, thank you very much," he said.

"Why don't you go up to the foredeck so the rowers can work freely?" Sostratos said.

"Oh, of course. I don't mean to be a bother." Dionysios picked up his bag and headed for the bow.

Sostratos went back to the stern and climbed up onto the poop deck. He waited for Menedemos to rake him over the coals; his cousin had earned the right. But Menedemos just clicked his tongue between his teeth and said, "Well, well—the biter bit."

"I never dreamt he'd give me Ptolemaios' money," Sostratos said. "He's as cocksure as an Athenian ought to be; he speaks good Attic Greek; I expected owls. This does make it all the more likely he's Ptolemaios' man."

"Because he uses coins from Egypt? I should say so."

"Well, that, too, but it isn't what I had in mind. I was thinking that he acts like a rich cheapskate, the way Ptolemaios did when we were haggling over the price for the tiger skin," Sostratos said.

"A rich cheapskate." Menedemos savored the paradox before dipping his head in agreement. "That's good. He can get anything he wants and pay anything he wants, and he knows it, but he still doesn't want to pay too much."

Up at the bow, capstans creaked as sailors brought up the

anchors. Rich cheapskate or not, Dionysios son of Herakleitos knew enough to stay out of their way. Sweat and olive oil sheened their naked bodies. Sostratos swiped a forearm across his brow. It came away wet. "I'm going to get a hat for myself, too," he said. "I don't care to bake my brains today."

His cousin wet a finger and tested the breeze—or would have, had there been any breeze to test. He sighed. "That's a good idea, however much I wish it weren't."

Diokles said, "I'm only going to put half a dozen men on a side at the oars, and I'll change shifts more often than I usually do. Otherwise, we'll lose somebody from heatstroke, sure as sure."

"As you think best," Menedemos told the keleustes.

With shouted orders from the captain and the oarmaster, the *Aphrodite* left the little harbor of Sounion and started east across the Aegean toward Kos and then toward Rhodes and home. Sostratos kept looking back towards the north and west, towards Athens, toward what might have been. He cursed the pirate who'd stolen the gryphon's skull—and every other pirate who'd ever lived. Those curses felt weak, empty. The skull was gone, and he'd never see its like again. He wondered if the world would.

RATHER THAN MERELY cursing pirates, Menedemos got ready to fend them off, serving out weapons to the crew as he had on the voyage towards Attica. Seeing that, the *Aphrodite*'s passenger took a hoplite's shortsword from his bag and belted it on around his waist. He had the air of a man who knew what to do with it.

In a dead calm, the Aegean lay smooth as polished metal under that fierce, broiling sun. Sweat rivered off Menedemos as he stood at the steering oars. He guzzled heavily watered wine to keep some moisture in him. So did the rowers. They couldn't pull their best, not in heat like this. Diokles didn't chide them. The oarmaster knew they were giving what they could.

Halfway between Sounion and Keos, the *Aphrodite* slid past a becalmed round ship. Sailors on the tubby merchantman shouted in alarm when they spied the merchant galley. Had she been a pirate ship, they couldn't possibly have escaped. The sailors on the round ship shouted again, this time in relief, when the akatos didn't turn toward them.

Well before noon, Menedemos decided to put in at Keos. "We'll fill up our water jars and hope for wind tomorrow," he told Sostratos. "I know we've only come about a hundred stadia, but even so. . . ."

To his relief, his cousin didn't feel like arguing. "We wouldn't have made Kythnos by sundown, anyhow, and we need the fresh water."

"That's right." Menedemos dipped his head. "And the water here is better than the nasty stuff they have on Kythnos."

Keos did look greener and more inviting than its southern neighbor, though the savage sun was baking it, too. As the *Aphrodite* came into the harbor at Koressia, one of the little island's four poleis, Sostratos remarked, "This was the place where, in the old days, they made people drink hemlock when they turned sixty—they didn't want any useless mouths to feed."

Menedemos snapped his fingers. "I knew that was one of the Kyklades, but you could have given me to a Persian torturer and he wouldn't have squeezed which one out of me."

Sostratos said, "I remember useless things—you know that. It's also where Simonides the poet came from."

" 'Go tell the Spartans, passerby, that here, obedient to their laws, we lie.' " Menedemos quoted the epitaph for the men who'd died at Thermopylai.

"He wrote a lot of other verses besides that one," Sostratos said.

"I know, but it's the one everybody recalls," Menedemos said. "I'm not like you, my dear—I don't come up with the strange things at the drop of a hat."

Sostratos took off his hat. Menedemos wondered if he would drop it, but he only fanned himself with it and put it back on. One of his eyebrows rose. He studied Menedemos the same way he'd examined the gryphon's skull—analyzing him, classifying him, finding a place for him in the bigger scheme of things. Menedemos didn't know that he cared for the place to which his cousin had assigned him. It would be higher on the scheme of things than the gryphon, surely, but how much higher?

Before Sostratos could give him the answer there—in greater detail than he would like, he guessed—Dionysios came back to the stern. "Considering the price I'm paying, I hoped to get closer to Kos my first day out than one miserable little hop," the dapper man said.

"I hoped to get closer, too," Menedemos answered, "but there was no wind, and I don't intend to kill my rowers. Maybe we'll do better tomorrow."

"We'd better," Dionysios said darkly.

With a smile even cooler and nastier than the one he'd just bestowed on Menedemos, Sostratos said, "Well, O marvelous one, if our pace doesn't suit you, I'll give you back all but five drakhmai of your fare, and you're welcome to find another eastbound ship here."

The dull red Dionysios turned had nothing to do with the heat. The harbor at Koressia, into which the Elixos River ran, held no other ships besides the *Aphrodite*: only little fishing boats that never got out of sight of the island. How long would the traveler have to wait for another vessel bound for Kos? Menedemos had no idea, and neither, plainly, did Dionysios.

With twin splashes, the akatos' anchors went into the sea. Sailors wrestled water jars into the boat and went ashore with them. The men made for the Elixos to fill the jars. Menedemos said, "Shall we go into the market square with some perfume and a little silk and see if we can sell 'em?"

"Here?" Sostratos' glance was eloquent. "I don't think they've done anything here since they sent a couple of ships to fight the Persians at Salamis."

Menedemos laughed. "You're probably right. Even so, though, they're bound to want their women to smell sweet and look pretty."

"I suppose so," his cousin admitted. "But can they pay for what they want?"

"Always a question," Menedemos admitted. "I think it's worth finding out."

Next to no one in Koressia was stirring as the two Rhodians made their way to the agora. Men stayed in wineshops or squatted like lizards in whatever shade the walls gave them. A couple of drunks lay snoring, empty cups or wine jars beside them. Sostratos raised an eyebrow. Menedemos only shrugged.

They nearly had the market square to themselves. A man hawked raisins, while a farm woman displayed eggs and cheeses. Neither had any customers or seemed to expect any—they were going through the motions of selling, no more. Menedemos had seen that before; it always made him scornful.

"Come on," he told Sostratos. "Let's show these people not everybody sleeps all the time."

His cousin yawned. "I'm sorry, best one. Did you say something?"

Snorting, Menedemos raised his voice till it filled the agora: "Perfume from Rhodes! Fine silk from Kos! Who wants to buy? We won't stay here long, so you'd better come quick. Who wants to buy?"

The man with the raisins and the woman from the farm both stared at them. Sostratos took up the call and joined with Menedemos. For a while, though, Menedemos wondered if anyone cared but a couple of doves grubbing whatever they could from the ground. Koressia wasn't just a sleepy town; it might have been a dead one.

At last, though, a middle-aged man strolled into the agora. " 'Ail," he said, dropping his rough breathings as did those who used the Ionic dialect. "What 'ave you got for sale?"

Why. I'm selling doors and roof tiles. Haven't you heard me crying them? Menedemos thought. But Sostratos was already displaying a bolt of filmy silk. Grudgingly, Menedemos admitted he and his cousin also sold perfume.

" 'Ow about that?" The Kean gaped as if he'd never heard of either commodity. " 'Ow much do you want for 'em?"

Menedemos named his prices, adding, "That's in Athenian drakhmai, of course." Keos was part of Antigonos' Island League, but had more intimate connections with nearby Attica.

"All right," the local said. "Let me 'ave a couple of jars of the perfume, and maybe two-three bolts of silk. Sounds like a pretty good deal."

"You . . . have the money?" Menedemos tried to hide his astonishment.

"I'll be back directly," the Kean replied. "Don't you go away, now." Off he went, no faster than he had to. He did come back, and started piling Athenian owls in front of Sostratos. "That should do it," he said when he was done.

"Why, so it does." Maybe the local couldn't hear how amazed Sostratos was. Menedemos could. But, at his cousin's gesture, he gave the man the perfume and the silk.

"Thank you kindly," the fellow said. "You got anything else?"

"Well . . ." Menedemos hesitated.

"Come on. Spit it out. I'm not going to buy it if you don't tell me what it is," the local said. "If I want it, though, I will. I've got the money. You've seen I do."

"So we have," Menedemos said. "All right, then, most noble: the other thing I have is a single Egyptian emerald."

"Now, that's something that doesn't come along every day." The Kean held out his hand. "Let's see it." Reluctantly, Menedemos produced the stone, half expecting the local to run off with it. But he didn't. He held it in the sunlight, murmuring, "Isn't that pretty?" When he returned it to Menedemos, he asked the right question: "How much?"

Without blinking, Menedemos said, "Ten minai."

The Kean handed back the emerald and spoke in mild protest: "That's a lot of silver, friend." But he didn't turn on his heel and walk away. Instead, he said, "I'll give you six."

Menedemos felt like shouting. Beside him, Sostratos inhaled sharply, but he didn't think the local noticed. He tossed his head. "I'm sorry, but I can't sell it for that without costing myself money." The money he was talking about was all profit, but the Kean didn't have to know that.

"Well, six minai, twenty drakhmai, then," the fellow said.

In a quick, neat dicker, they settled on eight minai, fifteen drakhmai for the stone. That was even more than Nikodromos had paid on Aigina. *The more I ask for emeralds, the more I seem to get,* Menedemos thought dazedly, and kicked himself for letting others, earlier in the trading run, go so cheap.

"See you soon," the Kean said, and strolled away. Menedemos hated to let the man out of his sight. Would he really come back? Some of the sweat pouring down the merchant's face had nothing to do with the beastly weather. In due course, the Kean did return, this time with a bigger leather sack, which he handed to Sostratos. "Count 'em out, friend. If I'm one or two light, I'll give 'em to you."

Count them Sostratos did. "As a matter of fact, best one, you're one drakhma over," he said, and handed the Kean an owl.

"I thank you." The man popped it into his mouth. It was heavy enough to make his cheek sag slightly. "A pleasure to know I'm dealing with 'onest men."

He put that extra coin in on purpose, to see what we'd do, Menedemos realized as he passed the Kean the emerald. The fellow might move slowly and talk like a rustic, but he was no fool. Nikodromos had played the same game, but only after he'd been caught cheating himself. This felt different—not nearly so annoying.

"A pleasure to know our goods please you," Sostratos said.

"You might say so." The local dipped his head. "Yes, you just might say so. 'Ail, the two of you." Without any fuss, he turned and ambled out of the market square.

I never even found out his name, Menedemos thought. He called out to the fellow selling raisins: "*Ea*, friend, who's that man we were doing business with?"

The fellow's eyes got big. "You don't know Kallimedes son of Kallias?" By the way he said it, everybody on Keos knew him. Sure enough, the raisin seller went on, " 'E's got bigger wheatfields and more olive trees than anybody else on this island, maybe more than everybody else on this island put together—I wouldn't be surprised."

"No wonder he could afford what we were selling," Sostratos murmured.

"No wonder at all," Menedemos whispered back. He asked the man with the basket of raisins, "Was he buying our dainties for his wife or for a favorite hetaira?"

"Kallimedes?" The raisin seller stared again. "You *must* not know him. Those are bound to be for a pretty boy. 'E's mad for boys, Kallimedes is."

"Oh," Menedemos said in slightly crestfallen tones.

"Ha," Sostratos said. Menedemos tried to step on his foot,

but missed. His cousin laughed. Menedemos muttered under his breath. He hadn't really intended *doing* anything with Kallimedes' wife, if the Kean had one. He'd just asked out of curiosity. And he'd got his answer.

"I think we're done here," he told Sostratos, who dipped his head in agreement. As they headed back toward the *Aphrodite*. Menedemos wished he were wearing his sword. He hadn't expected to be carrying so much silver. But he and Sostratos had no trouble. Not even the panting scavenger dogs found a couple of strangers worth barking at.

On board ship, Dionysios son of Herakleitos remained in a foul mood. "You've certainly gone and wasted the best part of the day."

"Wasted? I should say not, O marvelous one." Menedemos held up the two sacks of coins he'd got from Kallimedes son of Kallias. "Do you see these? Which do you suppose is more important to me, the business I did here or your paltry fare?"

"Paltry?" Dionysios said. "You've got your nerve, calling it that."

"Next to this, it is," Menedemos said. "You'll get to Kos soon enough, but you're out of your mind if you think I won't do business along the way."

"And you're out of your mind if you think we didn't need fresh water," Sostratos added. "We're not going to have our rowers fall over dead from working the oars too hard in this heat."

Dionysios looked back toward Cape Sounion, whose headland was still plainly visible in the west. "I could have swum this far," he grumbled.

"If you keep complaining, you *will* swim from here on out," Menedemos said, no trace of smile on his face. That got through to the passenger, who fell silent.

The following day dawned as hot and bright as the one before. The breeze that came up from the south might have blown from a smithy's furnace. But it *was* a breeze; Menedemos ordered the akatos' sail lowered from the yard. By the time the sun came up over the eastern horizon, the *Aphrodite* had left Keos behind.

"Are you going to make Syros tonight?" Sostratos asked.

"I'm going to try," Menedemos answered. "If the wind holds, we shouldn't have any trouble."

"And if we don't run into pirates," his cousin added. Menedemos spat into the bosom of his tunic. After a moment, Sostratos did the same. He went on, "Shall I pass out the weapons again, just in case?"

"Maybe you'd better," Menedemos said with a sigh.

They saw no pirate galleys on the Aegean, only fishing boats and one round ship that took the *Aphrodite* for a pirate and sped away, running before the wind. Syros rose from the sea ahead of them: a sun-baked island much longer from north to south than from east to west. The only polis on the island, also called Syros, lay by a bay on the eastern coast; Menedemos brought the *Aphrodite* down from the north into the harbor.

He quoted from the *Odyssey* as the akatos' anchors splashed into the Aegean:

" 'There is an island called Syrie, if perhaps you have heard of it,
Above Ortygie, where the turning points of the sun are.
It is not very populous, but it is good—
With fine cattle, fine sheep, full of wine, rich in wheat.
Famine never enters that folk, nor does any other
Dire plague come upon wretched mortals.
But when the race of men grows old in the city,
Apollo of the silver bow comes with Artemis.
He assails them with his painless shafts and kills them.
There are two cities there, and everything is divided in two between them.
My father was king over both:
Ktesios son of Ormenos, a man like the immortals.' "

"That's Eumaios the swineherd talking to Odysseus, isn't it?" Sostratos asked.

"Yes, that's right," Menedemos said.

Sostratos took a long look at Syros, then clicked his tongue between his teeth. "Well, if Eumaios was telling as much truth about his ancestors as he was about the island, he must have been a pigkeeper from a long line of pigkeepers."

"Scoffer!" Menedemos said, deliciously scandalized. But, the more he eyed the dry, barren landscape beyond the steeply rising streets of the polis of Syros, the more he realized Sostratos had a point: he saw not a tree, hardly even a bush. Still, he went on, "It must grow *something*, or no one would live here."

"I suppose so," Sostratos said grudgingly. "All the same, this is one of those places that prove Homer was a blind poet." He pointed ahead. "Even the polis is a miserable little dump. Herodotos never says a word about it, and neither does Thoukydides. I see why not, too."

"Why should they?" Menedemos said. "Nothing much happens here."

"That's what I mean," Sostratos said. "You could live out your life in this polis. You could be as big a man here as that Kallimedes son of Kallias was back on Keos, and nobody who's not from Syros would ever hear of you, any more than we'd heard of Kallimedes. In Rhodes or Athens or Taras or Syracuse or Alexandria, at least you have a chance to be remembered. Here?" He tossed his head.

Menedemos wondered if bright young men, ambitious young men, left Syros and crossed the sea to some other polis where they could seek their heart's desire. He supposed some had to. But most, surely, lived out their lives within a few stadia of where they were born. All through the civilized world, most people did.

The heat wave broke that night. The northerly breeze that blew the next morning had a distinct nip to it, a warning that autumn, even if it hadn't got here yet, would come. Menedemos enjoyed that, but he enjoyed its steadiness even more. "Now we'll show that son of a whore what the *Aphrodite* can do," he muttered, dipping a chunk of bread into olive oil and taking a big bite.

"If the wind holds, we'll make Naxos easy as you please," Diokles agreed, "and that's a pretty fair day's run."

Wind thrummed in the rigging and quickly filled the sail when Menedemos ordered it lowered. The merchant galley seemed to lean forward, letting that wind pull her along. Naxos lay at the heart of Antigonos' Island League. With malice aforethought, Menedemos asked Dionysios son of Herakleitos, "When we get there, shall we tell the Naxians how eager you are to go on to Kos?"

The passenger's eyes were cool as marble. "Tell them anything you please, O best one. It's all the same to me." He was probably lying about that, but he'd made his point, and Menedemos stopped twitting him.

From Naxos to Amorgos the next day was an even better run. Menedemos steered past several little islands that housed a few shepherds and fishermen. He'd almost gone aground on one of them in the rain on his last trip through the Kyklades, with Polemaios aboard. No danger of that here; not with the weather fine and sunny, but he did have to do several usual days' worth of steering before he left them astern. Sostratos said, "Any one of those horrid little rocks makes Syros look like Athens."

"And if that's not a frightening thought, Furies take me if I know what would be," Menedemos replied.

He took the *Aphrodite* south and west again the following day, to Astypalaia, where they spoke Doric Greek like his own rather than Ionic. A great many fishing boats bobbed in the offshore waters; a fertile valley stretched behind the polis, which lay in the southeastern part of the island.

"One more place where nobody ever made a name for himself," Menedemos said.

To his surprise, Sostratos tossed his head. "Don't you know the story of Kleomedes of Astypalaia?" he asked.

"Can't say that I do," Menedemos admitted. "Who was he?"

"A pankratiast, back around the time of the Persian Wars," Sostratos answered. "He would have won at the Olympic Games, but he killed his foe in the all-out fight and got disqualified. He must have gone mad with grief after that. He came back to Astypalaia and pulled down a pillar that held up the roof for a boys' school—fifty or sixty people died. He fled to Athena's temple and hid in a wooden chest there, but when the Astypalaians broke it open he wasn't inside, either: not alive, not dead, just . . . gone."

Menedemos felt the hair at the back of his neck try to prickle up in awe and dread. "What happened then?" he asked.

"They sent to Delphi to find out what they should do, and the verse they got back was,

'Last of the heroes—Kleomedes the Astypalaian.
Honor him with sacrifices, he being mortal no more.' "

"Do they?" Menedemos asked.

"I've never heard otherwise," Sostratos said.

"A demigod, from as late as the Persian Wars," Menedemos mused. "That's strange all by itself . . . although people are saying Alexander was divine, too."

"They're saying it, all right," Sostratos agreed. "What do you think of it?"

"I don't know," Menedemos answered. "He did things no ordinary mortal could do. Maybe that does make him divine. Who knows where humanity stops and divinity starts? It's not as though there were a neat line between gods and men." He poked his cousin in the ribs. "What do *you* think?"

"I don't know, either." Sostratos sounded uncomfortable, even a little annoyed: he always hated not knowing. He went on, "He was just a man—Ptolemaios and Polemaios knew him. I'm not comfortable with calling anyone a god—but, as you say, he did things you wouldn't think a mere man could do. I wish I had a better answer, but I don't. I wonder what Ptolemaios would say if we asked him."

"Well, we're only a couple of days from Kos," Menedemos said. "You can do that, if you've got the nerve."

"Oh, I'm sure he'd talk about Alexander—Alexander's dead, divine or not," Sostratos said. "Now, if I were to start talking about Antigonos . . . I don't think I'd want to do that." He glanced toward Dionysios son of Herakleitos, who'd dropped a fishing line over the side to see if he could catch some opson to go with his sitos. In a low voice, he added, "You never can tell who might be listening."

Just then, Dionysios tugged on the line and hauled a plump mackerel up into the ship. It wasn't a mullet or a dogfish—no opsophagos' delight—but it was a lot better than nothing.

He gutted it, threw the offal into the sea, and took out a little charcoal brazier to cook his catch.

"He's got good luck," Menedemos remarked.

"So he does," Sostratos said, still quietly. "I wonder where he stole it." To that, Menedemos had no answer.

The run from Astypalaia to Kos the next day proved harder work and slower than he'd hoped, for the wind died away to next to nothing and the rowers had to go to their benches. Even with a good following wind, though, Menedemos would have been amazed to make the polis of Kos before nightfall. The *Aphrodite* did reach the western end of the island, where he grounded her on a broad, fair beach on the north coast. "She'll be easy to get into the water again tomorrow," he told Sostratos. "We're not carrying enough to weigh her down."

"True," his cousin said. "And we ought to be safe from pirates, with so much of Ptolemaios' fleet in the neighborhood."

"If we're not safe here, we're not safe anywhere outside the great harbor at Rhodes," Menedemos said.

A couple of peasants came up with honey and olives to sell. As Sostratos did when buying anything, he clicked his tongue between his teeth and gave other signs of distress, but after they left he said, "If people here know it's likely to be safe to come up to a beached ship, that's the best sign pirates don't come sniffing around very often."

Menedemos dipped his head. "And tomorrow we'll put Dionysios ashore, and then we can head for home ourselves."

"I wonder whether Halikarnassos has fallen," Sostratos said.

"Me, I hope Ptolemaios' men sacked it," Menedemos said.

His cousin laughed. "Of course you do. That would mean what's-his-name, the fellow with the friendly wife there, was likely dead. And then we could trade there again without worrying about your getting murdered."

Ears hot, Menedemos said, "Well, that's not the only reason." Sostratos laughed again, sure he was lying through his teeth. Since he was, he changed the subject in a hurry.

AS THE *APHRODITE* came into the harbor at Kos, Sostratos shaded his eyes from the sun with the palm of his hand and peered northeast across the narrow channel separating the island from Halikarnassos on the mainland. "No smoke," he said. "No sea battles. Either the place fell a while ago or it hasn't fallen at all." Menedemos didn't answer. "Did you hear me?" Sostratos asked. "I said—"

"I heard you," Menedemos answered. "I'm just not listening to you."

"Oh," Sostratos said. "All right." The anger lying under Menedemos' quiet words warned him he'd pushed things about as far as they would go, or perhaps a little further. *Now if only Menedemos were as good at noticing when he goes too far with me*, he thought, and then laughed. *Wish for the moon, while you're at it.*

"Harbor's crowded," Diokles remarked. "Ships stuffed tight as olives in a jar."

"There's the likely answer," Sostratos said. "If Ptolemaios' fleet is back here, Halikarnassos probably still belongs to Antigonos."

"Too bad," Menedemos said. Then, suddenly, he took his right hand from the steering-oar tiller and pointed. His voice rose to a shout: "There's a spot we can squeeze into! Row, you bastards, before somebody steals it from us."

"Rhyppa*pai*! Rhyppa*pai*!" the oarmaster called, giving the rowers the stroke. The merchant galley slid into the wharf space. "Back oars!" Diokles commanded, and then, as she came to a halt, "*Oöp!*" The men rested at the oars.

Dionysios son of Herakleitos, leather duffel on his shoulder, hurried back to the poop deck as longshoremen caught lines from the *Aphrodite* and made her fast to the quay. "Put up the gangplank," he barked at Menedemos. "I have to be on my way."

Menedemos tilted his head back and looked down his nose at the passenger. "You talk to a skipper like that aboard his ship and he'll throw you overboard. You won't need to worry about the gangplank then, by Zeus."

"And you don't go anywhere till you pay us the twenty-five drakhmai you still owe us," Sostratos added.

Fuming, the dapper man gave him the second half of his fare—again, in Ptolemaios' light drakhmai. Even after that,

Menedemos took his own sweet time about running the gangplank over to the pier. When he finally did, Dionysios sprang onto it and went down the pier and into the polis of Kos at a dead run.

"What's chasing him?" one of the longshoremen asked.

Sostratos shrugged. "Who knows? Some people are just glad to get off a ship." The longshoreman laughed. Sostratos asked a question of his own: "What went wrong with the siege of Halikarnassos?"

"Oh, you were here when that started?" the longshoreman asked. Sostratos dipped his head. The Koan, a disgusted look on his face, spat into the sea. "Ptolemaios' army was on the point of taking the place when who should show up but Demetrios son of Antigonos, with the army he'd brought back from fighting somebody or other way off in the east."

"Seleukos?" Sostratos suggested.

"I think so," the longshoreman answered. "Anyway, he relieved the place and put a big new garrison into it, so there's no point going after it any more."

Menedemos made a horrible face. "Too bad," he said.

"I think so, too," the Koan agreed; Halikarnassos was his polis' longtime trading rival.

"Demetrios came back to Anatolia from fighting Seleukos, you said?" Sostratos asked, and the longshoreman dipped his head. As was his way, Sostratos found another question: "How did he do out in the east?"

"Well, I don't know all the battles and such, but I don't think he won the war," the Koan replied.

Demetrios beat Ptolemaios' army here, but he couldn't beat Seleukos' army there, Sostratos thought. *Isn't that interesting?* Ptolemaios had let Seleukos go off to the east to cause trouble for Antigonos in a new quarter. By all appearances, Seleukos was giving the lord of Egypt everything he wanted and then some.

"What other news besides Halikarnassos?" Menedemos asked.

"You should have got here half a month ago," the longshoreman told him. "The festival Ptolemaios gave when his lady had a boy . . ." He grinned reminiscently. "I drank so much wine, my head ached for two days afterwards."

"What did he name the baby?" Sostratos asked: he wanted to know all the details.

"Why, Ptolemaios," the Koan said.

Sostratos frowned. "Doesn't he already have a son named Ptolemaios? His wife bore the other one, not his mistress."

"I think you're right," Menedemos said.

The longshoreman shrugged. "I don't know anything about that. He's the richest fellow in the world. Who's going to tell him he can't have two boys with the same name, if that's what he wants? Not me, by Zeus."

"Nor me," Sostratos agreed. "But I wonder how happy his wife will be, knowing his mistress has a little Ptolemaios, too."

"You're too young to have a wife of your own, aren't you, best one?" asked the longshoreman, whose hair was thinning on top and gray at the temples. He didn't wait for Sostratos to answer, but continued, "You must be—you're nowhere near thirty. But I'll tell you something: you've got that right, whether you learned it from your own wife or not. She'll be steaming, sure as sure."

"Of course, Eurydike is back in Alexandria, and Berenike's here along with Ptolemaios—the grown-up Ptolemaios, I mean," Sostratos said.

"He'll go home sooner or later, and so will his lady—and so will their brat," the Koan said. "And how long he's been away won't matter a khalkos. What's-her-name back there will have plenty to say to him, no matter how long it is." He spoke with a mixture of glum certainty and gloating anticipation; Sostratos wondered who ruled the roost at his house. No, actually he didn't wonder—he thought he could guess.

Something else struck him: "Eurydike is Kassandros' sister, remember. He won't be happy if she loses her place."

"One more reason for a fight, maybe," Menedemos said.

"Don't the Macedonians have enough already?" Sostratos said. "It's not as if they need more."

"They're like a gang of pankratiasts fighting it out," the longshoreman said. "They won't quit till only one's left standing."

Sostratos thought uneasily of Kleomedes of Astypalaia.

He'd slain his foe, and been disqualified for it. Nobody disqualified a Macedonian marshal who killed a rival or a royal heir. Unlike athletes, the marshals advanced their positions through murder.

Menedemos said, "Now that we've put Dionysios ashore here, to the crows with me if I'm not tempted to head straight for Rhodes and not spend even a night."

Diokles gave him a reproachful look. "Seeing how hard the men worked through the hot spell, skipper, and seeing all the miserable, good-for-nothing places we stopped at on our way across the Aegean, don't you think they deserve one night's fun in a real polis?"

"Oh, I suppose so." Menedemos donned a lopsided grin. "I may even deserve a night's fun in a real polis myself."

"Sounds fair," the oarmaster said. "Except that once over in Aigina, you had yourself a pretty quiet run this year."

"We were talking about pankratiasts a minute ago," Menedemos said. "I didn't realize everyone was keeping score on *me*." Diokles and Sostratos solemnly dipped their heads at the same time. Menedemos made faces at both of them. Diokles laughed.

And Sostratos said, "Well, my dear, even if you do go out drinking and wenching tonight, I'm glad you sound as though you want to go home. When we set out this past spring, you didn't seem to care if you ever saw Rhodes again."

Menedemos' face froze—and the expression on which it froze was one not far from hatred. Sostratos took a startled, altogether involuntary step away from him. After a moment, his cousin's bleak look faded . . . a little. Menedemos said, "I'd almost forgotten about that, and you went and made me remember." He sighed and shrugged. "I don't suppose I can blame you much. It would have come back to me when we got into the great harbor."

"*What* would have?" Sostratos had known something was bothering Menedemos, but he'd had no idea what. And he still didn't; Menedemos had been unusually close-mouthed—astoundingly so, for him—all through this season's sailing.

He still was. He smiled at Sostratos and said, "However strange and sorrowful you may feel about it, O marvelous one, there *are* some things you aren't going to find out, no matter how much research you do."

"No, eh?" Sostratos almost made a crack about going on with his investigations, but the memory of the look his cousin had given him a moment before made him hold his tongue. Whatever reasons Menedemos had for wanting to stay away from Rhodes, he was serious about them.

"No," he said firmly. Maybe he'd expected a crack from Sostratos and was relieved not to get it, for his manner lightened again. He went on, "Why don't you come drinking and wenching tonight, too? It'd do you good."

"Me?" Sostratos tossed his head. "Going around with a thick head the next day isn't my idea of fun." He held up a hand before Menedemos could say anything. "Oh, once in a while—in a symposion, say. But getting drunk in a tavern isn't my idea of fun."

"Well, don't get drunk in a tavern, then. Get laid in a brothel instead." Menedemos smiled once more—or was that a leer? Whatever it was, his good humor seemed restored. "You can't tell me that's not your idea of fun, not after that girl in Taras last year, the one with hair like new copper."

"Every now and then," Sostratos admitted, "but not tonight."

"Wet blanket."

"I am not," Sostratos said irately. "No such thing, by Zeus! You can do whatever you want. Do I complain about it?"

"Only when you talk," Menedemos assured him.

Since he was right, or at least partly right, Sostratos tried a different tack: "Did I tell you not to go drinking tonight? Did I tell you not to go to a brothel tonight?"

"Not yet," Menedemos said.

"Funny man," Sostratos grumbled.

His cousin bowed, as if thinking he'd meant it. "Thank you very much."

That evening, most of the sailors, and Menedemos with them, went into Kos to revel. "Try not to drink up all our profits, anyhow," Sostratos said as Menedemos strode up the gangplank.

"You sound like the pedagogue who took me to school

every morning when I was a boy," Menedemos said. "But you haven't got a switch, and he did."

Sostratos spent the night aboard. He ate bread and olives and cheese and a fish he bought from a little boy who'd caught it at the end of the pier, and washed the supper down with wine. *If I wanted to get drunk, I could do it here*, he thought. If he wanted a woman . . . He tossed his head. He wouldn't have cared to do that aboard a ship, even one called the *Aphrodite*.

He got little sleep. Drunken sailors kept reeling back to the merchant galley at all hours. At some point, Menedemos must have come back, too, though Sostratos didn't remember that. Morning twilight was beginning to make the eastern sky turn pale when he jerked awake yet again at a snatch of drunken song and found Menedemos snoring on the planks of the poop deck beside him.

Sunrise woke Sostratos for good. It also woke his cousin, who looked none too happy about being awake. "If I jump into the sea, do you suppose I'll turn into a dolphin?" he asked. "I'm sure dolphins don't get hangovers."

"By the way your eyes look, I'd say you were more likely to turn into a jellyfish," Sostratos answered. "Was the good time you had worth the sore head you've got now?"

"From what I remember of it, yes," Menedemos said, which wasn't the conclusion Sostratos had hoped he would draw. Menedemos peered through half shut eyes at a couple of well-dressed men coming up the quay toward the *Aphrodite*. "What do they want? Tell 'em to go away, Sostratos. I don't want anything to do with 'em, not this early in the morning."

"Maybe they're passengers," Sostratos said.

"Tell 'em to go away anyhow," Menedemos answered, something Sostratos had no intention of doing.

His intentions turned out not to matter. One of the men said, "Menedemos son of Philodemos and Sostratos son of Lysistratos? Come with us at once, if you please."

There was breathtaking arrogance. "Who says we should?" Sostratos demanded.

"Ptolemaios, the lord of Egypt," the man answered. "He

assumed you would come peaceably. If not, we can make other arrangements."

"What does Ptolemaios want with us?" Sostratos asked in surprise.

"That's for him to tell you, not me," his man answered. "Are you coming?"

Sostratos dipped his head. After a moment, so did Menedemos. He ran his fingers through his hair to try to make it a little less disheveled. "I'm ready," he said, seeming anything but.

By all the signs, the tramp through town did little to improve his spirits. He paused once to hike up his tunic and piss against a wall. City stinks—dung and unwashed bodies and tanneries and all the others—were nastier away from the breezes of the harbor. His squint got worse as the sun rose higher in the sky.

When he came before Ptolemaios, he gave only a perfunctory bow, muttering, "My head wants to fall off."

"You should have thought of that last night," Sostratos said out of the side of his mouth. Menedemos sent him a horrible look.

"I hear you're thieves," Ptolemaios said without preamble.

"No, your Excellency," Sostratos said. Menedemos said nothing, but cautiously dipped his head to show he agreed with Sostratos. *I'm going to have to do this by myself,* Sostratos thought, annoyed at his cousin for being useless here. *But who would have thought Ptolemaios would want us? Be fair.*

"No, eh?" the Macedonian marshal rumbled. "That's not how Dionysios tells it, and I agree with him. Fifty drakhmai from Cape Sounion to here? That's piracy."

"Piracy? No, sir. By the dog of Egypt, no, sir!" Sostratos said.

Ptolemaios raised a bushy eyebrow at his vehemence. "I tell you it is."

"And I tell you you're talking like a fool . . . sir," Sostratos retorted. Both of Ptolemaios' eyebrows flew upwards. A couple of his bodyguards growled ominously. Sostratos didn't care. He was past caring. Rage almost choking him, he went on, "I'll tell you what piracy really is. Piracy's really a pack of howling whoresons swarming onto your ship and killing your men and stealing your goods, your . . . your most precious goods." He'd thought some of the pain from the loss of the gryphon's skull had eased. Now it stabbed him again. "It happened to us between Andros and Euboia. So Furies take your precious Dionysios if he calls us pirates. Nobody held a knife to his throat and made him come along with us. He could have taken any other ship he chose."

Furies take you *if you call us pirates*. He didn't quite say that to Ptolemaios, but it hung in the air. A vast silence fell over the andron. Some of Ptolemaios' servitors stared at Sostratos. More eyed the lord of Egypt. *How long has it been since anyone called him a fool to his face?* Sostratos wondered. *Years, probably*.

Something glinted in Ptolemaios' eyes. Amusement or anger? Sostratos couldn't tell. The marshal said, "If you think you can insult me as you please because you come from a free and autonomous polis, you're badly mistaken."

Sostratos made himself meet the older man's stare. "If you think you can insult us as you please because you rule Egypt—"

"I'm right," Ptolemaios broke in.

"You may be right, sir, but are you just?" Sostratos asked. "The last time we were in Kos, you said you wished you'd gone to Athens and met Platon. Would he have called that just?"

Ptolemaios grimaced. Sostratos hid a smile. A lot of the leading Macedonians craved acceptance as cultured Hellenes, and Ptolemaios was indeed an educated man. Every once in a while, someone could turn that longing for acceptance against them. Ptolemaios gave a sudden, sharp dip of the head. "Very well. I withdraw the word. Are you happy now?"

"Thank you, best one," Sostratos replied. Bodyguards and courtiers relaxed.

"But I still say that was an outrageously high fare," Ptolemaios went on.

Shrugging, Sostratos answered, "We're in business to make a profit, sir. As I said just now, Dionysios didn't have to come with us if it didn't please him."

"He might still be in Sounion if he hadn't," Ptolemaios said. Sostratos only shrugged again. Ptolemaios' gaze sharpened. "You say you lost your most precious cargo? That's not what I heard."

Ice ran through Sostratos. "Sir?" He had to force the word out, for he was dreadfully afraid he knew what Ptolemaios would say next.

And the lord of Egypt said it: "I heard you were selling emeralds. No, not you—your cousin." He pointed at Menedemos. "This fellow. He talked a lot more the last time I saw him. I wonder why that is. If you were selling emeralds, they were smuggled out of Egypt. I don't like smugglers. I don't like people who deal with them, either."

To Sostratos' amazement—and maybe to Ptolemaios', too—Menedemos burst out laughing. Bowing to the ruler of Egypt, he said, "Search me, sir. Here are your guards—they can look at whatever I have. So long as your men don't steal, they're welcome to come aboard the *Aphrodite* and search the ship, too. If they find a single emerald aboard, you can do what you like to me."

He sold the last one back at Keos, Sostratos remembered. He dipped his head. "My cousin is right, sir," he told Ptolemaios. "Dionysios is trying to get us in trouble because he's angry at the fare he had to pay."

"It could be," Ptolemaios said. "Sure enough, it could be. But, on the other hand, you may be bluffing. Who knows what kind of abandoned rogues you are?" He turned to his guards. "They've given you the invitation. Go ahead and search them. Do a good job of it."

"Yes, sir," the bodyguards chorused. They took Sostratos and Menedemos into separate rooms. Sostratos didn't know what Menedemos went through, and hoped it was as unpleasant as his own experience. After making him get out of his chiton and examining the garment, his belt, the little knife on it, the leather sheath for the knife, and the pouch in which he carried odds and ends, they turned their attention to his person.

They had more practice or more imagination than he'd expected. Their leader ran a finger around inside his mouth and discovered an obolos he'd entirely forgotten was in there. "Keep it," he told the fellow.

"Not me," the bodyguard said. "I'm no thief."

He might not have been a thief, but he would have made a good torturer's apprentice. He ran a straw up Sostratos' nostrils. That produced no emeralds, but did bring on a sneezing fit. He probed Sostratos' ears with a twig. He made Sostratos bend over and probed another orifice, too. He didn't go out of his way to hurt the Rhodian, but he wasn't gentle about it, either. He also made Sostratos pull back his foreskin.

Before the fellow got any other bright ideas, Sostratos said, "Let me piss in a pot. If I'm hiding anything up *there*, that will flush it out."

"Mm—all right," the guard said, and, to Sostratos' vast relief, tossed aside another twig. "Lift up your feet, one after the other, so I can make sure you haven't got anything stuck under your arches."

As Sostratos obeyed, he said, "How likely am I to have an emerald glued to the bottom of my foot, especially when I had no idea coming here that I would be searched?"

"I don't know how likely you are to have one there, friend," the bodyguard answered. "That's why I'm looking: to find out."

Finally, for good measure, he used a very fine-toothed comb, one suitable for getting rid of lice and nits, on Sostratos' hair and beard. Since his hair was wavy and his beard curly, and since he hadn't combed them out too well himself, that hurt as much as anything else he'd been through.

"Are you satisfied now?" he asked when the guard tossed the comb aside.

"Pretty much so," the man replied. "Either you haven't got any or you're a sneakier bastard than most."

After that less than ringing endorsement, he and his comrades let Sostratos put his tunic on again. He'd just slid it down over his head when the other group of guards led Menedemos past the doorway and toward the andron. His cousin, he was not at all sorry to see, looked at least as put upon as he felt himself—but his hair was well combed now. The men who'd searched Sostratos took him back to the andron, too.

"Well?" Ptolemaios barked.

"No emeralds, sir," chorused the men who'd searched Menedemos, and the ones who'd searched Sostratos dipped their heads. A guard asked Ptolemaios, "Shall we take their ship apart, too, the way this fellow told us we could?"

Ptolemaios thought that over, but not for long. Then he tossed his head. "No, no point to that. Too many places to hide such small things; you'd only find 'em by luck." He glowered at the two Rhodians. "I'm not convinced you're telling me the truth, not by a long shot. But I can't prove you're not, so I'm going to let you go: you did serve me well before."

"Thank you, sir," Sostratos said before Menedemos could come out with anything that might land them in more trouble.

"I suppose you're welcome," the ruler of Egypt replied. "I suppose." He jerked a thumb toward the front door. "Meanwhile, why don't you go somewhere else and not give me any reason to call you here again?"

"Yes, sir," Sostratos said. "Thank you again, sir." He hurried out of the andron, Menedemos in his wake. Only after they were out in the street did he pause to let out a sigh of relief.

"Many goodbyes to that Dionysios," Menedemos said.

"Yes, he tried to cover us in dung, didn't he?" Sostratos agreed. "I say we head for home first thing tomorrow morning."

"Oh?" Menedemos asked. "Why's that?"

"Two reasons." Sostratos looked around to make sure nobody was paying any special attention to them, then stuck his thumb in the air. "For one thing, Ptolemaios wouldn't find any precious stones hidden on the *Aphrodite*, but he would find the account books that talk about them. And, for another"—he stuck up his forefinger, too—"he might decide to hold us here till he sends to Keos or even to Aigina. Do you want to take the chance?"

"Now that you mention it, no," his cousin said.

"Good. Neither do I."

Menedemos said, "We bought the emeralds in Rhodes, not in any of the lands Ptolemaios rules. We didn't break any of his laws to get them. I don't see how he really could condemn us for that."

"He's lord of Egypt, the richest man in the world, one of the four or five strongest men in the world," Sostratos pointed out. "He doesn't need a reason. He can do as he pleases. That's what being one of the four or five strongest men in the world means. If he catches us lying . . ." He shivered. "And we brought those stones through Kos before, and what do you want to bet he's made laws against that?"

His cousin pulled a sour face. "You're probably right. No, you're certainly right. Very well, best one—you've convinced me. We go out tomorrow morning."

"Good," Sostratos said.

Menedemos chuckled. "Besides, I'd want to spirit you away before Ptolemaios makes you shorter by a head for calling him a fool in front of his men. Did you see how far his eyes bugged out?"

"I'm a free Hellene, by the gods," Sostratos said. "If he's not used to hearing people speak their minds, too bad for him."

"He being who he is, though, it's liable to be bad for anyone who does speak his mind," Menedemos said, and Sostratos could hardly argue.

He and Menedemos had almost reached the *Aphrodite* when someone called to them from behind. Alarm ran through Sostratos: had Ptolemaios decided to be difficult after all? But when he looked back over his shoulder, he recognized the fellow waving to them from up the street. "Hail, Pixodaros," he said. "What can we do for you today?"

"Hail, both of you," the silk dealer answered. "When I heard you'd come back to Kos, I thought it was a gift from the gods. Have you any more crimson dye?"

"Certainly," Sostratos answered. "How much do you need?"

"How much do you have?" Pixodaros asked.

"Let me think." Sostratos plucked at his beard. "I believe we have . . . fifty-three jars. That's based on what we sold. It might be fewer, though. We had to fight off pirates, and they might have stolen a few when they went back to their own ship."

"By Zeus Labraundeus, I'm glad to see you well and safe,"

Pixodaros said. "May they all go up on crosses!"

"May they indeed." Normally, Sostratos was among the most mild-mannered of men. Now he sounded thoroughly grim. Whenever he thought of a pirate picking up the leather sack that held the gryphon's skull and leaping back into the hemiolia from the *Aphrodite*, his blood boiled.

"How do you keep such good track of what's sold and what isn't?" Menedemos asked him.

He shrugged. "I write up the accounts, and I remember them." It didn't seem remarkable to him. He asked a question of his own: "How do you carry so much of the *Iliad* and *Odyssey* around in your head?"

"That's different. For one thing, the words don't change. For another, they're worth remembering." Menedemos turned back to Pixodaros. "Please excuse us, best one. We do go back and forth at each other, I know."

The Karian smiled. "Kinsmen will do that."

"How much dye do you need?" Sostratos asked him.

"As much as you have. If you had more, I would buy it. I have a lot of silk to dye, and my, ah, client wants the cloth as soon as he can get it."

"You can dye a lot of silk with fifty or so jars of crimson," Sostratos said. Pixodaros nodded, then remembered himself and dipped his head. Sostratos plucked at his beard again. He lowered his voice to ask, "Does Antigonos want to give his officers silk tunics, or is this for the officers' women?"

Both Menedemos and Pixodaros started. "Not Antigonos—Demetrios, his son. But how can you know that?" the silk merchant demanded. "Are you a wizard?" The fingers of his left hand twisted in an apotropaic gesture Sostratos had seen other Karians use.

He tossed his head. "Not at all. Who but a Macedonian marshal could afford so much crimson-dyed silk? If it were Ptolemaios, you would have come out and said so. It might have been Lysimakhos or Kassandros, but they're on good terms with Ptolemaios now, and old One-Eye isn't. He's the one you have the best reason to be cagey about."

"Ah. I see," Pixodaros said. "True—it is all simple enough, once you explain it."

Anything is simple, once someone else explains it, Sostratos thought sourly. But before he could say that out loud—and he might have—Menedemos contrived, almost by accident, to tread on his toe. After apologizing, his cousin asked Pixodaros, "And what will you give us for the dye?"

The merchant looked pained. "You have me where you want me, I know. I only ask you to remember this: if you hurt me badly now, we have years of dealing ahead where I can take my revenge." He gave Sostratos half a bow. "I too have a long memory."

"No doubt," Sostratos said politely. "Well, what does fifteen drakhmai the jar sound like to you?"

"What does it sound like?" Pixodaros exclaimed. "Piracy. Robbery. Extortion. In your dreams, you sell it for half that much. Because you have me, because I need it, I will give you half that much."

"You gave more than half that much in silk when we stopped here in the springtime," Sostratos said.

"Silk is one thing. Silver is another," Pixodaros replied. He haggled as fiercely as he could, but found himself at a disadvantage: the Rhodians knew how much he needed the dye. That meant they could bargain fiercely, while he couldn't. At the end, he threw his hands in the air. "All right, twelve drakhmai the jar it is. Bandits, both of you. How much silver is that altogether?"

"Let's see exactly how many jars we have." Sostratos called orders to the sailors. They brought forty-nine jars of crimson dye up onto the quay. He muttered to himself. "That would be . . . 588 drakhmai all told—*not* Ptolemaios' light drakhmai," he added.

"I understand. I'll be back." Pixodaros hurried off into Kos.

Menedemos snapped his fingers. "I promised to give a sheep at the Asklepeion here if the men healed well after the fight with the pirates. Now I won't be able to."

Sostratos thought, then tossed his head. "No, you promised to give a sheep here if you could, or on Rhodes if you couldn't. As long as you offer the animal to the god, you're not forsworn."

"Are you sure?" his cousin asked.

"Positive."

"All right. Good. That's a relief," Menedemos said. "We do want to leave as soon as we can. And then"—he sighed—"it's back to Rhodes." Sostratos still had no idea what troubled him there. He wondered if he would ever learn.

WALKING INTO THE ANDRON OF THE family house, Menedemos felt himself shrinking from a man to a youth, perhaps to a little boy. When he sailed the Aegean, he dealt with prominent merchants—some of them older and richer than his father—as equal to equal. They saw him as he was today. In Philodemos' eyes, he fell back into the past. He knew he always would, as long as his father lived.

"Not as good a run as you had last year," Philodemos said.

"We made a solid profit, sir," Menedemos said. "And we took fewer risks than we did last year."

When he'd come home the previous fall, Philodemos had done nothing but complain about the chances he'd taken in Great Hellas. Now his father said, "Well, those risks paid off. Here, you might as well have stayed in Rhodes and done your trading at the harbor, the way Himilkon the Phoenician does."

That wasn't fair. Even so, Menedemos didn't argue. In his father's eyes, he was almost certain to be wrong. Instead, he changed the subject: "I'll want to talk with Himilkon before we go out again next spring. Sostratos thought we might sail east to Phoenicia and get rid of one set of middlemen on goods from that part of the world."

"Your cousin has good sense," Philodemos said. That was true. Had he left it there, Menedemos wouldn't have minded. But he added, "Why don't you ever have good ideas like that?"

Menedemos could have claimed going east as his own notion; it had been as much his as Sostratos'. Had he done so, though, he knew his father would have found some reason not to like it. *I can't win*, he thought. But arguing with his father wouldn't get him anything, either. He gave up, saying, "It's good to see you well."

"I could be better," Philodemos said. "My joints pain me, as those of a man with my years will. Old age is a bitter business, no doubt about it." After a sip of wine, though, he admitted, "It could be worse, too, I will say. My teeth are still mostly sound, and I thank the gods for that. I wouldn't want to have to live out my days on mush."

"I don't blame you," Menedemos said.

His father said, "You did well with those emeralds. How much were you getting for those last few?" When Menedemos told him, he whistled. "That's good. That's very good."

"Thank you." *Are you well?* Menedemos wondered. *Are you sure you won't hurt yourself, saying I did something right?*

"I feel I ought to pay my fair share of what you made for them, not what they cost you," Philodemos said.

Oh, so that's it, Menedemos thought. *Say what you will about him—and I can say plenty—my father's as stubbornly honest as Sostratos.* Aloud, he said, "You can do that if you feel you must, sir, but if anyone's entitled to buy at wholesale, not retail, it's the founder of the firm."

That won him a smile—no mean feat, seeing how spikily he and his father got along. Philodemos said, "You may be right. I'll talk with my brother and see what he thinks."

"All right," Menedemos said. That was where things would matter, sure enough. As far as this line of the family was concerned, it was just a matter of two accounts for the same silver. But, to Uncle Lysistratos, it would be a question of whether the money belonged in the firm's account or out of it. Menedemos went on, "I still think he'd do the same thing."

"He might well," his father replied. "But if he did, he would ask me, and so I'll ask him."

"How does your wife like the stone?" The question put Menedemos on dangerous ground: not so dangerous as it might be, for his father had no inkling of what he felt for Baukis, but dangerous even so. He knew as much, and asked anyhow.

Philodemos smiled again, this time not at Menedemos but at the world at large. His lean, rather pinched features softened. For a moment, he seemed a different man, and one much easier to like. He said, "Timakrates the jeweler mounted it in a splendid ring, and she was glad to get it."

How glad was she? How did she show it? Menedemos could picture the answers to those questions readily enough. He shook his head, trying to get the pictures out of his mind. To keep his father from thinking he was unhappy—and to keep him from jumping to more unfortunate, and more accurate, conclusions—he said, "I hope she gives you a son."

"Seeing as another son would make your portion less, that's a generous thing for you to say." Philodemos didn't sound suspicious, but did sound surprised. "Maybe you're growing up after all."

"Maybe I am." Menedemos was convinced he'd grown up some years before. He was also convinced his father would never believe it. He asked, "How are things between her and Sikon?" That was a safer question.

His father snorted. "You know cooks. He's convinced he rules the roost. If you try to tell him anything else, he starts screaming that nobody will be able to eat his food any more, and that we'll never manage another proper dinner party again. He spends money as though he stamped it himself."

"He doesn't steal much," Menedemos said. "Everything he makes is good. If we can afford good opson, why shouldn't we enjoy it?"

On the instant, Philodemos' features returned to the hard cast Menedemos knew so well. "Yes, *if*. If, on the other hand, mullet and squid and dogfish bankrupt us, then we should keep a closer eye on what he spends. *You* may not care about such things—"

"Who says I don't?" Menedemos broke in.

His father ignored him. "—but Baukis believes in watching where the drakhmai go. We still eat well, but we'll have some silver left for you to squander when you do come into your inheritance."

"That's not fair. I'm making us money," Menedemos said.

"Less than last year," Philodemos said again.

Menedemos made as if to tear his hair. "Last year you called me an idiot for taking some of the chances I took. I took fewer chances this year, and we made less money. Now you complain about that! How can I please you?" *It's simple*, he thought. *I can't.*

"Lower your voice. Do you want the slaves hearing all our business?" Philodemos said.

"No." All Menedemos wanted was to get away. That was generally true whenever he talked with his father. It had been true before Philodemos wed Baukis, and was doubly true these days. Now he wanted—he needed—to escape Rhodes altogether, not just the andron or the house. And he would be stuck here till spring. With a growl that might have come from the throat of a cornered wolf, he got to his feet. "If you'll excuse me, Father . . ."

He went into the kitchen, where Sikon was expertly shucking boiled prawns out of their shells. The cook was chewing as he worked, which meant he'd sampled a few, or maybe more than a few. Philodemos fed his slaves well; he wouldn't mind that. And who'd ever heard of a scrawny cook, or at least of a scrawny cook worth having?

But when the door opened, Sikon looked up in alarm. When he saw Menedemos coming in, he relaxed. "Gods be praised, it's just you, sir. I was afraid it might be the lady." He rolled his eyes and let his head twist bonelessly in a gesture he must have filched from the comic stage.

"She'll learn," Menedemos said uncomfortably. He didn't like to hear anyone criticize Baukis. That had little to do with her position as manager of the household, much more with the position he would have liked her to . . . *Stop that!* he shouted at himself, as he did several times a day.

Sikon, of course, had no idea what he was thinking. Had the cook known, he wouldn't have dared roll his eyes again and say, "Maybe she will, but when? And will she drive me daft before she does? She fusses over every obolos I spend."

"You've got to make her happy," Menedemos said, and sternly told himself not to pursue that line of thought, either.

"Make her happy?" Sikon howled, peeling another prawn. "How am I supposed to manage that, short of serving nothing but barley porridge for the next six months? I think her mother must have been frightened by a tunny while she was in the womb."

Menedemos pointed to the prawn shells and the tiny bits of flesh clinging to them. "Instead of throwing those in the street in front of the house, why don't you give them to her to bury in the garden? They'll make her flowers and herbs grow better, and she's bound to like that."

"Is she? If you want to know what I think, I think she's more likely to grill me about how much the polluted prawns cost," the cook said. As Menedemos did when his temper began to rise, he drummed his fingers on the outside of his thigh. Sikon recognized the danger sign. "All right, all right. I'll give them to her, and I hope it does some good, that's all I've got to say."

It wasn't all he had to say, nor anywhere close to it. And he said still more when Menedemos reached out and hooked a fat prawn from the bowl into which he'd been tossing them. Mouth full, Menedemos retreated.

A moment later, he wished he hadn't: Baukis had come down from the women's quarters and was picking up a hydria so she could water the garden. "Hail," she called to him.

"Hail," he answered. His gaze flicked to the andron. Sure enough, his father still sat inside. He would have to be all the more careful about what he said, then.

But before he had a chance to say anything, Sikon stormed out of the kitchen, both hands full of prawn shells. He all but threw them at Baukis' feet. "Here you are, my lady," he said. "They'll make good manure for the plants, I hope."

She looked startled; plainly, Sikon had never done anything like that before. "Thank you," she said. "You're right. They will." But then she asked, "How much did you pay for the prawns?"

The cook glared at Menedemos. *I told you so*, his eyes said. Then, reluctantly, he turned back to Baukis. "I got a good price for them."

"I'm sure they'll be very tasty," Menedemos said. "In fact, I know they'll be very tasty, because I tasted one." Since he'd suggested this course to Sikon, he had to back him now.

Baukis said, "Tasty is one thing. Expensive is something else. What *exactly* did you pay for the prawns, Sikon?" Having no choice, the cook told her. She fixed him with a stony glance. "What would you call a bad price, if that's a good one?"

Defiantly, Sikon answered, "I've paid plenty more in years gone by. And"—he folded his arms across his chest—"nobody complained, either."

The Macedonians and Persians lined up against each other at Gaugamela could not have glowered with greater ferocity. Menedemos, in the middle, feared he might be torn limb from limb. "Peace, both of you," he said. "That isn't a dreadful price." He found himself wishing his father would come out of the andron and help him. If that wasn't a measure of his alarm and desperation, he couldn't imagine what would be.

Philodemos stayed where he was. He had too much sense, or too little courage, to jump into the middle of this battle. Under Menedemos' protection, Sikon preened and swaggered. Baukis looked as if he'd stabbed her in the back. "If you care more about your belly than about what this house really needs . . ." She didn't finish the sentence, but turned on her heel and stalked toward the stairs leading up to the women's quarters.

Menedemos watched—he couldn't help watching—the furious roll of her hips. Beside him, Sikon cackled with glee. "Thank you kindly, sir," the cook said. "I guess you told her."

"I guess I did," Menedemos said dully. He scowled at Sikon. Could those prawns possibly be good enough to make up for getting Baukis angry at him? He doubted ambrosia from Olympos would be good enough for that.

"—AND I LOOKED under the rower's bench," Sostratos said, "and the sack with the gryphon's skull in it was gone. One of those polluted pirates had stolen it. What I'd do to that son of a whore if I could . . ."

"I'm sorry," Erinna said, and then, with something like awe, "I've never seen you so angry before."

Sostratos looked down at his hands. Of themselves, they'd folded into fists. When he willed them open, the marks of his nails were printed on his palms. More than a little sheepishly, he smiled at his younger sister. "If you think I'm angry now, you should have seen me when it happened. So much knowledge that might have been so important, gone forever . . . I was beside myself."

A fly landed on Erinna's arm. She brushed at it, and it darted away. Gyges, the majordomo here, had heard from Philodemos' cook next door that Baukis was using fish offal to fertilize her garden. Erinna had started doing the same thing. Maybe the plants appreciated it. Sostratos was certain the flies did. The one that had been on Erinna's arm landed on his leg. He smashed it. It fell in the dirt. A tiny gecko darted out from between two stones, seized it, and disappeared again. Sostratos wiped his hand on his chiton.

His sister sighed. "Being a man, being able to do all those things, go all those places, must be wonderful."

"Not always," Sostratos said dryly. "I could have done without pirates trying to kill me or sell me into slavery."

Erinna flushed. "Well, yes. But most of the time . . . You know what I mean. You usually know what I mean."

Sostratos coughed. "Thank you." That was a rare compliment. He couldn't imagine anyone else saying such a thing to him. Menedemos? No, not likely. And he couldn't imagine saying such a thing to anybody else himself, not even to Erinna.

She asked him a question that surprised him: "You know Damonax son of Polydoros, don't you?"

"Of course I do," Sostratos answered. "I took the gryphon's skull to show him this past spring, remember? He tried to buy it from me. Now I wish I'd let him do it." He frowned. "Why do you want to know?"

"You were at the gymnasion yesterday when he stopped by," Erinna said. "He might be interested enough in marrying into the family not to care so much about how old I am."

"You're not old," Sostratos said loyally. "You're only nineteen."

"That's old for a girl to be marrying," Erinna said.

He couldn't very well argue with her, because she was right.

She'd been only fourteen when she wed for the first time. But he said, "Isn't Damonax already married?"

"He was." Erinna's face clouded. "His wife died in childbirth not long after you set out for Kos. He's looking to marry again. Of course, from what Father said, he wants a bigger dowry because I'm older."

"He would," Sostratos said. But that wasn't anything out of the ordinary.

"What's he like?" Erinna asked. "I got a glimpse of him as he was leaving, and he's more than good-looking enough, but that only goes so far. What's he *like*?"

Sostratos had never thought he might be describing Damonax as a possible husband. *Would I want him for a brother-in-law?* he wondered. He wasn't sure. He said, "He's bright enough—he studied in Athens before I did, you know. I don't think he's as bright as he thinks he is, but how many people are? He's not stingy, not from anything I've ever seen. I've never heard anything bad about him." He hadn't heard that much praise for Damonax, either. He went on, "When he wants something, he *really* wants it—I have noticed that about him. But that's not necessarily good or bad."

"Would you want him in the family?" Erinna asked.

That was the very question Sostratos was asking himself. Since he had no good answer for it, he gave back a question of his own: "What does Father think?"

"He didn't send Damonax away with a flea in his ear," his sister said. "He's—thinking things over, I guess you'd say."

"Good. These dickers can take a long time," Sostratos said. "The one for your first marriage did. I probably remember that better than you do—you were still a girl then."

"I didn't have much to do with it," Erinna agreed. "But it's different now. I'm not a girl any more. And I don't want this dicker to take a long time, because I'm not getting any younger."

"Time is a terrible enemy. Sooner or later, it always wins."

Erinna sprang to her feet and hurried upstairs to the women's quarters. Sostratos stared after her. *Oh, dear*, he thought. *That wasn't what she hoped I'd say at all.* Then he realized something else: *no matter what Father thinks*, she *wants to marry Damonax. He must feel like a second chance for her.*

Do *I want Damonax in the family? If I don't, have I got any good reason for not wanting him? And why does he want to join us? We're tradesfolk, and he's got land. Is he in debt?*

Those were all good questions. He had answers for none of them. He couldn't ask his father; Lysistratos was down at the harbor. From what Erinna said, his father was at least thinking about the match. That was interesting. Erinna, no doubt, found it much more than interesting.

A bumblebee buzzed through the garden. Sostratos went into the andron. He'd been stung before, and didn't care to get stung again. After a while, the bee had drunk its fill and went away. Sostratos returned to the courtyard.

Threissa, the family's redheaded Thracian slave girl, came out with her arms full of freshly washed tunics and mantles. She started spreading them in the sun to dry. "Hail," Sostratos said.

"Hail, young master," she answered in her oddly accented Greek. Carrying a load of wet clothes had got the front of her own tunic wet, too, so that it clung to her breasts. Sostratos eyed her. She noticed him doing it, and spoke quickly: "You excuse me, please, young master? I terrible busy."

He took her up to his bedroom every so often. She was only a slave girl; how could she say no? Even asking him to wait would have landed her in trouble in some households. But taking her for his own pleasure while she was in the middle of work would have landed *him* in trouble with his mother and sister. And, since she was more resigned to their occasional couplings than eager for them, he was less eager for them himself than he might have been. And so he said, "All right, Threissa," though he didn't leave off eyeing the way the wet wool displayed her nipples.

"I thank you, young master," she said. "You a kind man." Despite such praise, she stood with her back to him as much as she could.

Terrible to be a slave, Sostratos thought. *Terrible to be a woman and not a man. And if you're unlucky enough to be both, what can you do? Turn your back and hope, no more. Gods be praised I'm a free man.*

He might have gone upstairs with her when she finished spreading out the clothes, but his father got back while she was busy there. Lysistratos looked pleased with himself, saying, "I may have a deal for some olive oil of the very first pressing. That won't be long now; the fruit's getting on toward being ripe."

"That's good, Father," Sostratos said, "but what's this I hear about Damonax son of Polydoros sniffing around after Erinna?"

"Well, I don't quite know what it is," Lysistratos answered. "It's all very tentative right now. But she should be married again if we can arrange it—you know that. And I wouldn't mind a connection to Damonax's family—I wouldn't mind that at all."

"I understand—they've owned land for generations," Sostratos said. "Why do they want anything to do with us, though? Have they fallen on hard times?"

"That occurred to me, too, but not that I know of," his father said. "I *am* sniffing around—I'm sniffing around like a scavenger dog sniffing for garbage, as a matter of fact. Haven't found anything out of the ordinary yet."

"There must be something. Otherwise, he wouldn't be willing to join with mere tradesmen." Sostratos smiled a sour smile. People whose wealth lay in land always looked down their noses at those who made money by their wits. Land was safe, stable, secure—*boring, too,* Sostratos thought.

"Actually, son, you had something to do with it," Lysistratos said.

"Me?" Sostratos' voice was a startled squeak. "What? How?"

"Seems you impressed Damonax no end when you wouldn't sell him the gryphon's skull this spring," Lysistratos told him.

"I wish I had. Then it would still be here."

"That's as may be," his father said. "But Damonax thought all merchants were whores, and they'd do anything for money. He knew you'd gone to Athens, to the Lykeion, but when you put knowledge ahead of silver, that opened his eyes. 'Not many gentlemen would have done the same,' was how he put it."

"Did he?" Sostratos said, and Lysistratos dipped his head. "That's . . . surprising," Sostratos went on in musing tones. "What I was afraid of at the time was that he would call for half a dozen burly slaves and keep the gryphon's skull. I thought he was admiring that, not my integrity. You never can tell."

"No, you never can," Lysistratos agreed. "Would you want him in the family?"

"I've been thinking about that. Before what you said just now, I would have told you no," Sostratos answered. "Now . . ." He shrugged and let out a rueful chuckle. "Now I'm so flattered, my advice probably isn't worth a thing."

"Oh, I doubt that. If there's one thing I can rely on, son, it's that you keep your wits about you."

"Thank you," Sostratos said, though he wasn't quite sure his father had paid him a compliment. He might almost have said, *Coldblooded, aren't you?* Sostratos chuckled again. Compared to, say, his cousin, he *was* coldblooded, and he knew it. After some thought, he went on, "Do I want Damonax in the family? Erinna wants the match; I know that. It would be a step up for us, if he's not after our money to repair his fortunes. Actually, it would be a step up for us even if he is, but I don't think I care to take *that* kind of step."

"I told you you keep your wits about you," his father said. "I don't care to, either."

"I didn't think you did, sir." Sostratos plucked at his beard. "Damonax isn't bad-looking, he isn't stupid, and he isn't a churl. If he's not hiding something from us, Erinna could do worse."

"Fair enough," Lysistratos said. "I was thinking along the same lines. I'll keep talking with him, then. We have some haggling to do. He wants a big dowry—you already knew that, didn't you?"

Sostratos dipped his head. "He has some reason to ask it, because Erinna's a widow, not a maiden. But if he won't come down, if he cares more about the dowry than he does about her, that's a sign his own affairs aren't prospering."

"Good point—very good," Lysistratos said. "We'll take a few steps forward and we'll see, that's all."

MENEDEMOS SPENT AS much time as he could away from the house. That kept him from quarreling with his father, and it kept him from having much to do with his father's wife. He exercised in the gymnasion. He strolled through the agora, looking at what was for sale there and talking with other men who came there to look and to talk. All sorts of things came to the marketplace at Rhodes. He kept hoping he would see another gryphon's skull. If he did, he intended to buy it for his cousin. He had no luck there, though.

And, when he wasn't at the gymnasion or the agora, he went down to the harbor. Not many ships came in much more than a month after the autumnal equinox, but the harbor stayed busy even so, with new vessels a-building and old ones—the *Aphrodite* among them—hauled up on the beach for repairs and refitting. The talk was good there, too, though different from that in the market square: centered on the sea, much less concerned over either the latest juicy gossip or the wider world.

"You're lucky you're here, and not in shackles in a slave market in Carthage or Phoenicia or Crete," a carpenter said, driving home a large-headed copper tack that helped secure lead sheathing to a round ship's side.

"Believe me, Khremes, I know it," Menedemos answered. "A pestilence take all pirates." Everyone working on the merchantman dipped his head. In a savage mood, Menedemos went on, "And if the pestilence doesn't take 'em, the cross will do."

"I'd like to see that myself," Khremes said. "But those whoresons are hard to catch. Remind me—I heard your story, but this bit didn't stick—was it a pentekonter that came after you, or one of those gods-detested hemioliai?"

"A hemiolia," Menedemos said. "To the crows with the whoreson who first thought up the breed. He must have been a pirate himself. I hope he ended up on a cross and died slow. They're only good for one thing—"

"Might as well be women," Khremes broke in, and all the men in earshot laughed.

That hit closer to the center of the target than Menedemos would have liked. To keep anyone else from guessing, he took the gibe a step further with a bit of doggerel:

"Every woman's gall,
But she has two moments:
In bed, and dead."

"*Euge!*" Khremes exclaimed, and put down his hammer to clap his hands. The other carpenters and the harborside loungers bending an ear dipped their heads.

"Thanks," Menedemos said, thinking, *I'll have to remember that one and spring it on Sostratos when he's got a mouthful of wine—see if I can make him choke*. He made himself go back to hemioliai: "Cursed ships are only good for darting out to grab a merchantman—and for showing a pair of heels to anything honest that chases 'em."

"Sometimes a trireme'll catch 'em," Khremes said, picking up the hammer once more and choosing another short copper tack.

"Sometimes," Menedemos said morosely. "Not often enough, and we all know it."

The Rhodians dipped their heads again. A lot of them had pulled an oar in one of the polis' triremes, or in one of the bigger, heavier warships that were fine for battling their own kind but too slow and beamy to go pirate-hunting despite their swarms of rowers.

Khremes started hammering away. A man who looked as if he had a hangover winced and drew back from the round ship. As the carpenter drove the tack home, he said, "Don't know what to do about it. Triremes are the fastest warships afloat, and they have been for—oh, I don't know, a mighty long time, anyways. Forever, you might almost say."

Sostratos would know how long—probably to the hour, Menedemos thought. He didn't himself, not exactly, but he had some notion of how things worked. He said, "Biremes are faster than pentekonters because they can pack just as many rowers into a shorter, lighter hull. Hemioliai are especially little and light—the back half of that upper bank of oars only gets used part-time."

"Triremes are a lot bigger'n two-bankers," one of the loungers said.

Menedemos dipped his head. "Truth. But they pack in a *lot* more rowers, too, so they go just about as fast, and the extra weight makes 'em hit a lot harder when they ram. What we could really use is a trireme built fast and light like a hemiolia, maybe with the same way to stow mast and yard where the back half of the thranite bank of oarsmen work."

He'd been talking to hear himself talk. He hadn't expected anything particularly interesting or clever to come out. But Khremes slowly put down the hammer and gave him a long, thoughtful look. "By the gods, best one, I think you may have thrown a triple six there," he said.

Menedemos listened in his own mind to what he'd just said. He let out a soft whistle. "If we wanted to, we really could build ships like that, couldn't we?" he said.

"We could. No doubt about it—we could. And I think maybe we should," Khremes said. "They'd be quick as boiled asparagus, they would. And they'd have enough size and enough crew to step on a hemiolia like it was a bug."

"One of them would *be* a hemiolia, near enough," Menedemos said. "An oversized hemiolia, a hemiolia made from a trireme's hull. You could call it a . . ." He groped for a word. He didn't think the one he came up with really existed in the Greek language, but it suited the idea, so he used it anyway: "A trihemiolia, you might say."

Whether that was a word or not, it got across what he wanted, for Khremes dipped his head. Excitement in his voice, the carpenter said, "When I close my eyes, I can see her on the water. She'd be wicked fast—fast as a dolphin, fast as a falcon. A trihemiolia." It came off his tongue more readily than it had from Menedemos'. "You ought to talk to the admirals, sir, Furies take me if I'm lying. A flotilla of ships like that could make a big pack o' pirates sorry they took up their trade."

"Do you think so?" Menedemos asked. But he could see a

trihemiolia in his mind's eye, too, see it gliding over the Aegean, swift and deadly as a barracuda.

Khremes pointed north and west, toward the military harbor. "If you don't find one of the admirals at the ship sheds, I'd be mighty surprised. And, by the gods, I think this is something they need to hear."

"Come with me, will you?" Menedemos said, suddenly and uncharacteristically modest. "After all, you're one of the men who'd have to build a trihemiolia, if there were to be such a thing."

The carpenter stuck the hammer on his belt, carrying it where a soldier would have worn a sword. "Let's go."

Ship sheds lined the military harbor: big, wide ones that held the fives Rhodes used to defend herself against other naval craft; smaller ones for the triremes that hunted pirates. When not on patrol or on campaign, war galleys were hauled up out of the water so their hulls stayed dry and light and swift.

A few guards tramped back and forth by the ship sheds. When Menedemos and Khremes came up to one of them and asked their question, the fellow dipped his head, which made the crimson-dyed horsehair plume on his helmet nod and sway. He pointed with his spear. "Yes, as a matter of fact, Admiral Eudemos just went into that shed there. The *Freedom*'s been having trouble with her sternpost, and he wants to make sure they got it fixed."

When Menedemos walked into the shed that housed the five, his eyes needed a few heartbeats to adjust to the gloom. He heard Eudemos before spotting him up on the deck of the war galley: "You really think she's sound this time?" he was asking a carpenter.

"Yes, sir, I do," the man answered.

"All right. She'd better be," Eudemos said. "Nothing much wrong with having trouble—that's going to happen. But taking three tries to fix it? That's a shame and a disgrace." He noticed Menedemos and Khremes at the mouth of the shed and raised his voice to call out to them: "Hail, the two of you. What do you need?"

For a moment, Menedemos didn't know what to say. *Come*

on, fool, he told himself. *You've got something to sell, same as you would in the agora.* That steadied him. "Sir, I've had an idea that might interest you," he said.

"It's a good one, Admiral," Khremes added.

"That you, Khremes?" Eudemos said. He might not have recognized Menedemos' voice, but he knew the carpenter's at once. "You've got pretty good sense. If you say it's worth listening to, I'll hear it."

He came down the *Freedom*'s steeply sloping gangplank and hurried toward Menedemos and Khremes. Menedemos got the notion he did everything in a hurry. He was somewhere in his forties, with a graying beard, a jutting nose, and hard, watchful eyes. "Ah, Philodemos' son," he said to himself, placing Menedemos. "All right—you know a little something about ships, anyway. Say on."

Menedemos did, finishing, "Too many pirates get away. If we had some ships like these, maybe some of them wouldn't. That's what I'm hoping for." He waited to see how Eudemos would take the idea.

The admiral had heard him out without giving any sign of what was in his mind. Once Menedemos finished, Eudemos said not a word to him, instead turning to Khremes and asking, "Can we build such ships?"

"Yes, sir," the carpenter answered. "Yes, sir, without a doubt we can. They might even be cheaper than ordinary triremes. You'd want 'em light—you wouldn't close in the whole deck or build on an oarbox of solid planks, so you'd save timber."

That got Eudemos' attention. "I—see," he said, and turned back to Menedemos. "You've given me something new to think about, and that doesn't happen every day. A whole new class of warship . . . *Euge!*"

"I was just passing the time of day with Khremes when I said something that struck both of us," Menedemos said. "That was when we came looking for you."

Eudemos briskly dipped his head. "Having a good idea is one thing. *Knowing* you've had a good idea is something else again. People have lots of good ideas when they're just passing the time of day. Usually, they keep right on talking and forget all about them. You didn't. A trihemiolia, eh?" He tried the unfamiliar word, then dipped his head again. "A lot of pirates may be sorry you didn't, too."

"By the gods, I hope so," Menedemos growled.

"Yes, you're another one who got attacked, aren't you?" the admiral said.

"I certainly am, sir."

"Well, as I say, the pirates who struck you and a lot of their mates may be sorry they did it. That may prove one of the most important bits of piracy since Paris stole Helen, but not the way the pirates had in mind." Eudemos sounded as if he thought it was.

Sostratos thought it was one of the most important bits of piracy of all time, too, on account of that polluted gryphon's skull, Menedemos thought. *But then, the admiral has to think straighter than my cousin.*

"Do you read and write?" Eudemos asked Khremes.

"Some, sir. Nothing fancy," the carpenter answered.

"This doesn't need to be fancy," Eudemos said. "Write me up a list of what all would go into making a trihemiolia, as best you can figure. Base it on what goes into a trireme, of course."

"I'll do it," Khremes said.

"Good." Eudemos clasped Menedemos' hand. "And good for you, too. You've earned the thanks of your polis."

Menedemos bowed low. Those were words that struck home. "What Hellene could hope for more, most noble one?"

"A TRIHEMIOLIA, EH?" Sostratos said as he and Menedemos made their way through the streets by the great harbor toward Himilkon the Phoenician's workhouse.

"That's right," his cousin answered. "Like I was saying, the gods might have put the word on my tongue day before yesterday."

"If the gods gave you the word, why didn't they give you one that was easier to pronounce?" Sostratos asked. "A 'three-one-and-a-halfer'? People will be trying to figure out what that is for years."

"Admiral Eudemos didn't have any trouble," Menedemos said.

"He's an admiral," Sostratos retorted. "He worries about the thing itself, not about the word."

"Do you know what you remind me of?" Menedemos said. "You remind me of Aiskhylos down in Hades' house in Aristophanes' *Frogs*, where he's criticizing Euripides' prologues. But I don't think the trihemiolia is going to 'lose its little bottle of oil,' the way the prologues kept doing."

"Well, all right," Sostratos said. "I'd be the first to admit Eudemos knows more about such things than I do."

"Generous of you," Menedemos remarked.

Sostratos wagged a finger at him. "You shouldn't be sarcastic, my dear. You don't do it well, and that's something I do know something about." Menedemos made a face at him. Sostratos laughed.

Hyssaldomos, Himilkon's Karian slave, was puttering around by the ramshackle warehouse, looking busy while actually doing nothing in particular. Sostratos snorted. Every slave in the world learned that art. Seeing the two Rhodians approach gave Hyssaldomos a legitimate excuse for doing something that didn't involve much real work: he waved to them and called, "Hail, both of you! You looking for my boss?"

"That's right," Sostratos answered. "Is he there?"

"You bet he is," the slave said. "I'll go fetch him. I know he'll be glad to see you." He ducked inside.

"Of course he will," Sostratos muttered. "After we bought the peafowl from him, he's got to be sure he can sell us anything."

"We made money from them," Menedemos said.

"By the time we got rid of them, I'd sooner have served them up roasted at a symposion," Sostratos said. Familiarity had bred contempt; he was, and would remain, a hater of peafowl.

Before Menedemos could answer, Himilkon emerged from the warehouse, Hyssaldomos behind him. The Phoenician wore an ankle-length wool robe not badly suited to the raw autumn day. Gold hoops glittered in his ears; a black, bushy beard tumbled halfway down his chest. He bowed himself almost double. "Hail, my masters," he said in gutturally accented but fluent Greek. "How may I serve you today?"

Sostratos found the Phoenician's oily politeness excessive. As far as he was concerned, no free man should call another one *master*. "Hail," he answered, doing his best to hide his distaste. "We'd like to talk with you about your homeland, if you don't mind."

Himilkon's bushy eyebrows leaped upward. "About Byblos?" he said. "Of course, my friend. To you I shall gladly reveal the secrets of my heart." He bowed again. Sostratos didn't believe him for a moment. On the other hand, he didn't think Himilkon had expected to be believed.

"Not just about Byblos," Menedemos said. "About Phoenicia in general, and the countries thereabouts, and the kinds of goods we might expect to find in them."

"Ah." Intelligence glittered in Himilkon's black, black eyes. "You think to sail east next spring?"

"We've talked about it," Sostratos said. "If we do, we'd like to learn as much as we can beforehand."

"Wise. Very wise." Himilkon gave him yet another bow. "Most Hellenes, if you will forgive my saying so, charge ahead first and think of questions afterwards—if they ever do. I might have known *you* would be different." One more bow.

"Er—thank you." Sostratos wondered if that was a real compliment aimed at him or just more Phoenician flattery. He couldn't tell.

Himilkon rounded on his slave. "Don't stand there with your ears flapping in the breeze, you lazy, worthless, good-for-nothing rogue. Go inside and fetch us some wine and a bite to eat, and don't take all day doing it, either."

"Right, boss." If his master's outburst frightened Hyssaldomos, the Karian hid it very well. He sauntered into the warehouse.

"I ought to give him a good whipping—find out if he's really alive," Himilkon grumbled. "What do you have in mind buying, my masters, and what will you take east to sell?"

"Well, obviously, as long as we're in the country, we'll look to buy some of the crimson dye they make in the Phoenician towns," Menedemos said.

Himilkon nodded. He'd lived in Rhodes a long time, but still didn't usually show agreement as a Hellene would. "Yes, of course," he said. "You already know something of the qualities to look for there, for it comes west often enough. What else?"

"Balsam," Sostratos answered. "We bought some in Knidos from a couple of Phoenician traders, and we did well with it—better than I thought we would. If we could get it straight from the source, we'd make even more."

Before Himilkon could reply, his slave came out with wine and cups and some barley rolls and a bowl of olive oil on a wooden tray. "Just set it down and go away," Himilkon told him. "I don't want you snooping around."

"Wait," Sostratos said. "Could we have some water first, to mix with the wine?"

"Go on. Fetch it," Himilkon told Hyssaldomos. But the Phoenician also let out a mournful cluck. "Why you Hellenes water your wine, I've never understood. It takes away half the pleasure. Would you wrap a rag around your prong before you go into a woman?"

"One of the Seven Sages said, 'Nothing too much,' " Sostratos told him. "To us, unwatered wine seems too much, too likely to bring on drunkenness and madness."

Himilkon's broad shoulders went up and down in a shrug. "To me, this is silly, but never mind." He drank his wine neat, and with every sign of enjoyment. Smacking his lips, he went on, "You spoke of balsam, my master."

Sostratos had been chewing on a roll, and answered with his mouth full: "Yes. Certainly."

"You want the best, the balsam of Engedi?" Himilkon asked. Sostratos and Menedemos both dipped their heads. Himilkon said, "You won't get it straight from the source, not in Phoenicia you won't. Engedi lies inland, perhaps twelve or fifteen parasangs inland—you would say, let me see, about, oh, three hundred stadia."

"Isn't that Phoenicia, too?" Menedemos asked.

"No, no, no." Himilkon shook his head. "The Phoenician

cities are along the coast. Inland, down there, is the country of the Ioudaioi. And the Ioudaioi, my friends, are very peculiar people."

Menedemos sent Sostratos a quick glance, as if to say anyone not a Hellene was of course a peculiar person. Sostratos would not have disagreed, but didn't care to say any such thing where Himilkon could hear. What he did say was, "I don't know much about these Ioudaioi, O best one. Tell me more."

"Foolish people. Stubborn people. About what you'd expect from ignorant, back-country hillmen." Himilkon sniffed and poured himself more wine, then shook his head. "And they're slightly daft—more than slightly daft—about their religion. You need to know that if you decide to go inland."

"Daft how?" Sostratos asked. "If I go into their country, will they want me to worship the way they do?"

"No, no, no," the Phoenician said again. He laughed. "But they may not want to have anything to do with you, because you don't worship the way they do. Dealing with you might cause them ritual pollution, you see. They're very prickly about that sort of thing."

"They sound as bad as Egyptians," Menedemos said.

"They're even worse," Himilkon said. "They worship their own god, and they say nobody else's gods are real."

"What? Zeus isn't real?" Menedemos burst out laughing. "Oh, my dear fellow, that has to be a joke."

"Not to the Ioudaioi," Himilkon said. "Not at all."

"That holds an obvious logical flaw," Sostratos said. "If theirs is the only true god, why is he worshiped by one little tribe nobody ever heard of, and by nobody else in the whole wide world?"

Himilkon shrugged once more. Menedemos said, "Well, my dear, if you deal with these strange people, I suggest you don't ask them that question. Otherwise, you won't be dealing with them long. If they're like Egyptians, they'll be touchy as all get-out about religion, and they won't care a fig for logic."

However much Sostratos might wish it didn't, that made good sense. "I'll remember," he promised, and turned back to Himilkon. "What else can you tell me about these Ioudaioi?"

"They are honest—I will say that for them," the Phoenician

answered. "This god of theirs may seem silly to everyone else, but they take him *very* seriously."

"What does he look like?" Sostratos asked. "Do they turn a crocodile or a baboon or a cat or a jackal into a god, the way the Egyptians do?"

"No, my master—nothing of the sort, in fact." Himilkon shook his head again. "If you can believe it, he doesn't look like anything at all. He just *is*—is everywhere at the same time, I suppose that means." He laughed at the absurdity of it.

So did Menedemos, whose ideas about religion had always been conventional. But Sostratos thoughtfully pursed his lips. Ever since Sokrates' day, philosophers had been dissatisfied with the gods as they appeared in the *Iliad*: lustful, quarrelsome, often foolish or cowardly—a pack of chieftains writ large. One cautious step at a time, thinkers had groped their way toward something that sounded a lot like what these Ioudaioi already had. Maybe they weren't so silly after all.

How can I find out? he wondered, and asked Himilkon, "Do any of them speak Greek?"

"A few may." But Himilkon looked doubtful. "You'd do better to learn a little Aramaic, though. I could teach you myself, if you like. I wouldn't charge much."

Now Sostratos wore a dubious expression. His curiosity had never extended to learning foreign languages. "Maybe," he said.

"I know how it is with you Hellenes," Himilkon said. "You always want everybody else to speak your tongue. You never care to pick up anybody else's. That's fine in Hellas, my friend, but there's more to the world than Hellas. Your other choice would be to hire a Greek-speaking interpreter in one of the Phoenician towns, but that would cost a lot more than learning yourself."

Mentioning expense was a good way to get Sostratos to think about acquiring some Aramaic on his own. "Maybe," he said again, in a different tone of voice.

Himilkon bowed once more. "You know I am at your service, my master."

After the Rhodians left the warehouse, Menedemos asked,

"Do you really want to learn to go *barbarbar*?"

Sostratos tossed his head. "No, not even a little bit. But I don't want to have to count on an interpreter, either." He sighed. "We'll see."

MENEDEMOS FELT TRAPPED in the andron. For once, that had nothing to do with Baukis. She was upstairs, in the women's quarters. But Philodemos' friend Xanthos shared with Medusa the ability to turn anyone close by to stone: he was petrifyingly boring. "My grandson is beginning to learn his alpha-beta," he said now. "He's a likely little lad—looks like my wife's mother. My father-in-law liked string beans more than any man I've ever known, except maybe my great uncle. 'Give me a mess of beans and I'll be happy,' my great uncle would say. He lived to be almost eighty, though he was all blind and bent toward the end."

"Isn't that interesting?" Menedemos lied.

He glanced over toward his father, hoping the older man would rescue both of them from their predicament. Xanthos was *his* friend, after all. But Philodemos just pointed to the krater in which the watered wine waited and said, "Would you like some more, best one?"

"I don't mind if I do." Xanthos used the dipper to refill his cup. *Oh, no*, Menedemos thought. *That will only make him talk more*.

Of course, by everything he'd ever seen, Xanthos needed no help in talking as much as any three ordinary men put together. After a couple of sips of wine, he turned to Philodemos and said, "Were you in the Assembly when I spoke on the need to keep good relations with Antigonos and Ptolemaios both—and with Lysimakhos and Kassandros, too, for that matter?"

"Yes, as a matter of fact, I was," Philodemos said quickly. Menedemos' father, a man of stern rectitude, seldom told lies, but desperate times called for desperate measures, and he didn't hesitate here.

That did him little good. "I believe your son was still at sea, though," Xanthos said. "I'm sure he'd be interested in hearing my remarks."

Menedemos had no idea why he was sure of any such thing. Philodemos said, "My son's met Ptolemaios. You might be interested in hearing his views."

He might as well have saved his breath; Xanthos was interested in no one's views but his own. He took a deep breath, getting ready to launch into his speech. Menedemos tried a different tack: "What about Seleukos, O marvelous one? You say we should stay friendly toward all the other Macedonian marshals"—which struck him as much easier to advocate than to do—"but what about Seleukos, out in the east?"

"A very good question, young man, and you may be sure I'll address it in great detail when next the Assembly convenes," Xanthos said. "Meanwhile—"

Out came the speech. Resistance was futile; it only delayed the inevitable. *A man can close his eyes*, Menedemos thought. *Why can't he close his ears, too?* Being unable to do so struck him as most unfair, and ever more so as time dragged on.

The worst part was, Xanthos expected praise once he finished. He always did, and pouted when he didn't get it. "That was . . . quite something, sir," Menedemos managed, which saved him the trouble of saying just what.

"Yes, well, I have some rather urgent business to attend to," Philodemos said. For a bad moment, Menedemos feared his father would go off and leave him alone with Xanthos. He'd known he annoyed his father, but hadn't thought Philodemos hated him that much. But then Philodemos added, "And I need my boy with me."

Xanthos had trouble taking a hint. After another quarter-hour of platitudes, though, he did make his farewells. "Oh, by the dog of Egypt!" Menedemos exclaimed. "Doesn't he ever shut up?"

"When he goes to bed, perhaps," his father said.

"I'll bet he talks in his sleep," Menedemos said savagely. "It'd be just like him."

Philodemos clucked in mild reproof: "That's not a kind thing to say." He paused, then sighed. "I'm not saying you're wrong, mind you, but it's not kind."

"Too bad." Menedemos stood up and stretched. Something

in his back crackled. He sighed, too, with relief. "The saddest part is, he's got no idea how dull he is."

"No, and don't tell him," his father said. "He has a good heart. He's just boring. He can't help that, any more than a man can help having a taste for cabbage stew. I don't want him insulted, do you hear me?"

"I won't be the one to do it," Menedemos said with another sigh.

"You'd better not." But Philodemos sighed again, too. "He's *dreadfully* dull, isn't he?"

Baukis walked purposefully across the courtyard—now that Xanthos was gone, she could come forth from the women's quarters. Menedemos followed her with his eyes, but didn't turn his head. He wanted to give his father no reason for suspicion, especially when he was doing his best not to deserve any. But he couldn't help noting that she disappeared into the kitchen. *Uh-oh*, he thought.

Sure enough, a moment later her voice and Sikon's rose in passionate argument. "There they go again," Menedemos said—that seemed a safe enough remark.

"So they do." His father dipped out a fresh cup of watered wine, which seemed to express his view of the situation.

"You really ought to do something about that," Menedemos said.

"And what do you suggest?" his father retorted. "A wife is supposed to manage the household, and a cook is supposed to come up with the best suppers he can, and to the crows with money. If I side with either one of them, the other will think I'm wrong, and that will just cause more trouble. No, I'll stay off to the side. Let them settle it between themselves."

That made good sense. Menedemos wasn't altogether happy about admitting as much to himself. He wondered why his father couldn't give *him* as long a leash as he let his wife and the cook have. *Whenever he thinks I'm the least little bit out of line, he slaps me down hard*, he thought resentfully.

In the kitchen, the yelling got louder. "—think you're King Midas, with all the gold in the world around you!" Baukis said.

Sikon's reply came to Menedemos' ears in impassioned

fragments: ". . . cheapskate . . . barley mush . . . salted fish!" The cook slammed his fist down on a counter. Baukis let out a rage-filled, wordless squeal.

"Oh, dear," Menedemos said. Philodemos drained that cup of wine and got himself another. He was starting to look a little bleary, which he seldom did in the afternoon. *First Xanthos and now this*, Menedemos thought, not without sympathy.

A moment later, Baukis stormed back across the courtyard, her back stiff with fury. She went up the stairs. The door to the women's quarters slammed. This time, Philodemos was the one who said, "Oh, dear."

And, a moment after that, Sikon rushed into the andron shouting, "I can't stand it any more! Tell that woman to keep her nose out of my kitchen from here on out, or I quit!"

"That woman happens to be my wife," Philodemos pointed out.

"And you can't quit," Menedemos added. "You're a slave, in case you've forgotten."

By Sikon's comically astonished expression, he *had* forgotten. With reason, too: in the kitchen, a good cook was king. And Sikon was more than a merely good cook. He said, "The way she goes on, you'd think we were trying to scrape by on five oboloi a day. How am I supposed to do anything interesting if I'm looking over my shoulder all the time for fear I spend a khalkos too much?"

"You've managed so far," Philodemos said. "I'm sure you can keep right on doing it. Naturally, my wife worries about expenses. That's what wives do. You'll find a way to go on making your delicious suppers, come what may. That's what cooks do."

No, he never took so soft a line with me, Menedemos thought. *Maybe I should have been a cook, not a trader*.

But Sikon wasn't satisfied, either. "Cooks cook, that's what they do. How can I cook when she's driving me mad?" He threw his hands in the air and stomped out of the andron. When he got back to the kitchen, he showed what he thought of the whole business by slamming the door as hard as Baukis had upstairs.

"Well, well," Philodemos said, a phrase Menedemos had

been known to use himself. Philodemos pointed to him. "You're closer to the krater than I am, son. Is there enough wine left for another cup?"

"Let me look." Menedemos did, and then reached for the dipper. "As a matter of fact, there's enough left for two." He filled one for his father, one for himself.

"That man is so difficult," Baukis told him a couple of days later. "He simply will not see reason. Maybe we just ought to sell him and try someone else."

Menedemos tossed his head. "We can't do that. People would talk—he's been in the family his whole life. And he's a very good cook, you know. I wouldn't want to lose him, and neither would my father."

Baukis made a sour face. "Yes, I've seen as much. Otherwise, he would have laid down the law to Sikon." She threw her hands in the air. "What am I supposed to do? I'm not going to give up, but how can I make a proper fight of it? Maybe you have the answer, Menedemos." She looked toward him, her eyes wide and hopeful.

Why did she appeal to him against his father, her husband? Because she was looking for a weapon to use against Philodemos and Sikon? Or simply because the two of them weren't so far apart in years, and Philodemos' beard was gray? Whatever the reason, Menedemos knew she was giving him his chance. He'd made the most of far less with plenty of other women. Why not here, with Baukis?

It would be easy, he thought. He bit down on the inside of his lower lip till he tasted blood. "I don't know," he said woodenly. "I just don't know."

And then, to his horrified dismay, his father's wife hung her head and quietly began to cry. In a small, broken voice, she said, "Maybe he's angry with me because I haven't got pregnant yet. I've done everything I know how to do—I've prayed, I've sacrificed—but I haven't caught. Maybe that's it."

My father is an old man. His seed is bound to be cold. If I sow my seed in the furrow he's plowed, it would almost be doing him a favor. Menedemos sprang to his feet from the bench in the courtyard, so abruptly that Baukis blinked in surprise. "I'm sorry," he mumbled. "I've just remembered—I've got an appointment down by the harbor. I'm late. I'm very late."

The lie was clumsy. Baukis had to know it was a lie. Menedemos fled the house anyway, fled as if the Kindly Ones dogged his heels. *And so they might*, he thought as he looked around on the street, wondering where he would really go. *If I stayed on the road I was traveling there, so they might.*

He squeezed his hands into fists till his nails bit into his callused palms. Did Baukis know, did she have any idea, of the turmoil she roused in him? She'd never given any sign of it—but then, if she was a good wife, she wouldn't. Not all the seductions Menedemos tried succeeded.

He laughed, a harsh, bitter noise having nothing to do with mirth. *This is a seduction I* haven't *tried, curse it. This is a seduction I'm not going to try.* Baukis trusted him. By all the signs, she liked him. But she was his father's wife. "I can't," he said, as if he were choking. "I can't. And I won't."

All at once, he knew where he would go to keep his "appointment." The closest brothel was only a couple of blocks away. That wasn't what he wanted, but maybe it would keep him from thinking about what he did want and—he told himself yet again—what he couldn't have.

SOSTRATOS GAPED AT Himilkon. "What?" he said. "The conjugation of a verb in Aramaic changes, depending on whether the subject is masculine or feminine? That's crazy!"

The Phoenician shook his head. "No, best one. It's only different."

"Everything's different," Sostratos said. "None of the words is anything like Greek. You have all these choking noises in your language."

"I have learned Greek," Himilkon said. "That was as hard for me as this is for you."

He was bound to be right. That made Sostratos feel no better. "And did you tell me your alpha-beta has no vowels, and you write it from right to left?" Himilkon nodded. Sostratos groaned. "That's . . . very strange, too," he said.

"We like our aleph-bet as well as you like yours," Himilkon told him. The Phoenician scratched his head. "Interesting how some of the letters have names that are almost the same."

"It's no accident," Sostratos answered. "We Hellenes learned the art of writing from the Phoenicians who came with King Kadmos. We changed the letters to suit our language better, but we learned them from your folk. That's what Herodotos says, anyhow."

"If you changed them, you should not blame us for leaving them the way they were," Himilkon said. "Shall we go on with the lesson now? You are doing pretty well, you really are."

"You're only saying that to keep me coming back." Sostratos didn't think he was doing well at all. Aramaic seemed harder than anything he'd tried to learn at the Lykeion.

But Himilkon said, "No, you have a good memory—I already knew that—and your ear is not bad. Anyone who hears you speak will know you for a Hellene (or at least for a foreigner, for in some of these little places they will never have heard of Hellenes), but people will be able to understand you."

"Will I be able to understand them, though?" Sostratos said. "Following you is even harder than speaking, I think."

"Do the best you can. When spring comes and you sail east, you may decide you want an interpreter after all. But even if you do, you are better off knowing some of the language. That will help keep him from cheating you."

"True. Very sensible, too." Sostratos thumped his forehead with the heel of his hand, as if trying to knock in some wisdom. "Yes, let's get on with it."

His brain felt distinctly overloaded as he walked back up toward the northern tip of the city and his home. He was going over feminine conjugations in his mind, and so engrossed in them that he didn't notice when someone called his name.

"Sostratos!"

The second—or was it the third?—time, that pierced his shield of concentration. He looked up. "Oh. Hail, Damonax. Where did you spring from?"

Damonax laughed. "Spring from? What, do you think Kadmos sowed a dragon's tooth and reaped me? Not likely, my dear. I've been walking up the street beside you for half a plethron, but you never knew it."

Sostratos' cheeks heated. "Oh, dear. I'm afraid I didn't. I'm sorry. I was . . . thinking about something."

"You must have been, by Zeus," Damonax said. "Well, Sokrates was the same way if Platon's telling the truth, so you're in good company."

Sokrates, Sostratos was sure, had never pondered the vagaries of Aramaic grammar. "I was talking about Kadmos just a little while ago," he said, "though not in connection with the dragon's teeth."

"What then?" Damonax asked. "How Euripides shows him in the *Bakkhai*?"

"No." Sostratos tossed his head. "In aid of the Phoenicians' bringing their letters to Hellas."

"Oh. That." Damonax shrugged. "History interests me less than philosophy. Did I hear rightly that your splendid gryphon's skull was lost at sea?"

"I'm afraid you did," Sostratos replied. "What are you doing in this part of the city?"

"Why, coming to see your father, of course. He must have told you I'd like to marry your sister," Damonax said.

"Yes, he did. The news surprised me more than a little. We aren't a family with land out to the horizon." *And you come from that kind of family—or you did*, Sostratos thought. *Have you squandered everything? Is that it?*

Damonax's smile, bright and bland, told him nothing. "Of course I expect she'd bring a suitable dowry with her," he said, "but that would be true of any man seeking her hand, is it not so?"

It was so, and Sostratos knew it perfectly well. He did say, "What one side finds a suitable dowry may seem outrageous to the other."

Damonax surprised him by saying, "Oh, I hope not, not here. I knew your sister's first husband—we weren't close, but he was good friends with my older brother, who was nearer his age. He would sing Erinna's praises by the hour, in the areas where a wife should be praised: her spinning, her weaving, the way she ran the household. So I already have some notion of what I'd be getting, you might say, and I'm looking forward to it."

"Really?" Sostratos said. Maybe that explained why he was paying court to a widow and not to a maiden. Maybe. Sostratos still had his suspicions. He knocked on the door. When Gyges opened it, he told the Lydian majordomo, "Here's Damonax, whom I ran into on the street. He's come to talk with Father."

"Yes, of course, sir—we're expecting him." The house slave turned to Damonax and gave him a polite little bow. "Hail, most noble one."

"Hail," Damonax answered. "Is Lysistratos in the andron?"

"That's right," Gyges said. "Just come with me. I'll take you there." He glanced toward Sostratos. "You may find this interesting yourself."

"So I may," Sostratos said. "One of these days, I may have a daughter myself. I'd like to see how the dicker goes."

"You've already missed a good deal," Damonax said.

"That's all right. I expect you and Father will start raking things up again."

The older man chuckled. "You're probably right."

In the andron, Lysistratos waited till a slave had served out wine and olives and cheese before getting down to business. Sostratos' father said, "So Damonax, you don't think a dowry of two talents of silver is enough?"

"No, sir," Damonax answered with polite firmness. "Neither do my kinsfolk."

Lysistratos sighed. "I'm sorry to hear that, best one. Don't you think two talents would help you redeem some of your olive crop?"

Damonax flinched. "Redeem it? From whom?" Sostratos asked.

"From creditors, I'm afraid," his father answered. "Damonax's family sank a lot of silver into part of a cargo on a round ship—and the ship either met pirates or it sank, because it never got to Alexandria. The year's olive crop is collateral."

"How did you find that out?" Damonax demanded. "Our creditors swore they wouldn't blab."

"They didn't," Lysistratos said. "That's why I needed so long to figure this out. But I'm not wrong, am I, even if I pieced things together from hither and yon?"

"No, you're not wrong," Damonax said bitterly. "It's a pity, though—the match would have been a good one."

Sostratos got to his feet. "Father, walk out into the courtyard with me for a moment, would you?" he said.

Looking a little surprised, Lysistratos followed him out of the andron. In a low voice, he asked, "Well? What would you say to me that you don't care to have Damonax hear?"

"Only that he *would* be a good match for Erinna, if he'll settle for the dowry we want," Sostratos answered. "I do think he wants her for herself as well as for the money; he told me how her first husband praised her as a housekeeper to him. And Erinna does want to marry again, and we saw matches for her aren't so easy to come by when that other family chose a younger girl in her place."

His father looked thoughtful. "Something to that," he admitted. "And Damonax would be beholden to us for going forward, and his family's fortunes may recover." He sighed. "You're right about your sister—she *does* want children of her own. A father's not supposed to put much weight on such things, but how can I help it?" He dipped his head in sudden decision. "If he agrees to the dowry, I'll make the match."

When Sostratos and Lysistratos came back into the andron, Damonax rose. "I'll be going," he said. "Not much point to any more talk, is there?" Pained resignation had replaced bitterness.

"That depends," Lysistratos said. "You're not going to squeeze more than two talents' worth of dowry out of me, but we'll go on from there if you can live with that."

Damonax sank back onto his stool as if his legs didn't want to support him. "You would do that?" he whispered.

"Hard to blame a man too much for wanting to keep his family's money problems to himself," Sostratos said. Not all Hellenes would have agreed with him, but he was an intensely private man himself, and understood the urge to put such embarrassments in chests, as it were, and hope no one else found out about them.

His father said, "Tell me one thing very plainly, Damonax: you've lost your crop for the year, is it not so, but not the land itself?"

"Yes." Jerkily, Damonax dipped his head. "Yes, that is so. I swear it by Zeus and all the other gods."

"All right, then," Lysistratos said. "You people can recover from that, and even if two talents is less than you would have wanted, it will go a long way toward keeping you and your family afloat."

"Thank you, sir," Damonax said. "I am in your debt—we're all in your debt." Sostratos smiled to himself. That was what he'd had in mind. Gratitude and a sense of obligation didn't always last, of course, but sometimes they did. Damonax went on, "The marriage will give you legitimate grandchildren, sir."

"That's the point of marriage, after all," Sostratos' father said. "Now go on home. Make sure your kin are satisfied, and we'll take it from there."

After Damonax had left, Erinna came down from the women's quarters. When Sostratos told her of the agreement, she whooped with delight and threw herself into his arms. "This is wonderful!" she said. "It's like a second chance. It *is* a second chance."

"May everything go as well as it possibly can, my dear," Sostratos said. "Gods grant it be so."

"Gods grant it indeed," Lysistratos said. He eyed Sostratos. "One day before too long, son, we'll find you a match, too. Thirty's a good age for a man to wed, and you're getting there."

"Me?" Sostratos hadn't thought about it much. Marriage seemed neither real nor important to him. He patted his sister on the shoulder. She wanted a home to manage, but every port on the Inner Sea was his. *The gods made me a man, not a woman; a Hellene, not a barbarian*, he thought. *Truly, I'm the lucky one*.

HISTORICAL NOTE

The Gryphon's Skull is set in 309 B.C. I found the idea for the novel—that the skull of a *Protoceratops*, weathered out of its stony matrix, might have given the ancient world the basis from which it invented the gryphon—in John R. Horner's fascinating book, *Dinosaur Lives: Unearthing an Evolutionary Saga* (co-written with Edwin Dobb; HarperCollins: New York, 1997). It was first advanced by classical folklorist Adrienne Mayor. During early Hellenistic times, Greek cities were founded as far east and north as modern Afghanistan; if ever a dinosaur skull from Mongolia could—almost—have come to Athens, that was the era. Obviously, such a skull never truly reached the Greek scholarly community. I hope I've made this near miss plausible and interesting, which is, I think, the most one can reasonably expect from a historical novelist.

Real characters appearing in the story are Menedemos, Euxenides of Phaselis, Ptolemaios of Egypt, and Antigonos' rebellious nephew Polemaios (whose name is also spelled as Ptolemaios in the surviving histories, but Polemaios in inscriptions—I gladly seized the difference to differentiate him from his more famous contemporary). Others mentioned but not on stage include Alkimos of Epeiros, Antigonos, his sons Demetrios and Philippos, Lysimakhos, Kassandros, Seleukos, Polyperkhon, Eurydike, Berenike, and Ptolemaios' son Ptolemaios, who was indeed born on Kos in this year. Over this entire era hangs the enormous shadow of Alexander the Great, now dead fourteen years.

Exactly how Polemaios came from Euboia to Kos is not known; it might well have been by stealth, as plenty of people between the one island and the other wanted him dead. Equally unknown is Menedemos' connection, if any, to the invention of the trihemiolia. A few years later, however, he is the first man known to have captained such a vessel, so the connection might well have existed.

I have for the most part spelled names of places and people as a Greek would have: thus Knidos, not Cnidus; Lysimakhos, not Lysimachus. I have broken this rule for a few place names that have well-established English spellings: Rhodes, Athens, the Aegean Sea, and the like. I have also broken it for Alexander the Great and his father, Philip of Macedon. This helps distinguish them from the large number of men named Alexandros and Philippos, and they deserve such distinction.

All translations from the Greek are my own. As in *Over the Wine-Dark Sea*, I claim no particular literary merit for them, only that they convey what the original says. Menedemos' bit of doggerel in Chapter 12 is a poem of Palladas' from the *Greek Anthology* that actually dates from the fourth or fifth century A.D. I concede the anachronism—but Menedemos might have said it, even if he didn't.